BOOKS BY PAUL BISHOP

Fey Croaker Novels

Twice Dead

Kill Me Again

Calico Jack Walker/Tina Tamiko Novels

Sand Against the Tide

Citadel Run

Other Novels

Chapel of the Ravens

Shroud of Vengeance

TEQUILA MOCKINGBIRD

A Fey Croaker Novel

PAUL BISHOP

SCRIBNER

SCRIBNER
1230 Avenue of the Americas
New York, NY 10020

SCRIBNER and design are registered trademarks of
Simon & Schuster Inc.

Designed by Brooke Zimmer
Text set in Electra

Manufactured in the United States of America

1   3   5   7   9   10   8   6   4   2

Library of Congress Cataloging-in-Publication Data
Bishop, Paul.
Tequila mockingbird: a Fey Croaker novel/Paul Bishop.
p.   cm.
I. Title.
PS3552.I7723T47   1997
813'.54—dc21   97-24569   CIP

ISBN 0-684-83009-4

For Roger Bowles,
Links Road School alumnus.
His humor, friendship, and courage
a constant inspiration.

What lies behind you,
and what lies ahead of you,
are nothing compared with
what lies inside you.

THE PLAN

In the beginning there was the plan.
And then came the assumptions.
and the assumptions were without form,
and the plan was completely without substance.
And darkness was upon the faces of the detectives.

And the detectives spoke unto their supervisor,
saying, "The plan is a crock of shit
and it stinks!"

And the supervisors went unto their lieutenants
and said, "The plan is a pail of dung
and none may abide the odor thereof."

And the lieutenants went to their captains
and sayeth unto them, "The plan is a container
of excrement that is very strong, such that
none here may abide by it."

And the captains went to their commander
and said unto him, "The plan is a vessel of
fertilizer and none may abide its strength."

And the commander went to the deputy chief
and spoke, saying, "The plan contains that which
aids the growth of plants and is very strong."

And the deputy chief went unto the assistant chief
and said unto him, "The plan promotes growth
and is very powerful."

And the assistant chief went unto the chief
and sayeth unto him, "This powerful new plan will
promote the strength and efficiency of the department."

And the chief looked upon the plan and saw
that it was good and the plan became
policy, and thereafter, as always,
the detectives were stuck with it.

Anonymous

THE LINEUP

The chief

Deputy Chief Vaughn Harrison

Lieutenant Mike Cahill

Los Angeles Police Department chief of police

Commanding officer over LAPD specialized units such as Robbery-Homicide and the Anti-Terrorist Division

Commanding officer of the West Los Angeles Area Detective Division

WEST LOS ANGELES AREA HOMICIDE DETECTIVES

Detective III Fey Croaker — Unit supervisor
Detective II Monk Lawson — Unit second-in-command
Detective I Arch Hammersmith — AKA: Hammer
Detective I Rhonda Lawless — AKA: Nails
Detective I Abraham B. Cohen — AKA: Alphabet
Detective I Brindle Jones — Partnered with Alphabet

ANTI-TERRORIST DIVISION (ATD) DETECTIVES

Captain Ron Harper — Division commanding officer (deceased)
Lieutenant II John Dancer — Division acting commanding officer
Detective II Alex Waverly — Murder victim
Detective II Prester John "P.J." Hunter — Surveillance expert
Detective I T-Bone Rawlings — Partnered with P. J. Hunter
Mary DeFalco — ATD commanding officer's secretary

ROBBERY-HOMICIDE DIVISION (RHD) DETECTIVES

Detective II Frank Hale — Lead homicide investigator
Detective I Derek Keegan — Partnered with Frank Hale

OTHER CHARACTERS

April Waverly — Wife of Alex Waverly
Daniel Sousa/Danny Ochoa — Undercover mockingbird
Art Melendrez — University of California at Los Angeles police officer

Ash	Deceased FBI agent. Involved with Fey Croaker at time of his death.
Zelman Tucker	Ex-tabloid reporter turned true-crime writer
Linda Harper	Widow of Ron Harper
Gina Kane	Police records clerk

ORO DE DIOS CARTEL

Don Diego Santiago	Cartel leader
Adrian Santiago	Son of Don Diego Santiago. Assassinated by Catalan cartel.
Lucian Santiago	Grandson of Don Diego Santiago. Leader of Los Juniors.

CATALAN CARTEL

Don Emil Catalan	Cartel leader
Jorge Ramos	Catalan enforcer
Ignacio Ramos	Son of Jorge Ramos. Also a Catalan enforcer.
Ricardo Alamar	Political candidate supported by the Catalan cartel. Related to the Ramos family.

THISTLE ONE — PRIVATE SECURITY ORGANIZATION

Ethan Kelso	Retired ATD detective. Owner of Thistle One.
Boone Coltrayne	Thistle One operative
Trinity Valance	Thistle One operative
Blue MacKenzie	Thistle One operative
Ramon Quintana	Thistle One operative

TEQUILA MOCKINGBIRD

Prologue

APRIL WAVERLY *pushed open the heavy glass entrance doors and walked into the cavernous lobby of Parker Center. She had been inside the Los Angeles Police Department's headquarters building only once before, but her determination wiped away her usual self-doubts and stifled any feelings of intimidation.*

In the center of the lobby, several uniformed officers stood behind a wooden counter, which formed a square around them. April approached without hesitation.

"Can I help you?" one of the uniformed officers asked. He didn't appear very interested in talking to a pregnant Hispanic woman who looked as if she were going to pop any second.

Knowing she wouldn't be allowed direct access to her destination, April was ready with a lie. "I was told to come here to have photos taken of my injuries." She touched the huge sunglasses she was wearing as if she were self-conscious because of a hidden black eye. Alex had told her about battered women coming to the building to get their photos taken.

The cop didn't look twice. "You want the photo lab on the fourth floor," he told her in a bored voice. He handed her a paper clip and a small visitor's ID card. The card was pink and bore the words "Fourth Floor and Below." He pointed to the floor in front of April. "Follow the red line to the elevators. Get off at the fourth floor and turn right."

April did as she was told, following the red line as opposed to the green, yellow, and orange lines, which led in other directions.

At the elevators, April waited until she was able to enter an empty car. When the doors closed, she pressed the seventh-floor button.

The elevator stopped at the third floor, and April felt her mouth go dry. A woman with an armload of files entered the elevator and smiled at April. She pressed the sixth-floor button.

April felt her knees getting weak. She hugged her purse to her chest to hide the fourth-floor pass. The woman, however, looked straight ahead at the elevator doors. At the sixth floor, she walked out without saying a word. The doors closed again.

April let her purse drop to her side. It was a large purse that did not match the style or color of her long maternity dress. The purse appeared heavy, its weighty contents pulling the drawstring top tight. Carrying it was making April's arm throb.

On the seventh floor, April stepped out of the elevator and looked around. A sign on the wall to her left indicated her destination. She turned right down a short corridor to follow the arrow on the sign.

She stopped outside a door blocking access to the rest of the corridor. On the door was a stylized cutout of a hooded figure carrying an assault rifle. The figure had a thick circle around it with a line crossing the circle at an angle. The words ANTI-TERRORIST DIVISION ran below the logo.

The obstacle threw April. She had thought she could simply walk right into her husband's office. She hadn't figured there would be other security measures once she was beyond the front desk.

She almost turned around and walked away. From somewhere inside, however, she felt her resolve strengthen. Taking a deep breath, she pressed the intercom button. Somewhere in the distance a buzzer sounded faintly.

"Yes?" a female voice responded through the intercom's speaker box.

"I'd like to see Alex Waverly," April said. "I'm his wife."

There was a pause before the same voice said, "Just a minute."

April put her hand in her purse and stood waiting.

• • •

Inside the ATD office, Mary DeFalco stared at the intercom. She had been the divisional commanding officer's secretary at ATD through several changes of the guard, and was well aware that a cop's wife turning up at the job always spelled bad news.

She walked through the open door and into the office behind her desk without knocking.

"What's up, Mary?" Lieutenant John Dancer asked from his seat behind the captain's desk. The divisional captain, Ron Harper, had died almost a year earlier. As the division's second-in-command, Dancer had been appointed acting commanding officer. However, a promotional freeze guaranteed Dancer would still be "acting" for the foreseeable future.

"Trouble, I think." Mary stood far enough back from the desk to give Dancer a good view of her legs, which were encased in black hose and high heels beneath a shortish skirt. "Alex Waverly's wife is out front. She buzzed the intercom and asked to see him."

"How the hell did she get up here without an escort? Why didn't the front desk call us?"

Mary shrugged. "Beats me."

"Damn it," Dancer said, standing up. "Where's Alex?"

"I'll check," Mary said, quickly leaving the office.

Dancer looked down at the board on his desk where he had been adding to the list of threat assessments and security details that were a main part of ATD's mission directive.

The president was due in town, but there was little demand for ATD's assistance, as the Secret Service handled almost all of the security arrangements.

Two weeks later, Prince Charles would be passing through on a three-day goodwill junket. The only problem might come when the prince visited the Santa Monica Area—a bastion of British immigrants, both legal and illegal. Dancer made a mental note to have the detective team responsible for monitoring the IRA give him an update on any recent activity.

Next on the list was the Central American Solidarity Conclave. On the surface, this was also a junket. After making a series of unity speeches in downtown Los Angeles, a group of ambassadors from Central America would be attending a United States versus Mexico World Cup qualifying soccer match.

The junket, however, was actually a cover for the ambassadors to meet with California officials to discuss numerous items of mutual concern, from drug smuggling to illegal immigration to human rights issues. The meetings could become confrontational, leading local Latino activists to organize demonstrations should word leak out.

Dancer sighed and shook his head. Analysis of potential terrorist problems was a guessing game at best, and at ATD the guessing was often done in the dark while wearing a blindfold. He tried to clear his mind to deal with the new problem of Waverly's wife. As far as Dancer was concerned, women comprised the world's biggest terrorist organization, and he couldn't even begin to guess what this one wanted.

He was on his way to the front entrance when Mary called out Dancer's name from the detective squad room. Dancer leaned his head inside and saw Mary holding the sign-in/sign-out clipboard. There were a couple of detectives working at their desks, but otherwise the room was deserted.

"Waverly shows signed out to West Los Angeles Division," Mary read from the form.

"Okay," Dancer said. He headed toward the flimsy front security door, laughingly nicknamed the Spy Stopper.

April wondered what was taking so long. Her heart was pounding so hard she thought she was going to faint.

As the door began to open, April slowly began to remove her hand from her bag.

John Dancer stepped into view.

April almost dropped her purse, recovering to remove her empty hand.

"Hello, April," Dancer said. He'd met her once before at a divisional Christmas party. She had flat, dark, peasant features and a

*shrill personality. Dancer wondered what Alex had ever seen in her.
Now he saw a look of confusion cross her face.*

"John Dancer," he said, explaining, thinking her puzzlement
was over his name.

"Is Alex here?" April asked, eyes darting, voice anxious. Dancer
could see she was tense. He could also see she was bursting with
pregnancy.

"No. I'm sorry."

"Do you know where he is?"

Dancer looked at her. "Are you all right? Is this something to do
with the baby?"

April took a deep breath. "I need to see Alex. Please, I really
need him now." Her voice was pleading, on the verge of hysteria.

"He's out at West L.A. Station," Dancer said, his fear for April's
obvious condition overriding his natural caution.

"I bet he is," April said almost nastily.

Dancer wasn't sure what that meant, but put it down to pregnancy stress. "I can try to get hold of him on the radio and bring
him back here."

"No," April said. "I can't wait."

Dancer wasn't sure what to do. "Do you need to go to the
hospital?"

"No. I need Alex!"

"Okay," Dancer said. "I'll get somebody to contact Alex and
have him wait at West L.A. I don't think you should be driving, so
how about I take you there myself?"

April seemed to consider this. "Okay," she said.

Dancer hadn't even known April Waverly was pregnant. Alex had
never mentioned it. That didn't surprise Dancer. Alex Waverly was a
gregarious, one-of-the-boys type of detective who rarely talked about
his home life. Usually he was too busy playing grab-ass with anything resembling a female.

Waverly had applied for a position with ATD after making a
spectacular arrest while assigned to RHD—the elite Robbery-

Homicide Division. Arresting a team of carjackers who had been terrorizing the city had been a major coup, so it came as a surprise that Waverly would want to leave RHD, or that RHD would willingly let him go.

Still, despite the odd circumstances, Waverly had been snapped up by ATD, and quickly fit into the strange world of intelligence gathering that his new unit inhabited. During the last year, he'd been part of several outstanding investigations.

On their way to West Los Angeles, Dancer tried making small talk, but when April answered only in monosyllables, he gave up on conversation.

Dancer could see the woman was in distress, clutching her purse to her chest. His only hope was that she wouldn't go into labor before he could turn her over to her husband.

The radio crackled once during the trip. Mary was on the other end telling Dancer that she had reached Alex Waverly, and that he would meet them in front of West L.A. Station. Dancer acknowledged the arrangements, and with a quick look at April, he pressed harder on the accelerator.

In heavy traffic, the drive to the west side took almost forty minutes. When the Santa Monica Boulevard off-ramp came into view, Dancer offered up a silent prayer of thanks. He brought his new department Monte Carlo to a stop at a trilight, then turned left under the freeway overpass and traveled the five blocks to Butler Avenue.

Dancer turned left on Butler. West L.A. Station was a short distance down on the right side. A familiar, maroon detective sedan was parked at the front curb with Waverly sitting behind the wheel. Dancer pulled in behind it and tapped his horn.

Almost before it stopped, April Waverly was out of Dancer's car and striding toward her husband. Still in the car, Dancer was surprised that Alex hadn't exited his own vehicle to greet them.

Levering himself out of the Monte Carlo, Dancer looked up to see April Waverly stop at the rear of the maroon sedan. At first he thought she might have been stopped short with a labor pain, but then he saw her pull a gun out of her purse.

"Holy shit! April!" he screamed, lunging forward.

April Waverly spread her feet apart, took the gun in both hands, just as Alex had taught her when they were first married, pointed the gun through the maroon sedan's rear window, and shot her husband twice in the back of the head.

1

"**I** CAN REMEMBER when safe sex meant being sure your gearshift was in park," Fey Croaker said, eliciting the amusement of the other detectives in the WLA homicide unit. Before the kibitzing could continue, the intercom line on Fey's phone buzzed.

Fey punched the line and barked, "Croaker."

"Fey, get down here right now! There's been a shooting in front of the station." It was Sergeant Terry Gillette, the uniformed watch commander who worked in the patrol office downstairs.

"What the hell's going on?" Fey demanded, but the line was dead. She pulled off her glasses and dropped them on her desk.

"Trouble?" Monk Lawson asked. He'd recently been promoted to the rank of Detective II and was the homicide unit's second-in-command.

"Downstairs," Fey said, already in motion. She grabbed her shoulder holster from a desk drawer and slid into the rig. A Smith & Wesson stainless steel .38-caliber revolver, with a four-inch barrel and custom wood grips, was snugged inside.

West Los Angeles is one of eighteen geographic areas within the Los Angeles Police Department. Situated between the jurisdictions of Beverly Hills and Santa Monica, it is home to almost as many of the rich and famous as its affluent neighbors. The WLA Station is a two-story brick and concrete building with no windows and a low profile, a fortified bunker in the middle of a residential neighborhood.

The detective squad room and several specialty units, such as vice, narcotics, and bunco-forgery, are housed on the second floor. Uniformed patrol, the front desk, and the area jail operate out of the first floor. A level belowground contains locker rooms, the roll-call room, and the boiler room.

Followed closely by Monk Lawson, Fey moved quickly through the squad room and down the front stairs. Two other members of the homicide unit, Arch Hammersmith, and Rhonda Lawless, known as Hammer and Nails, fell in right behind them.

Bursting out the door at the bottom of the stairwell, Fey almost collided with Terry Gillette as he spilled out of the watch commander's office.

"Where?" Fey asked in verbal shorthand.

"Right out front," Gillette said. "Shot a detective in his car parked at the curb. Shooter is still out there."

That was all the explanation there was time for as Fey and Gillette, followed by the other members of the homicide unit, tried unsuccessfully to push through the station's glass doors together.

Directly across the street from the station was the police garage, where the area cars were serviced and gassed up. Two uniformed officers were leaning over a retaining wall with their guns drawn and aimed.

Fey could see that the guns were pointed at an obviously pregnant woman who was crying so hard she was shaking. One hand was covering her face. The other was by her side holding a gun. Beyond the woman was the shattered back window of a detective sedan.

"Oh, hell," Monk said.

There was another detective sedan, a Monte Carlo, parked behind the victim's vehicle. A detective whom Fey didn't recognize was crouched behind the trunk of the vehicle. He appeared to be more in hiding than taking cover. His gun was out, but he was not pointing it at anything in particular. He looked in shock, and Fey sensed he could be a bigger hazard than the woman.

Several other uniformed cops were on the sidewalk and in the street, all pointing guns at the pregnant woman.

"What are you waiting for?" April Waverly screamed, taking the hand away from her face. "Come on, kill me! Kill me!" She didn't raise her gun.

"Drop the gun!"

"Put it down!"

"Freeze!"

"Relax! Everyone just relax!" Fey's bellow overrode all other sounds. "Don't shoot!" She even surprised herself with the power of her voice.

There was obviously something going on that nobody understood yet. Fey, however, was sure of one thing: No matter what the justification, if they shot and killed this pregnant woman, the press would make the police look bad.

"Relax!" Fey yelled again. "Put your guns down."

The officers on the scene were young, assigned to uniformed positions within the station. Most had never been in a shooting situation. Fey's voice of reason was a welcome relief. They were more than glad to follow directions from somebody—anybody—who was willing to take control.

Fey brought her attention back to April.

The woman continued to cry, slowly sinking to her knees, the gun still in the hand at her side.

Swallowing, Fey stepped forward.

"Don't do it," Terry Gillette said sharply.

"Shut up, Terry," Fey snapped. "What are we going to do? Kill her and the kid she's carrying? This is a police station, not an abortion clinic. She isn't going to shoot anyone else."

"How can you be sure?"

"She would have done it by now." Fey wasn't sure she believed herself, but it sounded good.

Moving with determined deliberation, Fey walked toward the kneeling woman. When she was standing directly behind April, Fey stopped. The only movement April made was the shaking brought on by the sobs racking her body.

Fey reached out a hand and touched April on the shoulder. There was a soul-wrenching wail from April, and Fey knelt to wrap her arms around the woman. April turned into the embrace, allowing the gun to fall with a clunk to the sidewalk. Monk was there instantly to retrieve it.

Down on her own knees, the fabric of her slacks scraping on the hard concrete, Fey held April tight in her arms. She could feel the tremors in April's body being absorbed into her own. How odd, she thought, to embrace a killer.

"Monk," Fey called out. She moved one hand up to the back of April's head, pulling it forward to bury it in her shoulder. "I want everyone holstered up, and take care of the plainclothes guy behind the other car. I want him isolated. Put him in an interview room." She knew Monk was sharp enough to understand she was talking about the unknown detective behind the Monte Carlo.

"You got it," Monk said. "How about the crime scene?"

"Get Hammer and Nails to close off the entire street," Fey said. "We need a complete cordon around the station. I don't want a three-ring circus when the press hears about this." Fey was rocking April in her arms now as if comforting a child.

"Find out where Alphabet and Brindle are and get them down here," she said, referring to the other two homicide unit detectives. "Tell them to find some way to screen off the victim's car. I want to know who he is as soon as possible. I don't recognize the car, so I don't think he's from West L.A."

Terry Gillette was now standing beside Fey. He had a blanket in one hand.

"Any idea who she is?" Fey asked Gillette as she took the blanket from him.

"April Waverly," Gillette said. "Apparently, the guy she shot is her husband, Alex Waverly. He's a detective with ATD."

"Where did you get your info?" Fey asked.

Gillette nodded his head toward the detective who had been hiding behind the other vehicle. "That's Waverly's boss, Lieutenant Dancer. He drove the wife here to meet her husband."

Fey could see Monk talking to Dancer, but that wasn't her immediate priority. Monk would keep him on ice until she had the chance to get to him. Making soothing noises, she wrapped April in the blanket and eased her to her feet.

Slowly, with her arms still encircling her, Fey led April toward the station entrance.

2

FEY WAS barely through the front doors of the station before everything hit the fan again. With her arms still around April, Fey heard a scream of anguish from the records room located behind the front desk.

"No! No! No!" It was a high-pitched, hysterical yowl.

Gina Kane, a police records clerk, exploded out of the records room and crashed into the front desk. She pushed herself off and ran toward the side door that secured the rear area of the front desk from the lobby.

Gina was a twenty-something bubble-gummer with round heels and a taste for married men. She had long legs, and her chestnut brown hair tumbled down her back in a cascade of waves. The breasts underneath her too tight cashmere sweater had cost her a fortune and were large enough to keep her feet out of the sun.

Gina suddenly spotted Fey with her arms around April.

"You bitch!" Gina yelled, the expression on her face turning from anguish to hatred in a split second.

Fey looked up to see Gina coming straight at her with long, blood red nails bared.

"Gina!" Fey yelled. She released April and turned.

Gina, however, ducked past Fey and cannoned into April. Knocked off her feet, April fell to the floor. Gina leaped on her, scratching and slapping at April's face.

"You bitch!" Gina screamed again. "I loved him! I loved him!"

Fey grabbed two handfuls of Gina's hair. Viciously, she yanked backward, pulling the records clerk away from April.

Gina screamed in pain as Fey dragged her upright and thrust her into Monk's arms. Before he could get her under control, one of Gina's flailing elbows struck Monk a glancing blow under his right eye.

"Crap," he swore, an unusual occurrence for Monk, and stopped trying to be gentlemanly in his handling of the still hysterical woman.

"Cuff her," Fey said, "until we figure out what's going on." She turned to tend to April.

April lay very still, the blanket fallen away. She was on her side, her legs pulled up to protect her belly. Her eyes were glassy, and blood seeped out of long scratches on both cheeks.

"April?" Fey said, but there was no response. She went down on her knees beside the pregnant woman.

April's hands moved to her stomach and she gave a grunt of surprise and pain.

Fey suddenly felt something wet soaking her knees. She looked down and saw a puddle of water on the floor. Her heart started pounding.

"Don't do this to me," Fey said. She reached out and touched April, whose face was contorted in pain. "Damn it," Fey said.

"What's wrong?" Terry Gillette demanded.

"Her water has broken and she's going into labor. Get me a black-and-white unit out front right now, and clear us for a Code three run to the hospital. We're having a baby!"

3

BY THE TIME Fey returned to the station, she felt as if she had given birth herself. All she wanted was to go home, crawl into bed, and be left to die in peace. She knew there was no way that was going to be allowed to happen. Some days it just didn't pay to get up in the morning.

A full cordon was still blocking all public access to the station. The Division had been placed on an official tac alert. Uniformed officers had been held over from day watch to man the barricades while their night watch counterparts handled radio calls as usual. Other crimes didn't stop simply because the police were busy with one particular incident.

When she checked her watch, Fey was surprised to see that it was only late afternoon. *And miles to go before I sleep,* Fey thought with a mental shrug.

At the hospital, the baby had slid out of its womb like a runner stealing home. Hammer and Nails had remained with April. Fey would have preferred to stay with them, but she knew her place was back at the station supervising the crime scene.

Pulling into the station parking lot, Fey could see a temporary screen of blankets had been rigged around Alex Waverly's vehicle. The van from the coroner's office was already on-scene. Fey was sure, however, that they wouldn't move the body until she gave the word.

Monk met her as she entered the station. He wore a dark brown suit with a purple dress shirt and a gold tie. The colors went well with his ebony skin, and the double-breasted cut of the jacket complemented his slender build. As the homicide unit's second-in-command, he was Fey's closest confidant.

It was clear he had been hanging around, waiting to intercept Fey and brief her before she went upstairs.

"Did she have the baby?" he asked.

"About thirty minutes after we arrived. I think the lights-and-siren treatment all the way to Santa Monica Hospital was more than enough fanfare to hasten the birth." Fey still wasn't used to seeing Monk's bald head. He'd shaved it two weeks earlier at his wife's request. The rude squad room jokes about why his wife made the request were only now dying down.

"Boy or girl?"

"Girl."

"Is she going to name it after you?" Monk asked with an amused grin.

"Shut up," Fey said in a friendly manner. "I'm too tired to be jerked around." She ran a hand over her face. At forty-something, rapidly approaching fifty-something, she found she didn't have the same energy as when she was younger. She was still a good-looking woman with shoulder-length black hair and soft curves.

"Mother and baby seem to be doing fine physically," she said. "But mother hasn't said a word. She's working on the thousand-yard stare to beat all thousand-yard stares. The doctor called it a dissociative state—a complete mental shutdown. And there's no telling when or if it will pass."

"Just what we need," Monk said.

"What's the situation here?" Fey asked.

"Everything at ground zero appears to be under control. Hammer and Nails took care of the cordon before they followed you to the hospital. Alphabet and Brindle are standing by with the coroner's investigator."

"Who is it?"

"Lily Sheridan."

Fey nodded her approval. "Did Alphabet organize the makeshift screens around the scene?"

"Yeah, and it's a good thing he did."

"Why? Is the press everywhere?"

Monk nodded. "Most of them are set up across the street at the courthouse. They've all got long-range lenses pointing at us from there."

"Bloody vultures," Fey said. "What's the score with Gina Kane? How does she fit in?"

"I questioned her briefly while you were gone," Monk reported. "She was having an affair with Alex Waverly. She thought he was going to leave his wife and marry her."

"Silly bitch," Fey said. "Women who fall for that never cease to amaze me."

"It happens."

"Yes, it does," Fey agreed. "But not to women like Gina."

Monk held both hands up in front of his chest. "I won't argue with you."

Fey's expression was thoughtful. "So, the play on this is that April Waverly found out about the affair and decided to do hubby in?"

"In the absence of April Waverly making a statement to the contrary, that's the way it's playing right now."

"How about upstairs?" Fey asked.

"A nest of vipers," Monk told her. "The chief is here along with Commander Searls from Bureau. Cahill is trying to keep them both entertained. Keegan and Hale just showed up from Robbery-Homicide along with Deputy Chief Harrison."

"Oh, man. What are those cowboys doing here?"

"Looking to take over the case," Monk said.

"You're kidding?" Fey said.

"It's their jurisdiction," Monk replied, raising his eyebrows. "Investigating homicides where a cop is the victim is part of their mandate."

Fey shook her head. "I know it is, but this case is open and shut. We could handle it with our eyes closed. They just want to jump in and take the credit for their clearance rate."

Monk shrugged. "Not much we can do about it."

Fey started up the back stairs to the squad room. "I guess not."

Upstairs, Fey could see all the players gathered in Lieutenant Mike Cahill's office. Cahill was the commanding officer of the detective division. He had a large office in the front corner of the squad room with a bank of interior windows. Blinds could be pulled down for privacy when needed, but Cahill liked to see what was happening in the squad room, so they were open most of the time.

Fey went in without knocking.

"Chief," she said, immediately acknowledging the department's chief of police, who was standing next to Cahill's desk. He was a big man with a moon face and curly hair cut close to his scalp.

"Hello, Fey," he responded. He didn't smile, which added to the tension Fey could already sense in the room.

Deputy Chief Vaughn Harrison stood next to the chief. He was tall and wiry with gun-sight eyes. His right hand was a mangled and scarred hook of thumb, index, and middle finger. The two missing fingers had been torn off by shrapnel from a pipe bomb he'd been diffusing earlier in his career.

Standing beside Harrison was Dan Ayala, the chief's aide, a nervous ferret on a caffeine high. Ayala was the ultimate suck-up. Fey checked his nose for brown stains.

Keegan and Hale leaned against the back wall of the office like matched bookends. Wearing black suits and morose sneers, they were renowned as Vaughn Harrison's hit squad.

It was significant that nobody was sitting in the padded chairs surrounding the office conference table. Fey didn't know what it meant, but knew it couldn't be good.

"What's the status of April Waverly?" Cahill asked. So much brass in his office was making him sweat.

Fey deliberately sat down at the conference table. Normally, she wouldn't want to be on a lower plane than the person with whom she was talking, but in this instance, she felt the need to defuse the tenseness of the situation.

"She and the baby are fine physically. The kid shot out of the womb like a rocket down an ice chute. No complications for the kid, but April has gone into a dissociative state—hasn't said a word since we took her into custody."

"Is she aware of what's going on?" Cahill asked.

Fey tilted her head, thinking. "The doctor doesn't think so. She's out of it big time, and it's impossible to tell when or if she'll start functioning again."

There was silence in the room. Fey decided to wait it out. She looked at the chief. The big man slowly batted his eyes and then sat down at the conference table across from Fey.

Everyone else suddenly scrambled for seats. The image of kids playing musical chairs popped into Fey's head.

"We have a difficult situation here, Fey," the chief said. His forearms were flat on the table, his hands clasped. An old Rolex showed below an inch of monogrammed cuff.

Fey didn't answer. She didn't know the ground rules yet, and felt the best course was to keep her mouth shut.

"As you know," the chief continued, "a situation like we have here would normally be handled by Robbery-Homicide." He paused again.

"But?" Fey said, giving the chief a slight prompt.

"But there are some extenuating circumstances, and as a result, I'd like your unit to run with the investigation—get it cleaned up as quickly as possible."

Fey leaned forward in her chair. She could feel Monk Lawson watching her. In fact, she could feel everyone's eyes on her. "Extenuating circumstances?" she asked.

"Nothing that should affect the investigation," the chief told her. "I'd just prefer your unit handle the case."

Fey cut her eyes to Keegan and Hale. Both of them stared straight ahead, purposely not looking at her.

Fey turned her attention back to the chief. "I take it we're playing this as a domestic dispute that turned deadly? Nothing to do with Alex Waverly being a cop?"

"Is there any indication to the contrary?" The chief's voice was as hard as his stare.

"Not that I've come across yet, sir," Fey told him truthfully.

"Fey," the chief said, his voice softening. "Something like this hurts us all. I want it wrapped up quick and tidy. No muss, no fuss. The department has taken more than its fair share of bad press in the last few years. Let's clean our own doorstep and move on."

Fey realized that now was not the time to argue. The orders were coming straight from the chief. She knew she wasn't being given the whole story, but she'd been forced to fly blind on other occasions. She just hoped this wouldn't be the sortie in which she crashed and burned.

Fey looked at Monk. "We'd better get busy."

4

F EY FELT BLOOD zinging through her veins. She took a deep breath to ease the tightness in her chest, and then another to take the edge off jangling nerve endings. This moment defined police work for Fey. The seconds before stepping into the deep end of an investigation were as deadly an addiction as any needle Nirvana.

April Waverly's shooting of her husband appeared cut and dried, a routine *domestic* that would look as sordid on paper as it did in real life. It was a classic triangle of love, lust, and betrayal that was mildly out of the ordinary because it involved a cop. But there was an intangible something about the case that Fey could sense as if she were an animal anticipating an earthquake.

Leaving Cahill's office, she moved quickly to her desk. Her mind was whirling as she rapidly formulated a mental game plan. Monk followed behind her, stopping only to pour two mugs of coffee.

The squad room itself was a wide-open work space with no dividers or private cubicles. Desks were grouped together in domino patterns, each cluster defined by an investigative priority.

Connected to the homicide unit's desks were those of major assault crimes (MAC) and sex crimes. In WLA, both units had previously been under the jurisdiction of the homicide supervisor. However, with the department's current emphasis on spousal abuse and community policing, the workload had become overwhelming. Homicides citywide were not getting the attention they demanded.

As a result, a new supervisory position had been created strictly for the MAC and sex crimes units. Homicide went back to their original mandate of handling murder, kidnapping, and high-grade deadly weapons assaults.

Scattered elsewhere around the squad room were the other investigative units—burglary, auto theft, juvenile, robbery, and the CRASH unit, which specialized in gang crimes.

Monk placed a mug of coffee in front of Fey, adding another moisture ring to the collection on her blotter.

"When I was in Egypt," he said softly, "I watched a man castrate a camel."

"Really?" Fey said. "How very interesting." She took a sip of coffee and wondered where this was leading.

"It was a pretty quick operation," Monk told her. "The guy walked up behind the camel with two bricks and then slammed the camel's testicles between them."

"Ouch," Fey said, wincing.

"No kidding," said Monk. "I talked to the guy afterward and asked him if it hurt."

"And?" Fey asked, realizing she was playing straight man.

"He told me it only hurt if you got your thumbs in the way."

Fey laughed. "What's your point?"

"I don't want to be a squashed thumb."

Fey knew exactly what Monk was talking about. The scene in Cahill's office had explicitly shown that lines were being drawn in the sand behind the chief and Robbery-Homicide. Fey wasn't sure what it was all about, but she knew she'd better be quick on her feet if she didn't want to get slammed between two bricks.

She toasted Monk solemnly with her coffee mug and took another sip. The tar black liquid scalded across the back of her throat with a familiar bite.

Over the three years Monk had worked for her, Fey had come to have faith in his judgment. He was the only homicide detective left from the original unit Fey had been assigned to command. He'd been inexperienced then, but he'd learned fast and a mutual admiration had quickly been established.

Now Monk was not only Fey's second-in-command, he was also

her bellwether and sounding board. She trusted his opinion and his advice, even if she didn't always heed it. The fact that he was black or that she was a woman had never been an issue between them. The discriminations that each had overcome were mutual battle scars that didn't bear whining about.

"You make a good point," Fey said. "We don't want this caper coming back to bite us in the butt. Robbery-Homicide's nose is already out of joint over this case, so we'd better do this by the numbers and nail everything down."

Robbery-Homicide Division worked out of Parker Center. All high-profile murder cases, or any other homicide investigation that would overwhelm the manpower of a geographic homicide unit, were routinely assigned to RHD. As a result, the detectives working RHD thought of themselves as the police aristocracy, and copped an attitude to match.

The five or six detectives assigned to a homicide unit, such as Fey's, couldn't afford to be assigned to a case that would remove them from their duties for extended periods of time. RHD, on the other hand, could throw thirty or forty detectives into a task force to chase a serial killer until he was caught. RHD had enough manpower to assign detectives to high-profile cases, which would sometimes involve them full-time for two or three years.

RHD was also responsible for major robberies, serial rapists, and murder inquiries in which LAPD officers or detectives were involved as victims or suspects.

Unless, of course, the chief of police decided differently.

"What about the media circus this is going to generate?" Monk asked. "They're already howling like hyenas out there."

Fey bared her teeth. "I've suffered through the worst those pricks have to offer. This should be a piece of cake."

Fey had always hated dealing with the press. A year earlier, she had come under intense pressure while investigating a murder case in which a major sports celebrity had been arrested. Keegan and Hale from RHD had taken over the case, which had appeared open and shut until Fey unearthed evidence to the contrary.

The media had torn into Fey's private life and even published transcripts of a taped therapy session between Fey and her psychiatrist. Through it all, Fey had fought to maintain her dignity, and in the end she had earned a level of grudging respect from the media.

"Until we're ready to make an official statement, keep the uniforms on the cordon," Fey said. "Tell the blue-suiters to make sure all the looky-loos and reporters are kept at a distance. I don't want this turning into more of a soap opera than it is already."

"Got it," Monk said. He was penciling out a list on a notepad. A nerve pulsed under the skin covering his right temple. Like Fey, he was beginning to feel the *jazz*.

Fey swallowed the dregs of her coffee. "Come on," she said. She took a light jacket from the back of her chair and slipped it on to cover her shoulder holster. "It's show time."

5

OUTSIDE THE police station, Fey found that she didn't need to waste time waiting for the coroner's office or the crime scene techs from the Scientific Investigation Division—SID—to show. The whole dog and pony show was waiting for her for a change.

"How you doing, Lily?" Fey asked the coroner's investigator, who was leaning against her van.

"Fine, darlin'," Lily said in her southern drawl. She was a big woman, in the best sense of the phrase, but took little care with her appearance. The tail of her blouse hung out of her stretch pants, and the lining of her stained blazer was unstitched. Her hair was peroxide blond—a drastic change from the raven black it had been the last time Fey had seen her—but she still displayed the same wide smile that let everyone know they were her best friend.

"I'm sorry to keep you waiting," Fey said.

Lily laughed. "Honey, I've been keepin' people waitin' all my life. You don't have to apologize to me." She took a pair of thin rubber gloves from her pocket and pulled them on. She smiled at Monk and winked.

He nodded back to her in friendly reply.

There were two coroner's assistants—Lily referred to them as Igors—standing at the back of the van. "We'll call you when we need you," Lily told them. They were basically hired muscle sent along to lift and tote.

Walking toward the victim's car, Lily lowered her voice. "I'll need them most around ten o'clock tonight when I slip between the sheets."

Fey stopped herself from laughing only because she was very aware of the media barrage arranged on the other side of the police garage. Their long-range cameras were capable of capturing every nuance of expression. Laughing at a murder scene was understood by other cops, but never by the public.

The makeshift screens around the victim's car had been set up to allow free access for investigators, while blocking the view of the television and press cameras. Putting on their own latex gloves, Fey and Monk followed Lily behind the screen to the open driver's door of the detective sedan.

Waverly's body was leaning back against the seat, his arms relaxed at his sides, hands palm up. His face, or what was left of it, was turned toward the driver's door, his head lolled back against the headrest.

Fey was aware that the body had originally been slumped forward. Brain matter, hair, and other assorted gore still clung to the steering wheel.

Paramedics had been immediately called to the scene after the shooting, and had rearranged Waverly's position while checking for vital signs. It had obviously been a lost cause, but they had gone through the expected motions.

Eddie Mack, the SID photographer, suddenly appeared.

"Howdy, all," he said. Eddie's personality was congenial, but physically he was extremely unattractive. He was short and ugly, with thick black hairs exploding from his nostrils and ears and a lump the size of a tennis ball on his neck. He was dressed, as always, in Salvation Army rejects, but the photographic equipment slung from his neck was pristine and state of the art. Fey didn't care how Eddie looked. He was a good friend and took his work very seriously.

"Keeping well, Eddie?" she asked.

"Can't keep a good man down," he replied.

"That's what I always say," Lily chipped in.

Eddie looked into the car and grunted. "Nasty," he said. Waverly's face had been torn open by the exit wounds. "Bullets did their job, all right," Eddie observed as he brought his camera up and took a photo. "I heard his wife shot him for dipping his nib in a strange inkwell."

"It looks that way," Fey said.

Eddie took some more shots and then looked behind him. "These screens will have to be moved if you want full-coverage shots."

"I'll take care of it," Monk said.

"Get Alphabet and Brindle to help you," Fey told him. "I don't want the screens falling down. Pictures of the body on the six o'clock news could ruin someone's dinner."

"In this town," Monk said as he moved away, "they'd be considered appetizers."

Fey turned her head toward Lily. "You need help with this?"

"If I do," Lily said, "I'll call the Igors."

Lily began the task of moving the body, emptying the contents of its pockets, removing jewelry, taking its temperature, and other routine coroner responsibilities.

Fey moved around to the passenger side of the vehicle and opened the door. She looked at Waverly's body as Lily worked on it. The dead detective had been wearing a dark suit with a white shirt and striped tie. The white shirt was flecked with gore, but Fey was surprised there wasn't more blood.

Moving gingerly, she stuck her head into the vehicle and glanced around. There was a black leather briefcase on the backseat along with a carrying case containing a laptop computer. On the front seat was a map book, a leather-bound notepad with a pencil clipped to it, and a pair of sunglasses. A water bottle was lying on its side on the front passenger floorboards. The squirt cap was open, and some of the liquid had trickled out.

Fey picked up the map book and notepad before opening the rear door of the vehicle and removing the briefcase and the laptop computer.

She piled the items on the curb before turning back to look in the glove box. It was empty except for a stack of napkins and two unpaid parking tickets. Fey retrieved the tickets.

With keys from the ignition, Fey walked to the back of the car and opened the trunk. There was the usual mishmash of radios and police equipment along with a workout bag. Fey pulled out the bag and added it to her pile. By the time she had finished, Lily was almost done with her preliminary procedures.

"Anything interesting?" Fey asked, indicating the plastic bag of personal possessions Lily had retrieved from the corpse.

Lily shook her head. "Just what you would expect," she said. "You want to look through it now or at the autopsy?"

"At the autopsy is fine," Fey replied. "Is Rex Powers still butchering? I heard he was going to retire."

"He's still there for at least another couple of months."

"Great. Could you tag this body for him? He does good work, and I need this one wrapped up neat and tidy."

"No problem," Lily said.

"What are the chances of getting Waverly on a slab today?"

"I think you're pushin' your luck," Lily said.

"How about if the chief makes the request?"

Lily gave Fey an odd look. "Sounds as if you're callin' in the heavy hitters."

Fey shrugged. "I know this is a smoking gun case," she said. "Even though there's no forensic priority, Waverly was a cop, and I've got orders to put the case to bed as fast as possible. Surely the other stiffs aren't going to complain."

"You're bad," Lily said, chuckling. "If you can pull the strings, I'll see what can be done."

Monk had finished moving the screens around the car, and Eddie Mack was happily preserving Kodak moments.

Seeing the pile of items Fey had gathered on the curb, Monk asked, "What do you want to do with this stuff?"

Fey turned to look at him and saw that Alphabet and Brindle Jones were with him. "Let's lock it all upstairs in the homicide room for now," she said. "We can book it later when we have a chance to catch our breath."

Alphabet and Brindle were an odd pairing, but over the past year they had become an efficient team. They weren't on par with Hammer and Nails—nobody was—but they were an integral and reliable part of the homicide unit.

Brindle Jones was a slender, ebony sculpture. With her high cheekbones and regal bearing, she would have looked more at home on a fashion show runway than at a murder scene. She was well dressed, as always, in a bronze two-piece suit that showed off her legs and complemented the explosion of honey-colored hair framing her face. Gold-colored high heels and real gold bracelets added further class to the ensemble.

Next to Brindle, A. B. Cohen resembled a trash truck on legs. Affectionately known as Alphabet, he was short, round, bald, and myopic. A luxurious Snidely Whiplash mustache grew in the shade of his hooked nose. His tie was loosened and the sleeves of his white shirt rolled up to the elbows.

"Okay if we take the body?" Lily asked from the other side of the car.

"The sooner the better," Fey said.

Lily put two fingers in her mouth and whistled a piercing note. The two Igors, slouched against the side of the coroner's van, pushed themselves vertical and unfolded a black body bag.

"What do you want us to do with Gina Kane?" Monk asked, referring to the records clerk who had attacked April. "We've still got her on ice along with Waverly's boss, John Dancer."

Fey thought for a moment. "I'll deal with Dancer, but I'm not sure what to do about Kane. You've interviewed her, right?"

"Yeah. She's pretty torn up."

Fey snorted. "I'd say more than fifty percent of that is an act, but I don't know what more we can do with her at the moment. We have to play this by the book, so let's crank out a battery report against her for attacking April Waverly, and then let her go home. Make sure she knows she's not off the hook and that I'll want to talk to her. We'll present the battery case to the city attorney when we're tying up loose ends. I also want a personnel complaint initiated." She looked at Brindle. "You take care of it. Okay?"

"Sure," Brindle said. "But isn't that going a bit far? The woman was distraught. Who knows how any of us would react in the same situation?"

"She was out of control," Fey said. "She deserves everything she gets."

Brindle shrugged her acceptance, knowing it wouldn't do any good to argue.

The detectives watched as the Igors helped Lily manhandle the remains of Alex Waverly into a body bag and carry the awkward package away to the coroner's van.

"Thanks, Lily," Fey called out.

"Anytime, sugar," Lily said with a backward wave.

Fey turned her attention to Alphabet. "All right, let's get this scene cleared up. See if you can recover the slugs from the dashboard, and then get the screens down and impound the car. Tell the tow yard I want it secured in a print shed until I tell them differently."

"You want it held for prints?" Alphabet asked. The request didn't make sense.

"No," Fey said. "I just want the car kept in a locked print shed for security. I don't want any of the police gear disappearing."

Alphabet nodded and started to get busy.

"What do you want me to do?" Monk asked.

"After we take all this gear upstairs, I want you to get down to the coroner's office. Use the cellular phone and get the chief's adjutant to call ahead. Make sure Waverly gets autopsy priority. Get Rex Powers to do the cutting if you can. I want the results before we go home tonight. It should be straightforward."

"I'll take care of it," Monk said.

"Okay," Fey said. She was still running on the adrenaline high. "While you're doing that, I'll handle this Lieutenant Dancer character. Where have you hidden him?"

6

BACK AT her desk, Fey found a message to call Arch Hammersmith at the hospital. She dialed Hammer's mobile phone.

"Hammer," came the brusk response after two rings.

"What's up?" Fey asked.

"Hi, boss," Hammersmith said. "April Waverly is still out of it, but the doctor tells us she's okay to move."

"Great. Get her down to the jail ward at County Hospital and book her."

"I'm in the ambulance with her now," Hammersmith said. "Rhonda is already there getting the paperwork started."

Rhonda Lawless, aka Nails, had been partners with Hammersmith for over four years. They had transferred to West L.A. two years earlier from Internal Affairs. Speculation was strong at the time that they had been sent to investigate rumors of racism and sexism within the area. The speculation almost turned to certainty when they were assigned to different investigative tables and, within thirty minutes, pressure had come down from above to give them an assignment together.

Fey still wasn't quite sure if the pair were connected to Internal Affairs in some way, but she did know they had influence in many different spheres. It wasn't exactly a case of whatever Hammer and Nails wanted, Hammer and Nails got, but it was close. You almost never saw one without the other, either on duty or off. They clicked with a rare form of nonverbal communication, and there was an unspoken sexual tension between them that was electric.

"Make sure you arrange for a suicide watch," Fey said. "I don't want April offing herself in custody."

"You suck eggs this way, Grandma," Hammersmith said with friendly sarcasm. "We've already taken care of it. We've also done the protective custody petition to make the baby a ward of the court until DCS can find a suitable placement."

"Okay, okay," Fey said. "Don't rub my nose in it. I'm the boss. I'm entitled to be a mother hen."

"Trust me," Hammer said. "You're in good hands."

"I've heard you have good hands," Fey said.

"Someone must have been telling tales out of school."

Fey laughed. "Call me when you get clear," she said, and rang off. Hammer and Nails were the unit's Dobermans, and Fey had learned it was best to let them run loose.

Even though it had been several years since she'd smoked, Fey had a sudden urge for a cigarette. To fight the craving, she poured a cup of coffee and walked into Lieutenant Cahill's office. Cahill was at his desk writing. John Dancer, Waverly's ATD lieutenant, was sitting at the conference table fiddling with a paper clip. All the brass who had been there earlier were in the wind.

"Sorry to have kept you waiting, Lieutenant Dancer," Fey said. "It's been a hell of a day so far."

"You can say that again," Dancer agreed.

"Do you know Detective Fey Croaker?" Cahill asked Dancer.

"We've never met," Dancer replied. "But I've certainly heard of her." He stood up and extended his hand. Fey shook it.

"How is everything going?" Cahill asked. "The chief is going to want an update."

"Alphabet is clearing the scene outside the station. He'll curtail the cordon and we can release the day watch officers." Fey looked at her watch. It was almost five o'clock. Day watch had been held over on tac alert only for an hour and a half, which would keep the overtime mavens happy. "Brindle is handling Gina Kane. We're letting her go, but filing the appropriate crime reports and initiating a one-eighty-one. Hammer and Nails are transporting April to the jail ward at County Hospital. She's not talking, but the doctors have okayed her for booking. Monk is following the body to the coroner's office. He's going to ramrod the autopsy through. I told him I want the results before we go home."

"And the press?"

"I'll deal with them personally when we're done here."

Cahill nodded. "I'm impressed, and I'm sure the chief will be pleased."

"Just don't hog all the brownie points," Fey said.

"Fey, would I—"

"Yes, you would," Fey said, interrupting Cahill's insincere plea. She returned her attention to Dancer. "I know you've already talked to some of my people," she said, "but could you run through today's sequence of events again?"

"Sure," Dancer said. "I have to admit that I'm still blown away by the whole thing."

Rapidly, Dancer took Fey through the series of incidents from April Waverly arriving at the ATD office to the shooting in front of the station.

"Any indication something was wrong?" Fey asked.

"I didn't even know Waverly's wife was pregnant. It looked as if she was ready to give birth on the spot when she turned up downtown. All I wanted to do was get her off my hands as fast as possible. Driving her here to meet her husband seemed the best way to accomplish that end."

"Did they have any other children?"

"I don't think so. As far as I know, they hadn't been married long."

"Has anybody notified Waverly's next of kin?" Cahill asked.

"I haven't had the chance yet," Fey said. I haven't even had the chance to void my last cup of coffee, she thought with a silent sigh and a tightening of her bladder.

"Let me take care of that issue," Dancer said. "We have Alex's emergency records at the division, and the notification will be better coming from somebody he worked with."

"Thanks. I appreciate it," Fey said before bringing the interview back in line. "What about Waverly's work performance?"

"Exceptional," Dancer said. "The team he worked with have recently pulled off a couple of terrific scores."

"What kind of work did he do?" Fey asked.

"I'm afraid that's classified," Dancer said.

"Classified?"

"Before anyone comes to work for ATD they have to receive a top secret government clearance."

"I think I'm offended," Fey said.

"Don't be," Dancer told her. "The world of intelligence is a whole different ball game from regular police work. We trade in secrets, and everything is handled on a need-to-know basis."

"And if I decide I need to know something for this investigation?"

Dancer shrugged. "Why would you? Waverly was shot by his wife in front of witnesses. She isn't a terrorist. I would have thought the whole situation was abundantly clear."

Cahill's secretary stuck her head into the office. "Fey," she said. "Monk Lawson is on the phone for you. Line one."

"Okay," Fey said. "I'll take it in here." She punched line one. "Hi, Monk."

"Are you alone?"

Fey looked around at Cahill and Dancer. They were both watching her. "No."

"Be cool, then," Monk told her.

Fey turned her back to the room. "What's up?"

"I'm at the coroner's office. The chief's adjutant came through like a charm. Waverly was rushed right onto a slab as soon as we arrived."

"Good," Fey said.

"Not exactly," Monk said. "Rex Powers is doing the cutting , and he's come up with a problem."

"Really?"

"A big problem." Monk sighed audibly. "Waverly was already dead when his wife shot him."

7

"I'M NOT talking dead as in natural causes here," Monk said into the phone when Fey didn't reply. "I'm talking dead as in murdered."

"Are you sure?" Fey knew the question was stupid, but asking it was an automatic reaction.

"For shit's sake, Fey!"

Fey was silent again, her brain kicking into overdrive. Somehow, she had to buy enough time to figure out what was going on.

"Okay," she said eventually. "Have you called your problem into shop tow yet?"

"What the hell are you talking about?" Monk asked.

Shop tow was the generic term applied to the city-owned tow trucks. If a police car broke down or crashed, shop tow responded to the scene.

"All right." Fey carried on as if oblivious to the fact she wasn't making sense to Monk. "I'll pick you up, and we'll both go to the autopsy."

"I'm already at the autopsy," Monk said. "I told you—oh, wait a second—you can't talk freely, can you?"

"That's right." Fey gave up a mental prayer of thanks that Monk had caught on.

"You're coming down here?"

"You bet. I'll leave now."

"See you when you get here," Monk said. "I'll have Doc Powers put everything on hold."

Fey hung up the phone, pokerized her face, and turned toward Cahill and Dancer.

"Problems?" Cahill asked. His trouble-sensing antennae were working overtime.

"Nothing major," Fey said. She was constantly amazed by her ability to lie. "Monk's car broke down on the way to the autopsy. He was driving the unit's old Taurus, which has over two hundred thousand miles on the clock. It was only a matter of time before it went belly-up."

"You're going to pick him up and go on to the autopsy?" Cahill knew something was in the air, but he couldn't pin it down.

"Yeah," Fey said. "The chief wants this case put to bed properly, so somebody needs to be there when the canoe makers start hollowing out the body." She had remained standing and was now making her way casually toward the door.

Dancer seemed oblivious to what was going on, but Cahill was still giving Fey the eye.

"Monk called shop tow," she continued. "They'll tow him to Wilshire station, and I'll pick him up there."

Cahill grunted, obviously still not satisfied. "Okay. Call me with the results."

"You got it," Fey told him. "And do me a favor—give the press a statement."

Cahill's scathing reply came too late. Fey was already out the door.

"Heart attack?" Fey questioned. "I thought you said it was murder?"

"Powers thinks the heart attack was induced," Monk said. He was standing next to Fey in the autopsy gowning room.

"He thinks? What good is 'he thinks'?" Fey said with disbelief. "We have to know for sure before everything goes off the rails." She was busy slipping into hospital greens, rubber boots, gloves, mask, and goggles. With quick hand movements, she tucked her hair inside a green cap and was ready to go. The age of AIDS had made the procedure necessary. During an autopsy, it was impossible to tell when an infected body might spew its contents over the closest bystander.

Fey opened her purse and took out a small jar of Mentholatum. She twisted the top off and smeared a dab of the snot green, Vaseline-like substance under her nose.

Like the rest of the coroner's office, the gowning area was chilled below comfort level and smelled of chemicals and death. The harsh strip lighting brought normally shadowed human features into stark relief and made even the living look dead.

Entering the hallway leading to the autopsy room, Fey could hear the intermittent buzzing of wall-mounted bug zappers. With dead bodies breeding an infinite number of flying pests, the zappers were a necessity for the health and cleanliness of the morgue, the decomposition room, and the autopsy area. The zappers glowed with an electric purple light that gave them the appearance of possessed, hungry life-forms.

Monk noticed Fey glance up at the electronic killing fields. "The sound always reminds me of Dr. Frankenstein trying to jump-start his monster," he said.

"Funny," Fey said. "It always reminds me of a vibrator with a short."

Monk laughed. "Let's hope your sense of humor is still intact when this autopsy is over."

Rex Powers had been a staple at the coroner's office for as long as most cops on the job could remember. When Fey and Monk entered the autopsy room, Powers was stitching together the scalp of an infant whose brain had just been removed.

"Hello, Fey," he said in greeting. Their long friendship was cemented with professional respect on both sides.

Powers nodded at the small female body on the guttered stainless-steel table. "Massive subdural hematoma," he said. "The parents are trying to claim she fell out of her crib and hit the floor headfirst." He reached over and removed the brain from the scale bowl and held it out for examination.

Both Fey and Monk looked closely at the swollen and bruised area of the brain Powers was pointing out. Each of them had attended enough autopsies to keep their gag levels under control.

"There are only two things that can cause subdural hematomas in children," Powers said. "A high-velocity impact like a car crash—"

"—or a violent, head-snapping assault by an adult," Fey finished the short list. "Mommy or Daddy must have smacked her hard enough to knock the poor thing into the next zip code."

The pathologist nodded his agreement. "More than likely, but it's going to be tough proving which one did the deed."

As far as Fey was concerned, getting a parental confession was nowhere near as tough as cutting open and gutting infant bodies. Claiming a child fell out of a crib was the oldest excuse in the book for everything from broken bones to death. No way was the impact from a crib fall hard enough to cause the damage Powers had uncovered. It was only a matter of time before a detective would be booking either one or both of the parents for murder. The case would be solved, but it wouldn't reanimate the lump of innocent clay that had once trusted and depended.

Alex Waverly's body rested on his own slab two stainless-steel tables over. Powers put the child's brain back in the scale bowl and then turned on his heels to lead the way.

The autopsy room sported an assembly line row of eight operating tables. Each had its own sink and scale at one end, and was surrounded by a variety of instrument hutches. For most of the day, all eight tables were filled as deputy coroners worked their way through the city's constant flow of victims. Coroner's assistants hosed down the tables and dealt the bodies in and out as the macabre work was completed.

"You've got yourself a doozy this time," Powers said to Fey.

"I don't need a doozy," she told him. "Can't you ever give me a break?"

"You asked me to handle the autopsy because you wanted it done right," Powers said with a shrug.

"That was my first mistake," Fey said, bantering. Then she became more serious. "So tell me why this guy wasn't killed by the two bullets his wife put in his head."

Waverly had been a good-sized man. Even in death, it was easy to see he had been tall and muscular. His barrel chest had been sliced open by the Y incision that crossed his pectoral muscles and then ran down to the top of his pubis. The incision had been pulled open to expose the inner organs.

While Fey was experienced enough not to be disturbed visually by the gory tableau presented before her, she had never been able to adjust to the smells. Standing next to Waverly's body while Powers talked, she made a conscious effort to breathe through her mouth, and was thankful for the pungent smear of Mentholatum spread under her nose.

Powers pointed toward Waverly's face. "The first clue came from the wounds themselves."

The gore spewed out by the bullets' exit holes had been cleared away, but what remained still wasn't a pretty sight.

"There was some brain matter and crap thrown around when the bullets exited, but there was no bleeding of any consequence," the pathologist continued. "The wounds were basically as clean as the thermometer incision Lily Sheridan made to check the liver temperature—a wound made after death doesn't bleed because there isn't any blood pressure to force the blood out of the hole. This one died sitting up. All his blood had already settled in lower parts of his body before he was shot."

"Well, crap," Fey said. "I should have seen that for myself. I remember thinking there wasn't a lot of blood, but it didn't register as a problem."

"You were seeing," Powers said, "but you weren't looking. Why should you? The victim had been shot twice in front of witnesses. How were you to know the scenario was any different?"

"I still should have caught it," Fey said.

Powers had already used the heavy shears to cut through the rib cage and expose the interior organs. He reached in and brought forth the heart. "You can easily see the spread of heart disease without the clue from his personal effects."

"What clue?" Fey asked. "I haven't had a chance to look through the stuff from his pockets yet, but Lily said there wasn't anything unusual."

"There wasn't," Powers said. "Many people carry medications. But meds can often clue us to a cause of death."

"Waverly had a prescription bottle?"

"Yes. Probably just picked up a refill, because it wasn't something he needed to have with him. He would have simply taken his dosage daily."

"What was the drug?"

"Digoxin. And before you ask, it's used—"

"—to control heart arrhythmia," Monk said, finishing Powers's sentence.

Powers nodded his agreement.

"How do you know about dig-a-what's-it?" Fey asked her partner.

"Digoxin," Monk said. "My mother took it for years."

Fey shrugged. "So the digoxin made you look at the heart after you decided the bullet wounds were postmortem?"

"I would have looked at the heart anyway, but the presence of the drug, coupled with the diseased condition of the heart, made the victim a prime candidate for a killer heart attack."

"Let me get this straight," Fey said. "You're telling me that a few minutes before his wife slams a couple of lead pellets into his head, Waverly conveniently has a heart attack while sitting in front of West L.A. Station? He steals his wife's thunder by being already dead?"

"In essence, yes," Powers said. "But I would have said the heart attack was more ironic than convenient."

"It's convenient if you're facing a murder-one charge."

"You have a point," Powers said. "But that's something you'll have to handle."

"I can handle coincidence," Fey said. "I don't like it, but I can handle it. However, Detective Lawson," she jerked her thumb at Monk, "tells me you think Waverly was murdered."

"Most likely."

"Most likely? Give me a break, Doc. You said he had a heart attack. I can live with that—maybe it's an entry in *Ripley's Believe It or Not*, but it can be handled. Murder is another ball game. If April Waverly didn't kill him, and you say it's still murder, then where the hell does that leave me?"

"Probably up the proverbial creek," Powers said. "His wife may have murdered him, but she didn't do it by shooting him."

"Let's back up," Fey said. "I'm getting confused. What makes you think it's murder and not a simple heart attack?"

"The victim regurgitated before he died."

Fey gave Powers a hard look. "Waverly pukes, and you're ready to call it murder?"

"Regurgitation is a very common symptom in overdose cases."

Fey shook her head.

"Look." Powers held up a hand to forestall Fey's next outburst. "I knew you would be ready to fight me on this issue. I understand how difficult the situation is becoming for you, but I didn't murder the victim. I'm just telling you how he died. Don't kill the messenger."

Fey took a deep breath and gave Monk a twisted smile. "He thinks he understands how difficult this situation is becoming." There was a trace of the earlier easy banter in her voice.

"He has no idea," Monk said in the same tone.

Fey looked back at Powers. "I'm sorry, Doc. We're being set up like fall guys on this one. If we don't get it right, it's impossible to tell how deep things are going to get."

Powers nodded sympathetically. "Trust me. I'm doing the best I can for you. Normally, you would have to wait at least twenty-four hours for a toxicology return," he said. "But I played a hunch while we were waiting for you to get here."

"I've learned not to bet against your hunches," Fey said.

"Wise choice, because it turns out I was right."

"Are you going to share this happy news with us?"

"I did a quick test on the vitreous fluid from the eye," Powers said. "I chose the eye fluid instead of blood because the blood enzymes could have absorbed the drug I was looking for—"

"Doc, I love you, but could you give us the bumper sticker version?" Fey asked. "The suspense is killing me."

"Heathen," Powers said.

"I confess."

Powers sighed. He pulled off his gloves and cracked his knuckles. He flexed his fingers several times, trying to restore circulation. "Bottom line?" He shrugged. "Alex Waverly's heart attack was brought on by a massive overdose of digoxin."

8

I T WAS after seven in the evening and the silence on the eighth floor of Parker Center was as affecting as that of an empty church. Window offices for the power players in the police administration ringed all four sides of the floor, with claustrophobic, worker bee offices in the middle. The dividing lines between being somebody and not being somebody were long corridors filled with harsh yellow lighting that was never turned off. It was as if an effort were being made to catch anyone trying to escape from the rat warrens of the middle offices to the coveted window locales.

Fey and Monk stepped out of a central elevator and turned down the long corridor leading to the building's east wing. Fey's low heels tapped a staccato calypso in time to the squeaking of Monk's crepe soles.

To the left of each door, small signs protruded at right angles proclaiming the individual or unit inside. Neither Fey nor Monk spoke until they reached the corner office that was their destination. The sign sticking out from the wall was no different in size or style from any of the others. It simply proclaimed CHIEF OF POLICE.

Fey stopped outside the closed portal with her hand on the doorknob. Monk shot her a quick glance.

"Why do we always get the complicated cases?" she asked in a weary voice.

"Because the fates that decide such things find it amusing," Monk told her. He ran a hand over his bald pate and tried to smile.

Fey's mouth twitched. "Are you saying it's my destiny to be the straight man in some cosmic joke?"

"Don't you mean straight person?"

"I'm too tired to care about political correctness."

"Hey, if you couldn't take a joke, you shouldn't have joined," Monk said, invoking a shopworn punch line used to explain away difficult situations.

"Your insight is amazing," Fey said before twisting the doorknob and stepping inside.

The office was a huge square set on the corner of the building. The chief's inner sanctum was a smaller square set into the corner of the outer square. This arrangement gave the chief's personal office two walls of windows—the ultimate power office.

In the outer office, desks belonging to the chief's personal staff sat on upgraded carpet along with a Xerox copier, a shredder, several rows of filing cabinets, and a bank of computer terminals. Files were stacked everywhere in what looked like a paperwork logjam.

A small alcove housed a desk belonging to the chief's adjutant. Dan Ayala stood up from behind the desk as Fey and Monk entered. He was the only person in the outer office, and he greeted them with a sycophantic grin.

"The chief is on the phone," he said, jerking his thumb over his shoulder in the direction of the chief's actual domain. "I'll let him know you're here."

Ayala had the confidence of those born with natural athletic abilities. Aside from his duties as adjutant, Ayala was also the chief's driver and bodyguard.

Fey looked at the phone on Ayala's desk. One of the lines glowed orange, indicating it was in use. She moved closer to the desk, trying to get a look at the file on which Ayala had been working. She only had time to focus on Alex Waverly's name before the light on the phone went dead. She moved back from the desk quickly as Ayala returned.

"He can see you now," Ayala said. His expression changed as he looked at Fey. It was as if he sensed he'd almost caught her hand in the cookie jar. He cut his eyes toward Monk, who gave him a stone face in return.

"Thanks, Dan," Fey said with more assurance than she felt.

The chief was alone. Fey was surprised. Usually there were so many toadies around, you couldn't get near the chief. If bootlicking were a merit badge, the PD's upper echelon would all be Eagle Scouts.

Sitting at his desk, the chief looked up through deep-set, heavily hooded eyes that betrayed the strain of his position. Behind the desk, an American flag and a California flag hung dramatically on separate poles. A carved wooden Seal of California was mounted on the wall between them. The seal was placed high enough on the wall to be directly above the chief's head. It was a great set for photo ops.

The desk was a miniature landing carrier that looked as if it had taken a full stand of walnut trees to build. The stock price for Pledge, providing the desktop with its mirrorlike shine, had probably doubled. A lonely pen on a marble stand and a plastic city phone were the only accoutrements to grace the work surface.

The big man stepped forward to greet the detectives. He ushered them toward comfortable chairs arranged around a low coffee table and dismissed Ayala. "If we need anything, Dan, I'll shout.

"You have bad news for me?" he said, turning to Fey.

Fey didn't reply at first, wondering if somebody had already told him the news.

"It's clear your news is bad," the chief said, explaining his assumption. "If you had good news, you would have reported it telephonically."

"Yes, sir," Fey said. "It's bad news. Alex Waverly died from an overdose of heart medicine before his wife shot him."

"You're saying he was sitting in his car already dead?"

Fey shrugged. "There doesn't seem to be any other way around it, sir."

"Hell of a coincidence."

"Yes, sir."

The chief held her eyes. "That's all you've got to say—'yes, sir'?"

Fey blew out a deep breath through pursed lips. "I don't know what else you expect me to say." She deliberately left off the *sir*. "I feel like I've been thrust into some kind of bullshit game without being told the rules. You seem to want me to pull a rabbit out of a hat, and do it without either the rabbit or the hat."

The chief chuckled in a deep tone that reminded Fey of James Earl Jones. "You've done it before," he said. "Your career has been interesting."

"The old Chinese saying 'May you live in interesting times' is a curse, not a blessing," Fey said.

"You said an overdose of heart medicine. Suicide?"

"Possibly, but I don't think so. Waverly had a full vial of his prescription in his jacket pocket. Obviously, they weren't used for an overdose."

"Accident?"

"No way. The pathologist said there was too much of the drug in his system for it to be taken accidentally."

"You're aware of the only option left?"

"Absolutely," Fey said. "Waverly was still murdered, only now we don't know who did it."

The chief shifted in his chair. "What about the wife? Why did she shoot him?"

"She's still dissociative. We haven't had a chance to get into motive yet."

"Well, we certainly can't hold her for murder any longer."

"No," Fey said. "But we can hold her for attempted murder. Even though she shot a corpse, she is still technically guilty of attempting to murder her husband. She didn't know he was dead."

"The DA's office agrees with this?"

Fey shrugged. "They're the ones who advised me. I don't think they'll actually file a formal charge, but it's enough to hold her in our custody until we can sort things out."

The chief walked over to the glassed corner of the office and gazed out over the city.

"Detective Lawson," he spoke to Monk directly for the first time, but did not turn to face him, "I hope you won't think me too rude, but I would like to speak to Detective Croaker alone." The chief turned back to face the detectives. "Please do not take offense. This is not a reflection on you," he told Monk, spreading a hand in a gesture that asked for understanding.

"Sure, Chief," Monk said, levering himself out of his chair. "No problem." He winked at Fey and left the room to join Ayala in the outer office.

The chief sat down again. "With your partner outside," he said, by way of explanation, "I know my aide will not be trying to eavesdrop with a water glass pressed against the door."

"You're joking?"

The chief smiled. "Politics is an interesting exercise," he said. "But it does tend to raise one's paranoia level."

Fey sat back in her chair and waited. This was the chief's game, and it was up to him to make the first move.

"I understand, Fey, that you disagree with many of the modifications and restructurings I've made within the department." The chief had been with the LAPD for four years. He had been appointed as chief from an outside agency—a move that had ruffled the feathers of many who had come up through the ranks. The time period had been one of turbulent changes for the department— changes that had been very hard for Fey and many others of the old-time rank and file to accept.

From the chief's statement, Fey realized she had to be very, very careful.

"The department was overdue for change," Fey said. "I'm just not sure the changes you have brought about are the right ones."

"Such as?"

Fey shrugged. "It would be faster for me to list the changes I think were right," she said, regretting the words the instant they passed her lips. So much for being careful. She knew she had a problem with speaking her mind too freely. It was something she was working on, but obviously still had a long way to go.

Fey looked down at her hands in her lap, expecting to be verbally blown apart any second. Instead, she heard the chief laughing softly.

"I've always known you were a pistol."

"I'm sorry," Fey said, looking up. "I care about this department. I care about what happens to it, and I'm not going to sit here and tell you that I think you're making correct changes when I don't."

"There's no need to apologize. Believe it or not, I also care about this department. We simply have different visions of its purpose and future."

Fey didn't respond, wishing she'd remained silent from the start.

The silence dragged until the chief spoke again. "How much can I depend on your loyalty, Fey?"

Talk about minefields, Fey thought. How the hell was she supposed to answer that question?

"The LAPD can always depend on my loyalty, Chief. I think I've proven that time and again over the years."

The chief sharpened his stare, making Fey uncomfortable. "There has never been any doubt about your loyalty to the department," he said. "But I'm asking, if *I*, personally, can rely on your loyalty."

Fey realized she was in a tough spot.

"Your hesitation speaks for itself," the chief said when Fey didn't immediately reply. His voice held something else beside disappointment. "Let me be more specific. Would you lie for me?"

Fey didn't hesitate this time. "No."

"Would you cover up something I was involved in if revealing it would damage the department?"

"No." Again, no hesitation.

"What if there was personal gain in it for you?"

"No."

"Not even if I could guarantee you promotion and the choice of plum assignments?"

"No." Fey could feel anger building within her.

"What about my predecessor? I know you were loyal to him. Your personnel file shows you've twice worked assignments that answered directly to him. Would you have lied for him?"

"This is getting ridiculous," Fey said, standing up.

"Just answer the question, Detective Croaker."

The chief locked eyes with Fey. She sucked in air to calm herself and she again felt the sudden urge for a cigarette. She really hated being a nonsmoker.

"Let's get real here," Fey said, returning to her chair. "If you want to know if I've ever covered for a good cop who has made an honest, minor mistake, the answer is yes. If you're asking me if I have ever, or would ever, cover up something that was illegal or immoral, then the answer is no. Not for you. Not for anybody." Fey's voice rose an octave as anger surged through her. "And if you think some stinking promotion or other personal gain would make me compromise my personal integrity—"

"Whoa!" Holding both hands out in front of him, the chief sought to staunch Fey's verbal tsunami. "I have no intention of compromising your integrity. But I have to know where you stand."

"What did you expect me to say?" Fey asked. "Would you expect anyone to tell you anything different than I did?"

"Yes," the chief said, taking the wind out of Fey's sails. "Perhaps they wouldn't tell me anything different verbally, but their dishonesty would be revealed in a myriad of other ways—body language, tone of voice, facial expression, past track record. You may not like the direction I'm taking this department, but that doesn't mean I'm an incompetent idiot."

Even though she remained silent, Fey's eyes revealed her opinion of that statement, and the chief was quick to read the message.

"Don't overstep your boundaries, Detective."

"What do you want from me?" Fey asked, tiring of the game but refusing to back down.

"What I want is for you to use your vaunted integrity to find out who killed Alex Waverly. And I want you to do it no matter what the cost to yourself, to me, or to the department."

9

"THERE MUST be something about this division that attracts the most off-the-wall cases," Arch Hammersmith said. He was broad shouldered with a tapered waist and long legs. His face, under short-cropped hair, was full of angles and shadows. He was intense and impatient, always a step ahead of everyone else—except his partner, who operated on the same wavelength. "What the hell is going on here, boss?"

"That's the exact same question I asked the chief," Fey replied. "And he told me exactly what I'm going to tell you—I don't know."

Fey had brought Monk up to speed as they drove back to the station, and they had discussed strategy. Now they were doing the same with the other members of the homicide unit.

Fey sat at her desk, with Monk at the desk to her left and Brindle Jones at the desk to her right. Alphabet had pulled his own chair up next to Brindle, while Hammersmith and Rhonda Lawless leaned against the file cabinets behind Monk.

Lieutenant Cahill sat on the edge of the desk next to Brindle's. He was part of the group, but not part of the team—an untrusted outsider. In the them-and-us mentality of the police versus the public, Cahill was one of *us*, but in the microcosm them-and-us of the rank and file versus management, Cahill was one of *them*.

"It's no secret that a lot of people from the top down are not happy with the direction the chief is taking the department. It's not a long stretch to acknowledging there's a movement within the department to get the chief removed," Fey said. "The chief has survived so far because of his political pull outside the department—the people who appointed the chief can't afford to have him removed without irreparably damaging their own power base."

"All that means," Alphabet interjected, "is that there are a lot of politicians within the city who want to see the police department torn apart in order to advance their own agenda."

"The same people who pissed themselves silly with delight when Bates and Milton finally went down in flames. And since then the carrion have been happily picking the corpse of the city clean," Brindle said. She was referring to the prior chief of office and prior mayor. Their personal enmity had been legendary, with political infighting ultimately destroying them both while almost crushing the city in the process.

"I agree," Fey said. "But they don't pay us to care about that kind of philosophical shit. They pay us to solve murders, and the process of doing that hasn't changed since Cain and Abel."

"What about Robbery-Homicide? Shouldn't this be their baby?" Rhonda asked. "They must be having a fit." Tall and catlike with dark, spiked hair, she was Hammer's matching bookend both in temperament and physicality. Fey had seen Rhonda naked in the locker room on several occasions and was always amazed by her bodybuilder's physique.

"I can see us handling this thing if it was a straight smoking gun—a domestic: wife kills husband because he's dipping his wick in a strange honey pot," Rhonda continued. "But now it's a genuine whodunit." She accented the word *genuine* to make it sound like *gen-u-eyene*.

"I agree it shouldn't be our responsibility," Fey said, "but Vaughn Harrison is the deputy chief over Robbery-Homicide Division, and the chief trusts him about as far as he can spit," she explained. "Everyone knows that Harrison is a back-stabbing son of a bitch who wants to be chief of police so bad, just thinking about it makes him shake like he's crapping peach pits." Fey picked up a pencil and tapped it on her desktop. "Harrison is the chief's top rival, and there's no love lost between them. The chief knows this investigation is going to get ugly, and he doesn't want Harrison being able to stir the pot at every turn."

Monk picked up the thread. "There's also something funny in the fact that Waverly was a big success at Robbery-Homicide before moving to the Anti-Terrorist Division. Hotshot units like RHD don't give up their star players to a rival unit without reason. Whatever that reason was, it died at Harrison's level."

"Cover-up?" Hammer asked.

Fey shrugged. "Who knows? But if Waverly's murder has anything to do with the department, the chief feels putting RHD in charge of the investigation would be like putting the fox in charge of the henhouse."

"Harrison is also the deputy chief over ATD, isn't he?" Hammer asked.

"He's in charge of all specialized divisions," Cahill confirmed.

"Are you telling us we're looking for a killer from inside the department?" Rhonda Lawless decided to stop dancing around the question that was on all of their minds.

"Maybe," Fey said bluntly. "I damn well hope not, but maybe." Nobody wanted it to be true. The department still had not recovered from the bloodletting and scandals that came to a head with the Rodney King case and the Days of Rage riots in 1992. Events such as those took years, if not decades, to recoup from.

The homicide crew sat silently, absorbing the implications. Department morale was now worse than ever, and trust between management and the troops was nonexistent. A murderer within the ranks would do more than enough damage—but a murderer within the ranks who was killing cops didn't bear thinking about.

Monk stirred in his chair and stood up. He walked to the coffee room and came back carrying a pot of leaded. He filled his own cup and Fey's, and then handed the pot off to Alphabet.

"There's a bottom line here," he said. "The chief has ordered Fey to run with this case personally—wherever it leads. She can't do it alone, and that's where we come in."

"I knew there was going to be a catch in this somewhere." Brindle sighed.

Monk flashed his teeth at her. "You don't like the hot seat?"

"This caper isn't just a hot seat," Brindle said. "You're talking about riding the lightning." Her slang was a reference to the electric chair.

"There's no doubt sparks are going to fly before this is over," Fey said. "And that's why it's more important than ever we do things precisely by the book."

"Right," Hammer said with a laugh. "I've worked with you too long to believe that resolution."

Fey shot him a dirty look. "When this investigation gets nasty, people, we're only going to have each other to rely on. We don't take anybody else's word for anything. Got it?"

"What about the regular workload?" Alphabet asked.

"Brindle, you, and I are going to handle it," Monk told him. "We're the home team. Fey will take Hammer and Nails and run with the Waverly investigation. The rest of us will be there if they need backup." This was the plan that Monk and Fey had discussed driving back to the station.

Alphabet nodded and patted Brindle on the shoulder. "Always a bridesmaid, never a bride," he said resignedly.

"Don't worry," Fey said, her voice hard. "I have a feeling by the time this is over, there's going to be more than enough crap to cover all of us."

10

WHEN THE phone shrilled, Lieutenant John Dancer was in the middle of boffing his wife, an all too infrequent occurrence since the birth of their third child. The couple's actions could not have been referred to as making love, as that was an emotion which neither participant had felt for a long time.

Mandy Dancer sighed when her husband broke his rhythm and pushed away from her. She was a skinny woman with no breasts and a shrewish temperament. She had been born into money—money that Dancer had married her for but found he could not tap. For her part, Mandy had married Dancer for no better reason than he made her wet when she first saw him in uniform. Neither reason was good enough to sustain the relationship, but three children blinded them to the futility of continuing to claw each other to death.

Dancer's body snapped to attention when he realized Vaughn Harrison was on the other end of the phone line. With his heart still pounding from his sexual exertions, Dancer fought to listen intently as Harrison quickly explained the change in status of Alex Waverly's murder investigation, including Fey's new role as special investigator.

"Oh, shit," Dancer said. He knew better than to ask Harrison where he had obtained the information, but it worried him. The fact that Waverly was already dead when his wife shot him certainly wasn't public knowledge. The press had covered the event strictly as a tragic example of domestic violence. There hadn't even been a hint of anything more sinister.

"I want Croaker shut down hard," Harrison barked at Dancer. "She gets nothing from ATD the easy way. If the chief wants to play hardball, then we're going to come up to the plate with the big bats. Got it?"

"But what about Alex? Somebody murdered the poor bastard," Dancer replied.

"I'm as sorry as you are, John, that Alex is dead," Harrison said, "but the guy was a cock hound. This is clearly a domestic fracas. Somehow, someway, his death is going to be connected to tomcatting. What else could it be?"

"I don't know," Dancer said, sounding unsure.

"Come on, John," Harrison implored. "Poison is a woman's choice of weapons. Who the hell do you think murdered Alex—some female terrorist out of a Robert Ludlum book?"

"Of course not."

"I'm telling you, turning Croaker loose instead of letting Robbery-Homicide take over the case proves the chief doesn't give a damn about catching a cop killer. His only interest is in starting a witch-hunt. This is the excuse he's been looking for to take us on." Harrison paused and Dancer could almost feel the strength of the man's personality flowing down the phone line.

"How many times have you said yourself the chief is nothing more than a pawn of the mayor and the city council?" Harrison continued. "We've got to get rid of the bastard before he ruins what's left of this department. This city is already tearing itself apart, and if the department is allowed to get any weaker, the predators are going to take over."

"I hear you," Dancer said firmly. He was well aware of the razor's edge of potential violence upon which the city balanced.

"Clean this up, John," Harrison directed. "Get your people in line quickly. We can't have the rug pulled out from under us because Alex was cock-happy. Don't let me down!"

Harrison hung up, leaving Dancer with a dead phone and a

heart still pounding. The racing of his pulse, however, no longer had anything to do with his derailed libido.

Mandy Dancer looked at her husband's flaccid manhood with a smirk. Feeling superior, she pulled the covers up around her neck, turned her back on her husband, and went to sleep.

Left sitting in the bed, darkness filling the room around him, Dancer could have done with a sympathetic touch. He thought of Mary DeFalco, the ATD secretary with the legendary legs, and felt his loins stirring. He looked over at the sleeping form of his wife and realized the fruitlessness of trying to interest her again.

You bitch! he silently screamed at her in his head. Dragging himself upright, he padded naked into the bathroom. His clothes for the next morning were already laid out. He felt claustrophobic, his mind swirling with the implications of Harrison's phone call. His pulse was pounding. If he left now, he could get his people rolling on Croaker.

11

JOHN DANCER was not the only person to receive an unsettling phone call in the middle of the night. Jangling rings penetrated Fey's exhausted sleep and forced her to consciousness. She fumbled for the phone, knocking the receiver from its cradle. Cursing, she tried to sit up in bed, dislodging the two cats that had been sleeping peacefully on her feet.

She groped for the receiver in the dark, made contact with the phone cord, and reeled the receiver in hand over hand like a young boy trying to land a fish. Through bleary eyes she tried to focus on the red glow of her alarm clock. One thirty-eight A.M. She'd been in bed for a little over an hour, but had been exhausted enough to immediately go dead to the world. The last thing she needed was another homicide call-out.

"Croaker," she said into the phone's mouthpiece. Her voice was muzzy with sleep, her brain not yet sharp.

"That's right," a semifamiliar male voice slurred from far away down the line. "If she digs too deep, they're gonna *croak her.*" The voice giggled.

"Who the hell is this?" Fey was not at her best after being rudely awakened.

"Croaker? Is that you?" The giggling had stopped, but the voice still held a slight slur.

Fey fought to recognize the voice. She knew it, but couldn't place it. "Yeah, this is Croaker. You've got five seconds to stop farting around and tell me what you want."

"Jeeze, you're a hard bitch, Croaker. Do you know that everybody thinks you're a hard bitch?"

Fey had the voice now. "Keegan? Is that you? Do you know what time it is?" Keegan was one of the Robbery-Homicide dicks who'd been in Cahill's office earlier in the day. Fey knew he'd been pissed when the chief had told her to run with the case.

"I've always fancied you, Croaker. You've got something—"

"Something you're never going to get," Fey cut in. She'd heard this kind of bar-closing crap too many times before. "You sound drunk, Keegan. Do you have something to say, or is this a pathetic attempt at an obscene phone call?"

Brentwood, a white furball on legs powered by a whipcord tail, jumped back onto the bed. Fey reached over to scratch the fluffy white cat behind the ears.

"Watch your step on this caper, Croaker. There's stuff you don't know. If you get in the way, they'll run right over you."

"What are you talking about? What stuff don't I know?"

"I got a fifteen-year-old daughter, Croaker. Did you know that?"

"Can't say as I did."

"Well, they do."

"Who's *they*, Keegan?"

The line hummed with silence. Another, larger fur ball, this one black in color, pushed into Fey's lap. Marvella added her purring to Brentwood's. Fey pushed both cats aside and swung her legs over the edge of the bed.

"Keegan? Are you still with me? Keegan?" Fey knew he was there—she could hear him breathing. A picture popped into her head of Keegan holding on to the receiver of a pay phone in the back of a bar, his head pressed against the wall. For some reason she imagined he was crying.

"Talk to me, Keegan. Tell me what I need to know."

The line went dead. The caller had hung up.

"Damn!" Fey slammed down the phone on her end. Quickly, she picked it up again and pressed the *, 6, and 9 buttons, which dialed back the number of the last incoming call.

A phone rang at the other end and went on ringing. After fifteen rings, somebody picked up the phone. "The Gunnery."

Fey recognized the voice. "Harry, it's Fey Croaker."

"Hey, Fey. What are you doing calling in on the pay phone?" Harry Cross was the bartender at The Gunnery, a well-known cop watering hole.

"Sorry to drag you from behind the bar, Harry," Fey said. "But have you seen Derek Keegan tonight?"

Harry laughed. "Do you and Derek got a thing going on now? Are you checking up on him?"

"Give me some credit," Fey said. "The only person Keegan has a thing with is himself."

"Whew," Harry said. "For a moment there, I'd almost lost faith in you."

"This is important, Harry," Fey said.

Harry had known Fey for a lot of years and could read the urgency in her voice. He stopped messing around. "Derek was here," he said. "But I don't see him now."

"Are you sure?"

"Yeah. He was drinking heavier than normal, but Hale was with him so I figured he'd be okay."

"Is Hale still there?" Hale was Keegan's RHD partner.

Harry took a second before replying. Fey mentally pictured him scanning the bar. "No," Harry said, coming back on the line. "It's almost closing. Things are pretty quiet."

"Okay," Fey said. "Thanks."

"Catch you on the flip side," Harry said and hung up.

Damn, Fey thought as she put her end of the phone down and dropped her torso backward onto the bed. Here we go!

Fey sipped from an oversized coffee mug while splashing lactose-free milk into two bowls. Brentwood and Marvella both knew a treat was coming, and were bouncing around as if trying out for a Broadway chorus line.

"What's with you two this morning?" Fey asked her feline buddies as if she expected an answer. "You'd think you haven't been fed in a week." She put the milk bowls down on the kitchen floor, where the cats attacked them.

The cats had both been gifts to Fey from the Grim Reaper. Brentwood had been the only witness to the murder of a woman who had supposedly been killed ten years earlier. It had been a big case for Fey, and solidified her reputation as an investigator.

Brentwood had been with Fey for a couple of years now, but Marvella was a more recent addition to Fey's menagerie. She had inherited the huge, bad-tempered lump of claws and teeth when Ash, an FBI agent who had been both a lover and a friend, lost a bitter battle with ALS—amyotrophic lateral sclerosis.

Following shortly after the violent death of her brother, Ash's decline and passing had left Fey feeling hollow inside. For several months, she had simply gone through the motions of breathing and being alive.

Coupled with the deaths had been the impact of shattering public revelations about Fey's sexually abusive childhood. The laying bare of her most private secrets had resulted from the intense media coverage of a high-profile murder case. The secrets themselves had no bearing on the case. But when a high-priced defense lawyer came into possession of Fey's taped psychiatric sessions, he saw a way to smear the investigation and direct attention away from his client.

Piled on top of each other, these events had become a crushing emotional burden. Looking to withdraw into herself, to streamline her life, Fey had retreated to the rambling ranch-style home that had always been her sanctuary. Built after the demise of her third marriage, the house stood hard against the foothills of the San Fernando Valley suburb of L.A. It defined Fey's personal space, giving her room not only for herself but also for her horses and other assorted animals.

Though she continued as the homicide unit supervisor in West L.A., Fey had cut herself off from most social contacts. She took care of her horses, Thieftaker and Constable, and worked to establish Ash House, a private children's hospital that was part of her deceased lover's legacy.

With more time than normal on her hands, she had taken up running—not jogging, but running—and had come to exhilarate in the physically cleansing and mentally purifying aspects of that activity. The running had helped her to find her center gain, to go beyond the pain that had seared her soul, and recently she was beginning to feel back in control. Life was becoming of interest again.

Leaving the cats to lick up their breakfast, Fey took her coffee back to the bathroom. She ran a brush rapidly through her black shoulder-length hair and then secured it behind her head with a large, antique brass clip.

She applied minimal makeup, making sure none dusted down onto her blue silk blouse, black knee-length skirt, and black hose. She'd dropped weight during the stresses of the past year and, checking the trim of her stomach in the mirror, wryly reflected on silver linings. Her muscle tone had always been good from hours spent riding hard in the saddle, but her recent exercise and running regime had added definition. *Not bad for an old broad*, she thought before snapping off the bathroom light and moving back to the bedroom for a pair of low black heels.

The call from Keegan in the early hours of the morning had left her disturbed and sleepless. She knew Keegan was a conscientious if unimaginative detective. He was a slogger, solving cases more by sheer determination than astute deduction. She hadn't known Keegan had a fifteen-year-old daughter, and as she finished her coffee, she wondered who the *they* was who did know about Keegan's daughter, and exactly what that meant.

Keegan had sounded drunk on the phone. Something had obviously been eating at him—something that scared him. Fey realized the call had been a warning, not a threat—a warning to Fey to bury Waverly's death in a shallow grave lest she dig too deep and unleash a monster. But Fey knew about monsters. She'd been battling them all her life, and it would take much more than a midnight phone call to make her back down.

She rinsed her mug in the kitchen sink, then refilled it to take with her. As she absently took a sip, she thought briefly about the chief's order not to reveal the circumstances arising from Waverly's autopsy to the press.

Fey had gladly agreed with the directive at the time. She certainly didn't need the pressure. But now she wondered if stonewalling the press was really wise. The media could be brutal under the best of circumstances. When they found out Waverly's death was not the simple domestic killing the department claimed, the caca would hit the fan big time, and information leaks were inevitable. Between the coroner's office, RHD, ATD, the chief's aides, the department's top brass, and Fey's own crew, too many people knew the true facts. Leaks would happen. Fey's only hope was to solve the case quickly.

Setting her mug back on the kitchen counter, she squatted to stroke both cats. She checked her watch. It was still early, before six, but the day ahead was going to be longer than an hour in a dentist's chair.

Pulling her ancient black Datsun Z car out of the garage, Fey tuned the radio to a news station. Preoccupied with all of the things needing to be done, she didn't notice the dark blue Buick that pulled away from the curb a block behind her.

12

FEY WAS NOT surprised to see Hammer and Nails already at work when she walked into the squad room.

"Don't you two ever sleep?" she asked, dropping her purse on her desk.

"Life's too short," Hammer replied without looking up from his laptop. As usual, he was pushing the envelope of acceptable detective fashions. In a world where pale blue shirts and polka-dot ties were considered avant-garde, Hammer was a constant challenge to convention. Today, his traditional, all-black outfit over cowboy boots had been dressed up with a colorful Indian bead belt that sported a huge silver buckle, a silver conch bolo tie, and a black vest with silver brocade.

A detective who didn't know Hammer might think he was some kind of drugstore cowboy, but Fey knew that the silver belt buckle had been the top prize for bull riding at the International Police Rodeo in Calgary a year earlier. Hammer had earned his spurs and then some.

"Anybody else in yet?" Fey asked.

Rhonda shook her head. "The rest of the crew is due around eight, as usual. Apparently, it was a quiet night."

"Let's be thankful for small favors," Fey said. "We could do with a whole string of slow nights right now."

Rhonda put a hand over her eyes in a dramatic gesture. "You had to say something, didn't you?" she said. "Now we'll be throwing more chalk on the ground than a kid on eraser duty."

"Touch wood and bite my tongue," Fey said, quickly matching actions to the statement, hoping against hope to ward off a plague of homicides. Every detective knew you shouldn't challenge fate. If there had been any salt around, she would have thrown it over her shoulder.

Fey walked into the small coffee room and poured a cup of black syrup. Rhonda followed her in.

Brindle might be the unit's obvious fashion maven, but Rhonda had a style all her own—subtle beauty and power in one package. She was wearing a black jumpsuit that was cinched around her waist with a belt of silver conchs that matched Hammersmith's bolo. Below her spiked, raven black hair, silver earrings dangled moons and stars halfway to her shoulders. She was as tall as Hammersmith and model slender without the fragility. Fey felt a twinge of jealousy knowing that they were both the same age. Although she was older, Rhonda could still pass for early thirties.

"What's he so busy cranking out?" she asked Rhonda with a nod of her head in Hammersmith's direction.

"Search warrant for Gina Kane's pad and another for Waverly's house. We were talking about the obvious suspects in this case, and the love triangle is still the simple solution." Rhonda added cream to Hammersmith's coffee, but left hers black.

"April Waverly shoots her husband because he's cheating on her with Gina Kane," Fey said, "but Gina beats her to the punch by poisoning Waverly because he won't leave April?"

"It could happen," Rhonda said. "We've got to consider it as an option."

"I agree," Fey told her. "But it reeks of coincidence."

"Coincidence happens."

"I know, but I still don't like it." Fey chewed down another bite of coffee. "How about this angle?" Fey said, deciding to throw out a theory that had been bugging her for a while. "April Waverly poisons her husband and then later shoots him. In her mind, she figures she'll be cleared of murder charges as soon as it's discovered—as she knows it will be—that Waverly was already dead. Furthermore, by shooting him—making out as if she was murdering him—she figures that nobody would think twice about her being the culprit in the original poisoning."

"Nasty," Rhonda said. "Being a cop's wife, April knows enough about how the system works to realize that she'd walk on the attempted murder charge because no DA in their right mind is going to go into court behind that kind of case."

"I don't buy it," Hammersmith said, having entered the coffee room and overheard the conversation. "You've got even more coincidences and logistic problems than the first theory. You're also talking major premeditation. Somehow, I don't think we're going to find that type of behavior consistent with April Waverly's personality."

"We don't know that yet," Rhonda said.

Hammersmith shrugged. "We spent a lot of time with her yesterday. Do you think she's faking this dissociative stuff?"

Rhonda shook her head thoughtfully. "No—I don't think she's faking. And that level of emotional distress is not consistent with the cool calculation needed to first pull off the poisoning and then follow up with the shooting. The timing would have to be almost perfect."

"She could be a hell of an actress," Fey said.

"No way," Hammer and Nails said in unison.

Fey laughed. "Okay, I'll take your word for it. But even if April is only responsible for shooting Waverly's corpse, we still need to know the motive behind her actions. If we can discover her reasoning, perhaps it will give us a lead to the motivation behind the poisoning."

The trio moved back into the squad room with their coffee mugs and sat down at their desks. All three liked the early morning hours at the station, when the phones were quiet and the daily bustle of investigative work had not yet begun. It was as if they were wrapped in the lull of an ongoing storm, giving them a time to plan and prepare for the next onslaught of rough sailing.

For most detectives, the squad room was more than a simple workplace. It was a second home, a private place where they were secure. As police departments across the country continued to come under siege from the political agendas of outside sources, the squad room still remained a sanctuary where what it took to be a cop was understood and accepted. It was the final bastion of the them-against-us mentality that had pervaded law enforcement since its inception.

"Do you really think Gina Kane could have had anything to do with the poisoning?" Fey asked.

Hammer and Nails looked at each other before answering. It was a habit that had irritated Fey at first, as it always seemed as if they were holding out on some vital piece of information. However, she had long ago come to accept the custom as part of the pair's inner communication.

"We don't think so," Hammer said, shifting his eyes back to Fey's. "But we can't afford not to check it out. After April Waverly, Gina is the next logical suspect. Like you said earlier, it smacks of too much coincidence. But you never know. The possibility can't be ignored."

"And even if Gina didn't poison Waverly," Rhonda added, "pillow talk with Waverly could have given her at least some idea about April Waverly's motives, if not about other reasons somebody may have wanted Waverly dead. She may hold the key to this whole thing."

"If she does," Fey said, "she could be in danger herself."

"Now, there's a thought," Hammer said. Fey could almost see the self-chastisement he was going through for not coming up with that idea himself. "We'd better get out there as soon as possible."

"Do we have enough probable cause for a warrant?"

"No sweat," Hammersmith said. "I always got A's in creative writing at school."

"What about Waverly's work locker or anywhere else he may have stashed stuff?"

"One thing at a time," Hammersmith said. "I can only type so fast, and we don't want to go off half-cocked on this thing."

"You're right," Fey said. "So let's take a couple of minutes to break this investigation down." She pulled a yellow legal pad out of her desk and uncapped a black, thin-tipped marking pen. She took her glasses out of her purse and slipped them on. "As I see it, we have two forks to the investigation." She scribbled on the pad as she talked. "We have the love triangle involving Waverly, April, and Gina Kane. On the other hand, there is Waverly's professional position as a member of the ATD and any possible threat from the investigations he was conducting. If he was close to making a major arrest, perhaps the bad guys got wind of the deal and decided to take him out."

"How does that tie in with his wife shooting him?" Rhonda asked.

"I don't know," Fey admitted. "Maybe it doesn't, or maybe we'll uncover a connection between the two on down the line."

"I love this job," Hammersmith said.

Fey shot him a look, thinking he was being sarcastic.

Hammersmith interpreted the expression. "I'm serious," he said. "There isn't another job in the world that gives me this kind of a jazz."

"People are dying here," Fey said.

"Yeah. Isn't it great?"

Fey laughed. "You're nuts." She looked up at Rhonda and saw that she was grinning. "And you're just as bad as he is."

"Why, thank you, ma'am."

Fey shook her head in mock disgust. "Okay, you two, let's really get serious here. Since you're ready to go on the warrants, why don't you take responsibility for serving them and interrogating Gina Kane."

Hammer and Nails both nodded.

"We'll also keep track of April Waverly's condition. If she wakes up, we'll be there," Hammer added.

"Good," Fey agreed. "I also want you to question everyone here at the station who saw Waverly yesterday. I want a rundown of who he saw and what he did while he was here. If he came by and saw Gina Kane on a regular basis, I want to know what his normal routine was. If you can, take it even further back and track his movements for the entire day."

"You got it," Rhonda said, starting a notepad of her own.

"Meanwhile," Fey said, "I'm going to start out looking through the stuff we took out of Waverly's car. Then I'll make the initial overture down at ATD."

"They're not going to be easy to crack," Hammersmith warned.

"Don't I know it," Fey agreed. "But I'm going to take the weight of the chief in behind me and see how far I get. I also have an idea of the medium used to get the poison into Waverly's system, so I'll be going out to the impound lot." She looked up from the legal pad. "Did we book the items we took out of the car into property yet?"

"No. We didn't get a chance. They're still locked up in the homicide room."

Fey finished making notes and then checked her watch. "What do you say we meet back here around one and compare findings?"

"Fine with us," Rhonda said, after first making eye contact, as usual, with Hammer.

Fey took another swig from her coffee mug and stood up. Hammer turned back to his laptop, and Rhonda went back to playing on the NECS computer.

Taking a key from her desk, Fey walked down the short front corridor to the homicide room. Two years earlier, the room had been renovated for the specific use of the homicide unit. Funds had been raised in the community to construct the interior and update the unit's equipment, which was stored inside.

Fey began to examine the items that she'd removed from Waverly's car. There was one item in particular that, although she didn't want to examine it immediately, she knew could play an important part in the investigation.

As she began to go through the still sweat-wet clothes in Waverly's workout bag, another part of her mind was looking for Waverly's laptop.

It wasn't there.

With anxiety turning her stomach into a Mixmaster, she walked casually back into the squad room.

"Hey, you guys," she said to Hammer and Nails. "What happened to the laptop we took out of Waverly's car?"

Hammer looked at Nails. "We locked it up with the rest of the stuff in the homicide room," he said.

"Are you sure?"

"Absolutely." Hammer paused. "I hate to ask this, but why?"

"It's gone," Fey said. "And I have a damn good idea who took it."

13

T-BONE RAWLINGS and P. J. Hunter cruised into John Dancer's office looking like top draft picks for a sleep deprivation experiment.

"What kind of a wild goose chase are we running here, boss? The least you could have done was give us an interesting assignment if you expected us to stay awake all night." P.J. flopped his bantam-sized frame into a reclining desk chair and started in with his usual complaining. "I don't know if I can get behind following cops to work. I mean, aren't there enough bad guys to follow around without checking up on our own people? Have we been reassigned to Internal Affairs or something? And where were the regular surveillance teams? Why couldn't they handle this?"

Dancer listened silently as P.J. wound down. He knew from long experience that trying to answer the flood of questions only led to more virulent complaining.

Prester John "P.J." Hunter was a cocky redhead with a bad case of small man's complex. Detectives who didn't care for his personality referred to him as Napoleon. They never did it to his face, however, unless they were willing to go two out of three falls with him right then and there.

Despite his diminutive stature and whining nature, he was considered by Dancer to be a highly effective anti-terrorist detective. It was for that reason alone that Dancer ignored the detective's constant complaining.

By contrast, T-Bone Rawlings was a golem of epic proportions. A native of Tonga, his massive upper body was covered by a Hawaiian shirt of blatantly loud colors. At six-eight and a heavily muscled three hundred pounds, Rawlings could have been a star in the World Wrestling Federation. He rarely spoke, but when he did, people generally listened. If they didn't, he had numerous other ways of getting their attention. C-clamping someone to a wall was one of his more subtle methods.

The two detectives had been staked out on Fey since Dancer put them on the job following his phone call from Vaughn Harrison. After trailing Fey to work, they waited patiently until she left again, this time with Hammer and Nails. From West L.A., P.J. and T-Bone shadowed the trio as they drove downtown to Parker Center.

The West L.A. detectives were now in another ATD office waiting to talk to Dancer.

P.J. rubbed his hand across the stubble of his beard and made as if he were falling into a deep sleep accompanied by snores that would have put a lumberjack to shame.

"Shut up, P.J.," T-Bone said. The Tongan's eyes shifted away from P.J. and pinned Dancer in their stare. "What's going on?"

Dancer gave him a hard look. "We have a major problem. Alex was already dead when his wife shot him."

"Whoa," P.J. said, sitting up straight. "What are you talking about?"

Dancer filled in his men on the information Vaughn Harrison had shared with him.

"Are you telling us that the chief thinks somebody working ATD murdered Alex? Another cop?" P.J. was getting agitated. "That's crap! Alex was our partner. There's no way somebody on the job did him."

"Calm down," Dancer told him. "You and I both know it's foolishness, and so does the chief. I don't know who killed Alex, but I know it wasn't another cop. This is politics, pure and simple. The chief knows he's in trouble. His contract with the city is up for renewal next year, and he's on his way out unless he can do something to consolidate his position. Vaughn Harrison is the front runner to fill the chief's shoes, so the chief is using this as an excuse to go after Harrison's power bases—the department's specialty divisions, like RHD or us."

"So, while Croaker is conducting the chief's witch-hunt, whoever killed Alex is away smiling," P.J. said. He stood up and looked at his stoic partner. "Like I said, total crap with a capital C."

"It may be," Dancer agreed, "but Croaker could still put us in a bad position. This division has always had to fight for its survival. Our files are sacrosanct. If we open them up to Croaker, it would be accepting the thin edge of the wedge. The pricks who think they're running this city would love to get their hands on our files."

P. J. Hunter nodded his agreement. "The ACLU and all their butt buddies would have a gigantic orgasm if they could get us disbanded. They hate the fact that we follow *innocent citizens* around and force them to commit terrorist acts so we can arrest them."

Almost all law enforcement personnel considered the American Civil Liberties Union the true enemy of justice—a hated check and balance, as far to the left as law enforcement was to the right.

T-Bone grunted his acceptance of the statements. The taciturn giant was well aware of the political pressures constantly being brought to bear on the division.

ATD had originally been a mutation of the department's Public Disorder and Intelligence Division. PDID had been forced to disband in the late seventies when it was found to be keeping elaborate files on politicians, Hollywood celebrities, union leaders, professional athletes, reporters, media magnets, and all manner of normal citizens.

The gathering of raw information and gossip on its unauthorized targets had eventually become the main focus of PDID's existence. Real police work such as terrorist suppression, solving crimes, and making arrests became less important than PDID's constant search for dirt and political pressure points.

Using an intricate intelligence network of informants, telephone taps, surveillances, and electronic eavesdropping, detectives assigned to PDID considered themselves to be elite and untouchable. They patterned their lives after the flashy images of detectives portrayed in movies and television. Their expense accounts were liberal and unchecked. Detectives were able to pick and choose their investigations, work what hours they deemed best, and report only to the department's top brass.

Arrests were not encouraged. Arrests meant publicity, and publicity brought outside scrutiny, anathema to the ultra-secretive world of criminal intelligence. When information was uncovered implicating suspects in crimes, the information would be fed to concerned detectives through the use of anonymous phone calls, or by sending the information to the national We Tip center to be funneled back to the appropriate source—going north to go south.

Arrests would also have led to court time for the PDID detectives. Court cases were to be avoided, as they would lead to defense attorneys subpoenaing files when detectives tried to explain where their information came from. The possibilities of these actions were not acceptable as they would endanger the continued accumulation of facts and rumors that kept the police department in its position as the tail that wagged the dog.

Eventually, in the seventies, the intrusions into the lives of private citizens came to light. A major investigation into the activities of PDID had been instigated and resulted in orders to destroy all files not specifically targeting terrorist or other public disorder groups.

PDID insisted they had complied, but a few months later, the supposedly destroyed files were found in the private garage of one of the PDID detectives. The illegal surveillances and information gathering on private citizens had been continuing unchecked, despite orders to the contrary. The American Civil Liberties Union had sued the city, and PDID was disbanded in public disgrace.

Still, as terrorism continued to become a growing and immediate threat to the city of Los Angeles, the need for true intelligence gathering became clear. Reluctantly, the city powers acquiesced to the establishment of a new intelligence unit with a full set of checks and balances and audits.

Working from guidelines established by the ACLU, the department created the Anti-Terrorist Division. The ACLU guidelines were to be held in force for ten years. Problems, however, were immediate as the new rules and regulations were purposely established to be contrary to any semblance of effective intelligence-gathering procedures.

The fledgling ATD struggled through its first years, battling constant internal upheaval as its four sections—legal, analytical, deep cover, and detectives—fought with one another to establish a pecking order. Eventually, however, as the need for an efficient terrorist unit to protect the city became imperative, ATD began winning more of its legal battles with the ACLU, and the disparate sections within the division began to blend and pull together.

Gradually, ATD started to find ways to do its job despite outside pressures. As the division proved itself, the constant harassment by the left was counterbalanced by support from both the right and moderates. The ten years of the ACLU's moratorium on the guidelines came and went, and ATD began to thrive.

Establishing a multiagency task force with the FBI, the Los Angeles Sheriff's Department, and the Secret Service, ATD eventually became a gem in the LAPD crown, admired and revered by other law enforcement intelligence units nationwide.

But intelligence units are secretive by nature, the information they gather potentially explosive, and none of them relished the thought of scrutiny by an outsider—even if the outsider carried the same badge.

"So, Croaker is a problem," Rawlings said.

Dancer nodded his agreement. "She has a reputation for being so tough her tits clank when she walks. The last thing we need is somebody like that poking their fingers in our pie."

"Clank! Clank!" Fey said, entering Dancer's office.

The three men looked at her.

Mary DeFalco, her impeccably nyloned legs swishing angrily, lurched into the office behind Fey. She was almost spitting fire. "I'm sorry, Lieutenant. She walked past me while I was at the copy machine."

"I was tired of waiting in your isolation room," Fey said. " I wanted to do this with some semblance of decorum, but obviously, you're not on the same sheet of music."

Hammer and Nails quietly drifted into the room, taking relaxed positions behind Fey. The small office was suddenly cramped.

"Let's not get off on the wrong foot, Fey," Dancer said, trying for familiarity. "Rawlings and Hunter were just bringing me up to date on a priority investigation." He indicated the two ATD detectives with a wave of his hand. "I'm sorry I kept you waiting."

"Stop pissing down my back and telling me it's raining," Fey said, her eyes hard as stone. "Cheech and Chong here need a surveillance school refresher course. I've seen elephants who are more invisible than these two."

"Hey!" P.J. said.

Dancer reached out a restraining hand and put it on the small man's arm.

In actuality, Fey hadn't spotted the tail. Hammer picked it up on the way to Parker Center. He'd also recognized Rawlings when the pair pulled a little too close at the bottom of the freeway off-ramp. Fey did realize, however, that the tail must have been with her from home.

"If I've all of a sudden become a surveillance subject for ATD, I want to see your justification and authorization. Or is this division as off the rails as the *Los Angeles Times* and the ACLU claim it is in their regular attacks?"

"You are not a surveillance subject," Dancer said. He was fuming, peeved that P.J. and T-Bone had allowed themselves to be burned, but now was not the time to fight a battle. "There must be some mistake."

"There's no mistake," Fey said, "but let's not squabble over little things. Why did you take Waverly's laptop computer out of property? It's evidence in a homicide case."

Dancer ponied up a tight smile. "The laptop computer did not belong to Waverly. It's ATD equipment. And I did not take it out of property. At my request, Lieutenant Cahill removed it from your homicide room and gave it to me. Since it had not been booked into property, I assumed it wasn't evidence. As a hotshot homicide detective, surely you book your evidence without delay?"

Fey took the statement in full stride. Dancer was right, the evidence should have been booked into property in an expedient fashion, but it didn't negate the fact that Dancer was playing semantics.

"You're pissing down my back again, Lieutenant, and I don't appreciate it," Fey said. "I want that laptop back, and I want it back now."

"The laptop is the property of ATD—"

"It's the property of the Los Angeles Police Department," Fey interrupted. "And I don't give a damn if it's the property of the pope. I want it back. It's evidence in an ongoing homicide investigation. I am here on the authority of the chief of police. If you do not cooperate, I'm sure he would be more than pleased to personally come down and discuss the situation with you."

Silence followed Fey's proclamation until Hammer removed the toothpick he had been chewing on from his mouth and quietly said, "Clank, clank."

Keeping a poker face, Dancer rolled his chair back to give himself access to his desk drawers. Without further argument, he opened the middle drawer on the left-hand side and removed a laptop computer in a black nylon carrying case. He set it in the middle of his desktop.

Fey looked at it, knowing she couldn't prove one way or the other from the exterior if it was the same computer recovered from the back of Waverly's vehicle.

"Anything else we can do to assist you, Detective Croaker?" Dancer drew out Fey's title, pronouncing it *dee-tective* to emphasize the difference in their ranks.

Fey moved forward and unzipped the nylon carrying case. "You can show my detectives Waverly's desk and locker. We have search warrants for both. They were telephonically confirmed by a judge this morning." She opened the screen on the laptop computer and hit the power button.

"You didn't need to get search warrants," Dancer said. "Department lockers and desks are subject to administrative searches at any time."

"I'm well aware of department regulations," Fey said, waiting for the computer to warm up. "But you never know when administrative rules will be challenged in court, so it's always nice to have a judge's order to back your case."

"Are you planning on going to court?" Dancer asked. A small smile threatened his lips.

Fey took her eyes off the computer screen and locked them on Dancer. "A cop has been murdered. I didn't know him, but I'm damn sure going to find out who killed him. He worked for you. I'd have thought you'd be all over me like a cheap suit, pushing to get this case solved and get the villain into court."

The C-prompt showed on the computer screen. Fey looked back at it and signaled to Hammersmith. "Do your stuff," she said.

Hammer stepped forward, bent over Dancer's desk, and started tapping keys.

Fey looked at Dancer. Dancer stared back.

After a few seconds of concentrated effort, Hammer turned off the computer and pushed the screen shut. "There's nothing on the hard drive," he said. "It's been wiped clean."

14

VAUGHN HARRISON held up and flexed the partial claw that was
his right hand. He placed it on the desktop in front of him and flexed
it again. He refused to give in to the pain of arthritis, which plagued
him more often with each passing year. Pain pills, even aspirin, were
anathema to Harrison. He believed if a man couldn't control his
own body, then he couldn't control his life or the lives of those
around him. And Harrison believed emphatically in control.

"You did well getting Waverly's computer cleaned. That was fast
thinking on your part, John, but why did you clean the whole hard
drive? It kind of gave the game away." Harrison's voice betrayed only
a slight hint of chastisement.

John Dancer was sitting in a chair in front of Harrison's desk.
Not used to having search warrants served on his unit, he was still
shaken by the storm trooper tactics. He was further unsettled at
being immediately summoned to Harrison's office, where the
deputy chief already appeared to know what occurred.

Dancer cleared his throat. "I wasn't even sure if there was anything in Waverly's computer that needed to be wiped, but Alex was
very computer savvy," he said. "He was always keeping the divisional
system up and running. If anyone had a computer problem, Waverly
was the one they went to. He could have had files hidden somewhere in his hard drive that I couldn't find, so I had to wipe the lot.

You told me to get the computer and clean it. I did what you ordered."

Harrison grunted. "Okay, you did good."

"I'm sure Alex had another computer setup at his house. His laptop was just an accessory. He was always talking about new stuff he was adding, and all this Internet access crap. I don't understand a whole lot of it."

"Don't worry. It's being handled."

Dancer paused for a breath. It crossed his mind to ask how it was being handled, and who was handling it, but he didn't. Instead, he stated, "Croaker wasn't very pleased."

Harrison gave a low chuckle this time. "I can imagine. She has no idea about the tiger she's trying to grab by the tail."

"I'm not so sure we're doing the right thing," Dancer said, worried Harrison was dropping him into a pit of quicksand from which there was no return.

"John, I have to know I can rely on you." Harrison's facial features became intense. "We're playing for very high stakes. When this venture comes together, we will all share the glory. But this is not just about us as individuals. This is about the department—the LAPD. This is about saving the city from itself." Harrison was becoming fervent, like a Bible Belt tent preacher.

"Did Ron Harper know this was going on?" Dancer asked, referring to the ATD captain who had died in harness, and whose job Dancer was filling.

"Ron was a good man. He knew a lot of things. However, he wasn't particularly good at making the right decisions. He couldn't handle pressure." Harrison stroked his clawed hand. "How good are you at making right decisions, John?"

Dancer hated talking to Harrison. You could never get a straight answer out of the man. "I'm one of the old guard; you can rely on me," he stated, not knowing what else to say.

"I hope so, John. For all our sakes. The future of this city rests with those of us who all share the same vision."

"How do we know Croaker doesn't share the vision? She's been around a long time. She can't like the way things are going any more than the rest of us. Why are we trying to hinder her? Somebody killed Alex. We should be doing everything we can to help her find the murderer."

"Even if that means opening our files to her and her team?"

"Why not?" Dancer asked. "What are we trying to hide?"

Harrison leaned forward and grasped his good left hand around his disfigured right. "It's not what we're trying to hide. It's who we're hiding it from."

"The chief—" Dancer started.

Harrison cut him short. "The chief of this department is nothing more than an appointed political buffoon. If he knew what was going on, he'd cut and run on us in a heartbeat. The chief wants to open all aspects of this department to public scrutiny. He wants everyone to hold hands and help one another." Harrison's voice was full of contempt and sarcasm. "It's ludicrous. You can't hold hands with predators and jackals—they'll eat you alive."

Dancer squirmed in his chair. "Okay, I understand, but what about Alex?"

Harrison's face hardened. "Damn it, John. I told you last night, Alex's murder has nothing to do with the cases he was working on. If you really want to help find out who killed him, then we keep Croaker out of the ATD files and get her to focus on Alex's private life. That's where the killer came from. For hell's sake, he may have been dead already, but his own wife still shot him. How can there be any doubt in your mind that his murder is anything but domestic related?"

Dancer shook his head. "Croaker will push for the files." His voice was almost a whine.

Harrison shook his head in frustration. "Then give her files. Give her more files than she'll know what to do with—but we don't give her Los Juniors. There are people out there who will not understand that what we're doing is for the good of the department and the city. Got it?"

Dancer felt his bowels rumble. "Yeah, I got it."

Harrison let a small smile run across his lips. His pristine white shirt was complemented by a perfectly knotted blue silk tie with white polka dots. Under the tie knot, a gold tie bar held the shirt's collar tips in perfect symmetry.

"Do you know how I ended up with this?" Harrison asked, holding up his mangled hand.

"A pipe bomb blew up in your hand when you were with the bomb squad." Dancer stared at the cruel-looking appendage. If the truth were told, he was afraid of Harrison. The cause of the deputy chief's hideous injury was well known, but Dancer's own terror of mutilation was multiplied through the absurd notion that handicaps might be contagious. He avoided shaking hands with Harrison.

There was more to Dancer's fear of Harrison, however, then simple irrational phobias. Harrison's aggressive, controlling persona intimidated him. At his core, Dancer knew he wasn't man enough to stand up to Harrison.

Harrison had come up the hard way. He'd played hardball in Vietnam and come home a hero. As a cop, he had not allowed his injury or anything else to stand in his way.

Starting at the bottom as a rookie patrolman, Harrison had charged through every rotten, bloody, deadly situation the dregs of society could throw at him. He lived for the job. Day and night, he was always in the middle of the action. An adrenaline junkie, he pushed every situation to the limit.

While still in uniform, he earned a Police Star for bravery during the Watts riots. A year later, he was awarded the Medal of Valor for taking three bullets while saving a young girl caught in the middle of a gang war crossfire.

When he was promoted to detective, his arrest/crime clearance record was second to none. His reputation preceding him, he rapidly moved from divisional detective into specialized units, where his star continued to rise. Harrison had scaled the department ranks in record time. He studied hard for the required civil service exams, and breezed through oral interviews with superiors who owed him a favor, or whom he had something on.

As a deputy chief, he was now admired by the men who worked for him, and feared by toadying administrators.

In Dancer's eyes, Vaughn Harrison was a true man—a genuine

hero, a personage of vision—the real thing, not the facade of manhood Dancer believed he represented himself. Vaughn Harrison scared Dancer because he felt Harrison could see right through to the coward in his soul.

Unlike Harrison, Dancer had climbed through the departmental ranks with a pen in his hand instead of a gun. He knew others looked at him as little more than a glorified clerk who knew exactly which ass to kiss to get ahead. It also bothered Dancer that he knew this assessment to be true. He'd never proven himself under fire, and was not sure he would be able to do so even if given the chance. He was not a cowboy.

It didn't matter that he was actually a good administrator who cared about the department and the personnel who worked for him. He was still a paper pusher in a department that valued macho behavior over evenhanded, community-related interaction—despite public relation mouthings to the contrary.

Harrison now looked at his clawed hand, pointed it as if it were a limp fish in Dancer's direction, and then suddenly snapped it into a rigid, accusatory rod of mangled flesh and bone that seemed to cavort like a malicious puppet to its owner's command.

"You're damn right it was a pipe bomb! A puny, no-account excuse for an explosive device. The simplest, by-the-numbers diffusion in the book." Harrison's voice rose in pitch, and then returned to normal. He sounded like an evangelist trying to get the last dollar out of a hayseed's pocket. "But I learned one thing by my stupidity, and that is you can't trust anybody. Even your best friend can be your worst enemy."

Harrison read the look in Dancer's eyes and wiggled his disfigured fingers. The hand had been rebuilt by surgeons using bone from Harrison's ribs and tissue from his backside. Before the surgery, Harrison had forced a promise from one of the surgeons to use a pistol as a mold so Harrison's grip and trigger finger would be preserved.

"It was 1984, on the last day of the Olympics here in L.A. Three pipe bombs had been discovered sitting on the bumper of a bus that was used to transport athletes from the Olympic village to the closing ceremonies. A SWAT officer spotted the bombs and prevented the loaded bus from leaving the village. He was with a SWAT sergeant, who stopped the officer from removing the bombs from the bus. The sergeant called the bomb squad. Joe Brasher and I caught the call-out."

Dancer sat quietly, entranced as he always was by the exploits of other men. His eyes were riveted on Harrison's clawed fingers still held in the air.

"Today, we would have simply removed the bombs by remote control robot and exploded them in a controlled environment. Back then, however, we still did things by hand. The first two bombs turned out to be ghosts—casings only, with no explosives inside. Brasher got careless with the last bomb, expecting all three to be a hoax. I saw the inner wire for a split second when he removed the upper cap."

"What did you do?" Dancer couldn't help asking. He felt like a kid attending story time at the library.

Harrison took a deep breath and brought his clawed hand down to the desktop again. His voice when he spoke was mild—not coming from the here and now, but from a past that could never be changed.

"There was no time to give a warning. All I could do was react and try to slap the bomb out of Brasher's hands."

"It exploded?"

"Hell, yes," Harrison said, holding his hand up and dropping it back on the desk again. "They said I was lucky. The only major damage the bomb did to me was to tear off two of my fingers. Brasher lost a leg and had his guts torn up with shrapnel. Two weeks of incredible pain later, he was dead."

Harrison fell silent.

"I don't understand—" Dancer started.

"You don't understand what that story has to do with not trusting anyone?" Harrison finished the question as if he had been anticipating it. "I'll tell you. The official version of the incident indicates that the bombs were of an unknown origin. No terrorist group came forward to claim credit, and blame for the incident was put down to a crank, since the bomb itself was actually too small to have done any major damage to the bus or the athletes inside. The case was closed due to lack of leads, and the city and the department were able to bask in the glow of an Olympics unsullied by terrorist actions."

"You're saying there were terrorists?"

Harrison snorted. "Not even close. I told you that I learned that nobody could be trusted. The bombs were planted by the SWAT officer who so conveniently discovered them."

"What?"

Harrison shrugged. "He wanted to be a hero. He planned on dramatically grabbing the bombs off the bumper and throwing them into an open field on the other side of the Olympic Village compound. He'd designed the one live bomb to explode on contact with the ground, and he would get all the credit for saving the athletes. His plan was derailed by his sergeant, who stopped him from touching the bombs and made the call to the bomb squad."

"What happened to the officer? He couldn't be allowed to just walk away."

"Why not? The officer quietly resigned, and the whole incident was buried. The department and the city couldn't afford the scandal. The whole world was watching, and the LAPD was supposed to be the best of the best. We couldn't have one of our own accused of trying to disrupt the Olympic showcase. Too much had already been expended to make things look perfect."

"I don't see you accepting that outcome."

Harrison gave an evil smile. "There is another thing I believe in," he said. "You take care of your own. Joe Brasher was my partner. He died because of some jerk with a Lancelot complex—and then the jerk was allowed to walk away for the good of the organization. It wasn't right, and something had to be done—just like we're doing something with Los Juniors." Harrison flexed the clawed fingers, not saying anything further.

"What did you do?" Dancer pushed again.

With an effort, Harrison tore his gaze away from his clawed hand. "When the time came," he said softly, "I hunted the sorry son of a bitch down."

Dancer swallowed. "Did you kill him?" It was an awkward, stupid question, but he felt forced to fill the silence—half scared of the answer.

Harrison caught Dancer's stare and held it hard. "No. But he still wishes I had."

Dancer didn't even want to know what that meant.

"John, the situation with Los Juniors is no different," Harrison said. "We're playing for all the marbles here. Don't let me down." He paused. "Don't make me come hunting you."

After Dancer left his office, Harrison sat at his desk letting his mind run through the situation. He sometimes believed the disfigurement of his hand was responsible for the inner demons that drove him. Raising hell in Vietnam had not prepared him for any other type of work in civilian life, nor did he want any other kind of work. He loved raising hell. In peacetime America, he saw big-city police work as the only viable venue to ply the lessons taught to him in war. The enemy was different, but the tactics and the power rush were the same.

More than any other department, the LAPD's reputation for proactive police work—kicking ass and taking names—appealed strongly to Harrison's nature. He had heard all the stories of how Chief Parker took control of the department in the fifties and dragged it kicking and screaming out of the slime and corruption in which it had been mired.

He had also admired how the LAPD's paramilitary structure continued under new chiefs, protecting the sprawling city with fewer police officers per capita than any other department in the country. The department's iron fist provided answers for a population demanding law and order.

The LAPD had been a vanguard—a universe unto itself that was admired and emulated by police departments across the nation and around the world. LAPD defined professionalism to Harrison then, as it still did despite the internal changes.

In his current position, one step away from the brass ring of full department command, Harrison was still a cop to the core of his soul. Tough, hard-bitten, and unforgiving, he was a bastard through and through—no quarter given, and none asked.

Whether he was a good cop or not depended on point of view. He was alternately glorified and reviled by different segments of the city's power structure, but all respected him as a force to be reckoned with. Harrison didn't give a damn either way.

In the moderate politically correct atmosphere, when the LAPD's iron fist approach to law enforcement was being attacked by every liberal cause in the barrel, Harrison still firmly believed he had the wider vision—the commitment to the majority of citizens who needed protection from the predators.

As far as Harrison was concerned, anyone who stood in the way of his vision would not be tolerated—including Fey Croaker, who was not only blocking Harrison's vision, but thumbing her nose.

Harrison looked up as Mary DeFalco walked into his office without waiting for an invite. The ATD secretary was radiating coiled sexual energy. Harrison reacted to her—as most men did—as if she were a bitch in heat.

"You must have put the fear of Hades into John Dancer," she said. There was smoke and whiskey in her voice. "He came back to the division grayer than the sheets at a no-tell motel."

Harrison smiled at the quip. Mary walked forward and sat on the corner of the desk closest to Harrison, the full length of her sculpted legs on display.

Harrison placed his clawed hand on her right thigh. He could feel the heat of her emitting through the silk texture of her nylons. "I'm worried about him," Harrison said, referring to Dancer. "I need you to keep close to him. If he looks as if he's going to fold, I need to know immediately."

"How close?" Mary asked, sin in her smile.

For an answer, Harrison pulled her to him, and she laughed as he buried his face in the exposed cleavage of her breasts.

15

"WELL, THAT was a total waste of time and energy," Fey said after returning to West L.A. Station with Hammer and Nails.

On her desk, Rhonda plopped down a cardboard box of miscellaneous items taken from Waverly's desk and locker. There did not appear to be anything of real interest in the box, but they had to take something for their efforts if only to irritate Dancer and his crew. "Did you expect anything different?" she asked.

"No," Fey said. "But I'd hoped for some sort of intradepartmental cooperation. After all, Waverly worked for ATD. They should want his murder solved more than anyone else."

Hammer carried a small tray containing three cups of Starbucks coffee into the homicide room. "Do you think ATD wants to keep us out of their files badly enough to run a renegade investigation?" he asked, picking up on the conversation.

Fey gave him a funny look. "You mean trying to solve the murder themselves?"

"Yeah."

Fey shrugged. "It's a stupid move, but I wouldn't put it past them. There's something going on there that we are not even close to getting a handle on."

Rhonda took her coffee from Hammer's tray. "Dancer and his buddies sure appear to be scrambling to protect themselves," she chipped in. "Blanking Waverly's computer and sanitizing his desk and locker smack of cover-up."

"I don't see it," Fey said. "A cover-up would be much more discreet. They would want to look like they were cooperating. Waverly's desk and locker couldn't have been any cleaner if Martha Stewart had been let loose on them. I think it was a message."

"A message?"

"Yeah. *Butt out!*"

Faced with both the proper administrative powers and the backup of legal search warrants, there had been little Dancer could do to stop Fey from searching Waverly's desk and locker. However, when Fey demanded to see the investigative files assigned to Waverly, Dancer had brought out his big guns. Detectives from ATD's legal section entered the picture to throw down roadblocks and spikes.

The confrontation had become heated, with Fey threatening air strikes from the chief's office. Go ahead, she was told, take your best shot.

Fey backed off a notch. She wasn't ready to flex that particular muscle just yet. There would be more need later. If Waverly's desk and locker had been any indication, his investigative files would be just as sanitized. Bringing in her own heavy artillery simply to prove a point would be fruitless. The issue of the files was not going to be the decisive battle of the war, at least not yet. All things considered, Fey felt there might be some advantage to letting ATD think they had won this round.

It had been hard to back down and walk away, but Fey had done so with as little bloodletting as possible.

Fey knew that sooner or later she would have to access the files for the cases Waverly had been working on. The possibility that Waverly had been murdered because of something he was investigating could not be ignored. Everything in his life both on the job and outside the job had to be considered until it had been eliminated.

"If what happened this morning was only department politics," Rhonda said, "what do you think is really going on?"

Fey shrugged. "Beats me. But whatever it is, I don't think anyone is going to like it much."

The three detectives all sipped their coffee, considering Fey's statement. From the main squad room they could hear phones ringing and the bustle of everyday police work.

"How do you want to play it from here?" Hammersmith asked, bringing everyone back into focus.

"We still need to handle this as we would any other homicide investigation," Fey said. "I want to follow up at the impound lot on Waverly's car. While I'm doing that, why don't you two take a patrol unit and a uniformed sergeant with you to serve the search warrant on Waverly's house. When I'm done, I'll catch up with you, and we'll all go out and take on Gina Kane together."

"That girl isn't going to know what hit her," Rhonda said.

"Storm warning," Hammer said. "Hurricane Fey is about to hit shore."

When he saw Hammersmith and Lawless exit the squad room, Monk Lawson wandered back to speak with Fey.

"How are you doing?" he asked.

Fey grinned. "Stop the world, I want to get off."

"Glad to see you're taking things in stride."

"I can do without your sarcasm."

Monk grinned.

"How are things on your end?" Fey asked.

"Mostly under control. Brindle and Alphabet are swamped, but coping without too many problems. Cahill has reassigned Corrigan from autos and Bliss from burglary to help handle our scut work."

"Detective trainees working the homicide unit," Fey said, referring to Corrigan and Bliss. "What's the world coming to? When I started in detectives, you had to have at least ten years' experience before you would even be considered for homicide."

"It's a different department these days," Monk said.

"Maybe," Fey said, shaking her head. "I don't know if it's really that much different, or if I'm just getting old. I just can't get into all this current touchy-feely, social service crap they keep shoving down our throats. Community policing was around twenty-plus years ago when I first came on the job. We called it team policing, and it didn't work then and it won't work now. The price of manpower is too high, and quite frankly, the community doesn't want to dirty its hands doing police work. It's what they hired us to do."

"Everything goes in cycles," Monk said.

"I agree," Fey said. "And I can't wait to get back to being a police department again. Whatever happened to putting villains in jail and making sure that was where they stayed?"

"Gypsies in the palace," Monk said.

"Don't go enigmatic on me. What the hell does that mean?"

"In England, when the knights went off to fight in the Crusades, bands of roving gypsies took over their castles and destroyed everything while the knights were gone."

"Are you saying that's what's happening in L.A.?"

Monk shrugged. "Well, L.A.'s not exactly a palace, but between post-riot retirements and young coppers leaving LAPD for greener pastures with higher pay and better equipment, blue knights are leaving the city in hordes, and the gypsies appear to be taking over."

"I think you may be reaching for an analogy," Fey said. "But it's clear that every butt hair with a political agenda, or an ax to grind against the police, has certainly made L.A. 'the place.'" Fey's tag line mocked the mayor's new city motto. She waited a beat and then asked, "So what happened when the knights returned from the Crusades?"

"They slaughtered the gypsies and brought the kingdom back under their control."

"Are you trying to tell me something here?" Fey asked.

"All I'm saying," Monk spoke softly, "is that if the knights don't come back soon, there may not be anything left of the palace."

When Monk took himself back to the squad room proper, Fey tried to shake herself out of her lethargy. Gathering her keys and purse together, she made herself ready to leave for the impound lot.

Before she left, however, she picked up the homicide room phone and punched in the number for RHD downtown.

"Robbery-Homicide Division." A voice that Fey didn't recognize answered the phone.

"Can I speak to Keegan?" Fey asked.

"He's not here."

"Okay, how about Hale?"

"Hold on."

Fey waited for almost a minute before a gruff voice came on the line. "Hale."

"Frank, it's Croaker. I need to speak to your partner."

"He's not available."

"I understand that," Fey said. "When will he be back?"

"Beats me."

"Come on, Frank. Don't jerk me around. Taking this case wasn't my choice."

"I'm not jerking you around," Hale said. "I don't know when he'll be back. He called in this morning before I arrived. Said he needed to take some vacation days—was maybe going to run his time until he retired."

"You're kidding? I didn't know he was thinking about retirement."

"I didn't either." Hale's statement, delivered in a flat monotone, intimated volumes.

"What's going on, Frank?"

"It's not your business."

Fey wasn't to be put off. "Did you call him?"

There was a pause before Hale replied, "No answer."

"Did you go out to his residence?"

"He has an apartment. I have a key. He wasn't there. Neither was his suitcase or his toilet kit, and some of his clothes were gone."

"No note?"

"Not a line."

"What about the wife and daughter?"

"Ex-wife. The divorce was final last year."

"I'm sorry. I didn't know."

"No reason why you should." Hale's voice had softened. "Derek took it hard. He misses his kid. I checked with them. He'd called and said he was going to be out of town for a while. Told them he needed a break, and that he would keep in touch."

"At least that's something."

"Yeah, but it's not much."

"Are you worried?"

"He's my partner." The flat monotone again, filled with unstated meaning.

"Derek called me late last night," Fey said, probing.

"Did he?" Hale tried to sound innocent.

"He called me from The Gunnery. He was drunk."

"Very possible, but tell me something new."

"He was crying."

Hale didn't respond.

"Frank," Fey probed more directly, "I know something's going on that is threatening to get out of control. I don't know what it is, but I know it's there. I've been around for too long not to be able to smell the storm coming."

"I told you before," Hale said. "It's not your business."

"It became my business when Alex Waverly was murdered," Fey said. "It became even more my business when Derek phoned me. He was scared, Frank. He's a good cop, and he was scared."

There was a pause on the line again.

"Well, that makes two of us," Hale replied finally. He broke the connection.

16

HAMMERSMITH CASUALLY steered the gold-colored detective sedan with one hand. His other hand rested lightly on Rhonda Lawless's thigh, where it was covered by one of her hands. Each detective was an effective and efficient separate entity, but together they formed a formidable force—the total of the whole becoming more than the sum of the already impressive parts. As longtime partners, they had come to accept and revel in this duality.

"I have a bad feeling about this case," Hammer said.

"I agree," replied Rhonda. "There's too much ground to cover and not enough manpower. We're scattered, without focus."

Hammersmith nodded in agreement.

The detective sedan cruised north on the freeway through the Sepulveda Pass, cresting the foothills at Mulholland Drive and descending into the San Fernando Valley.

Five of the LAPD's eighteen geographic divisions were spread across the San Fernando Valley, but currently the Valley was causing major consternation within the department. Strong political forces were being brought to bear in an effort to secede the San Fernando Valley from Los Angeles and incorporate it as a separate city. For years, the myriad bedroom communities and business districts comprising the Valley had sought to distance themselves from downtown L.A., and the atmosphere to actually make the break was quickly becoming ripe. If and when the break did occur, the status of the LAPD could be changed dramatically—especially if the San Fernando Valley, as a newly incorporated city, chose to contract their law enforcement needs from the Los Angeles Sheriff's Department and not from the LAPD, which had served there for so long.

Hammer moved his right hand to turn up the air-conditioning and then returned it to its position on Rhonda's thigh.

"We have to start digging into what led April Waverly to shoot her husband," he said. "Her motives could be the key to the whole case. I'm not willing to accept the shooting and the poisoning as unrelated acts. They have to tie together."

"Especially because of the timing," Rhonda said. "We're talking about a twenty-minute window from one person poisoning Waverly to another shooting him."

"It's got to connect. If April remains catatonic, we're going to have to find some other way to uncover her reasoning. She was pregnant with the man's baby, for hell's sake. You would think the last thing she would do was kill the father of her unborn child."

"Pregnancy mood swings?" Rhonda suggested lightly.

Hammer rolled his eyes. "Just remember you made the sexist woman problem comment, not me."

Rhonda laughed. "I just beat you to it."

Their association had started twelve years earlier when Hammersmith had responded to Rhonda's officer-needs-help broadcast. Between them, they had rescued Rhonda's arrogant training officer, who had driven into an ambush. It had been their first experience with the clicking, nonverbal communication that provided the basis of their partnership.

Several years later, they were able to manipulate positions together in Internal Affairs, where their official on-the-job partnership had begun. As they worked together, the legend of Hammer and Nails had grown rapidly. Hammer's indefatigable work ethic coupled with Nail's pit bull tenacity made them the scourge of bent coppers in every corner of the department.

On the other side of the coin, the duo proved they were willing to go to the wall for any officer they believed was being politically railroaded or shafted by the department. Their refusal to go along with the "best interest of the department," or to kowtow to superior officers, judiciary pundits, or city political entities, made them a dangerous liability that could not be handled through normal damage-control channels.

Several campaigns had been mounted to discredit them or to break up the partnership. In each case, however, the duo had quietly produced sources, or revealed knowledge of information, that gave them leverage over their detractors and kept their positions secure. Their list of enemies within the department and the city was impressive. Their list of powerful friends and admirers, however, was even more impressive.

Hammer's face was creased with concentration. "I have a feeling Waverly's murder is not going to turn out to be cut and dried. Something stinks about the way he bounced to ATD after his big arrest success with RHD. It doesn't wash."

Hammer exited the freeway at Ventura Boulevard and headed west toward Sherman Oaks. Turning off the main drag into a quiet, upscale residential neighborhood, he started checking house numbers.

Two years earlier Hammersmith and Lawless had left Internal Affairs and brought their act to West Los Angeles. There, Lieutenant Cahill had made the mistake of assigning them to different investigative tables. Within thirty minutes he received a call from the upper levels of the department chain of command to reassign them as partners on the same investigative unit. The directive was not a request.

Reluctantly, Cahill had agreed, but the duo had never given him cause to regret the arrangement. Like Fey, Cahill had come to rely on them. They were the go-to team when any major investigation stalled and results were needed. Left alone to do things their way, they produced results and handled anything that was thrown at them. Try to push them, and they pushed back—hard.

Other detectives in the squad room speculated about the duo's relationship outside the job, but it was purely speculation. Hammer and Nails kept their private lives to themselves and enforced an attitude of live and let live.

Hammer parked at the curb in front of the older but well-kept bungalow belonging to Alex and April Waverly. It was at least twenty years old, but like its surrounding neighbors, it looked to have been recently painted.

Two black-and-white patrol units from the Van Nuys Area were already parked at the location. Rhonda had radioed ahead for a uniformed sergeant and a pair of uniformed officers to meet them at the location. The backup was standard procedure when serving a search warrant.

Exiting the car, Rhonda and Hammer conversed briefly with the sergeant and the uniforms before heading for the house. The neighborhood was quiet, but it would be only a matter of time before neighbors began wandering over to see what was going on. The uniforms were assigned to keep the looky-loos at bay. The patrol sergeant, Rich Foster, would use his camera to record the condition of the house prior to the search, any evidence that was found, and the condition of the house when the search was finished. Civil liability demanded proof these days.

Walking up the brick and concrete driveway, Hammer bent down to scoop up the day's newspaper. He tossed it on the porch.

Rhonda put her hand on the glass beside the front door to shade the glare as she looked inside.

"Appears empty," she said, being able to see through the living room and into the family room and kitchen area.

"Feels empty," Hammer said, ringing the doorbell.

They both stood back from the door, listening for movement. None occurred.

Hammer tried the door handle, but found it to be locked as expected. "Let's try around back," he said.

The wooden gate, closing off the front yard from the back, opened easily to the latch pull on its right side. Hammer moved through the gate quickly, aware and looking for any signs of a dog. Finding none, he led the way to the rear door.

"Must have a gardener," Rhonda commented, looking around at the small but well-trimmed backyard.

"Probably," Hammer said. "I doubt April Waverly was up to

pulling weeds and pushing a lawn mower in her condition." He tried the back door and found it also locked. "You guys see any joy with the windows?"

"All locked, as far as I can see," Foster said.

Hammer ran a hand quickly over the frame of the door, but encountered no hidden key. At the same time, Rhonda bent down and turned over a flowerpot near the back porch. A key lay beneath it. She picked it up. "Is this what you're looking for?" she asked innocently, holding the key out. "Let's see, that makes it thirty-two key finds for me, and still only seventeen for you."

"Okay, so two more key finds and you win a toaster," Hammer said. "What do you want, a medal?" Disgruntled, he took the key from her, twisted it in the lock, and opened the door.

Foster, the uniformed sergeant, had started to raise the Polaroid camera to begin recording the entry, when Hammer suddenly turned and charged away from the door.

"Gas!" he yelled, tackling Rhonda and driving her to the ground.

The explosion lifted Rich Foster off his feet and blew him head over heels across the yard and over the slump stone wall that separated Waverly's residence from its rear neighbor.

Hammer and Nails disappeared in a profusion of flame, smoke, and flying debris.

17

FEY WAVED to Mavis Fennelly, the grizzled widow who ran the local official police garage with an iron hand. Mavis waved back at Fey through the trailer window she used to keep an eagle eye on her crew.

Each LAPD Area had an OPG tow yard. The contracts awarded to the OPGs were eagerly sought after, as they amounted to a license to print money. The lots were filled with cars impounded by meter maids and traffic officers, as well as cars used in crimes or impounded as evidence. The lots were always full and their fees were high.

Fey walked through the closely parked cars toward the hold-for-prints evidence shed, where Alex Waverly's detective sedan had been deposited.

"Hey, George," she called out to one of the OPG employees using a forklift to move cars. "Can you open the evidence shed for me?"

"Sure thing," George said. He shut down the forklift and leapt nimbly to the ground. He wore overalls and had a blue bandanna tied around his head. With thick thumbs and fingers, he twirled the combination lock on the shed door until it clicked open. "There you go. You looking for anything special?"

Fey pointed to Waverly's car. "I just want to give it another going-over."

"No problem. If you need anything, just shout."

George went back to his forklift, and Fey made her way over to Waverly's car. It was hot and stuffy in the enclosed shed, and Fey could feel herself beginning to sweat. She ran a hand across the back of her neck and felt it come away wet.

Waverly's maroon Chevy was a standard, stripped-down detective sedan. Too obviously a police car to be used for surveillance or undercover-type work, it was nothing more than on-duty transportation for whatever plainclothes detective checked it out.

The car was eight years old with almost more miles on it than the odometer could count in one trip around the clock. The paintwork was dull and cloudy, and there were numerous dings and scratches covering both sides that were unidentifiable in origin. Two thin antennas protruded from the trunk lid, indicating the presence of the department radio stored below.

The last time Fey had seen the car, she had been concentrating on Waverly's body inside. At that time, the case had been open and shut—Waverly murdered by his wife—and there had been nothing more the car needed to tell them.

Circumstances, however, had changed dramatically, and this time Fey was forced to treat the car as she would the scene of any murder, as the best possible source for clues to the killer.

Fey was glad that she had requested that the car be secured in the print shed. She had done it not because she was thinking about fingerprint evidence, but because she wanted to keep the police radios secure from wandering hands. Now she was thankful for her decision. On her way to the OPG, she had contacted the scientific investigation division and requested the car be printed. It might not do any good since so many people had gone through the car while removing the body and other evidence, but there was always a chance.

She had retrieved the car's keys from the homicide room, where they had been stored with the other items taken from the car, and used them to open the trunk. Inside, she observed the standard police radio system and made a mental note to request a tape of the prior day's radio traffic to identify any broadcasts made by Waverly. That would be a long, slogging job for somebody.

Also in the trunk were a box of flares and a standard AIDS kit that all police cars carried for dealing with victims or suspects who possibly had the disease. Putting on a pair of latex gloves, Fey opened the kit and saw that it held its complete complement of paper overalls, booties, gloves, and mouth-to-mouth protection. She set the kit on the ground behind her.

She dumped the box of flares out beside the AIDS kit. Nothing else was inside except the flares, with one missing to complete a full box. Next, she pulled out the spare tire and jack, cursing when she put a black smudge on her blouse.

Having to tug hard, but persevering, she pulled up the carpeting covering the trunk bottom. There was nothing hidden below. She didn't think there would be, but she had to check. She felt as if she were closing the barn door after the horse had bolted, but the barn door still had to be closed.

Moving around to the side of the car, she opened the rear passenger door. Leaning in, she shifted the back bench seat out of position. Underneath there was a Heath bar wrapper, a cluster of rotting sunflower seed shells, a stub of yellow pencil, three toothpicks, and a McDonald's straw still in its wrapper. Fey ignored the detritus and used her hand to search behind the seat back. Finding nothing, she pushed the bench seat back into position and closed the door.

She had been purposely putting off searching the front of the car, because she needed to force herself to follow the routine steps before she allowed herself to be distracted. Ever since she found out that Waverly had been poisoned, an image had been sitting in her mind, making her damn herself for the cursory way the investigation had been handled originally.

She had led her crew through the motions of a homicide investigation, but with April Waverly in custody—and numerous eyewitnesses to her actions—the full-scale, detail-oriented investigation had not appeared necessary. The shock of having a cop murdered in front of the station was a ready-made excuse for the shoddy work, but Fey knew herself better than to accept that explanation.

In 99.9 percent of homicides, the simple explanation was the right explanation. But procedure had to be followed every time, otherwise that .1 percent would come back and bite you in the butt. And Fey was certainly feeling teeth marks in this case.

Opening the car's front passenger door, she looked in but couldn't see the item that had been burning its image into her psyche. Her pulse was racing as she bent forward and reached her hand under the front seat. She couldn't feel anything; panic began rising in her chest.

Getting down on her knees outside the car, she bent herself around until she could actually look under the seat. With relief, she saw the plastic water bottle that she had failed to retrieve when the car had been parked in front of the station. It was wedged all the way in the back against one side. Somehow, the bottle must have rolled there when Waverly's body was being removed from the car, or during the process of towing the car to the impound lot.

Fey carefully pulled out the bottle, touching it as little as possible with her glove tips to preserve any latent fingerprints on the main surfaces. Obviously refillable, it was made out of clear plastic with a blue tinge. Screwed on the top was a plastic spout that opened and closed.

The spout was in the same open position as it had been when Fey had first noticed the bottle. Fey shook the bottle and there was the reassuring sound of liquid inside. Unless she missed her guess, the lab rats at SID would find the contents to be the medium of delivery for the digoxin that killed Waverly. It was the simple answer, and Fey hoped that this time it would be the right one.

As carefully as she could, she unscrewed the spout, knowing the ribbed surface would not yield any prints, and poured the contents into a glass evidence jar she had brought with her for that purpose. She screwed the jar's top closed tightly. Next, she placed the plastic bottle itself into a large, brown paper bag; now it was ready for printing.

It was imperative to try to establish Waverly's movements during the last hours of his life, but Fey was willing to bet that the agenda would include a workout in the WLA weight room, or a run through the nearby Veterans Hospital, which was favored by many WLA coppers and their FBI counterparts from the nearby federal building.

Her theory was supported by her knowledge of the damp workout clothes and bag that had been removed from the trunk in her first search. It would also provide the reasoning behind why Waverly had been drinking the copious amounts of diluted digoxin needed to kill him from his water bottle.

When the pager at her waist vibrated, Fey was deep in concentration, and the tickling sensation made her jump. She checked the number on the display, took her phone out of her purse, and dialed Lieutenant Cahill's number. Even though he had also entered 911, to indicate an emergency, it was just like Cahill to page Fey to call him rather than call her direct. This way it put the major cost burden of the call on her.

Asshole, Fey thought as the phone on the other end began to ring. What now?

18

DRIVING AS if the devil were at her heels, Fey was almost broad-sided by an ambulance as she pulled into the parking lot of Tarzana Hills Hospital. Rolling with the red lights and siren of her dual-purpose detective car activated, she swerved hard to avoid the ambulance, which was traveling under similar conditions. The difference was that the ambulance was authorized to roll Code 3; Fey wasn't. If there had been an accident, it would have been her fault.

Bringing her car to a rocking halt inches away from a parked minivan, Fey closed her eyes and white-knuckled the steering wheel as she got her breath back and tried to slow her heart rate. Blindly, she turned off her lights and siren, and took in several huge gulps of air.

I'm an idiot! she thought. There was nothing she could accomplish by driving as if she were a madwoman. There was nothing she could do at the hospital that would change a damn thing one way or another. Her presence wouldn't alter squat. It was only her own anxiety that would be temporarily relieved by her arrival—not much of a trade-off for the risks she had taken driving Code 3 in an unmarked car, cutting through traffic, half-running red lights, screeching around corners. She wouldn't have done anybody any good if she had crashed and injured herself or an innocent citizen.

But she couldn't bear to lose anyone else. She would truly go mad. Hammer and Nails had to be okay. They had to be. *They're okay. They're okay.* Fey repeated the mantra to herself over and over.

It was easy to harden herself to the lifeless bodies of strangers, but recently death had become too close an adversary for her. First, her brother at the hands of a vicious murderer, then Ash to the ravages of a vicious disease. At the very least, she'd had the primal satisfaction of killing the man who had tortured her brother before stealing his life. The loss was just as great, but even hollow revenge was better than nothing.

What could she do to get back at a disease? Hate God for allowing it to happen? Hate Ash for getting the disease? Hate herself for being too slow to save her brother, too ineffectual to save Ash—not good enough to deserve either?

Ah, there it was. Her father had always told her she wasn't good enough. Standing there in his police uniform, he told her that if she were good he wouldn't have to do the disgusting, painful things to her at night in her bed. But no matter how hard she tried, she was never good enough for her father, forcing him to keep doing those things.

"Damn!" she spoke out loud, opening her eyes and slamming an open palm on the steering wheel. Putting the car into gear, she backed up slowly and pulled into the parking spot vacated by the exiting ambulance.

The emergency room was a madhouse. Two traffic accidents and a gang shooting were taxing the available staff to the limit. Fey flashed her badge at a nurse behind a counter and was buzzed through from the waiting area into the emergency room proper.

Mike Cahill saw her coming and walked forward to meet her. He suddenly looked like an old man, and she realized he was probably seeing the same haggard expression on her own face.

"How bad is it?" she asked.

"They'll both live."

Fey dropped her head forward onto Cahill's shoulder, and he awkwardly put his hands on her shoulders.

"Thank God." Fey stepped back and took a calming breath. "Are they badly injured?"

"Rhonda is pretty badly shaken up. A few bruises and some minor flash burns. Nothing too bad. She says Hammer tackled her and was lying over her when the blast happened."

"How is he?"

Cahill grimaced. "It's not good. He was hit in the head by falling debris. He's unconscious. Doctor says there's a definite concussion, but we won't know how serious for a while. He has some pretty bad flash burns and various lacerations and scratches—a couple pretty deep. They'll do a CAT scan as soon as they can."

"Any broken bones?"

"They don't think so. When he regains consciousness, though, I'm betting he's going to be in so much pain he'll wish he was still out of it."

"Did they have any uniformed officers with them?"

"Yeah. The two in front of the residence were okay, but the sergeant who was in the back with Hammer and Nails was blasted into the next zip code."

"Dead?"

"Fortunately, no. He's got a broken leg and a couple of cracked ribs, but he's better off than Hammer even though he was thrown over a wall into the next-door neighbor's yard."

"I wonder if he can get frequent flyer miles." Fey's dark humor was a typical cop response to stress. "Do we have a clear idea of what happened yet?"

"I talked to the fire chief. His initial impression is a setup—gas left on in the kitchen flooded the house, a spark probably caused by remote control when Hammer opened the door."

"So somebody was watching?"

"Most likely. The bomb squad is out there now working through the rubble with the fire department's arson unit. I told them we want a report ASAP."

"I can't believe this crap—a detective murdered while parked in front of the station, poisoned before being shot. Now a house blowing up just as detectives are entering to serve a search warrant. What's going on?"

"Your guess is as good as mine."

"Are you sure?"

Cahill gave Fey a hard look. "What are you trying to say?"

"Let me make it clear for you. Yesterday, the chief makes it obvious he doesn't want RHD investigating this case. Last night, I get a cryptic call from Keegan basically telling me to cover my ass, and then he disappears. Today, I spend all morning butting heads with ATD. I get back a computer with its memory wiped clean, and the rest of our search at ATD is a well-orchestrated exercise in futility. Now I've got two detectives almost killed by a house blowing sky high before it can be searched. This stinks. There are a lot of deadly lines being drawn here, and I need to know which side you're on."

Cahill turned away from Fey and took several steps down the hallway. When he turned back, the expression on his face left no doubt he was having trouble restraining his temper.

"Now, you listen to me," he said, his voice gruff with emotion. "I don't give a damn what our differences have been in the past—you think I'm a first-class suck-butt, and I think you're a first-class bitch—but I have never tried to block any kind of murder investigation on my patch or any other. Hammer and Nails may be assigned to your unit, but they also work for me, just like you do. I will not have anyone get away with what's been done here. You go where the case takes you."

"Even if it means nine shades of shit hitting the fan and spraying everywhere?"

"Do what you have to do."

Fey held Cahill's eyes briefly and then gave a nod of her head. "Good enough," she said, and then changed the subject. "Has the chief been notified?"

"He's on his way."

"What about the press?"

"As far as the media is concerned, the explosion was a tragic accident."

Fey chuckled. "You think they're going to buy it?"

"They won't be able to prove different."

"They'll sure start speculating when they find out it was

Waverly's house that blew up. Sooner or later, they'll also find out he was poisoned, not shot. Then what are you going to do?"

"One bridge at a time. For now, Waverly was shot by his wife. Refer all press inquiries to me. I'll keep the wordsmiths off you for as long as I can."

Fey was surprised. Normally, Cahill would have dumped everything on her. Maybe he really was going to back her up. And maybe there would be a blue moon that month.

"Can I talk to Nails?" Fey asked.

Cahill turned and pointed. "Yeah. She's behind the third curtain."

Fey walked past the first two emergency room beds and pulled the curtain back that was encircling the third.

The bed was empty.

"What do you mean, she's gone?" Cahill asked in confusion.

"She's gone, left," Fey said. "Vamoosed, vanished, disappeared, no longer on the premises."

"Maybe she went to the bathroom."

"That was the first place I checked. Besides, I talked to the nurse on the desk. She saw Rhonda leaving through the ambulance exit."

"Why didn't she try to stop her?"

Fey shrugged. "She said she tried to catch up to Rhonda, but before she could, Rhonda was inside a cab and out of here."

"What the hell does she think she's doing?"

"I'm scared to answer that question."

There was a commotion at the entrance to the emergency room, and both Fey and Cahill looked over to see the chief and his entourage entering.

"Oh, hell," Cahill said. "How are we going to explain this situation?"

"Leave it to me," Fey said. She stepped in front of Cahill and moved forward to meet the chief.

"How are they?" the chief asked. It was the natural first question.

"Hammersmith is in bad shape, but Rhonda Lawless appears to be up and running." Fey excused herself for the pun. "There's also a sergeant with some broken bones."

"Damn!"

Fey could tell the chief was angry, but she wasn't sure if he was upset over coppers being hurt or the fact of the incident itself.

"What happened?"

Fey explained briefly, including Rhonda's disappearing act. She then pointed to a small conference room usually used to interview rape victims. "Can we talk?" she asked. "Privately?"

The chief nodded. He turned to his entourage—a lieutenant from press relations, a sergeant Fey recognized from Legal Affairs, and the chief's aide, Dan Ayala. "Do what you can to put together a press release on the incident," the chief said to the lieutenant. "Keep it short and sweet—nothing but an unfortunate accident."

The chief turned to the sergeant. "I want statements from all the involved officers and all the neighbors in the area. Get somebody on it now."

The sergeant moved away after the lieutenant.

"Okay," the chief said, entering the small conference room. "Let's talk."

Fey walked into the room behind the chief. She was followed by Dan Ayala.

"Dan," the chief said, "get me some coffee. And don't bring me any crap out of a hospital vending machine."

Ayala looked as if something had vomited on his shoes, but he turned around slowly, closing the door behind him.

"If you don't trust Ayala, why don't you get rid of him?" Fey asked. Steam had been coming out of Ayala's ears.

"Better the devil you know than the one you don't," the chief replied, plopping his enormous frame down into one of the room's comfortable armchairs. "Now, what's up?"

Fey sat down opposite the chief and crossed her legs demurely. She fiddled with the hem of her skirt, pulling it down evenly. "You said you wanted me to take this case wherever it needed to go."

"I'm not going to like this, am I?"

Fey leaned forward. "By the time this case is a wrap, I don't think there's anybody who's going to like it. I don't know exactly where it's going yet, but I know it's not going to be a walk in the park. People are going to get hurt. Hell, people have already been hurt—badly—and if we don't move fast enough, the body count is going to rise."

"What makes you say that?"

"Gut instinct."

The chief nodded. He knew all about gut instinct. Every cop did. "Bumper-sticker it for me. What do you need?"

"I've got one detective down and another one running around like a loose cannon. I need the rest of my team kicked free and assigned to this investigation. I know it's extraordinary, but can you assign detectives from RHD to handle any murders that happen within WLA Area while my team runs with this?"

"No problem. What else?"

"Do you have access to a slush fund?"

The chief looked slightly taken aback. "Why?"

"Do you want this case solved or not?"

"You know I do."

"Then I'm going to have to go outside the department."

"No way!" The chief stood up as if to emphasize his adamancy.

"There's no choice," Fey bit back. "Besides, it's someone I can trust."

"Who?"

Fey shrugged. "You don't want to know the details. Plausible deniability and all that stuff, remember?"

"Has it come to that?"

Fey shrugged again and then waited.

"There's money," the chief said eventually.

"A lot?" Fey asked.

"If there needs to be."

"I'll need open access to it."

The chief grunted and rubbed his stomach. He belched softly and sighed. "Okay, it will be handled," he said calmly. "Call your people. I'll get RHD slotted in."

Fey thought for a moment. "Oh, make sure Hale is one of the RHD detectives assigned."

The chief gave Fey a sharp look. "Why?"

"His partner has disappeared. Supposedly, he's running his vacation and sick time until retirement, but I don't like it."

The chief shook his head. "I've got another question. What's Lawless doing?"

It was Fey's turn to sigh. She was worried about Rhonda. "I have a hunch she's doing the same thing I would if somebody had tried to kill me and left my partner in a coma—especially if I was as close to my partner as Lawless is to Hammersmith."

"You'd better reel her in before she gets out of hand."

"Nobody reels Lawless in if she doesn't want to come in, but I'll do what I can."

The chief walked to the door. He partially opened it before turning back to face Fey. "I'm putting a hell of a lot of faith in you, Croaker."

"No, you're not," Fey said. "You're just setting me up as the perfect scapegoat if this all goes south."

19

I T WAS LATE in the afternoon when Fey escaped the hospital and grabbed a fast-food salad. While she ate, she felt her stress level rising as she mentally tried to list everything that needed to be done in the investigation. The list was almost overwhelming.

With an effort, she forced herself to concentrate on one thing at a time. Locating Rhonda Lawless and getting her back in line was top priority. A loose cannon in the investigation would only cause more problems. Rhonda was also one of Fey's team, and she cared about her. If Waverly's murder were solved, that was fine, but not at the expense of one of her own. Satisfied with her choice of direction, Fey finished her rabbit food and got back on the road.

Driving to Rhonda's house, Fey obeyed all speed and traffic laws. She found herself putting on her turn signal even when changing lanes, and slowing down when she observed yellow lights instead of speeding up to shoot through the intersection before the light could change to red. Objectively, she knew her actions were a classic neurotic trade-off—overobedience to the traffic laws to make up for her earlier blatant disregard.

The journey from the San Fernando Valley to Pacific Coast Highway—via the freeway and Sunset Boulevard—took about twenty minutes. Turning north on PCH toward Malibu, Fey quickly checked for house numbers. She had never been to Rhonda's residence before, but knew it wasn't much farther.

Another few minutes of driving brought her to a stretch of houses nestled together along the western side of the highway. Traffic was light, making it easy for Fey to turn across the incoming lanes and park parallel to the garage door of number seventy-eight.

Rhonda's address was the northernmost residence of the short enclave. Like its neighbors, it was box shaped with a rough wood and stucco exterior in varying shades of weathered brown and gray. The roof was shingled and appeared new. Two draped windows over the garage stared blindly out toward the street. Fey figured the front door had to be on the back or on the north side.

While not appearing lavish in size, design, or workmanship, Fey knew the house had to be worth a fortune because of the setting. Houses directly on the beach along Pacific Coast Highway were considered prime California real estate. That wasn't to assume that Rhonda was somehow living beyond her means by having the house, but the initial purchase—or perhaps she'd inherited it—of the house must have come from some source other than a police detective's wages.

The thought made Fey realize how little she really knew about one of her top detective's personal life. Hammer and Nails were simply an accepted entity. They did their job, and far more, in a fashion that left no room for questions or criticisms. It was a given that they were together as much off the job as on, but the duo never gave any indication of their lifestyle outside the department.

Not for the first time, Fey wondered where they went on vacation, what their plans for the future were, what were they like in bed together. The thought of Nails without Hammer wasn't worth contemplating. Fey knew how much Rhonda must be hurting.

The design of the beach house forced Fey to traipse along a sand-covered walkway running next to the house to where several steps led up to a small front porch. Long, stained-glass windows framed the carved front door, but Fey was unable to see anything through their color. Ringing the doorbell brought no response, and she pounded on the heavy wood door with the flat of her hand.

She called out loudly, "Rhonda! It's Fey. Open up."

There was still no response. "Come on, Rhonda! I know you're in there!" Fey cursed under her breath and left the front porch to struggle through the sand to the beach side of the house.

Mentally, she checked her reasoning for assuming Rhonda would come home. Fey knew if she had gone through the same experience as Rhonda, she would have wanted to get home as quickly as possible to regroup. She also knew Rhonda would be full of hurt and anger, and would need to take action against what she would perceive as a personal attack. Home would provide the base and equipment from which to launch such a counteroffensive.

If Hammer and Nails had a flaw, it was an innate belief in the righteousness of their own actions. Fey was well aware that the pair often used pressure points—hell, call it what it was: blackmail—to achieve their goals. However, since their goals were generally of benefit to Fey, she gladly let them run. But she also knew that their actions pushed the envelope of taking the law into their own hands. With Hammer out of action, Fey could see Rhonda losing perspective and crossing that line—and once crossed there was no way back.

"Rhonda!" Fey called out again. She had mounted the beach-side decking and was knocking on a sliding glass window.

She swore again, and then began poking through the potted cactus and other greenery that was scattered artfully around the deck. She ran her hand over the ledge above the sliding glass door, unknowingly mimicking Hammer's key search at Alex Waverly's residence.

"Do you think I'm stupid as well as crazy?"

Fey spun around at the sound of the voice and saw Rhonda at the base of the deck. She was wearing a red one-piece, which was recognizable as an old lifeguard swimsuit. Sand clung to her wet feet and ankles, and her wet hair was plastered to her skull.

"I know it's surprising how many people are fools and hide an extra key outside for burglars to find, but I'm not in that category," Rhonda said. She reached inside to the seam of her suit, unpinned a key, and held it up for Fey to see.

Looking at Rhonda, Fey was impressed and maybe just a bit jealous. Except for the toll on her skin from sun damage, Rhonda's lithe, taut frame was that of a female bodybuilder ten years younger than Fey knew Rhonda to be. She was all muscle and bone, no fat anywhere.

"You may not be foolish enough to leave an extra key accessible," Fey said, "but you're a fool for leaving the hospital."

"Who elected you mother all of a sudden?" Rhonda asked. She stepped onto the deck and used a low showerhead spigot attachment to rinse the sand from her feet.

"I'm not trying to be your damn mother." Fey sighed. "But I am your supervisor—and, I hope, your friend. Now, what the hell are you doing swimming around in the ocean?"

Rhonda shrugged. "I had to do something to get myself back to feeling normal. I still can't hear properly, and I couldn't think straight in the hospital. The ocean renews me. It's a place to hide." She turned to unlock the sliding glass door, but paused with the key in the lock.

She leaned her forehead against the glass. Her next words were only slightly above a whisper. "But there are some things you can't hide from," she said. As she spoke, her knees gave way and she slid down the glass, crying out, "Please don't let him die!" Tears choked her words.

Inside the house, Fey wrapped Rhonda in a huge white fluffy towel and sat her on a low leather couch. There was no hard liquor, but there were four or five bottles of wine in a rack on the kitchen counter. Fey opened a bottle of merlot and poured two glasses. She handed one to Rhonda and then settled down with her own in the couch's companion chair.

"Get that inside you," Fey insisted, and watched as Rhonda took a large gulp.

The house was decorated in a somewhat southwestern style, but the emphasis points were leather and roses. Fey couldn't see much of Hammer in the place. This was definitely Rhonda's sanctuary, not his.

Rhonda sat forward with the towel around her shoulders. The tears had stopped, but she had adopted a forever stare.

"He's going to be all right," Fey said.

"We were set up," Rhonda said, ignoring the platitude. "If it hadn't been for Hammer's quick reactions, we both would have been taken out by the blast. Somebody is going to pay."

"Come on, Rhonda. You can't be going off half-cocked over this thing."

"Watch me," she said, and took another large swig from her wineglass. She stood up and seemed to pull herself mentally and physically back into focus. "Arch Hammersmith is the only thing I've ever had of value in this crappy life. He *is* my life."

"So, what are you planning on doing? Taking on this whole investigation by yourself?"

"If I have to."

"That's bullshit, Rhonda, and you know it."

"Hammer would if the situation was reversed."

"And he'd be just as wrong as you are."

"You don't understand."

Fey felt as if she were talking to a teenage daughter. "Like hell, I don't understand! How do you think I felt when Ash died? Do you think you're the first person in the world to have a relationship as close as the one you have with Hammer?"

Rhonda was silent.

"I can understand your feelings for the man, but taking the investigation outside the lines isn't going to help him. And where would you start anyway?"

"That's easy," Rhonda said. "Somebody at ATD knows more than they're telling. I don't know if it's Dancer or somebody else above him pulling strings. But he's as good a place as any to start."

Fey tried to keep frustration out of her voice. "You can't simply strap on your guns and go out and kick ass. You're a cop. You're held to a higher standard. We have to do this by the book, or it's not worth anything."

"This is from somebody who in the past has joined forces with the FBI against the department. What are you preaching? Do as I say, not as I do? I've heard you say, 'I've never met a rule I couldn't break.'"

"That's different and you know it. Taking on the department is one thing. Even that's stupid, but I've never been accused of being too bright. However, the department isn't the law of the land. When you start taking that into your own hands is when you lose every-thing—not only Hammer but everything else you believe in." When Rhonda didn't immediately answer, Fey pushed her advantage. "I have worked with you long enough to know that Hammer may be the most important thing in your life, but he isn't the only important thing. You love the job the same as he does. It's important to you. It's how you define yourself. It's even how you define your relationship with Hammer. Don't throw all of it away because you're hurt and angry."

"What do you suggest instead?"

Fey sat forward on her chair. "That we do it by the book. We can play it by the rules and still beat whoever is out there playing outside the lines. We play hardball, but we do it right."

"And if that doesn't work?"

"Then we switch to playing by tequila rules."

"What are those?"

Fey shrugged, her eyes gleaming. "When you drink tequila there are no rules."

20

THE BLUE CAT was off the beaten track, but still drew a respectable crowd of regulars who came for consistently good jazz, full-measure drinks, and trendy coffees. In Brentwood off San Vincente Boulevard, the club's marquee posted nothing more than the silhouette of a large blue cat against a yellow moon. For those in the know, it was more than enough.

Fey and Rhonda sat at the bar, which was being overseen by Booker, the owner/bartender. He was a big black man with hang-dog jowls and bristled eyebrows that met in the middle. He placed another vodka and 7Up in front of Fey, and a goblet of white wine next to Rhonda.

"You ladies drinking to forget or drinking to remember?" he asked. The drinks were only their second of the evening, but the first ones had disappeared quickly.

"We're drinking to get drunk," Fey said. "And we both deserve it."

After Fey had convinced Rhonda to come with her, they had returned to the hospital to discover Hammer's condition had been downgraded from critical to serious. His vital signs were stable, but he was still unconscious.

Hammer's doctor was a bird-thin woman in her fifties wearing designer glasses that appeared to be two sizes too big for her narrow face. Lines of stress across her features spoke of too many nights working the emergency room. "I have a feeling he's close to the surface," she told them, in an uncharacteristic statement of something other than medical fact. "I'll let you know as soon as anything changes." Compassion tinged her voice, and Fey wondered how the doctor managed to constantly replenish her supply of the emotion.

Rhonda had stood by Hammer's bed in the private room, holding her partner's hand with a look of desolation on her face. She had wanted to remain there, but Fey refused to allow it.

"You know what a hardheaded bastard he is," Fey told Rhonda. "He'll come back to us in his own good time, and there's nothing you can do to speed things up."

Rhonda was still reluctant, but Fey finally convinced her to leave. In actuality, Fey wanted to keep Rhonda under her control. It might not be so easy to find her and stop her the next time.

Fey had driven first to her house, where Rhonda helped muck out Constable's and Thieftaker's horse stalls and bring in fresh hay. The row of three stalls and a small split rail corral filled the huge yard area behind Fey's house. The empty stall on one end of the row was used for tack and feed storage.

Inside the house, Rhonda petted and fed Brentwood and Marvella while Fey showered and changed. The two women then caught a quick bite to eat at a local *mamá-papá* Mexican restaurant before moving on to The Blue Cat.

Booker smiled at Fey, exposing horse-sized white teeth. "Drinking to get drunk doesn't sound much like your regular style."

"It is tonight," Fey told him.

Booker and Fey had become good friends since they had been introduced by Ash a year earlier. Ash would often sit in at The Blue Cat's piano, playing jazz arrangements of forties and fifties standards, before his debilitating disease stopped his fingers from responding to the commands of his still razor-sharp brain.

After Ash's death, Fey continued to patronize the club as a way of remaining close to her memories of a man that both she and Booker had cared about, albeit in very different ways.

"You'd better watch it," Booker said to Rhonda, to whom he had just been introduced. "She can be dangerous when she gets like this."

Rhonda lowered the level of her wineglass by almost half. She set the goblet down on the bar top. "So can I," she said with a smile that put a shiver on Booker's spine.

"Oh, Mama, two of you out of the same mold."

Fifteen minutes later, the quartet on stage was moving into some Muddy Waters when Fey caught the faint ringing of the phone in her purse. She pulled it out, catching Rhonda's eye.

"Hello," Fey spoke into the flip phone, plugging her other ear with a finger and turning away from the stage.

"Fey? It's Monk. I can barely hear you."

"Sorry," Fey said, speaking louder and annoying the other people at the bar. She stood up and walked toward the club's bathrooms. "What's up?"

"I need you up at UCLA. At Bunch Hall."

"You have a jumper?" Bunch Hall was the highest building on the University of California at Los Angeles campus, which made it the logical site for a handful of student suicides each year.

"Well, he *was* a jumper. Now he's squash."

"Then why do you need me? If it's a suicide, they don't even need *you*. Let the university cops handle it."

"There's a problem."

"A kid jumps off the building roof and goes splat. How can there be a problem? What did he do, bounce?"

"No, he didn't bounce. The kid is catsup, not rubber."

"So?"

"I don't want to talk about it over the phone. Just get here."

Fey was taken aback. Monk sounded shook, and it was unlike him to be so blunt. "I have Rhonda with me," Fey said. Instinct twisted in her gut. "We'll be there in twenty minutes."

The UCLA campus lies at the north end of Westwood village—a cluster of streets lined with trendy boutiques, movie theaters, and restaurants. The businesses were supported by tourists not rich enough to visit Beverly Hills, and staffed by students from the plethora of surrounding frat houses and student apartments.

The campus itself was a vast sprawl devoted more to athletic excellence than academic achievement. Nonetheless, the school was held in high regard and regularly churned out more than its quota of Ph.D.s and rocket scientists.

Security on the campus was controlled by the University of California Police Department. The UCPD was a state agency, its officers given actual peace officer status, and it had departments on each of the campuses throughout the University of California system. UCPD was responsible for handling all civil disturbances and criminal activity on campus except for murder, which was handled by the city department, within whose jurisdiction the campus was located.

Fey and Rhonda parked at the curb in front of Bunch Hall. Together, they walked slowly through the cool night air to meet Monk, who was standing at the top of the cement steps leading up to the hall. Yellow crime scene tape was strung around outdoor columns, marking off an area of the building's wide front walkway. The concrete expanse was clear except for what appeared, from a distance, to be a lumpy pile of dirty laundry.

Monk greeted the new arrivals with a nod. "Brindle and Alphabet are on their way," he said.

"How did you get here so quick?" Fey asked. There were several units of uniformed campus police standing around by their cars.

"Art called me," he said, nodding toward the tall, uniformed sergeant with a full black mustache who was standing beside him. "Caught me just as I was leaving the station. I'd been working late to keep everything caught up."

Fey smiled at Art Melendrez. "How you doing?" she asked.

"Fine," Art said. "Trying to stay out of trouble, anyway."

Both Fey and Monk knew Melendrez from previous contact. He had retired from the LAPD a year earlier, and had lateraled over to the campus police. He was a good, professional cop with a lot of experience behind him.

"Why all the fuss over a jumper?"

"The body was called in to our station anonymously," Melendrez said. The campus police station was located just inside the campus boundaries. "Most of our units were tied up with a problem at the student union, so I left Dave Brewster in the office and rolled out to have a peek for myself."

"Can't get it out of your blood, can you?" Fey said. "Got to be out snooping around."

Melendrez chuckled. "You know I hate being in the office."

Other than a couple of years spent training rookies at the police academy, Melendrez had spent the rest of his career with LAPD working the streets as a patrol cop. Some cops love the call of the street and have no desire to get out of uniform and take up the detective torch.

"What did you find?"

"What you see." Melendrez turned and pointed toward the pile of laundry. "The winner of tonight's hop, jump, and splat competition."

"A world record?"

"Hardly. It's only a five-story drop, but it's the best suicide venue the campus has to offer. This is the fifth one this year."

"Anybody see him go over?"

Melendrez shrugged. "Nobody was around when I arrived. I checked the body. Looks as if he hit the ground chin first—the face is broken beyond recognition. There was a wallet in his back pocket with a driver's license." Melendrez extended the small official rectangle toward Fey.

She took it and glanced down at it briefly. The face caught in the harsh light of the photo was young with a lot of hair. The name on the license was Daniel Sousa. According to the birthdate he was twenty-three years old. "Okay," she said. "I still don't see what's so special."

Melendrez took a deep breath and let it all out in a sigh. "Do you know what a mockingbird is?" he asked.

Fey knew the sergeant wasn't talking about something with wings. Her guts twisted again. "A deep-cover cop," she said. "They're usually recruited from the academy before they begin to pick up cop habits. The department uses them to infiltrate everything from biker gangs to organized crime factions to suspected terrorist groups."

"Do you know why we call them mockingbirds?"

"Because actual mockingbirds imitate the calls and sounds of other birds, and a deep-cover cop has to imitate the lifestyle of whatever group he is tasked to infiltrate."

A commitment to become a mockingbird was a career choice. You went under and you didn't usually surface until your career was over, or you got dead. How many mockingbirds the department actually ran and their true identities were among the department's most closely held secrets.

Mockingbirds, or simply birds, as they were often called, were provided with totally new identities, which left any family or loved ones behind. While under, their only contacts with the department were the two control officers who ran each mockingbird's operation. Suitable mockingbird candidates were a rare breed. When one was found, they were handled with the care of the last canteen in the Sahara.

Melendrez gave Fey a funny look. "You know I spent my last couple of years with L.A. training the peach fuzz at the police academy?"

"Yeah."

"The kid's real name is Danny Ochoa," Melendrez said. He was on the verge of tears. "Danny entered the academy a month before I retired. We watched him for a couple of weeks and checked him out nine ways to Sunday. He was perfect. We'd been looking for somebody like him ever since I'd been at Training Division." Melendrez stopped and shook his head. "The day before I retired, I recruited him as a mockingbird for ATD."

21

ONCE THE IMPORT of Melendrez's proclamation had sunk in, Fey realized that the true identity of the corpse would have eventually been discovered during the normal course of events. However, by then any investigation at the scene of the incident would have been tainted by the passage of time.

It was possible that Sousa/Ochoa was simply another tragic suicide statistic, but there wasn't a cop at the scene who believed it. A dead mockingbird meant murder. Deep-cover agents didn't die of natural causes, and if they did commit suicide, it was exclusively after surfacing, when the stress of adapting back to a normal way of life descended on them.

The loss of identity from a world of gangs, drugs, or terrorists was even more wrenching than the original loss of normal identity when a mockingbird first went under. There was also the stress of informing on people whom you had come to be friends with, people who trusted you, maybe even loved you, whom you were now betraying.

Anyone who became a mockingbird was changed forever. Sudden death or slow psychological destruction was his only future. Success as a mockingbird was considered a great achievement by those in control, but more often than not turned sour for the individual.

None of this was explained during the recruitment process. Rookies were eager to serve, their heads filled with visions of action and adventure nurtured by television and movies. When asked to become a mockingbird, they imagined a scenario of fantasy fulfillment. If they could have conceived the final cost, there would never be any takers—and the world would be a safer place for the bad guys.

Fey and Monk walked over to look at the body. Rhonda hung back to speak to Brindle and Alphabet, who had just arrived.

Fey bent down and picked up first the right hand and then the left hand. She pointed to the fingers of the left hand. They were abraded. "Looks as if he tried to save himself," she said.

Many jumpers change their mind as they leap and try to scramble back onto their perch. Some make it. Most don't.

Monk crouched down next to Fey. He took the hand from her and examined it.

"Are we getting in over our heads here?" he asked. His voice was low, and he did not look at Fey. It was clear he understood the complications of the bird's death.

"We've been in over our heads since we were plugged into this game," Fey said in the same low tones. "Starting tomorrow, RHD will be sending out detectives to take over the area homicide unit. Per the chief's orders, and my request, you, Brindle, and Alphabet are now on the Waverly murder investigation."

"I take it that was all arranged prior to this little debacle."

"Yeah. I was going to tell you in the morning," Fey said. She pointed at the body. "This makes having you three on the team that much more important. Everything has become tenfold more complicated."

"And tenfold more dangerous," Monk said.

Both detectives looked up as Rhonda let out a whoop. She ran toward them, stopping short of running over the body.

"Radio call just came through," she said, her voice high with excitement. "Hammer has regained consciousness." Rhonda was hopping around like a four-year-old with an urgent need for a potty.

"Calm down, girl," Fey said with a smile. "You're trampling possible evidence."

"Sorry," Rhonda said, looking down at the body as if seeing it for the first time.

Brindle and Alphabet, along with Art Melendrez, walked up behind Rhonda.

Fey took the car keys out of her pocket and tossed them to Alphabet. "Drive her to the hospital," she said, nodding toward Rhonda. There was no way she was going to let her drive in the state she was in. "Leave her there and come back. We've got a lot of work to do."

Alphabet nodded and turned to follow Rhonda, who was already halfway to the car.

"What is it with those two?" Brindle asked.

"Hammer and Nails?" Fey questioned.

"Who do you think? That girl sure ain't wearing her heart on her sleeve for old Alphabet."

Fey laughed. "That's for sure. I don't actually know what they've got together. I just wish I had even half of it with someone."

"You ain't talking nonsense," Brindle agreed. "Let them get married, though, and all that will change."

"Such a cynic at such a young age," Monk said.

Brindle gave him a dirty look. "You don't think it's true?"

"I love my wife," Monk said.

"That's not an answer."

"It's the best you're going to get from me."

"Bodies, children, bodies," Fey said, bringing her people back on point. "We have more than our fair share here." She turned to Art Melendrez. "Anybody been up to the roof yet?"

Melendrez shook his head. "Not yet. Once I recognized Ochoa, I sealed everything off and left it for you."

Fey smiled. "Are you sure you don't want to come back to LAPD? We could use an infusion of experience and efficiency."

"I'm too old to play with the big dogs anymore."

"Somehow I don't think so," Fey said. She nodded toward the entrance of Bunch Hall. "What's the best way up?"

"Straight ahead," Melendrez said. He took a ring of keys out of his pocket.

"Stay with the body," Fey told Brindle, who nodded. "The coroner shouldn't be too long. Melendrez already put out the request."

Inside the building, Fey and Monk traipsed behind Melendrez as he led the way up an interior stairwell.

"Any other stairs?" Monk asked.

"Not with roof access," Melendrez told him.

"I know you've had a lot of jumpers here in the past," Fey said. She was breathing through her mouth as they started up the third flight of stairs. "Don't you keep the roof locked?"

Melendrez shrugged. "Fire regulations won't allow it. It's one of the great mysteries of life," he said. "We've never had a fire, but every year a half-dozen kids take a double twisting back somersault into the concrete pool. You'd think we'd save more lives by locking the door, but then again, the jumpers would just find somewhere else to end it all."

After the fourth flight of stairs, Fey could feel the effort in her thighs. She paused fractionally before following the others up the last flight to the roof.

As Melendrez approached the roof door, he could see it was blocked open by a wadded-up T-shirt placed between the jamb and the door frame. He looked at the others, and pulled his baton out of its ring at his waist. To preserve any fingerprints, he used the baton to push the door open. The trio stepped through.

The door formed one side of a small structure that opened out onto the roof. Exiting into the night air, Fey crunched across scattered pea gravel to the two-foot-high balustrade that ran around the perimeter.

She looked over the edge and down to where Ochoa's body lay bloodied and broken. She felt a slight sensation of vertigo and closed her eyes. There had been times in her life when she had considered suicide herself—dark nights when eating a one-course bullet meal from her gun barrel was an almost overwhelming impulse. But she had seen enough suicides in her career to know the final outcome was nothing more than squalid and futile, not even a statement of defiance.

Fighting the feelings of dizziness that were swirling through her head, she turned back to speak to Melendrez and Monk. Behind them, to one side of the door structure, she saw a huddled figure.

Reaction kicked in and her hand flew to the gun nestled in her shoulder holster. Both Monk and Melendrez saw her movement, immediately interpreted it, and rolled away from each other. As they hit the roof, they turned to assess the hidden threat.

Fey had her gun out in a two-handed grip. "Freeze!" she yelled, her voice hard and guttural. "Put your hands where I can see them!"

The huddled figure didn't move.

"Do it now!" Fey said.

Monk and Melendrez both had their guns out and pointed at the figure. It was unmistakably human.

"Is it a drunk?" Monk asked, when no response was forthcoming.

"Put your hands up!" Fey yelled again. "I want to see hands!"

The body still didn't move.

Monk shuffled forward slowly, careful to stay out of Fey's line of fire.

"If this bastard moves, kill him," he said. Even though the comment was directed at Fey, it was meant for the ears of the huddled figure.

As Monk approached the figure, he could make out a mop of long black hair sticking out of an army fatigue jacket worn over jeans and battered combat boots.

"Don't be stupid," Monk said. "Put your hands where we can see them."

Keeping his gun ready, Monk snaked his free hand forward and grabbed the collar of the jacket. He pulled hard, dragging the figure out of its crouched position. As the figure moved, Monk released the collar and jumped back, his gun now fully extended in a two-handed grip.

As the body slumped over on the roof, one arm swung out with the momentum and then flopped down lifelessly.

"I don't believe this," Fey said. "Not another one."

She walked forward, gun still on point.

Monk leaned down beside the body and felt for a pulse. Close up, even in the darkness of the night, he could see the battered condition of the body's face. His fingers pressing against the cold neck could find no signs of life. He looked up at Fey and shook his head.

"Well, isn't that just dandy," Fey said in disgust.

22

WHEN FEY WALKED out of her house the next morning, she sighed in exasperation when she saw the beat-up, sixties vintage Cadillac convertible blocking her driveway. She easily recognized the figure dozing behind the wheel, and had to fight an urge to wake him up by spraying him with water from her garden hose.

The hours following the discovery of the bodies on the UCLA campus the night before had been extremely wearing. All routine homicide procedures had clicked into place easily enough, but there was more to the scenario than a routine double homicide—if such a thing could be said to exist. The two new homicides, piled on top of their possible ATD connections, the murder of Alex Waverly, the incapacitation of Waverly's wife, the explosion of Waverly's residence, the injuries to Hammer, and the stormy intradepartmental political waters had turned the investigation into a pressure cooker without a safety valve.

Fey had finally managed to crawl between the sheets for six hours, but her sleep had been closer to unconsciousness than rest. The last thing she needed before going back to work was to deal with Zelman Tucker.

"I can see I'm going to have to buy some fresh snail and slug killer," Fey said as she approached the Cadillac.

Tucker opened one eye and looked at her. "Give me a break, will ya? I didn't come banging on your door, or disturbing your beauty sleep by ringing the telephone. I've been waiting out here for two hours."

"I turned my phones off," Fey said. "And you knew if you woke me up by knocking on the door, I would have shot first and asked questions later."

"There is that," Tucker said with a smile. His brush-cut red hair clashed horribly with his lime green jacket and pink polo shirt. The top button of the polo shirt was fastened, and Fey could see the pink shirt tucked into a pair of brown Sansabelt slacks.

Fey shook her head and almost laughed. "You are a walking fashion statement, Tucker. Does GQ know about you?"

"Can we talk?" Tucker asked.

"Do I have a choice?"

Tucker smiled. "You know me better than that. Of course you don't have a choice."

"Okay, but not here," Fey said. "I need coffee. There's a Daily Grind on the corner of Ventura and Sepulveda." She hadn't felt like making her own coffee when she'd rolled out of bed. She'd barely felt like feeding the cats.

"Wherever you lead, I'll follow." Tucker fired the Cadillac's ignition.

From behind the roof peak of a house across the street that was tented for pest extermination, P. J. Hunter pulled loose his earpiece and closed down a parabolic microphone. Working rapidly, he stuffed the electronic surveillance equipment into a soft-sided bag.

He spoke rapidly into a handheld radio he unclipped from his belt. "They're moving. Ventura and Sepulveda. Some kind of coffee place. We need to beat them there." As easily as a spider moving across a web, he went down the backside of the roof in a controlled scramble. A collapsible ladder leaned against the back of the house, and P.J. slid down like a fireman on a call-out.

On the ground, he quickly collapsed the ladder, tucked it under his arm, and moved out of the backyard and into the alley behind it.

In the alley, T-Bone Rawlings had the trunk of the surveillance vehicle open. He took P.J.'s burdens from him and stuffed them inside. P.J. slid behind the wheel as T-Bone wedged his bulk into the passenger side. The front bucket seat on T-Bone's side had been removed. T-Bone sat on the rear seat, his heavy legs and huge feet resting where the original bucket seat had been.

"She knows him," P.J. told his partner. "Called him by name."

"Was she expecting him?"

P.J. shook his head. "Nah. I got the feeling she didn't want to deal with him, but didn't have much choice."

"Who do you think he is?"

"Zelman Tucker."

T-Bone growled dangerously. "I knew that much from the DMV check on his car registration and his driver's license. But who the hell is he?"

"Probably some sort of press. We can check later." P.J. started up the car and pulled away at speed. "Right now I want to see if we can get set up at this Daily Grind place."

As Fey drove toward the Daily Grind, she thought about Tucker. The fact that the guy was a first-class scuzball didn't alter the fact that she kind of liked him. If a muckraking journalist could be said to be good at his job, then Tucker was one of the best. And she couldn't deny that in the past, Tucker had made both her and Ash look good. Certainly he had made them look better than their respective agencies, a fact that had covered their butts for some less-than-standard procedures.

Tucker had started out as a tabloid journalist for the *American Inquirer*. He had come to know Ash's FBI work with serial killers, and had produced two true-crime novels, *The Vermont Vampire* and *The Wyoming Whacker*, from Ash's exploits. The notoriety of the books pushed him from tabloid journalism to tabloid television.

When Fey and Ash had been working the JoJo Cullen investigation the previous year, Tucker had been there with important information. The information came with strings attached, however, and he later received an insider's exclusive on the case. Tucker had turned the interviews into *Grave Sins*, a best-selling true-crime book about the case.

Tucker had also broken the news to Fey about Ash's medical problems, an act that had made her both angry and thankful — emotions that always seemed to go together when Tucker was around. Still, he'd played square with her, and he'd scored points with his sensitive in-print handling of her relationship with Ash and with Ash's passing. It was more than she had expected.

Sitting on stools by the Daily Grind's front windows, both Fey and Tucker sipped at steaming cups and chewed on croissants.

"So, what do you want this time?" Fey asked. Talking to Tucker was always a gamble.

"What? I can't just drop by to visit an old friend?"

"Tucker, you wouldn't drop by to visit your mother unless there was a story in it."

"Guilty as charged," Tucker said. He held his hand out in front of him. "Cuff me and take me away."

"Not in your wildest dreams, pal."

Tucker laughed, forcing a smile from Fey.

"See, I knew you liked me."

Fey shook her head and fought to straighten her lips. "Don't push your luck," she said, but her words held no rebuke. "What's up?"

"As if you didn't know."

"What?"

"What do you mean, what? This whole thing with Alex Waverly stinks to high heaven. How long do you think the press dummies are going to buy the crapola your department is putting out?"

"Until they can prove differently."

"Oh, come on, Fey. You know what the press is like. They're vultures. Sooner or later they will pick you clean. And you ain't going to keep them at bay much longer. They already know an ATD detective was murdered this week. How do you think they'll react when they find out that the jumper from Bunch Hall also worked for ATD—an undercover bird who tried to fly on clipped wings?"

Fey shot to a standing position. "Who gave you that information?" She had unconsciously moved forward, shoving her face into Tucker's.

Tucker put his hands up in surrender. "It was a lucky guess."

"Bull crap, Tucker. Now, give!"

"Relax. Drink your coffee." Tucker's voice was soothing.

Fey backed off a little. When Tucker didn't say anything, she climbed back onto her stool.

"I know most people think I'm a dog turd, but I thought you knew differently by now."

Fey grunted. She wasn't sure.

"All right," Tucker said. "I know what my image is, but I ain't working for the rags anymore. A television piece here and there still, but the books are where I make my bread and butter now. You and Ash saw to that scenario. I owe you guys. He ain't around anymore. So, I owe you."

"I don't know if I like you owing me anything."

"Better than the other way around."

"Perhaps, but why do I feel this is still going to cost me?"

Tucker sipped more coffee. "I can't give you my source."

"Tucker." Fey's voice was filled with menace.

"I'll give you the source when I can. When the source says I can. Until then, you'll just have to be patient."

"I don't have time to be patient, Tucker. I'll do you for obstruction of justice."

"Prove it."

The pair looked at each other.

"Crap," Fey said, looking away.

"It's not that bad," Tucker said. "I don't want anything now, and I won't spill the beans. All I want is the inside track when this breaks."

"Another book?"

"It's what I do."

"I think I hate you."

"A guy's got to make a living."

Fey stuffed the remainder of her croissant between her lips and spoke while she chewed. "Okay, what have you got?"

Tucker turned away from the window and leaned back on his stool. "Your other dead body on the roof. Have you identified him yet?"

"I'm sure you know we haven't. He had no identification on him. We ran a FIN on his fingerprints, but it came back negative. We're still listing him as a John Doe."

Several construction workers entered the coffee bar, full of early morning noise. Both Fey and Tucker looked up at them.

"Would you look at that?" Tucker said. "Where I grew up, guys like that wouldn't be caught dead in a coffee bar."

"This is L.A., Tucker. They probably even eat quiche."

"Yeah, but can they spell it?"

"Who cares?" Fey said, tiring of the banter. "Now, what do you know?"

Tucker put his lips close to Fey's ear. "Your John Doe," he whispered. "He's April Waverly's younger brother."

"Damn!" P.J. pulled the parabolic microphone's earpiece loose and slammed it down on the front seat of the car. The point of the microphone was resting on the car's beat-up dashboard, and was pointing at the front window of the Daily Grind. "I hate these pieces of crap. You can't make out nothing when there's background noise."

T-Bone grunted. "What did you get?"

"This piece of crap has got to be fifteen years old. How can a police department that classifies itself as the best in the world operate with antiquated equipment?"

"What did you get?" T-Bone asked again.

"No. Wait. I have a legitimate bitch here," P.J. ranted on. "How the hell are we supposed to do anything if we can't get equipment that's worth a crap?"

T-Bone turned his head and looked at P.J. through dark, wrap-around sunglasses. "What did you get?"

The tone of the Tongan's voice had deepened only slightly, but P.J. picked up the warning sign.

"I got squat, is what I got. Tucker knows about the bird, but he gave her something else. I didn't get it."

T-Bone grunted. "If he knows about the bird, we got problems."

23

SITTING IN HER CAR in the West L.A. Station parking lot, Fey tossed her head back and dry-swallowed three Tylenol gel caps. It was far too early in the day to let the pounding behind her temples overwhelm her.

Instead of invigorating her, Tucker's revelation had thrown her off-kilter. The case was still running her instead of the other way around. Events were moving faster than she could keep up with them, and there was simply no time to sit back and examine the case evidence.

Cops often made decisions or reacted out of gut instinct. But experience, which motivated that gut instinct, could only take you so far. In an investigation where every decision was made without having time to consider the big picture, disaster was always waiting nearby. Every gambler knows you can only run your luck so far. Hit one lucky number—no problem. Hit two, three, four lucky numbers in a row—still maybe no problem. But if you kept pushing things, sooner or later, Lady Luck was bound to take a coffee break.

So far, Fey knew that she and her crew had been lucky. Rex Powers, the pathologist, had been lucky for them when he came up with the true cause of Waverly's death—although, in the short run, Fey wanted to reserve judgment on that call. Despite their injuries, both Hammer and Nails had been damn lucky. Art Melendrez's being on the scene at UCLA had been lucky. They would have found out about the bird's identity sooner or later, but Melendrez had saved them a lot of time as well as preserving the scene. And now somebody somewhere was adding to her luck by sending her clues via Zelman Tucker.

Getting out of her car, she saw Rhonda Lawless pull her bright orange MG into the lot. Fey waited to get the latest medical update.

"How's Hammer?"

"He has a hell of a headache," Rhonda said with a big smile. "But he's out of danger and over the worst."

"What is the prognosis?"

Rhonda shrugged. "The flash burns are still painful, but they haven't caused any permanent damage. The doctors want to keep him in the hospital for a few days, but I have a feeling that isn't going to happen."

"Damn cowboy," Fey said, but she knew she wouldn't lie around in a hospital any longer than absolutely necessary herself. "Does he need anything?"

"Nothing I can't provide except perhaps a phone call from you telling him to chill out and not worry about coming back for a while."

"Consider it handled. I don't know how much good it will do, though. I have a funny feeling if I gave him an order to keep his nose out of the case, I would rapidly find him being insubordinate."

Rhonda opened the station door for Fey. "You're right, but let's hold him back for as long as we can."

Inside the station, Fey fought her natural urge to pick up any crime reports—usually involving serious assault with a deadly weapon, nonhomicide deaths, and a smattering of other incidentals—that had been assigned to the homicide unit from the night before.

Upstairs in the squad room, there were clearly some new faces sitting at the homicide unit desks. They did not look happy to be there, especially Frank Hale.

Hale was sitting in Fey's chair, taking a small dose of revenge by trespassing on her personal territory. "Was this your idea?" he asked Fey as she approached.

"Why, no, Frank. Whatever would make you think I'd want your size twelves trampling through my caseload? I just do what I'm told like a good little Indian. How about you?"

Hale glared, but didn't rise to the bait.

"Heard anything from Keegan?" Fey asked.

"Not so you'd notice."

"Must be sunning himself on a beach somewhere, happily running his time to retirement."

"Must be."

Spotting Monk and Alphabet standing in the hallway leading to the small private room that was also used by the homicide unit, Fey walked through to join them. Brindle was already inside, along with Mike Cahill.

Rhonda followed Fey, bringing coffee for both of them from the station pot.

"Ain't life just a barrel of surprises, Lieutenant?" Fey said to Cahill.

Cahill shook his head. "Just do whatever it takes to get things back to normal. I don't want these zoo escapees from RHD around here any longer than necessary."

"I'm with you," Fey said. "My chair will never be the same after it gets molded by Hale's butt heat."

Everyone sniggered like school kids at her comment.

"I have a visitor for you in my office," Cahill told Fey. "Alex Waverly's mother. She came in from Seattle this morning. The Protective League is picking up her costs and taking care of all the funeral arrangements. It's scheduled for tomorrow." The Police Protective League was basically a cop union, handling all salary contract negotiations with the city, and looking out for all manner of employee-related concerns.

"This is an open homicide investigation," Fey said. "I haven't authorized the release of Waverly's body."

Cahill shrugged. "The chief authorized the release. He wants the body in the ground before the press begin to question the delay."

Fey bit her tongue. "Okay," she said, taking a deep, calming breath. "Tell Waverly's mother I'll be with her as soon as I can."

Thinking about it, Fey realized the situation could be turned to her advantage. Waverly's mother could possibly fill in some blanks.

"Mrs. Waverly?" Fey asked the small, compact woman who was waiting for her in Cahill's office.

"Mrs. Slate, actually. Amanda Slate," the woman replied. Her face was pleasant but pointed, giving her the appearance of a friendly bird. "Alex's father died of cancer when Alex was a teenager."

"I'm sorry," Fey said for lack of a better response.

"No need, dear. It's a long time past. I remarried a good man." Amanda Slate was dressed in black, but wore it more as if it were her everyday color, as opposed to specifically for mourning.

"Is Mr. Slate with you?"

The woman gave Fey an almost amused look. "It appears I'm destined to outlive the men in my life. Mr. Slate passed away two years ago. A stroke."

Fey nodded, but didn't speak as there was suddenly a catch in her throat. Fey looked down at the floor, trying to compose herself.

Amanda Slate seemed to understand intuitively what was happening to Fey. She stood up and reached out for Fey's hand. "I am sorry, my dear," she said. "How long has it been since your loss?"

"Obviously, not long enough." Fey wiped at an eye with her free hand and moved to where the two women could sit down. "I'm sorry," she said again, but for a different reason. "You've just lost a son. I should be offering you support."

Amanda Slate smiled. "Alex was a difficult child. I loved him, of course. He wasn't bad, just problematic, but we were never close. A funny thing for a mother to say about a child, I guess, but true nonetheless. If I didn't know better, I'd have said we brought the wrong child home from the hospital."

"Do you have any other children?"

"Two girls from my second marriage. They're grown now with kids of their own."

"Will they be coming to the funeral?"

Amanda Slate shook her head. "No. Alex wasn't the kind of man who endeared himself to his siblings. It was never said, but I'm sure they were glad to see the back of him when he left home. Life became a lot less stressful."

"Did anyone tell you about April and the baby?"

The older woman nodded. "Yes. But nobody would tell me what happened to the baby." There was a note of genuine concern in the statement that belied her alleged lack of feelings toward her son.

"The child is safe," Fey told her. "She's being cared for at a place called Ash House. It's a home for children supported by a nonprofit organization and run by nuns. They specialize in infants." Fey didn't go into the facts that the home was located in the converted church that had once been Ash's residence, or that it was the money from Ash's legacy that funded the operation. She also didn't go into how she arranged for the child to be taken there as opposed to a traditional Department of Children's Services home. Ash House was state approved, but the available beds were few and far between.

"Can the child be released to me?" Amanda asked.

Fey sighed. "I don't know. April Waverly's status is still in question."

"What's the question? She shot my son, didn't she?"

"Yes, she did," Fey said, looking for a way to avoid the true details of Alex's demise. "But there is still her family to be heard from."

"She didn't have any," Amanda said a shade too quickly. "At least none in this country."

"Did you know April well?"

"No. I only met her twice. I think she had a brother, but she said he'd returned to Mexico or somewhere."

"I take it you didn't approve of your daughter-in-law?"

"That doesn't mean I don't want my grandchild."

"I understand," Fey said. "But could you tell me why you didn't like her?"

Amanda shrugged. "I have no idea why Alex married her in the first place. He was a lot older than her, and had never displayed the need to be married before."

"Perhaps he'd reached a point in his life where he wanted to settle down and have children."

Amanda Slate gave out a little laugh. "You obviously didn't know

Alex. Children would be the last thing on his agenda. He was far too selfish. As for settling down, it wasn't his style. He was like his father—couldn't keep his dick in his pants." The use of foul language was a jarring note. "The only thing I could think he wanted April for was as a housekeeper, someone innocuous to take care of the chores while he did whatever the hell he pleased. He would have been better off simply hiring somebody."

Fey could sense Amanda's grandmotherly image slipping. Beneath it appeared to be a core of bitterness spiced with more than a dash of prejudice. She wondered if Amanda's lack of emotional closeness to her son had sprung from her anger toward her first husband's extramarital activities.

"How long had they been married?"

"About seven months," Amanda said knowingly.

Fey gave the older woman a look. "You think she trapped Alex into marriage by becoming pregnant?"

Amanda shook her head. "Another man, maybe, but not Alex. He wasn't a man who could be made to do something by forcing him into a corner. As I said, I have never understood their marriage."

Fey wanted to mention the possibility of love, but caught herself when she thought of Gina Kane. Perhaps it had been love, but a love soon defeated by the habit of lust. Or perhaps not. Alex Waverly was remaining an enigma.

"Did you know of anything going on between April and Alex that would have led to her shooting him?"

"As I said, I didn't know her well. I only met her once. We lived too far apart for casual contact."

Fey changed tacks. "What kind of man was Alex?"

"The same as he was as a boy, I would imagine." Amanda shrugged rounded shoulders. "Self-centered, driven, one-tracked. In school, he would excel in one class that interested him, but give no effort in any of the others. If he got an idea in his head, he would pursue it single-mindedly."

"Were you surprised when he joined the police force?"

"Not at all. When he was eight years old, he said he wanted to become a policeman and he never changed his mind. It was typical

Alex. He had firm beliefs in right and wrong with little leeway for other points of view."

"Had he been in contact with you recently?"

"Not since Christmas—and then it was only a card and a phone call."

"So you had no idea what was going on between Alex and April? No idea why somebody might blow up your son's house?" Fey made the last statement come out hard and fast for its shock value. She wanted to shake something loose from this woman.

Amanda Slate was taken aback, but maintained her consistency. "Alex was not a person who made friends or endeared acquaintances. If his house blowing up was not an accident, then it was Alex's stubborn streak that would have led to the incident. His fixed ideas and refusal to compromise caused him numerous problems growing up. I can easily see how the same things could have led him to greater problems as a detective."

Fey nodded her head. "It's definitely a changing world," she said.

"And I can tell you," Amanda Slate said, "Alex was not one to easily change."

24

Leaving Amanda Slate to Lieutenant Cahill's ministrations, Fey returned to her team in the homicide room.

"Okay, I'm sure you've all met your coffee intake needs for this morning, so let's get down to it. Any news from SID or the coroner's office?"

Monk looked up from where he was putting together two new murder books for the incidents from the night before. "I spoke with the lab. They said the water in the sports bottle you sent down to them had enough digoxin diluted in it to fell an ox."

Fey had sent the sports water bottle she had taken out of Waverly's car to the lab with the SID people who had met them at UCLA the night before. With Waverly's residence exploding and Hammer being injured, she had almost forgotten about her trip to the impound lot.

Not having had time to do so before, she explained to the others where the bottle had come from and the significance of the lab findings. "We now know how the digoxin was administered, but it doesn't bring us a hell of a lot closer to who administered it." She made sure she had everyone's attention in the small room. "We're all obviously back on this together as a team, and the first thing we need to do is get this damn investigation rolling before any more bodies turn up. Three is enough, don't you agree? It's time we started scoring some points of our own."

Everyone in the room nodded.

"Okay, enough of the halftime speech. Murders are solved through good, solid, basic police work. In our favor, it's clear that things are getting out of hand for whoever is behind what's going on. They have to be making mistakes, and we're going to catch them through those mistakes."

"First, we've got to figure out what those mistakes are," Alphabet said.

"Exactly," Fey agreed. "So, let's split up the basic assignments and get to it."

"I'll handle the autopsies on the bodies from last night," Monk said. "I'll also see what's happening on identifying the John Doe."

"Good," Fey said. "But see me before you take off." For some reason, she was reluctant to share the information she had received from Zelman Tucker publicly. The hidden identity of Tucker's source still bugged her, but she didn't want Monk chasing his tail. There had been too much time wasted in the case already. "I also want you to snag Waverly's file from personnel. Check for prior personnel complaints—see if there are any skeletons in the closet. Then interview some of his old partners and commanding officers. Find out what kind of detective he was. You know the routine—did he have any regular snitches? What was his clearance rate?"

"I'm with you," Monk said, writing furiously in a small notebook.

"I had a thought," Brindle said, sliding off a desktop and straightening her skirt.

Fey caught Alphabet watching the movement.

Brindle continued, seemingly unaware of the scrutiny. "How did April Waverly get to Parker Center?"

Everyone looked one another, cognizant that it was an obvious question that should have been asked before.

"I figure she had to have a car," Brindle said. "And it's probably still parked down there somewhere."

"Excellent," Fey said. "You and Alphabet get on it. Whatever motivated her to shoot Waverly may have been blown up in the house, but it may also be still in her car." Fey paused for thought. "I also need you two to get out to the jail ward and check on her status.

Go in person and see for yourself. Don't just let some doctor give you the runaround over the telephone. While you're there go through the contents of her purse and anything else that was confiscated when she was booked."

"Would Waverly have driven a private car to work?" Alphabet asked.

Fey shook her head. "I doubt it. Most of these specialty divisions have take-home cars for their detectives, but we need to confirm the fact."

"I'll do a check on parking passes for the Parker Center lots. He wouldn't need a pass if he had a take-home car. If he has a pass, we'll look for the car."

"Great," Fey said, and then turned her attention toward Rhonda. "How about you and I brace Gina Kane? She's had enough of a reprieve."

"Sounds good," Rhonda said. "How about we also take another hack at getting information from ATD? We need something on the bird who was murdered."

"I agree, but I think that's going to have to come from the chief. It's time we pull out the big guns and see if Vaughn Harrison and his minions are as powerful as they think they are. I'll call the chief before we leave."

Everyone in the room was standing now, eager to go.

"People," Fey said, getting their collective attention and taking a beat to steady them. "We've been up against it before, but never like this. I've got a feeling there's a lot more riding on all of this than a simple murder inquiry, so cover your asses. Got it?"

"Got it," the team replied.

Gina Kane lived in a two-bedroom condo on the outskirts of Venice, the small bohemian beach community at one end of LAPD's Pacific Area. The community had once been planned as a West Coast version of the magnificent Italian city of romance and water. The vision of splendor had failed to fulfill its promise, however, and the dredged canals had turned into stagnant waterways lined with mismatched housing and crumbling edifices. The community had evolved to take on a circus-type atmosphere catering to an uneasy alliance of struggling artists, retired liberals, and Hispanic gangs.

Venice's Muscle Beach was a real location, but its reputation had been blown out of proportion by television shows such as *Baywatch* and *Pacific Blue*. On weekends, East Coast and foreign tourists flocked to the area to mingle with oddballs and perverts, have their pictures taken against graffiti-covered walls, haggle over local folk art, and pay exorbitant prices for leather goods and clothing that had fallen off a truck somewhere earlier in the week.

There were no beautiful girls. There were no bronzed Adonises. They all had the good sense to hang out at Malibu or Zuma. As a result, Venice was little more than a swap meet by the sea.

Gina Kane's condo complex housed about sixteen run-down units, as best as Fey could estimate. The architecture of the stuccoed two-story structures screamed of the 1960s and it looked as if they needed more than the obvious coat of fresh paint. The small greenbelts were weed ridden, crabgrass farms slowly turning to dirt and rock.

"You think she owns or rents?" Rhonda asked.

"I'd say she rents," Fey guessed. "Gina's a flake. I don't see her as the type to be making house payments and planning for the future."

"Maybe not, but it seems she had some kind of plans for Waverly."

Fey mounted the two concrete steps that led to a small slab in front of Gina's door. "I don't think the plans she had for Waverly included anything that touched base with reality."

When Gina answered the door to Fey's knock, she appeared to be in worse shape than her condo unit. She wore no makeup and her eyes were red and puffy. Her hair was an unwashed tangle pulled back in a makeshift ponytail. A cigarette dangled from the left side of her mouth, and she held a glass of clear liquid in one hand. Fey was willing to bet her next paycheck that the liquid in the glass wasn't water.

"It took you long enough to get here," Gina said when she saw who it was. Her words were slightly slurred, and when she turned to walk away from the door she was obviously unsteady on her feet.

Fey and Rhonda exchanged glances and entered the condo to follow Gina down a short hallway. The interior of the unit was surprisingly clean and bright. The walls had been recently painted and were host to numerous pieces of eye-catching artwork.

In the living room, the furniture appeared to have been bought for comfort as opposed to style, but it all fit together to form an inviting space. Gina had flopped down on an overstuffed burgundy and black couch and was taking a large slug from her glass.

"Did you do these?" Fey asked. She was looking at several of the wall-mounted artworks. They were framed multimedia pieces that formed an abstract combination of paint, lace, textured papers, old brooches, and antique photos.

"What? You think I'm not capable of creating them?"

Fey turned her head and looked directly at Gina. "Actually, I'd be surprised. From the job interest and your competence at the station, I wouldn't think you'd have the attention span."

Gina looked somewhat shocked despite the booze in her system. She hadn't expected her own aggression to be met with harsh reality.

When Gina didn't say anything, Fey returned her attention to the art pieces. Rhonda had drifted to the other side of the room to take up sentry near a window that looked out on to a decrepit courtyard with rusting lawn chairs. She knew her job was to disappear and listen unless Fey brought her into the interview.

Rhonda actually felt a bit strange. She had worked with Hammer for so long that it was decidedly odd to be partnering with somebody else. She liked and respected Fey, but it wasn't the same. With Hammer gone, she felt unbalanced, as if she were walking around with one shoe on and one shoe off.

"Your work is very appealing," Fey was saying, still looking at the art pieces. She ran her fingertips across the bottom of a frame. "Balanced and comfortable."

"What is this?" Gina asked. "You buttering me up for the kill? You want to make me think everything is going to be okay, so you can tear me apart?"

Fey dropped her hand and turned to face Gina. Her whole

demeanor appeared to undergo a transformation. It was a physical trick of squaring shoulders and rearranging facial features.

"Okay," Fey said. "Let's all be girls together here. Sharpen up the fingernails and get to gouging. Is that what you want, Gina? Is that how you want me to run this get-together?"

Gina swiveled her head toward Rhonda as if to ignore Fey, but she wasn't able to complete the motion. Fey had flashed across the space that separated the two women and grabbed Gina by the cheeks. She twisted the records clerk's features back to face her, and clamped her fingers tight.

Gina let out a tiny cry and dropped her glass. Fey's actions had knocked the cigarette from her mouth.

"Don't give me this aggressive, drunken bitch act," Fey said, her voice pitched low and gravelly. "I can spot a planned response a mile away, and you're no more drunk than I am."

Gina tried to pull away from Fey's grip but found it impossible. She put her hands up to Fey's wrist, but Fey slapped them away with her own free hand.

"You're hurting me," Gina said through twisted lips.

"I don't give a damn, Sunbeam," Fey said. "You're a round-heeled piece of dog turd as far as I'm concerned, and I don't have time to play games with you. Now, you either straighten up and fly right, or I'll have you booked for that little attack of yours in the station lobby, and we can have this conversation down at Sibyl Brand before we allow the bull dykes to have at your creamy flesh."

Real fear entered Gina's eyes. "You bitch," she said, still a little feisty.

"And don't you ever forget it," Fey said. "Now, are we going to play this nicely-nicely, or do I have to get nasty?"

Gina capitulated and Fey released her grip. Gina immediately rubbed her hands over the red marks that were left behind.

"I hate you," she said, but there was no aggression in the statement.

Fey smiled at her. "Join the line. It's a long queue. Now, let's talk about Alex Waverly."

Gina folded her arms across her chest and rubbed her shoulders. "What do you want to know?"

"Let's start with your relationship."

"We were in love."

"Cut the bullshit, Gina. You've been around too long to expect me to believe that crap. You were screwing him. What else?"

Tears welled up in Gina's eyes. She was quiet for a few moments and then the dam broke. She began sobbing and buried her face in her hands.

Rhonda made to move forward, but Fey held up a hand and stopped her. Fey moved forward herself and sat down on the couch next to Gina. She put her arm around the sobbing woman and gave her a gentle squeeze.

"Let me rephrase my last statement," Fey said. Her voice had softened. The change wasn't unusual, as Fey was adept at reading and manipulating the emotional fluctuation of an interview. "You may have been in love with Alex," she said. "You may also have believed in the dream of his loving you, but deep down you knew he was just screwing you. I know you knew that. You had to. You've been around men too long not to know it."

Gina began rocking back and forth. "The bastard," she said. "He said he loved me. Sent me cards and flowers. He hated that bitch he was married to. Hated her." Gina sobbed some more and then made a huge snuffling noise to clear her nose. She stood up and walked to a side cabinet for a box of tissues.

Fey had slid to the side of the couch opposite where Rhonda was standing. When Gina sat down again, Rhonda was behind her. The move on Fey's part was deliberate. She wanted all of Gina's attention. Wanted to keep her focused on her confession. The words were coming freely now, and Fey wanted no distractions to stem them.

"I knew Alex would never leave his wife until he didn't need her anymore," Gina said. "But I thought—I thought—" Tears started falling again. "Damn it," she said.

Fey let Gina cry for a few moments while she tried to digest her last statement. "What do you mean, Alex wouldn't leave his wife until he didn't need her anymore? Why did he need her?"

"I don't know," Gina said. "I really don't," she insisted when Fey gave her a sharp look. "It was just something he said once. Alex enjoyed playing the mysterious loner. It was a role he relished. He said there was something big cooking that would make all his previous busts put together look like small change."

"And it had something to do with his wife?"

Gina looked decidedly unsettled. "And her brother," she said.

"What do you know?" Fey practically leaped forward from her leaning-back position. The movement startled Gina, and Fey had to put a hand on Gina's arm to settle her. "I'm sorry," she said. "It's important."

Gina blinked her eyes. "Alex met a man here one day. He had a key and could let himself in. I came home early from work with a headache. Well, I didn't really have a headache—"

"Don't worry about it," Fey said. "I've had those kinds of headaches myself in the past."

Gina nodded. "When I saw Alex's car out front, I was excited. I thought he had come by to surprise me, and I hurried in to greet him. He was the one who was surprised, though. He was sitting in here with another man. They were very intent, speaking Spanish, and didn't hear me come in. When they did see me, they looked like two naughty boys caught looking at dirty magazines." Gina shrugged. "Alex jumped up and grabbed me. He hustled me into the bedroom and made me stay there until the other man left."

"How did you find out it was his wife's brother?"

"Alex told me when I asked him. Anyway, they looked enough alike to be twins—Alex's wife and her brother, that is. Alex said there was a family problem and he was just trying to straighten things out. He said he didn't want April's brother to see me or talk to me in case he said anything to April."

"And you bought it?"

"No. I knew he was lying."

"How?"

Gina shrugged again. "It was a stupid lie. It didn't make any sense. I also heard something they said in Spanish."

When Gina didn't say anything more, Fey prompted her. "Do you speak Spanish?"

"Yes."

Gina paused again, knowingly forcing Fey to push for the information.

"Okay," Fey said. "You've got me hooked. What did they say?"

"I actually didn't hear much," Gina said. "But I did hear one specific word—*asesinato*."

Rhonda's ears perked up and she joined the conversation for the first time. "*Asesinato*—it's Spanish for 'assassination.'"

25

GINA HAD OVERHEARD no other conversation of significance between Alex and the man he'd said was April's brother, nor could she remember any other statements that could shed light on what Alex had been mixed up in.

Fey did learn from Gina that ATD expected their detectives to be physically fit and mandated they exercise as part of their daily duties. Fey's guess had been correct: Alex was in the habit of using the weight machines in the West L.A. locker room, or running through the grounds of the local Veterans Administration. When he had finished, he would shower and take Gina to lunch. Alex followed this routine two or three times a week when he wasn't tied up on an investigation.

In Fey's mind, it was logical that after working out, Alex would drink from his water bottle. On the day of his death, Gina said Alex had just finished working out when the call came through for him to stand by at the station for John Dancer. Alex had left Gina and gone outside to wait in his car. Fey could see him sitting in his car, drinking deeply from the water bottle after his workout.

Gina also cleared up another little mystery. It was apparently common knowledge that Alex had won a civil lawsuit against a dentist who had botched a root canal job, leaving Alex with no sense of smell or taste. Even if the digoxin had given the water a funny flavor, Alex would never have noticed it.

It also interested Fey when Gina told her Alex had recently been particularly excited and on edge, as if the "something big" he had been talking about was close to fruition.

After leaving Gina, Fey knew she really wasn't much closer to the truth, but she felt she was making progress—getting there a tiny step at a time. If she kept pulling the loose strings attached to the case, it would unravel completely.

"Where to now, boss?" Rhonda asked.

"ATD," Fey said. "It's time to go back into the lion's den."

In his office, John Dancer was more than a little surprised when Fey and Rhonda barged through his door. Mary DeFalco was even more surprised, perched as she was on the edge of Dancer's desk.

"Well, isn't this cozy?" Fey said with a smug smile. Instinctively, she knew she'd caught the pair in a movement from the mating ritual.

"How did you get in here?" Dancer demanded.

"Your security is slipping. What if I'd been a Russian spy?"

Dancer stood up. "How did you get in?" he asked again. "You don't have an entry key."

"But I do," the chief said as he entered the office. He'd caught up with Fey and Rhonda on the seventh floor outside the ATD entrance in response to a call Fey had made from the lobby.

Dancer swallowed to clear his throat. "Chief. What's this about?" He felt as if he'd been caught with his pants down, which figuratively speaking was true.

"I want you to give Detective Croaker a copy of every file Alex Waverly ever worked on. I also want you to give her a complete—and I do mean complete—rundown on your bird Danny Ochoa."

The small office suddenly became even more crowded as Vaughn Harrison joined the party. "Just a minute, Chief."

The chief swung around to face the man who was a rung below him on the organizational chart. He sighed, knowing Harrison must have been alerted by somebody from his own office. "There is no 'just a minute,' Vaughn," the chief said, purposely using the deputy chief's first name. "This is my department, my game, my ball. What I say goes."

Harrison scowled. "Croaker and her crew do not have the clearance needed to view the Ochoa file. What he was working on is top secret." All personnel assigned to ATD were vetted and given a top secret clearance by the federal government.

"It must have been top secret," the chief said, "because I don't even remember you ever briefing me that we had another bird working the field. I know about two, but you never told me about Ochoa. Maybe there are others you haven't told me about."

Harrison's features clouded over. "This may be your department, but ATD is under my command," he said. "I am not required to run to you with every decision I make. I put birds underground wherever I decide they'll do the most good."

"Isn't that special?" the chief said. "ATD, RHD, and a whole bunch of other letters may be under your command, Vaughn, but you are under my command. I'm sick and tired of all this super-spy mumbo jumbo you're constantly throwing around. ATD is an investigative unit of the Los Angeles Police Department, not an arm of the CIA. You answer to me, I answer to the police commission, they answer to the city council, and they answer to the people of this city. So, let's cut through all the James Bond crap, shall we? If I have to come in and take over this unit to get those files, I will."

Fey had brought the chief up to date with the circumstances at the UCLA crime scene and Melendrez's information regarding the ATD bird.

The chief spread his legs and faced Harrison head on. "If Fey had not found out Ochoa's identity from another source, I'm wondering if you would even have told me Ochoa had been an undercover bird."

Harrison looked around at the assembled bodies in the office and then brought his stare back to the chief. Harrison knew better than to attempt an explanation of any kind. He brought up the three fingers of his deformed hand and wiped the tips of them across his upper lip.

"Your contract comes up for renewal next year," Harrison eventually said in a low voice, speaking as if he and the chief were the only ones in the office. "But don't bet you won't be removed before then. If you mishandle this quagmire, you'll be gone before you can draw breath. I'm telling you, Waverly's death had nothing to do with this unit. The fact that Ochoa fell off a building while meeting and apparently fighting with a known terrorist has no connection to Waverly. Waverly was not working on anything connected with Ochoa."

Harrison's version of what happened on the rooftop of UCLA's Bunch Hall was the party line. After the discovery of the second body on the roof, the idea that Ochoa was a possible suicide statistic had been abandoned. The body found on the roof had been badly beaten, but initial findings by the coroner's investigator indicated stabbing as the cause of death. There had been an entry wound in the abdomen pointing up toward the heart. There would be more information after the autopsy.

Fey wanted to wait for some kind of official identification, but what Zelman Tucker had told her about the body being April's brother, and Gina's story about Waverly meeting at her condo with a man he said was April's brother, went round and round in her head.

Although it had not been revealed to the press that Ochoa had been an undercover ATD agent, the departmental press release stated that the two men on the roof had been having a clandestine meeting. The speculation was that, at some point, there was a disagreement over drugs. A struggle ensued. One had stabbed the other, after which the injured man pushed his attacker off the roof before dying.

It was a great fairy tale for citizens to read over their morning coffee. Fey knew there was much more to the story, and in time she would find it.

"Vaughn," the chief continued, "I don't trust you. That's the bottom line. Now, unless you want to be relieved from duty, you will do as I am ordering. Give Waverly's and Ochoa's files to Croaker, or I will suspend you and initiate departmental charges against you for insubordination."

"Do what you have to do," Harrison said.

When the chief spoke, his voice was smooth and assured. "You don't want me to do that yet, Vaughn. I know you can't wait to push my hand, but believe me when I tell you this isn't the time. You're not powerful enough yet. The police commission may be disenchanted with me, but I still have enough influence in this city to put down any coup you might be able to ignite today." The chief shrugged his shoulders to straighten the jacket of his double-breasted suit. He then buttoned it across his vast bulk. "Pick your moment, Vaughn," he advised. "Don't let me push you into it."

All the other players in the room could feel the tension. Harrison's ambitions had been made nakedly clear. The chief, however, was proving that his castle wasn't going to be an easy siege. Harrison was going to have to take it one room at a time, and he didn't have control yet.

Harrison switched his eyes from the chief to John Dancer.

"Give them what they want," he said brusquely before turning on his heel and walking out of the office.

Alone in his office, Harrison snatched a small, round paperweight from his desktop and threw it across the room. The hard orb thunked loudly as it struck and dented the rosewood paneling. Harrison stared at the scar in the wood and swore at himself.

If he could keep everything going a little longer, however, he would soon be the one with the power. The chief had been right when he said it was the wrong time for Harrison to make his move. The chief still had a strong power base in the city's minority and liberal communities—communities, in Harrison's mind, which represented those with their hands out and those blind enough to fill them.

The city's new mayor understood what the city needed. He was more businessman than politician. He recognized the necessity for order. You couldn't do good business if you weren't in charge of your customers. Of course you had to let the customers think they were in control, but you made sure they were directed to the right choices.

In Harrison's view, the city was being turned over to the animals.

The chief's social worker approach to law enforcement was a waste of time. Street animals only understood the law of the jungle—raw power.

Subtly pushing for a return to proactive, iron-fist policing, Harrison was growing ever more powerful politically. With his core of supporters around him, he fervently believed he would soon be in a position to manipulate events and send the chief back to the oblivion from whence he came.

The chief might currently be in charge of the LAPD, but he would never be a member of the LAPD. He hadn't paid his dues to the city or to the men and women of the department. His appointment from the outside had been a mistake, and even those who had originally supported him were beginning to see the truth.

Harrison walked over and picked up the thrown paperweight. He held it in his good hand and ran the mangled fingers of his other hand over its smooth, solid roundness. He moved the fingers from the orb to the dent in the paneling, touching the scar lightly as if his touch could heal it.

Switching his thoughts to Fey Croaker, he realized it wouldn't take her long to realize she had been wound up. Harrison was well aware of Fey. He knew her work and her reputation. There were others on her team who could spell trouble also, especially Hammersmith and Lawless—nobody had ever seemed to be able to control those two.

If Croaker kept pushing, she could cause disaster. Harrison wondered if the best approach might not be a sharing of the spoils. Croaker was nobody's fool. Perhaps John Dancer was right in suggesting Croaker could be an ally instead of an enemy. The chief clearly thought Croaker was on his side, but perhaps that could be changed.

The minute Fey saw how much information ATD was providing, she realized she had been set up. Be careful what you wish for, she thought as she watched the paper pile grow. You just might get it.

It was clear Vaughn Harrison had been alerted that the chief was on his way to ATD. Fey figured Dan Ayala, the chief's aide, was the source of Harrison's early warning system.

It was also apparent that Harrison and Dancer had been prepared for Fey to make a big push for the ATD files. Their response had been to overload her with information. knowing there would be no way for her to find the time to sort through it all, and no way for her to determine if there was anything missing.

Fey opened one of the copier-paper boxes of files and riffled through it. "Talk about not being able to see the forest for the trees," she said to Rhonda.

Thirty boxes had been delivered to the ATD conference room. Stacked up against one wall, the boxes represented weeks and months of surveillance logs, threat assessments, terrorist group histories, analysis, and ephemera connected to cases Waverly had been investigating. Fey had no idea what she was going to do with it all.

"Can't we get somebody to encapsulate all of this for us verbally?" Rhonda asked.

Fey shrugged. "What good would it do? There's no way we'll know if what we're being told is the truth, just as there's no way we can tell if what we're looking for is actually contained in this mess." Fey gestured at the stacked boxes.

"How are we going to handle it?"

"I don't know. We're being given access, but none of the material can be removed from the premises. Somebody is going to have to come down here and wade through this stuff. I'll have to make a decision later."

Mary DeFalco came forward with a sheaf of papers. She thrust them onto the conference table in front of Fey. "You'll have to sign for access to these files," she said. Her smile was knife sharp, her eyes mocking.

Fey took the proffered pen and scribbled her name and serial number on a dozen forms.

"I'll send somebody else from my unit to make a start on looking through this stuff tomorrow," Fey said.

"Fine," Mary said. "They'll also have to sign for access." She shuffled the forms together and left Fey and Rhonda alone.

"Why are they doing this?" Rhonda asked, referring to Dancer and Harrison. "You'd think they would want to do everything they could to help. I mean, two of their own cops have been murdered."

"I hear you," Fey said. "We're not just dealing with a murder investigation here. We're also in the middle of a clash of empire builders. Murder apparently takes second place to protecting political butt."

"That sucks."

"Maybe," Fey said. "But it's also reality."

"What are we going to do about it?"

Fey examined the stacked boxes again. "What we always do—kick butt and take names, no matter what the consequences."

26

ETURNING TO West L.A. Station, Fey and Rhonda found
Monk in the homicide room busily clicking keys on the computer.
He glanced up as they entered.

"You two look like something the cat dragged in," he said.

"I'd argue with you," Fey said, "but frankly, I *feel* like something
the cat dragged in."

"Me too," Rhonda said. She flopped down into a swivel chair.
She knew the symptoms of exhaustion she and Fey were experiencing were more emotional than physical. Sooner or later, the siege
mentality that homicide investigations fostered would kick in and
the emotional fatigue would dissipate. Until then, however, they
simply had to slog forward.

"What are you bashing your way through?" Fey asked, nodding
her chin toward the computer.

Monk leaned back in his chair and rubbed his eyes. "Nothing
fancy—just a follow-up on the autopsies."

"Anything useful?"

Monk shook his head. "Basically, Ochoa's death was due to the
impact of the fall. The John Doe expired due to the knife wound that
punctured the right ventricle heart chamber. He bled to death—
mostly internally."

"Any sign of the weapon?"

"Funny you should ask," Monk said. "Art Melendrez searched the area again today in daylight. He found a switchblade under one of the redwood planters near where Ochoa fell. The planters are raised about an inch off the ground to allow for drainage. The knife must have skittered under there when it hit the ground."

"Did it match the wound?"

"As close as the pathologist could tell. The blade had been chipped and bent when it hit the ground. There were traces of blood in the hilt, however, that match type with the John Doe."

"Any prints on the knife?"

"Smears only, but as you know, that's not uncommon. Whenever a knife is used to stab something, the prints smear when the fingers slide with the stabbing impact."

Fey grunted her agreement with Monk's statement. "What about the facial bruising?"

Monk spun his chair around to face Fey. "Our John Doe was beaten pretty severely prior to death. Under the jacket he was wearing, his shirt had been cut to ribbons. There were welt marks all over his back. He'd been whipped by something like a belt. More than one, since there were two different widths to the welt bruising."

"That blows the party line theory about Ochoa meeting the Doe on the roof and arguing with him," Rhonda said.

"Not really," Fey said. "It will still play for the press as long as they don't find out Ochoa was a cop." Fey knew at least one member of the press who was privy to the truth, but it was currently in Tucker's best interest to keep his yap zipped. "Anyway, the beating could have taken place before Ochoa arrived. If the John Doe was one of Ochoa's snitches, he could have been turned by the beating and used to lure Ochoa out."

"So, you think there were more people up on that roof than Ochoa and the John Doe?"

Fey nodded. "I figure it's more than possible. Once Ochoa was tossed over the edge, the John Doe was simply a liability."

"So, whoever else was on the roof killed him and tossed the knife down to where Ochoa was playing splat?"

"Makes more sense than what we're being asked to swallow by the setup."

"We can't prove it," Monk said.

Fey switched her attention back to him. "Not yet," she said, and then changed the subject. "Did you get into Waverly's personnel file?"

Monk reached over and picked up a thick, buff-colored folder from beside the computer. "I got it eventually, but I had a bit of a runaround."

"Why so?" Fey asked. She reached over and took the folder Monk was proffering.

"It wasn't in personnel. It had been checked out to Internal Affairs."

"Why?"

"My question exactly," Monk said. "I asked it numerous times. Finally, they told me Waverly was being considered for The List of Forty."

The List of Forty had been established by the Christopher Commission after the riots in 1992. It was a controversial listing of forty police officers and detectives who had accumulated the most use-of-force entries in their personnel package. A UOF entry could be anything from putting a strong grip control hold on a suspect—wrist locks and twist locks—to punches, kicks, use of the baton, and all the way up to deadly force.

It didn't matter to the Christopher Commission that UOF entries for most of the officers on the list were minor and had always been found justified and in policy. It also didn't matter that most of the officers on the list were working assignments that routinely placed them in situations requiring the use of force.

There were a few officers who absolutely deserved to be on the list and needed to be retrained, controlled, or weeded out. But the majority of officers on the list found themselves being black-balled from promotions or plum assignments for simply doing their job in the justified and in-policy manner in which they had been trained.

If Waverly was being looked at as an addition to The List of Forty, the question in Fey's mind had to do with whether he deserved to be on the list, or if his inclusion was a matter of constantly being placed in harm's way.

"What do you think?" Fey asked Monk. She knew the same thoughts would have occurred to him.

Monk ran a hand across his bald scalp and then reached for a can of soda on the other side of the computer. "I did what you suggested," he said. "I went out and talked to several of the officers who partnered with him before he went to RHD."

"And?"

"He was fairly well liked, but all of them indicated he was very quick off the mark when it came to a punch-up. Apparently, he was the first to volunteer for any detail that promised to result in a ruckus—demonstrations, student protests, that kind of thing. In fact, if you look through his package, you'll see there's some speculation that he may have been the cause behind a couple of street scenes turning nasty. You know the kind of thing—throwing the first rock or bottle himself, blaming it on the crowd, and then wading in with baton drawn."

"Was he racially motivated?"

"It doesn't appear that way. He's an equal opportunity brutalizer. There's also two beefs in his package for domestic abuse. They were made by different girlfriends several years apart, but neither was sustained after the women refused to testify at the departmental hearings."

"Charming fellow, our Detective Waverly," Fey said. She flipped through the package, scanning quickly through the rating reports and other information it contained. "His arrest record probably kept him out of a lot of trouble. His clearance rate shows consistently among the highest in the city."

"Yeah," Monk agreed. "His arrest stats are brilliant. He made a lot of brass look good, and in return, they covered his butt. Waverly's reputation was for getting the job done, any job, as long as you didn't mind how he got the job done."

"A blunt instrument," Rhonda said.

"There are more of those around than we like to think," Fey said. "What about his move to RHD?"

Taking another sip from his soda can, Monk pointed back at the personnel file. "As far as I can tell, he was taken in by RHD because of his street knowledge of robbery suspects. Working street robberies, he started getting results at RHD right from the start. Eventually, he was assigned to this carjacking task force and wound up making the big bust that sent him on to ATD."

Fey shook her head in confusion. "I still don't like this RHD to ATD thing. It's not done. If you're a success in a unit such as RHD, they don't let you get away to another unit. It doesn't make sense unless there was some kind of major personality problem. Do we know anything about the big carjacking arrest?"

"Not yet. I've requested a Lexus/Nexus run through the library, but I haven't picked it up yet." Lexus/Nexus was a computerized print media information-gathering service. "Do you want me to see if I can get the files from RHD?"

Fey took the soda can from Monk's hand, took a sip, and handed it back. Neither gave the action any thought, making it an oddly intimate exchange through its sheer normalcy.

Fey shook her head in answer to Monk's question. "Let's see if we can leave them out of the loop. RHD are under Vaughn Harrison's thumb along with ATD, and I'd prefer to keep him in the dark about where we're focusing."

Rhonda spoke up. "It seems to me Vaughn Harrison is like a shark swimming silently in the background behind all of this political BS. Maybe we should be taking a hard look at him as well."

Fey looked at Monk. "What do you think?"

He shrugged. "I'll get on it."

"Have you heard from Brindle and Alphabet?"

"They called in from the hospital jail ward. There is no change in April Waverly's condition. She's still in a dissociative state. If anything, she's regressed. She is almost totally nonresponsive. They're having to feed and hydrate her intravenously, and they had to put a catheter in to cover urinary functions."

Fey pushed away from the desktop she'd been leaning against, and walked a few steps within the confines of the small room. "We can't get a break, can we? All I want to know is why she shot her damn husband. Is that too much to ask?"

Monk was reluctant to deliver more bad news, but he didn't have much choice. "The jail ward watch commander is also making noises about moving April if we don't charge her."

"Hell!" Fey said. "We're almost positive she didn't murder him, but I don't want her released until we get something out of her."

"What about the attempted murder charges you were talking about—for shooting a corpse without knowing it was a corpse?" Rhonda asked.

Fey shook her head. "It's a good charge, and I think the DA would go along with filing it to keep her in custody. I don't think they'd prosecute in the long run, but it's an option for the short term."

"Then what's the problem?"

"The problem is that if we charge her with attempted murder, it becomes a matter of public record and the press would be all over us wanting to know what the hell is going on. As far as the press is concerned, April murdered her husband. They have no idea he was already dead when she shot him, and we want to keep it that way for now."

"How about we compromise?" Monk said. "If we do the paperwork for a probable cause declaration, it will buy us another forty-eight hours before the arraignment."

"What's today?" Fey asked.

"Thursday," Monk told her.

"A PCD hearing would buy us more than forty-eight hours." Fey snapped her fingers. "It would delay the arraignment until Monday, which would get us through the weekend before we need to take action."

"Sounds good," Monk said.

"Where are Brindle and Alphabet now?"

"They were on their way to Parker Center to look for April's car. They got the license, vehicle make, and model from DMV registration."

"Great. Get hold of them and tell them to complete the PCD paperwork, find a user-friendly judge to sign it, and get it faxed to the watch commander at jail ward. Let's hope it buys us the time we need."

"I still don't have anything on the identity of the John Doe," Monk said. He was actually nudging at Fey, since she had told him in private, before he'd left for the autopsies, not to spin his wheels. He realized she had more information than she was telling.

Fey looked up at the ceiling and massaged the back of her neck with both hands. "I'll take care of it," she said with a sigh. She was going to have to get Zelman Tucker to give up his source. Fey believed she knew who it was, but she would need Tucker to get to him.

"Uhhm," Rhonda started to speak, stopped, and started again. "Do you think . . ." She trailed off.

"Yeah," Fey said, reading Rhonda's mind. "I think it's a good idea. You go check on Hammer, and I'll run with trying to identify the John Doe."

27

Tarzana Hills Hospital on Ventura Boulevard was known for having the most cop friendly emergency room on the Valley side of Mulholland Drive. Whenever patrol officers brought in victims or suspects for medical treatment, the officers were always greeted with enthusiasm. They were also assured of finding a fully stocked refrigerator in the lunchroom.

Blessed with a top-notch staff and a highly rated rape treatment center, the hospital—unlike a number of other city contract hospitals—was credited with performing surgery as opposed to committing surgery.

If statistics were ever compiled, Tarzana Hills would also hold the city records for the number of nurses married to cops, and the number of nurses divorced from cops. Romance, heartbreak, hormones, and testosterone were constantly in the air.

Rhonda parked her orange MG in a POLICE PARKING ONLY spot next to the ambulances. She placed one of her detective business cards on the dashboard and switched on the theft alarm.

Her stomach fluttered as she walked through the door of the emergency room and flashed her badge. She knew she could easily have walked through the front entrance of the hospital, but entering through the emergency room was a cop thing—a habit with just a hint of superstition attached.

Before leaving West L.A. she had grabbed a quick shower, slipped gold sandals over her painted toenails, and changed into a yellow sundress that showed off the glowing amber tan of her shoulders and bare legs. The dress was also scooped at the neckline to reveal a dusky swath of freckles across the tops of her breasts.

She waved at a female doctor whom she knew.

"You look dynamite," the doctor said.

"Thanks. How's Hammer doing?"

"Making a nuisance of himself. Go and see if you can calm him down. Although, in that outfit, you're guaranteed to send his blood pressure up."

Rhonda smiled and moved on. Something about the way the doctor watched her made her feel uncomfortable, but she shrugged it off and decided to take the compliments for what they were worth.

Waiting at the elevator, her thoughts were on Hammer. They had survived gun battles, fistfights, and the pressures of major investigations. She had learned so much from Hammer—not just about police work, but also about living life on the edge. However, Rhonda also knew Hammer had learned about commitment, trust, and teamwork through her.

Stepping out of the elevator, her heart pounding in anticipation, she walked down the hall to the room Hammer occupied. Even though the room was only semiprivate, the hospital had made sure Hammer had it to himself. Doctors and nurses, in a hospital such as Tarzana Hills, work with cops so much they extend them every courtesy.

At the nursing counter, a black heavyset woman in a pink nylon smock leaned out when she saw Rhonda. "Listen, girlfriend, I don't know how you put up with that boy. You tell him if he doesn't lay off the call button, I'm gonna come in there and shove it where the sun doesn't shine."

Rhonda recognized the sentiment was only half serious, but she also knew there was more truth than fiction to it. "I'll take care of him," she said.

"I don't know how," the black nurse said. "I don't see you carrying no whip and muzzle."

Rhonda scooted down the hall and turned into Hammersmith's room.

"What in the name of heaven have you been doing to these poor people?" she asked, catching Hammer as he was climbing out of the bed.

"Thank goodness you're here," Hammer said. "They won't give me my clothes."

"Get back up there," she said. She shooed him back toward the hospital bed with flapping hands.

"No. I want out of here."

"If you don't get back on that bed this instant, I'll come over there and knock you back onto it."

Hammer stopped his actions and looked at Rhonda. He paused before saying, "You can't be serious?"

"Do you want to try me?"

Hammer paused but only for a second. "No," he said, and hoisted himself onto the sheets. The back of the bed was raised, and he leaned against it.

"You're worse than that gargoyle they call a nurse who keeps coming in here and yelling at me every five minutes. I thought you were my partner."

"I *am* your partner. I also know what's best for you even if you don't."

"Now you sound more like my mother."

Rhonda came over and took Hammer's hand. "That's the nicest thing you've ever said to me. Do you mean it?"

Hammer rolled his eyes. "I'm not going to win this battle, am I?"

Rhonda laughed. "How are you?" she asked.

"Well enough to be making a pain in the butt out of myself."

"So I can see. Why?"

Hammer's color wasn't the best, and his short hair was plastered to his skull. Still, he looked better and stronger than he had the night before, when he'd been only barely conscious.

"I hate hospitals. You know I do. I'll get better much faster if I can get out of here."

"And where do you think you're going to go? I can't nursemaid you. I've got a killer to catch."

"And you think you can catch him without me all of a sudden?"

"I solved crimes before you came along, you know."

Hammer smiled, the lines and seams in his face smoothing out to make him look like a mischievous little boy. "I know that, but it's not half as much fun as when we do it together."

Rhonda laughed again. "No, it's not."

"Then get me out of here."

"Oh, no, big boy. We're going to wait until your body is as ready to leave as the rest of you."

"My body is just fine," Hammer said. He reached out a hand to cup the back of Rhonda's neck and pull her face toward him.

She moved forward with his guiding and they kissed, at first tenuously, moving on to passion, and then hunger.

Rhonda finally broke the clinch. "There's certainly nothing wrong with your lips, anyway."

"There's nothing wrong with the rest of me, either, that getting out of here won't cure."

"How are the burns on your back?"

"Minor. They're dressed and padded. They can't be too bad— I'm leaning on them."

Rhonda made to pull back in concern, but Hammer held on to her. "It's all right," he said. "Stay where you are. You're the best medicine I've had all day. You look incredible."

Rhonda gave him a big smile. "Thanks. I was beginning to think you hadn't noticed."

"The bang on my head wasn't that bad." Hammer reached a hand up to touch the white dressing that was still taped to the back of his skull. "They shaved the back of my damn head. It's going to look ridiculous when the bandage comes off."

"Ah," Rhonda said. "Vanity, thy name is hair."

"Yeah, well . . ." Hammer had the grace to look sheepish. "How's the investigation going?"

"Slow," Rhonda said. She gave him a rundown of the day's events.

"You realize somebody tried to kill us?" he said.

"I don't know if they were trying to kill us, but they were certainly trying to put us out of commission and delay the investigation."

"Okay, I'll buy it, but it still means somebody was lying in wait for us to go to Waverly's house. They wanted to destroy any evidence inside, and at the same time give us a good scare."

"What do you think they were trying to destroy?"

Hammer shrugged, and then tried to hide a wince. Rhonda made out as if she didn't notice.

"Somebody wiped Waverly's computer clean before we got it back from ATD. If I had to guess, I'd say whoever did the wash and dry on the ATD computer figured Waverly might have backup tapes or other computer files at home — especially if he was killed because he was running a rogue game."

"It's kind of hard to get away from the scenario of this whole thing being an inside game."

"I don't think we *can* get away from it. What's with this assassination thing you said Gina Kane was going on about?"

"Who knows?" Rhonda said. "But I think we should be taking a hard look at who the current prime targets are in L.A. for that type of action." She scowled slightly. "The problem is, there's no way to tell if it has anything to do with Waverly's murder. We don't even know if the guy he was talking to was really April's brother. Maybe that was just another lie Waverly made up."

"Do you have any better ideas?"

Rhonda shook her head. "No. I can't say that I do."

"Then it sounds as if we should pay Gina Kane another visit, see if we can't shake loose any further information."

"I don't know. I think Fey got all there was from the girl. Anyway, what's this *we* stuff? You're not going anywhere. Maybe, when you get out of here, you can start going through all the ATD files. That sounds about your speed for right now. You're going to have to leave the heavy work to the distaff team."

"Oh, come on."

Rhonda reached out a hand and pressed her fingers against Hammer's lips to staunch the flow of protests.

When Hammer was silent, Rhonda moved her fingers and leaned forward to kiss him lightly.

When she pulled back, she asked, "Do you know what I felt like when I thought I was going to lose you?"

Hammer didn't say anything.

"I felt as if my entire world had collapsed—as if I had stopped breathing."

"Rhonda—"

"Shut up," she said, moving her fingers back to his mouth. "You have to stay here, at least one more night, for me—please. I can't even think about being without you. I thought you understood how much I need you."

"No more than I need you."

Rhonda leaned forward and kissed him again. "I need you," she said again, but this time her meaning was different. She kissed him fiercely, biting at his lips.

Hammer reached out and pulled her onto the bed. The effort almost drained him.

Almost.

As he lay back, Rhonda moved to pull aside his hospital gown and straddle him. Under the sundress she was wearing nothing but girl, and she reached a hand down between them to grasp his readiness and guide him into her.

They both gasped from pleasure—and he, a little, from exquisite pain.

She leaned forward over him, her breasts almost spilling from the scoop of the sundress. Hammer reached his hands to them and caressed their firm roundness, using his fingers to bring her familiar nipples to erection.

Out in the hall, Hammer's gargoyle of a nurse gently pulled the room door closed.

28

FEY LEFT Monk to finish his follow-up report and wandered into the squad room. The afternoon was winding down. Many of the detectives who had started the early morning shift at six o'clock had gone for the day.

Fey knew Cahill would still be in his office, but she wasn't interested in updating him with her lack of major progress. She didn't want to worry about that until Cahill called her on it. Still, there were two things in her mind that she knew she needed to accomplish. The first was to track down Zelman Tucker.

As she thought about the information bombshell Zelman Tucker had dropped on her, she turned around and stuck her head back into the homicide room. "When you finish your follow-up, can you take some time to try and get a line on April Waverly's family?" she asked Monk. "I'm particularly interested in finding out about any brothers she may have."

"Are you thinking about what Gina Kane said?"

"That and something else."

"There always is with you." Monk's tone was friendly. "Do you want to talk about it?" he asked. He knew she would tell him what was going on when the time came, but it didn't hurt to let her know he was aware she was holding back.

"Not yet. I've got to run with it by myself for a while. If it looks as if it might pan out, I'll let you know."

Monk waved a hand in acknowledgment. "Okay. But don't get yourself into trouble."

"Why should today be any different?" Fey asked.

Back in the squad room again, she began to consider her second piece of business. Frank Hale.

The detective in question was sitting at Fey's desk chatting with a pair of patrol officers. From their posture and laughter, it was obvious they weren't discussing work.

Fey sighed and wondered why she'd bothered to ask the chief for extra help. She should have known better. It was clear from their attitude that Hale and his RHD buddies were only going to do the minimum amount to keep the West L.A. homicide unit's caseload flowing.

But Fey had also had another reason for her action. There was something going on with Frank Hale and his missing partner, Keegan. The pair were almost as close as Hammer and Nails, albeit not as efficient, but if Hale really didn't know what Keegan was doing, Fey would be very surprised.

She had asked the chief to make sure Hale came to West L.A. because she wanted to keep an eye on him. The lack of progress in the case was making her edgy, however, and she felt the need to press the issue.

She had a hunch about Keegan and Hale. She also had a hunch about Tucker's source. And somehow the two kept colliding.

Both Keegan and Hale knew Tucker. They were also aware of Tucker's connection to Fey. If Keegan's drunken warning had any substance, he might later have decided upon a less direct approach.

The two patrol officers moved away from where Hale was sitting. The heavyset detective swung his chair around to face the desk and saw Fey watching him. He scowled.

"You checking up on me?"

Fey shook her head. "No. But I'd like to buy you a cup of coffee."

Hale looked at his watch. "I've had more caffeine today than I can stand. Does your budget extend to beer?"

"Sure. Where do you want to go?"

"You're buying."

Fey thought quickly. "The Blue Cat is close. Happy hour is always fairly quiet there."

Hale nodded. "No cops?"

"No cops."

"Fine. Where is it?"

Fey related the information and agreed to meet Hale in the bar thirty minutes later.

Fey arrived first, parking at the curb and hanging the radio microphone over her rearview mirror instead of feeding the meter.

Inside, it was quiet, dark, and cool. Two pairs of lovers sat in booths at opposite ends of the main room. The bandstand was empty, giving way to a soft jazz CD playing through the sound system at low decibels.

Booker glanced up as Fey walked in. "You look like hell," he said.

"Why do people keep saying that to me?"

"You looked in a mirror lately?"

Fey shook her head. "I don't want to see the death of my youth."

Booker chuckled. "Coffee and brandy?"

"No. Give me a couple of beers. I have company coming."

Fey took the filled, frosty glasses to a corner booth and sat down to wait. The jazz CD ended, to be replaced by a CD of redigitized blues. The music was just loud enough to take the edge off the odd feeling of a bar caught in the quiet hours.

Hale walked through the door just as Fey thought she'd been stood up. She had finished her own beer and half of the one she had bought for him. Booker brought over refills without being asked.

"I was beginning to think you weren't coming."

"I almost didn't." Hale adjusted his bulk in the booth and swallowed half his beer.

"Why?"

"Why do you think? I know what you want from me, but I can't give it to you." Hale's voice betrayed his inner struggle.

"You came to tell me that? You were the one who suggested coming for a beer."

"Yeah. Well, I had second thoughts." He finished his beer and signaled for another.

Fey wasn't sure how to approach the situation. "Does this have to do with Keegan?"

Hale was silent. Booker brought another beer.

"Is he okay?"

"Hell." He paused. "I think so."

"Come on, Frank. What's happening that has the two of you so rattled? We may not see eye to eye, but I know you're both good cops."

"You don't know squat!" Hale's voice was low but fierce.

"Okay, okay," Fey said, holding up her hands and leaning back against the booth.

Fey waited. It was a good interview technique. You waited for a subject to plug the void of silence. It was human instinct to fill silence with chatter.

Hale polished off his beer and rolled the empty glass in his hand. "You don't have anybody to worry about, do you?"

"What do you mean?"

"I mean, you don't have a family. No husband, no kids, no relatives, no ties. You got a few animals, but who gives a damn about them?"

Fey did, for one, but she didn't jump in and object, now Hale was spouting off. Anyway, his jibe about no family cut deeply.

"And your point is?"

"My point is, some of us have a lot to lose."

Fey thought about her last phone conversation with Keegan. What was it he said? Something about knowing he had a fifteen-year-old daughter.

It hadn't registered at the time, but now Fey looked at Hale with widening eyes. "Keegan's daughter?"

Hale went silent again.

Fey prompted. "Somebody threatened his daughter?"

Booker brought over four more beers on a tray. He could recognize a heavy drinking session in the making when he saw one. He set the tray on the booth table.

Fey said, "Run a tab."

"These are on the house," Booker told her. "You just promise me you'll come back and sing with the guys again when you have a free evening."

"Booker, what do you want with a broken-down novice with a voice like shattered glass?"

"You have style, Frog Lady," he told her. "You don't find that too often." He moved away.

"Frog Lady?"

"Don't you start," Fey warned.

"I've seen you bite the heads off people for using that nickname."

"It's all in who says it, and how they say it."

Hale picked up a fresh glass and rubbed its chilled exterior across his brow. He brought the glass down and took a swallow. "Keegan is running scared. That kid of his is all he has. He took his divorce hard. He isn't handling pressure very well right now."

"Who's threatening him?"

"It's not just him."

"Frank, this is going too far. You have to tell me what's going on."

"I can't, damn it!" Hale's voice rose and his bulk lifted from the booth seat.

Fey put out a hand and rested it on his arm. "Whoa, big fellow. Whoa."

Hale sat back down, looking around to see if anyone was watching him.

"I promised Keegan," he said. "His daughter is almost as much mine as she is his."

Fey thought for a moment. "I'll tell you what. I'm going to run some thoughts by you. If I'm off base you tell me. Okay?"

Hale stared directly at Fey as he took another swallow. When he didn't answer, Fey started in.

"Whatever is going on is big?"

Hale didn't respond.

"Waverly was a threat to whatever or whoever is involved?"

Hale took another swallow of beer.

"You know why April Waverly shot Alex?"

Hale raised his eyebrows and shook his head negatively.

Fey went where her thoughts were taking her. "The threat to Keegan, to Waverly, and to everything else is from inside the department?"

Hale set down an empty glass and picked up a full one. He shrugged.

Fey was running on instinct, but it was experienced instinct. "Vaughn Harrison," she said, giving the name only.

Hale stared at her without blinking an eye.

29

TWO HOURS AND three beers later, Fey left Hale sitting in the booth at The Blue Cat. The RHD detective was working up to a good drunk, but Fey couldn't afford to hitch a ride along with him.

If she had thought alcohol would have loosened Hale's tongue, Fey might have stuck around. But she had seen Hale drink before, and knew he became mean and surly.

There was a pay phone near The Blue Cat's back entrance. Fey used it to dial Zelman Tucker's number. She had his listing on a business card in her purse. Fey left a message on the answering machine asking Tucker to contact her on her beeper when he arrived home.

Just as she was hanging up, she heard a strange sound on the line as if somebody had knocked Tucker's phone receiver over while picking it up to interrupt her message. Too late to stop herself from disconnecting, she immediately redialed the number. It was busy.

Fey waited for a few minutes and tried again, thinking the busy signal might have been due to the answering machine resetting. The line was still busy. Fey frowned.

Fey hung up again and called the operator. Identifying herself, Fey asked for an emergency breakthrough on Tucker's line.

The operator put Fey on hold, but came back a few seconds later to tell her that Tucker's receiver was off the hook, not engaged.

Crap, Fey thought. What does that mean?

She rummaged in her purse and retrieved Tucker's business card. The only address printed on the card was a P.O. box number, but Tucker had scribbled his home address on the back in his cramped reporter's handwriting.

Fey tried the phone one more time. It was still busy. She had no choice but to drive to his house.

With road construction and heavy traffic it took Fey thirty minutes to get to Tucker's high-rise apartment in the Wilshire district. Every mile of the way, she regretted the amount of beer she had imbibed. She felt bloated and needed a bathroom. Trapped in her car, she could only sit and suffer.

Her brain felt foggy. She had tried Tucker's number several more times from her cell phone, but it remained busy. She tried another operator to get an emergency break, but was again told the phone was off the hook.

Fey didn't know what it all meant. She had been talking on Tucker's answering machine when the receiver had been knocked off. Maybe Tucker had a cat or a dog that had jumped up on the phone when he or she heard Fey's voice. Maybe.

Cutting into oncoming lanes and turning down side streets, Fey finally arrived outside Tucker's apartment complex. She parked in a red zone and hooked the radio mike over the rearview mirror. How anyone could stand to live in such an overpopulated and overpriced area was beyond Fey. The heat and congestion would drive her mad. It was bad enough to have to drive around in it all day at work, but to have to come home to it as well seemed insanity.

Outside of the car, Fey removed her gun from her purse and secured it in the waistband at the small of her back under her short jacket. Her heart was pumping and her head was pulsing. Beer and adrenaline were working their usual black magic, including a dry mouth and a bursting bladder.

Like many of the mid-Wilshire residential high-rises, Tucker's building, The Lamont, was a ten-story monolith of modern architecture. However, unlike many of the surrounding buildings, The Lamont did not have a doorman standing watch over the lobby.

The glass entrance door was locked. Beside the door was a directory listing the residents and a corresponding number to be entered into the keypad of an intercom system. Fey found Tucker's number and punched it into the keypad. As she was waiting for the intercom to connect, she realized she was wasting her time. If Tucker couldn't answer the phone, he certainly couldn't answer the intercom.

The intercom line rang five times and then self-disconnected. Fey looked for a manager's number on the directory but couldn't find one listed. She put her hand up to the glass of the door as a shield, and looked through in hope of seeing a passing resident. The empty lobby stared back at her.

She thought about ringing another apartment number, but decided to try something else first. Reaching into her purse, she removed a Swiss Army knife. Choosing the large blade, she inserted it into the doorjamb and pushed the tip into the lock shaft. Wiggling the knife, she worked the shaft backward an eighth of an inch and then held it in place by pulling back on the door. She moved the knife to the front of the shaft again and performed the same operation.

Slipping only once, she popped open the lobby lock in under a minute. She tried to calm herself. What was the worst anyone who saw her could do? Call a cop? Slipping through the door, she bent down and blocked it from closing with a floor mat.

An elevator stood open at one end of the small but nicely decorated lobby. Without a doorman, Fey figured Tucker was still paying almost two grand a month for an apartment in this location. She wondered briefly how rich Tucker's true-crime books, and the television networks that kept buying them for movies and miniseries, had made him.

The elevator took Fey up to the eighth floor. The large and lavish apartments ran two on a floor, with Tucker's on the left as Fey stepped into the deep carpeting of the short hallway. She knocked on the door, again wondering why she was wasting her time. She heard a muffled noise from inside.

"Tucker?" she called out.

No answer.

"Tucker!" she called louder, and pounded on the door.

She heard the muffled, moaninglike noise again.

The door was locked. She ran her fingertips over the doorjamb but did not locate a key. She looked at the lock. This one was going to take far more than her Swiss Army knife.

The moaning came from inside again, louder, closer to the door.

"If you're in there, Tucker, relax. I'll get in one way or another." Fey felt slightly silly talking out loud, but she was convinced now something was wrong.

Jogging to the other end of the small hallway, she pounded on the door to the next apartment. Maybe Tucker had left a key with his neighbors.

Fey also needed a bathroom, and soon.

When there was no answer, Fey decided neither her bladder nor Tucker could wait any longer. She walked back to the door of Tucker's apartment, slipping her gun from its holster with her right hand. With her left hand, she took her cell phone from her purse and punched in the number of the West L.A. watch commander.

The phone seemed to ring forever, but once it was answered, Lieutenant Ruth Kopitzke, the P.M.. shift watch commander, responded to Fey's request without argument.

Knowing uniformed backup and an ambulance were on the way, Fey set the phone down next to her purse. She left the line open, with Kopitzke on the other end. Fey knew she should wait for the backup to arrive, but she was near to wetting her pants and there was no way she was going to live with that stigma.

Kicking off her low-heeled shoes, she braced herself, raised up a leg, and smashed her bare heel into Tucker's door just behind the doorknob. The door cracked, but didn't give completely.

Fey kicked twice more. Each time the door gave a little more, but refused to open completely.

"This never happens on TV," Fey said aloud. She examined the damage to the door and was relieved to see the dead bolt was not engaged. She kicked the door again. It budged some more, but didn't give.

"Hell!" Fey said. She backed up and ran at the door. As she approached, she turned the flat of her shoulder into the barrier and hit the door with everything she had. She burst into a tiled entry, lost her balance, and sprawled onto the floor, her gun spinning away from her as she bounced.

Picking herself up, she slid over and grabbed her gun, swinging it around to cover everything and nothing.

No baddies jumped out at her, but she could hear the moaning loud and clear now. She moved through the well-appointed rooms, looking for the source of the sound.

In the sparkling kitchen, she found Tucker sprawled on the floor—there was no mistaking the canary yellow pants and orange socks. Next to him, the phone and the answering machine were scattered across the okra-colored floor tiling, somehow pulled down from their normal counter perch. The phone was making the inhuman, off-the-hook moaning sound.

Fey scooped up the phone handpiece and placed it back on the receiver. The silence was blissful.

Turning back to Tucker, she saw there was a sack tied over his head. His arms were pulled back and taped behind him with silver duct tape, which had also been used to tape his ankles, thighs, and calves.

The thin shirt Tucker wore was torn and tattered. Beneath the shreds that ran across his back, thick red welts crosshatched the skin like vibrant snakes.

Fey took the time to untie and remove the sacking from Tucker's head, and to pull the gag out of his mouth, before she was forced to take care of her own miseries. Leaving Tucker bound on the floor, but breathing better, she ran to the bathroom.

As she moved through the apartment, Fey was surprised both by its neatness and by the good taste it displayed. She'd expected Danish make-it-yourself furniture and Day-Glo colors. What she got was earth tones, books, a little leather here and there, and homey comfort. Who was the real Tucker?

If Tucker ever asked her where she had gone, she was going to tell him she'd gone to retrieve her cell phone and purse from the hall, which was true. No way was she ever going to tell him she had to take a pee.

She didn't have to worry, however, as Tucker was barely conscious when she returned to his side. He had been badly beaten, but the extent of his injuries was hard to tell. There did not appear to be any external bleeding or obvious broken bones, but Fey had no way of knowing what internal damage had been done.

Moving quickly but gently, she cut through the duct tape binding his arms and legs with a kitchen knife. Tucker groaned with the painful surge of fresh circulation brought on by the freedom.

"Hang in there, Tucker," Fey told him. "Help's coming."

As Fey spoke, two uniformed officers pushed their bulk through the splintered door frame guns first. They were both over six feet tall and built like defensive linemen.

"Where were you two battering rams when I needed you?" Fey asked when she saw them. "You can put out a Code 4 for other units, but keep the ambulance rolling."

Tucker wasn't talking clearly and seemed to be fading in and out of consciousness. Fey cradled him in one arm, trying to be careful of the injuries on his back.

"Water—"

Fey could barely make out the word, but she understood a tongue that moved out to lick dry lips, and an Adam's apple that bobbed with the effort of dry swallowing.

"Get me some wet paper towels," she said to one of the officers. "Soak them."

The officer responded quickly, tearing paper towels off a kitchen rack and soaking them under the sink tap. He wrung them slightly so they weren't dripping, and handed them to Fey.

Fey gently pressed the towels against Tucker's lips, allowing a small amount of water to seep into the injured man's mouth. If there was internal damage, she didn't want to make matters worse by giving him copious amounts of water.

Fey retrieved her cell phone again and spoke into the receiver. "You still there, Ruth?"

"As ever was, dear girl."

"The situation is under control here, but I've got a badly injured victim of a beating."

"Tell me you didn't Rodney King somebody."

"Relax, Ruth. I didn't hit anybody. The bad guys are the suspects—just like it's supposed to be."

"How did you know there was somebody hurt in the apartment?"

"Long story. I'll buy you a beer sometime."

"I've heard that before."

Fey thanked the watch commander for her unquestioning assistance and hung up as Tucker stirred in the crook of her arm.

"Fey—" His voice was a whispered rasp.

"Easy, big boy. An ambulance is on the way."

"I told them. I couldn't help it."

"Don't worry about it. Whatever it is, we'll handle it. Do you know who it was that did this to you?"

Tucker coughed and groaned. Fey pressed the wet paper towel to his lips again.

"Damn, I hurt," he said. His voice was weaker.

"Who was it?" Fey pressed again.

"Didn't see." Tucker tried to shake his head, but the effort only caused him pain. "They took me from behind in the garage. Gagged me and put the sack over my head. They carried me into the elevator and up to the apartment."

"They took a chance on being seen."

"No." Tucker said. "Nobody is ever around. Place is half vacant."

"You say *they*. How many were there?"

Tucker swallowed. "I think two. One did all the talking. They both did the whipping."

Fey felt herself cringe thinking about the attack. "What did they want?" she asked.

"They wanted to know how I found out about the murdered bird. They wanted to know who told me."

"That seems to be the sixty-four-thousand-dollar question. What did you tell them?"

"The truth. It was a blind tip. I got a call. The guy on the other end told me about the bird. Then he told me to call you. He also told me about the other stuff."

"April's brother?"

Tucker nodded painfully. "Yeah. They didn't know about the brother."

"The guys who beat you?"

"Yeah."

Fey thought for a second or two. Tucker stayed quiet.

"They didn't believe you about the blind call?"

"No," Tucker said. "They kept whipping me until I convinced them I didn't know anything."

"I'm sorry."

"Not as much as me." Tucker tried to laugh, but it turned into a groan.

"Did you tell them about April's brother?"

Tucker stayed silent this time.

"It's okay," Fey told him.

"I had to tell them."

"Absolutely."

"I had to give them something."

"I know. There's no harm done."

"They knew I'd told you something, but they didn't know what. They kept asking me. I had to tell them."

"I'm glad you did," Fey said. "The secret wasn't worth keeping."

Tucker's breathing was labored. "You always think—" he said, before stopping and sucking more moisture from the paper towels. "You always think you can stand up in a situation—like in the movies."

"Life isn't like the movies. It isn't like your books either. Real life is painful. You're no longer an observer, Tucker. Somebody will be writing about *you* for a change."

"Say it ain't so, Joe." This time his smile hung around a little longer.

"At least your sense of humor is still intact, such as it is. Maybe you'll survive."

There was a commotion in the front room of the apartment as two paramedics arrived. Fey eased Tucker into their tender mercies and started to stand up. Tucker put out a hand and stopped her.

"They must have been watching us—long-range microphone," he said.

"I've got that part figured," Fey said.

She stood up, but before she could walk away, Tucker spoke again. "I really don't know the source," he said. "He called me. I had no way to get back to him. It was a blind pig."

"It's okay." Fey said. "I think I know who the information came from. He's paranoid. He must have piggybacked the information through you in case calling me direct could be traced back to his location."

Tucker grimaced as one of the paramedics moved him. "Remember," he said through gritted teeth. "I get the story at the end. I've earned it."

30

THE FOLLOWING morning, Fey dragged herself out of bed, dressed in black, and prepared to face Alex Waverly's funeral. Ceremonies for the dead were one of Fey's true hatreds in life. She had been through too many of them in the past—too many for victims, and far too many for friends, family, and lovers.

With the cremation of her brother followed less than a year later by Ash's quiet burial service at Forest Lawn, Fey'd had more than enough of funerals. But she had to attend Alex Waverly's. The killer might be there.

Like firebugs drawn to the scene of their fiery creation, undiscovered, a murderer often feels the need to pay last respects to his victim. Sometimes killers attend fearing that nonattendance will expose them. Sometimes a murderer comes to gloat and revel in his or her deed. And sometimes, a murderer is driven to attend the victim's funeral out of guilt. Whatever the compulsion, the funeral mourner's list provides a fertile field for a clue-farming detective.

Fey drove to the station, where she had arranged to pick up Rhonda and Monk. Brindle and Alphabet were still searching for April Waverly's car, and were under instructions from Fey to do another personal check on April's physical and mental condition.

Fey had called the hospital before leaving home and was told that Zelman Tucker had been treated and released. When she identified herself as a detective, Fey was also able to learn that Tucker's sister had come to the hospital to pick him up. Fey hadn't even known Tucker had a sister, but she was glad he had someone who could take care of him. Like many other aspects in this case, Tucker was going to have to wait until Fey found time for a more in-depth interview.

Upstairs at the station, Fey was pleasantly surprised to see Hammer sitting in the homicide room. He was wearing casual clothes—black jeans over boots topped with a lumberjack shirt—and still had a bandage on his head, but he gave Fey a crooked smile when he saw her.

"What is this?" she asked. "*Night of the Living Dead III?*"

"Do I look that bad?"

"All you need is a toe tag and we could ship you down for an autopsy."

Rhonda followed Fey's entry into the homicide room carrying two cups of the ever-present coffee.

Seeing Fey and Hammer talking, she rolled her eyes. "He stayed in the hospital overnight, but I couldn't get him to linger any longer," she said.

"Cowboys and cops," Fey said. "Thick skulls and crap for brains." She turned her attention back to Hammer. "You look as if you could be knocked over by a feather. What good do you think you're going to do anybody here?"

Hammer took his mug from Rhonda. "I understand there are a ton and a half of files down at ATD to be sifted through."

Fey had to admit the path of Hammer's reasoning had merit. "It's a crap job," she said. "It's nothing but a smoke screen."

"I guessed as much," Hammer said. "But somebody has to go through the motions. It might as well be me. I also want to go through all the stuff we recovered from Waverly's desk and locker again. Somewhere, there has to be a clue."

"Okay," Fey said. "But only if you're up to it."

Hammer nodded at Rhonda. "That's what she wanted to find out last night," he said. Fey was almost shocked. It was the closest either of the pair had ever come to saying anything public about their relationship.

• • •

The funeral held two particular points of interest for Fey. First, even though Waverly had died while on duty, he had not died exactly in the line of duty. As a result, the funeral was not the high-profile affair usually reserved for law enforcement personnel who are killed on the job.

As far as the press and the great majority of the department were concerned, Alex Waverly had been shot by his wife as the end result of a love triangle. The sentiment was "He who plays, pays." The detective's demise was something of an embarrassment, the circumstances tainting the usual blaze of glory flag-waving generated by the death of a cop in the line of duty.

In most cases when a cop is killed, he or she is turned into a public hero. The department ritualistically martyrs their dead, using them as shining examples of sacrifice and selflessness. Even if a cop's death is the result of screwing up tactics, or walking around with head up butt, he or she was still trying to do the job, and the department covers their own.

Alex Waverly's death, however, was spectacular in its own right, but no amount of public relations maneuvering could make it anything more than a sordid soap opera. It was hardly the stuff for recruiting posters and budget expansion guilt to be built on. The only approach was to downplay the entire incident and focus on the fact that a public servant had died.

The other interesting aspect of Waverly's funeral, which surprised Fey, was the number of women present. Though great strides had been made to recruit women in recent years, the LAPD was still top heavy with testosterone. At any given cop gathering, males generally still outnumbered women at least three to one, but Waverly's funeral appeared to be an exception.

If Waverly's burial had been a traditional cop funeral, officers from all over the LAPD would have been joined by officers from other local law enforcement agencies, and even out-of-state law enforcement representatives, in paying respect to a fallen comrade. Cops would have attended the funeral whether or not they knew Waverly. By attending, they paid respect not only to the newly dead, but to all those who had previously fallen in the line of duty.

For cops, attending a police funeral is a mandatory responsibility, a reminder of their own vulnerability and mortality. They go to fight the fear that the next funeral they attend could easily be their own.

But the small gathering at the nondescript cemetery had not been publicly broadcast outside the department. Even within the department, only those who actively sought out information pertaining to the funeral were made aware of the arrangements.

There was also no contingent at the funeral from April's side of the family. Amanda Slate had told Fey she didn't think April had any family beyond a brother, and from what Tucker had told Fey, it was clear the brother wasn't going to be attending.

For Fey, this scenario meant she was looking at mourners who almost all had a connection to Waverly. Detectives from both Robbery-Homicide and Anti-Terrorist Divisions were present, but that was to be expected—Waverly had worked for them, even been their star. Fey recognized P. J. Hunter and his partner, T-Bone Rawlings. Frank Hale stood next to him. Derek Keegan was conspicuous by his absence.

The top brass in the form of the chief, Vaughn Harrison, and a full complement of deputy chiefs and commanders all attended for the sake of appearances—and to make sure nobody put a knife in their backs for not showing up.

Amanda Slate was appropriately somber in black sheath and veil. When the chief handed her the tricorner of the folded American flag, Fey watched as Waverly's mother's shoulders shook with the sobs racking her body. It was impossible to tell if they were real or put on for effect. Fey decided to give her the benefit of the doubt.

More than the expected faces, however, Fey was interested in the number of other women present. Gina Kane stood in the middle of a group of feminine friends, who Fey recognized as the other civilian records clerks from West L.A. When she arrived, Gina had exchanged tentative nods with Fey, almost as if she expected Fey suddenly to begin another round of interrogation.

There were at least fifteen to twenty other women standing around the edges of the activity. Most were civilian employees from various divisions—records clerks, captains' secretaries, PSRs, and other similar positions. There were several female officers who were still in diapers as far as their time on the job was concerned, and one or two female detectives whose love lives were in constant turmoil.

As Fey surveyed the crowd, she spotted Mary DeFalco, the ATD captain's secretary, who was standing next to John Dancer, her arm linked through his for support. Now, that's cozy, Fey thought. She also thought that Mary's skirt was a little too short for the occasion. Dancer certainly didn't appear to be minding her attention. Fey remembered the almost compromising position she had caught the pair in on her last trip to ATD.

Fey wasn't sure what the presence of all the women meant beyond confirming Waverly's reputation as a womanizer. She wasn't even sure if it meant anything.

Seeing all these women attending the funeral also made Fey think about April Waverly, and what Waverly's mother had said about the union. While Fey had hardly seen April Waverly at her best, it was obvious that she did not compete looks- or charm-wise with even the least of the women present. What had possessed Waverly to marry her? Was the child even Waverly's? And what was Waverly's relationship with April's brother? Who was Waverly involved with first, April or her brother? Which came first, the chicken or the egg?

Fey was beginning to feel the rhythm of the case, and the back beat was becoming frenetic. It was time to make something happen, bust something free.

It was time to throw a spanner in the works. A spanner named Ethan Kelso.

31

E THAN KELSO had christened his thrity-two-foot Hammond sloop the *Corrienearn* after the small Scottish town where he had been born of English parents. Its long, sleek lines looked powerful even at rest in its accustomed slip in the Santa Monica Marina. There, the late-morning sun was burning through the overcast, promising fine weather for the afternoon.

After parking in the marina lot, Fey and Rhonda walked toward the sloop, enjoying the tangy, salt smell of the air, and the cool onshore breeze. Fey had only just told Rhonda why they were at the marina.

For her part, Rhonda had realized something was up before they left the funeral, when Fey had asked Mike Cahill to trade detective cars with her.

Cahill, who had been obligated to attend the ceremony, had initially balked when it came to switching his brand-new department ride for Fey's battered, eight-year-old detective sedan. To his credit, he soon realized Fey wouldn't have made the strange request if she hadn't had strong reasons.

Once in the lieutenant's car, Fey had driven the wrong way out the cemetery's one-way entrance, and immediately made an illegal left-hand turn across traffic. Rhonda figured they were both going to be killed before she could even yell at Fey to look out.

"What are you doing?" Rhonda had asked as the car finally settled into the correct lane and flow of traffic.

"Patience," Fey had replied, checking her rearview mirror while stopped for a trilight. Before the light turned green, Fey ran the red light and sped away from the intersection.

At that point, Rhonda knew Fey was dry cleaning—finding out if they were being followed and then losing or confronting the tail.

"You changed cars with Cahill because you were worried about a bug?"

Fey grunted. Watching her rearview mirror, she had accelerated to the top of a freeway on-ramp. Once into the flow of slow-lane traffic, she suddenly pulled over to the shoulder and stopped. Getting out of the car, she stood looking up at the sky, but was unable to spot any overhead surveillance.

Back in the car, Fey had carefully, and with much honking of horns, reversed down the shoulder and backed down the on-ramp she had used to enter the freeway moments before. No surveillance cars could have followed without being spotted.

"What if whoever you think is after us has a full surveillance team?" Rhonda had asked. A full surveillance team of eight to ten cars could prepare for and handle the type of dry-cleaning techniques Fey was employing.

"If there are that many players on the opposite team, then we are in worse trouble than I think," Fey had said. "In fact, if they have those kinds of resources, it might as well be game over, because we won't be able to stop them."

"Where are we headed?" Rhonda had finally asked.

"To see an old friend. We need reinforcements."

Now at the marina, Fey led the way toward the *Corrienearn*. As they walked, Fey told Rhonda that she had known Kelso a long time. She explained that the *Corrienearn* was Kelso's floating residence.

"How well did you know him?" Rhonda asked, her voice loaded with innuendo.

"None of your damn business. And anyway, it was a long time ago."

"Between marriages?"

"Not exactly."

"My, my," said Rhonda. "You were quite the little firecracker, weren't you?"

"Don't let my ancient visage fool you," Fey said. "I still am when I want to be." And then she realized she hadn't wanted to be for what seemed like a long time.

"Permission to come aboard, Captain?" Fey requested with mock severity as they approached the sloop.

"Since when have you ever waited for permission to do anything?" Kelso asked, politely offering his hand to help both women step from the gangplank to the deck. "Ever since I've known you," Kelso said, "you've acted first and asked for forgiveness later."

"She hasn't changed," Rhonda told him.

"Ethan Kelso," Fey performed introductions, "Rhonda Lawless."

"*The* Rhonda Lawless? The Hammer and Nails Rhonda Lawless?" Kelso asked.

"In the flesh," Fey told him. "Your reputation proceeds you," she said to Rhonda.

"So does this gentleman's," Rhonda said. "You retired from the Anti-Terrorist Division—what? Four years ago?"

"Five," Ethan told her. "But it still seems like yesterday."

"You wrapped up that investigation involving the Acropolis sports arena and the soccer teams back in the eighties?"

Ethan nodded. "I still have the bruises to show for it. Don't ever let anyone tell you that being shot while wearing a bulletproof vest doesn't hurt."

Kelso gestured with his hands and ushered his guests down into the sloop's interior. He was close to six feet with a physical build that had become stocky with middle age. His face was still youthful under the close-cropped blond hair, but it was hiding beneath crinkles brought on by stress, sunshine, and time.

Rhonda had immediately noticed his washed-out blue eyes. Despite the soft color, they were very hard under the surface twinkle. They were warrior's eyes. Rhonda recognized them easily since she saw a pair of them in the mirror every morning.

When the three had slid into a booth built in around a small table, Kelso poured hot tea from a silver teapot into three mugs.

Tequila Mockingbird • 205

Rhonda watched the ritual and then looked at Fey.

Fey nodded at Kelso while speaking to Rhonda. "Even though he came to America from Britain with his parents when he was barely out of diapers, he still hasn't cottoned to the way things are done in this country. He's still a tea and crumpets kind of guy."

"Twenty-five years with the department," Kelso said, "and I never could get used to drinking coffee." He set down the teapot and served up the steaming mugs. "Now, why all the cloak-and-dagger stuff of meeting away from my office? What's going on?"

While driving home the night before after seeing Zelman Tucker off to the hospital, Fey had stopped at a randomly chosen phone booth and called Kelso. She had arranged the current meeting, but had stipulated that she wanted it to be clandestine, as away from prying eyes as possible. The growing paranoia that had driven her to use a random pay phone for the call, as opposed to her cell phone or her home phone, extended to being seen in public with Kelso.

Fey looked again at Rhonda. "We need help with a murder investigation," Fey said. "I want to hire your crew."

Kelso looked surprised. Since retiring from the department, he had used the tools of the intelligence trade he'd learned with ATD to build a high-end, private-sector security firm. Thistle One specialized in industrial espionage and had rapidly become one of the more highly regarded names in the field.

"Since when has the department started turning to freelancers for help with murder inquiries?" he asked.

"Since the victim was an ATD detective and the internal politics are telling me that there are cops involved," Fey said. "Since somebody almost killed two of my best detectives trying to cover up a source of possible evidence. And since two more stiffs have turned up with ATD connections."

There was a sort of stunned silence for a few beats.

"I don't believe it," Kelso said, but the tone of his voice indicated he did believe. "You have to be talking about this caper with Alex Waverly, but I thought his wife shot him."

"Life couldn't be that simple," Fey said, explaining about the poisoning and everything else that had occurred since the shooting in front of the station.

When Fey finished, Kelso poured himself more tea, indicating the intensity of his thought process by his failure of manners in asking his guests if they wanted more.

He eventually shook his head and turned to Rhonda. "What's your gut feeling about Waverly's house blowing up?"

Rhonda shrugged. "I think it's tied into John Dancer taking Waverly's laptop computer back and wiping it clean before we could get to it. Waverly was sure to have another computer setup at home, and there was only one way to be sure he didn't keep backup disks there for his laptop."

"Do you think whoever blew up the house was trying to kill you?"

"I don't think so," Rhonda said. "I've thought about it a lot. It was pulled mighty close, but whoever set off the spark that ignited the gas could have done it quicker and taken out both Hammer and myself. I think they wanted to take us out of play for a while, not kill us. However, as the stakes get higher, I don't think they'll hesitate next time."

Kelso sighed. "This John Dancer guy is new since my time. Vaughn Harrison had just been promoted to deputy chief when I retired, so I don't know him too well either. A lot has changed in the division since my tour with ATD." He switched his attention to Fey. "What about these two guys you say were following you?"

"Hunter and Rawlings," Fey told him. "Hammer spotted the tail while we were on the way from West L.A. to Parker Center, but I think they'd been with me since home. And I don't think I ran them off when I called Dancer on the surveillance. Somebody was watching when I talked with Zelman Tucker. Somebody who wanted to know where Tucker was getting his information. Without any indication that other parties are involved, I'd have to put my money on those two."

"It's going to be hard to prove," Kelso said.

"It's also going to get more interesting when the welts on Tucker's body are compared with the welts from the corpse on the roof of Bunch Hall."

The implications of Fey's conclusion silenced the small group. If whoever had beaten Zelman Tucker had also beaten and killed the person on the Bunch Hall roof, then by extension, whoever it was probably also killed Danny Ochoa—the mockingbird who took the cement swan dive.

"What exactly do you want from my people?" Kelso asked eventually.

"I don't just want your people, Ethan," Fey said. "I want you as well. You've worked for ATD. You know how that system clicks. None of the rest of us do."

Ethan chuckled. "Let me tell you, nobody really knows what ATD does, not even ATD. I used to call it The Emperor's New Clothes Division."

Fey wasn't laughing. "I want you to set up a surveillance on Hunter and Rawlings. Maybe later we'll also need to set up on John Dancer and Vaughn Harrison."

"Whew," Ethan said. "You do realize how much manpower you're talking about?"

Fey leaned forward, placing her elbows on the table. "I've heard it said that Thistle One is some kind of hotshot enterprise. Your offices are in a fancy, high-tech building in Santa Monica and you billed over two million dollars last year. Are you telling me that surveillance on two or four subjects is going to break your bank?"

Kelso gave her a dirty look and then decided to play hardball. "What I'm telling you is that it's going to cost you big time. I didn't bill over two million dollars last year by trading on past relationships." He flashed a glance at Rhonda, but she remained stone-faced.

"I don't expect favors," Fey said. "We never were that close, and you weren't that good. Anyway, I don't trade on one-night stands."

"Meow," Rhonda said, interrupting to play mediator. "We also need your people to dig," she said, surprising both Fey and Kelso. She could see what was needed as well as Fey could.

"Dig?" asked Kelso.

"Yeah. Task some of your gunfighters with finding out what Rawlings and Hunter were into on the street. We need to know what their ATD investigations responsibilities are, and about their relationship to Waverly."

"The money is covered." Fey took the reins of the conversation back. "You tell me what your requirements are, and I'll make the arrangements."

"Slush fund?"

"Do you care?"

Kelso shrugged. "Okay. I'll get my people rolling."

"There's more," Fey said.

"There always is," Kelso replied.

Fey told him what Gina Kane had said about Waverly meeting with a man he introduced as April's brother, and the use of the Spanish word for assassination.

"So, you'll want to know what threat assessments are current?"

"Threat assessments?"

"Yeah. Whenever a prominent dignitary comes to town or a major demonstration is planned, ATD creates a threat assessment to determine the danger level. If we know what threat assessments ATD has in the works, it may possibly give us a clue to who or what may have been the focus of Waverly's conversation with his supposed brother-in-law."

"It will be more than we have now," Fey said.

Ethan stood up and walked to a small stove, where he turned a burner on under a kettle for more hot water. "I guess things have changed since I retired from ATD. Our old captain there, Ron Harper, wouldn't have let something like this get by him. It was a shame when he died. He was such a solid type of guy. I couldn't believe it when I heard he'd committed suicide. It actually scared the hell out of me. If Ron could do something like that, then anybody could."

Fey and Rhonda sat in the booth looking at each other.

"Holy hell," they said in quiet unison.

32

BRINDLE JONES stood at the edge of what seemed to her to be the fiftieth parking lot she had traipsed through. "How many does this make?" she asked Alphabet, who was shuffling along beside her.

"Twelve." Alphabet scratched inside his ear with the eraser end of a number 2 yellow Ticonderoga.

"You've got to be kidding me! Only twelve?"

"Yup." He switched the pencil to the other ear and continued his personal hygiene regime.

The search for April Waverly's car was taking on odyssey proportions. After procuring the car's description and license plate number from the DMV computer the day before, the duo had checked the curb parking around Parker Center, but without any joy.

Fey's instructions, sent to them via Monk, had pulled them off the car search in order to procure the PCD that would keep April Waverly in jail over the weekend without their being forced to charge her. By the time they finished the procedure and presented copies to the jail ward watch commander, it was too late to continue their search.

Instead of going to Waverly's funeral the following morning, they had resumed looking for the car starting with the employee parking lots for the police headquarters building—thinking that Alex Waverly may have put a pass in the window allowing April access to a controlled parking area.

When that failed, the partners switched their efforts to canvassing the pay parking lots closest to the station. They had already covered three sides of the building without success and were now embarking on the fourth.

Brindle stared at the expanse of cars baking in the downtown Los Angeles parking lot. "I had no idea there were so many white Buick Regals in this damned city. And all of them appear to have been parked downtown," she said. "My feet are killing me."

"I told you not to wear the cruel shoes," Alphabet told her. "Four-inch heels don't cut it on soft asphalt." Worn Converse high-tops covered Alphabet's own fallen arches.

"Yeah, but they do show off my calf muscles to perfection. I don't spend all my time in the gym to run around in flats."

Alphabet used the pencil to scratch under one arm. "Can we try and find this damn car? The only people down here looking at your legs are drunk and couldn't get it up if they tried." He started walking down the aisles of parked cars.

Brindle walked over to the attendant in the parking booth.

"Say, sugar. You be looking fine this morning." The attendant had been watching her with lust in his eyes since he'd spotted Brindle and Alphabet approaching his location. "What's that tubby white boy got to offer you that I don't?" The question was said with a smile, but Brindle could easily read the hustle underneath.

"You must get more than your share of trim with your silver tongue, Leonard," Brindle read the name tag on the attendant's blue uniform shirt. "But I'm too high maintenance for your league. Anyway, I don't think your taste for fuzz runs to my brand." Brindle swung back the edge of the mauve jacket she was wearing to show the badge pinned to the matching skirt. A white blouse revealing plenty of cleavage, combined with white hose and the mauve high heels, which Alphabet had ragged on her about, completed her ensemble. She looked ready for her own television series.

"Whoa, sorry, Mama. Didn't mean to get you riled." Leonard's eyes started doing the badgeaphobic skitter—looking everywhere for an escape route.

"Relax, Leonard," Brindle said, not wanting the attendant to rabbit. "I don't care if you've got warrants, and I ain't interested in anything you may have stashed in the booth—that is, unless you call me Mama again."

Leonard smiled weakly, showing off grime-encrusted teeth. "Sorry. I's just nervous. Don't ever remember seeing a lady cop as good-looking as you before."

Brindle almost laughed. "Cut the horsecrap, Leonard. It isn't going to get you anywhere. All I want to know is, has anyone left a white Buick Regal in your lot who hasn't come back for it in the last few days?"

Brindle sensed Leonard's hesitation as he judged how much his information could be worth.

Brindle held up her hand. "Twenty bucks," she said. To forestall any bartering she added, "You hold out for more and I start getting real interested in searching for the source of the dope that's got your pupils pinpointed. Worse comes to worse, I can always book you for internal possession."

"Twenty bucks sounds good to me," Leonard said, quickly relenting and holding out his hand.

Brindle looked at the outstretched palm. "Value for money, Leonard. First you tell, then I pay. That's the way business works." She pulled a folded twenty from her skirt pocket and flashed the cash. Somehow she was going to have to find a way to get reimbursed through the vice unit's secret service funds.

Leonard was quick to decide Brindle was not going to be pushed. "We had a Regal towed yesterday. We ain't no long-term lot. Thing had already been sitting there for a couple of days." He held out his hand for the money.

Rhonda was so relieved to get a lead she almost handed over the twenty without asking anything further. Fortunately, better judgment prevailed. She brought the cash halfway toward Leonard's palm and then held back. "What tow yard did the grab-and-run?"

"Mooney's. They're over on Twelfth."

Rhonda handed over the cash before turning to call out to Alphabet.

"Why you so interested in a piece-of-crap Buick? What the owner do?" Leonard figured he had nothing to lose by probing to see if there was another cash angle to play.

"A Buick isn't a piece of crap," Alphabet said, as he walked up and Brindle filled him in. "I've been driving Buicks for twenty-five years."

Leonard gave a gap-toothed bray. "My point exactly. I figured this lady be more the Mercedes type."

"The Buick is business, not pleasure," Brindle said. "I want to search it, not drive it home. I told you, I'm high maintenance." Her tone was flirtatious.

Alphabet scowled. "Let's stop screwing around and go find the car." He turned Brindle away from Leonard with a hand on her forearm and led her away.

Brindle tugged her arm free. "What's the matter with you?"

Alphabet stumped over to their detective sedan and opened the doors. Once in the car, Brindle repeated her question.

"Why are you wasting time being friendly with an idiot like Leonard?" He spun out the name with a sneer.

Brindle slipped her shoes off and rubbed her feet. "Why, I do believe you're jealous," she said, oozing southern charm. "I was simply greasing the squeak." Living with Alphabet's gruff exterior was not always easy, but Brindle enjoyed working with him because he kept his hands to himself and wasn't constantly trying to get into her pants. However, the thought that he might have enough feelings for her to be jealous was not unwelcome.

"I'm not jealous." Alphabet's scowl deepened. "It just pisses me off when you do that simpering woman thing. You don't need to bat your eyelashes and act coy and sexy to do this job."

"Why does it bother you that I do?"

Alphabet pulled into traffic in the direction of Mooney's impound lot. "It bothers me because it isn't professional. You have the potential to be a good detective, but you'll never get there acting the way you do. The short skirts and cleavage are going to backfire on you down the line when you want to be taken seriously."

Brindle stretched her long legs out toward the floorboards. The action made her hemline rise up her thighs. Alphabet did not appear to notice.

"I think you're wrong," Brindle told her partner. "Every good detective develops techniques that suit their own personality. You run around in thrift store clothes like a Columbo stand-in and act like a bulldog with a bad flea itch. People tell you things to make you go away, or they let things slip because they don't see the brain underneath your impersonation of an unmade bed. Sex works for me. It's a tool. A little teasing, a flash of thigh or breast, the scent of musk, a smile, a wink, the unstated promise of thong panties and wild nights in the sack, and I can get a male suspect, a male witness, or a male supervisor eating out of my hand."

"What about the distaff side of those coins?"

"I can switch to the woman bonding thing, or the all-dykes-together approach, just like throwing a switch. The only one who seems to call me on it is Croaker."

Alphabet gave a short laugh. "Yeah, and she's your boss."

Brindle grimaced. "She's not been so bad lately. I think all that crap she went through last year has mellowed her."

"Maybe so," Alphabet agreed. "But we're talking about you. This sex-on-the-hoof strategy may work, but you end up with a reputation as a tramp."

Brindle turned on Alphabet in anger. "Is that what you think—that I'm a tramp? Let me give you a clue, buster. If any cop on this job or anybody I've ever dealt with as a detective tells you they've slept with me, they're lying. I'm not as intellectually smart as you or anybody else in the unit, but I am street smart and I have to use what gifts I have to keep up with the rest of you. If that gives you a problem, tough nookie."

"First of all, I don't think you're a tramp," Alphabet said by way of apology. "I've worked with you long enough to know better. And maybe you were right—maybe I *am* jealous. Don't ask me why, or what right I have to feel that way, because I haven't figured that out. But, more importantly, what makes you think you're not as smart as the rest of us?"

"I'm just a colored girl from the projects." Brindle's accent had downscaled and added a sarcastic tinge. "We's always bin told we's ain't as smart as other folks."

Alphabet negotiated a right turn onto Twelfth Street. The big Mooney's sign loomed a block away. "Yeah, and I'm just a dumb Jew boy tied to his mama's apron strings. You're so full of crap, you'd choke a toilet."

"Well, thanks for that comparison. I sure as hell don't feel sexy now."

Silence reined as Alphabet signaled and turned into Mooney's lot. He pulled to a stop in the parking lot, put on the hand brake, and snagged his jacket from the backseat. Brindle slipped her shoes back on and straightened her blouse.

"When we're done here," Alphabet finally said as they were getting out of the car, "can we go back to the part in our conversation about thong underwear?"

"Hell," Brindle said in a tone of truce. "I thought you were different."

"I am different," Alphabet told her. "But I'm still male."

Fred Mooney was more than happy to confirm that it was indeed April and Alex Waverly's Buick that had been impounded from the lot where Leonard worked. Beyond that, however, he did not want to cooperate with Alphabet. He wanted his money for the impound fees before he let Alphabet in the car—cop or no cop.

When Brindle stepped forward and intervened, Fred's attitude changed completely. Suddenly, cooperation and civic duty were the name of the game. Fred turned away to get his logbook and look up the car's location.

Brindle stuck her tongue out at Alphabet.

"Does that mean 'I told you so'?" Alphabet asked quietly.

"Shut up," Brindle said in the same tone, and immediately switched on her smile as Fred returned.

"It's in lot three," he told them. "Out the gate and to the left. I'll take you over there."

Lot three was hidden behind a high chain-link fence covered with green sheeting of the same type used on tennis courts. Inside the fence, cars were stacked three and four high along the back three rows. In front of the stacked rows, an ocean of individual cars were crammed together with no room to walk between them.

Brindle winked at Fred, and he jumped up onto a yellow Cat

forklift and began moving cars around till he had freed the long-sought-after white Buick Regal. Using the forklift to maneuver the vehicle, Fred set the car down near the lot's gated entrance.

Brindle bent over to verify the license plate number. Fred appeared very happy with this view.

"Bingo," Brindle said. "This is what we've been looking for. We're going to have to get police tow out here to impound it as evidence."

"That's not going to please your new boyfriend," Alphabet said, referring to the current lot owner.

Brindle gave a wave of thanks in the direction of the forklift. "Don't worry about old Fred. I've got his number. Remember, we all have our own style of getting things done. But it's still professional, not personal."

With Brindle leading the charge, arrangements were made for police tow to take custody of the vehicle and transfer it to the same official police garage where Waverly's detective sedan was impounded.

Using legal impound/inventory search procedures, Alphabet crawled through the white Buick looking for evidence.

"What are we actually hoping to find?" Brindle asked.

"Evidence."

"I know." Brindle feigned exasperation. "But what kind of evidence?"

"I don't know. It's kind of like looking for pornography," Alphabet replied.

"Pornography?"

"Yeah," Alphabet told her. "I don't know what it is, but I'll know it when I see it."

It was clear somebody had been through the interior of the car before Alphabet. The radio/cassette player was missing from the dash, and the glove box was open with its contents scattered across the front seat and floor mats.

Alphabet shuffled through the mess. Tossing aside an L.A. freeway map, he caught sight of the black backing of a Polaroid photo. He noticed two other Polaroids, and a crumpled-up handwritten note within reach. He picked the items up and turned them over.

33

THE THREE Polaroid photos from the seat of April Waverly's car lay spread out on the conference table in the Area captain's large office. They were slightly bent as if they were about to be used in a three-card monte shuffle. The difference was all of these cards were jokers. Smoothed out next to the photos was the note, along with another sheet of paper transcribing the Spanish of the note into English.

While everyone had been pursuing leads in the field, Hammersmith had made a command decision and moved the investigation base from the small upstairs homicide room to the Area captain's office downstairs. Normally, this would not have been an option, but the Area captain was on vacation and Hammersmith had a passkey.

The homicide room upstairs was really nothing more than a converted interrogation room, and nowhere near large enough to accommodate the entire coven of the unit's detectives. Under normal circumstances, it could be used by one or two detectives while the other unit members utilized their desk areas in the main squad room. But with the RHD detectives working from the unit's regular desks, there was no space for the full spread of an investigation.

With his usual lack of respect for command, Hammersmith had commandeered the vacationing captain's office. What the captain didn't know wouldn't hurt him. In many ways, Hammersmith was the reincarnation of Sergeant Bilko, only without the humor.

"That's our John Doe, right?" Alphabet pointed a finger at the terrified face in the Polaroid photos. While at the crime scene, Alphabet had taken a good look at the face of the body removed from the roof of UCLA's Bunch Hall.

"It certainly looks like him," Fey said. She produced another Polaroid, this one taken of the John Doe while at the coroner's office. She placed it down next to the other photos. Everyone gathered around to take a look.

The photos were gruesome. In the first, the head of the John Doe was pulled back by fingers locked in his hair. A stiletto knife was pricking his throat, blood trickling down.

In the second photo, the face of another figure leered at the camera as he placed the glowing end of a cigar against the John Doe's cheek. Smoke from the searing flesh had been captured like a special effect from a bad horror movie.

"Any ideas who that is?" Fey asked, pointing to the face of the torturer.

"Not at the moment," Alphabet said. "But that's Ochoa, the ATD bird." He pointed at the third photograph, which showed Ochoa shoving the barrel of a gun into the John Doe's mouth.

The detectives all nodded their heads or grunted in agreement.

The camera that had taken the photos was sophisticated enough to imprint the date and time on the photos, placing the scene a few days before Alex Waverly's demise.

The pace and pressure of the case should have been taking its toll on the detectives. However, after following Hammersmith's trail of bread crumbs to the captain's office, each appeared to be brimming with fresh clues, giving them renewed energy.

Knowing him better than anyone else, Rhonda had intuitively noticed Hammersmith was almost vibrating like a tuning fork. Rhonda raised her eyebrows, only to receive a slight, negative shake in return. Hammer was going to save his bombshell for the right moment. He had remained silent, letting Alphabet and Brindle show off the photographs, which linked Ochoa and the John Doe to each other and, through being found in April's car, to Waverly.

"What the hell does it all mean?" Rhonda asked. "Why were the photos in April's car? Does the note make it any clearer?"

"A little, but not much," Brindle said. She picked the note and the translation up from the table. "The note is handwritten in Spanish. Basically, it's a threat demanding that April kill Waverly immediately or her brother dies." Brindle set the note and the translation back down. "Why she would kill her husband to save her brother is still a big question, but I would assume the victim in the photos must be her brother, which would make her brother our John Doe." Brindle sorted the situation out verbally.

Monk coughed. "I came up with a name for our John Doe."

Fey lifted her head from examining the photos. She had not told anyone what Tucker had said about the identity of the Doe. She had even told Monk that she would take care of that aspect of the investigation—thinking she would get more information out of Tucker. That route had not proved profitable, but it seemed as if Monk and the others had come up with the information through their own initiative.

"The Doe's name is Ignacio Ramos, and he is April Waverly's brother," Monk said casually. "But you already knew that, didn't you?" he asked Fey without malice.

Fey ignored the slightly accusing eyes the other detectives focused on her.

"I had unreliable information that the Doe was April's brother, but I didn't have a name." She explained about Zelman Tucker's informant. "I wanted to confirm the source before we all went off half-cocked."

"Who do you think Tucker's source was?" Alphabet asked.

"My best guess would be Derek Keegan," Fey said. She told them about Keegan's drunken warning and mysterious disappearance. "I think he wanted out of whatever is going on, and he's run away because of the threats to his family. I think he used Tucker to get to me rather than run the risk of contacting me directly again."

"Why?" Alphabet asked.

"It's possible our phones are bugged," Fey said.

Alphabet's expression showed disbelief. "Are you talking both private and public?"

Fey nodded. "I know it sounds far-fetched, but I still want us to take precautions just in case." She circled a finger around the room. "You're the gimmick king," she said to Hammer. "Can you get this place swept, and checks done on our private and public phone lines?"

"I'll see to it," he told her.

"What about you?" Fey asked Monk. "How did you come up with the Doe's name and relationship to April?"

"Routine slog," he said, pulling out some papers from a file in front of him. "I ran into a blank trying to find further information on the carjacking ring Waverly smashed. I pulled reports from Records and Identification Division, but they didn't tell me much except that Waverly had been working a tip from a confidential informant, the four arrestees were all Hispanic, and the stolen cars were all assumed to have been smuggled into Mexico for distribution in Central America."

Monk shuffled the papers from his file and placed them on the table in front of him. "I let the carjacking go for a while and, on a hunch, decided to take a closer look at April. I figured if we could discover her motive for shooting Alex, it might lead us somewhere."

"Good thought," Fey said. "What did you find?"

Monk shrugged. "Another puzzle. All of the information I uncovered was bogus or unverifiable. The maiden name listed for April on the marriage license, her Social Security number from bank records, her date of birth from DMV—nothing jibed." Monk pulled a form out of his pile and held it up. "The one item I thought might be true was April's place of birth, listed as Mexico." He pointed to the information on the Waverly's marriage certificate.

"I figured I'd play a long shot by shipping her fingerprints off to Interpol. I asked them to contact the Federal Judiciary Police, the Federales, in Mexico City and request a priority run."

"I take it you had some luck?" Fey inquired.

Monk nodded. "Somebody must have owed somebody a favor, because a Captain Vera was on the phone to me within two hours. It seems that April and her brother, Ignacio Ramos, were the only survivors of a mob-style massacre that left their father, two older brothers, their mother, and three sisters splattered across the landscape.

All of this took place in Tecate, a small industrial town about thirty miles outside of Tijuana. Tecate is known for brewing a number of Mexican beers. It's also known as the stronghold of the Catalan cartel. April's father and brothers were Catalan enforcers."

"The worm turns," Fey said.

"Exactly," Monk agreed. "Apparently April's father, Jorge Ramos, and her brothers were heavily into bank robbery, protection, murder for hire—the usual fun, family activities. The Catalan cartel employed them on a freelance basis when their interests in the area needed strong-arm attention.

"The Catalan cartel is also politically oriented, and April's family did a lot of dirty work for the incumbent political party, the Partido Revolución Instrucional." Monk paused to check his notes.

"The conservative PRI has been in power in Mexico for decades. Several years ago, however, the rival Partido Acción Nacional conducted a vigorous election campaign for local control over the Mexican state of Baja California.

"Captain Vera told me the hot PAN candidate, Adrian Santiago, was a little too popular. The police theory is the corrupt incumbent government panicked, turned to the Catalan cartel for help, and arranged for Santiago to be gunned down at a political rally by four men—April's father and brothers."

"Democracy in action," Alphabet commented.

Monk pointed a gunlike finger at him in agreement and continued. "There were a lot of PRI sympathizers in the crowd and all four men escaped, although it quickly became common knowledge who they were."

"I take it the police didn't get to them fast enough," Fey said, asking for confirmation.

"Obviously not," Monk said. "Adrian Santiago's father, Don Diego Santiago, is not only a powerful landowner, he also runs the Oro de Dios cartel—the Catalan's top competitors. Before the police could get to Jorge Ramos and his sons, Diego Santiago sent his own enforcers to pay a visit. Somehow, April and Ignacio escaped the slaughter, and Mexican law enforcement has been looking for them ever since."

"Are there any charges pending against April?" Fey asked.

"No. Vera said they were looking for April only because they believed she could lead them to Ignacio. Vera sent me photos and prints on Ignacio. I ran them against our John Doe and—bingo."

"Did you get back to Vera?"

"Not yet. I wasn't sure we needed to be that cooperative at this point."

"Escaping didn't do Ignacio much good," Fey said, picking up the photos and looking closely at April's brother. She was remembering the battered body they discovered on the roof.

"He has a record in Mexico for bank robbery. Apart from his involvement in his family's activities, he was also suspected of being part of a lunatic fringe group pushing for revolution in Mexico."

"Domestic terrorism south-of-the-border style," Alphabet put in.

"What about the other guy in the photos?" Brindle asked.

"No idea yet," Monk said. "Captain Vera might be able to tell us."

"If we can identify him, it might go a long way to unraveling this quagmire," Fey said.

"Chances are he has some connection to the Santiago cartel," Monk said.

"Probably," Fey agreed. "But that still doesn't tell us what the connection to Waverly is, or what the hell they were all doing at UCLA. Let's run the photos by Art Melendrez and see if they ring any bells with him." She turned toward Alphabet and Brindle. "I take it there was nothing else in April's car?"

"Some loose change, a couple of maps, a gas receipt—typical car junk," Alphabet told her. "Nothing else that appeared connected."

Hammer picked up each of the photos and stared hard at them. "Could Waverly have been manipulating April's brother?" he ventured. "Maybe he was using his marriage to April to force Ignacio into something dangerous?" He fiddled with the bandage on his head.

"Interesting," Fey said. "If Waverly was manipulating Ignacio Ramos and the plan went wrong . . ."

Rhonda took the photos from Hammer and examined them herself. "There has to be a connection to the slaughter of April's family. It's the only thing that makes sense."

"Very probably," Monk agreed. "We're going to have to check further."

"There's also something else we have to check," Fey said, watching Rhonda place the photos back on the counter. "It seems Alex Waverly and Ochoa are not the only recent violent deaths at ATD. John Dancer took over the unit after a captain by the name of Ron Harper committed suicide."

There were several suicides a year involving department personnel, but it was never discussed—a taboo subject best ignored.

"Whoa," Alphabet said, "I remember hearing about it. The department downplayed it as usual, and there wasn't press coverage. Are you saying it wasn't suicide?"

"No, not yet," Fey told him. "But remember, Waverly wasn't actually killed by April. He was already dead. What I am saying is we need to find out more about Harper's death and see if there's anything there that doesn't feel right. Let's get copies of the autopsy and the death reports. I'm thinking there are too many deaths for all of them to be a coincidence, but let's not jump to conclusions just yet."

"I've got something also," Hammer said.

"So, give," Fey told him.

"I went down to ATD today and plowed through the files they dumped on us. I can tell you this—there is nothing in there even remotely connected to Mexico or even Central America. I'd be willing to bet that Waverly wasn't even assigned to half the stuff. It was a waste of time. A dead end."

"But you said you had something," Fey said.

"Patience, patience." Hammer took a yellow slip of paper from his back pocket and unfolded it. "When I went over the stuff we took from Waverly's desk again, I found this stuck inside a folder he was using for reimbursement receipts." He handed the paper to Fey.

Holding the slip at arm's length because she didn't have her glasses on, Fey read the name of the company who issued the receipt. "Computec?" She studied the paper for a few seconds. "This is a receipt for repairs?"

"Specifically," Hammer said, it's a receipt for replacing the hard drive on Waverly's laptop, and it's dated the day before he was killed."

"I'm not exactly computer literate," Fey said. Can you drag me through why this is important?"

Hammer sighed. "Waverly was a computer geek. He used his laptop regularly, and supposedly had a good system at home. If the hard drive in his laptop crashed, he would have wanted to get it replaced right away. Computec is known for doing rush repairs. When a hard drive crashes, most repair shops simply install a new one that can be reprogrammed from backup disks to restore data. It's cheaper to replace a hard drive than fix one, but it doesn't mean a hard drive can't be fixed, or that the data on it can't be recovered."

Fey sat up a little straighter in her chair. "Are you saying that Waverly's old hard drive might still be at this Computec place where we could recover it?"

Hammer nodded. "It's probably in a trash receptacle with a lot of other broken hard drives and other computer clutter. But if it hasn't been thrown away, I think we could maybe find it and recover its secrets."

"Then what the hell are we sitting here for?" Fey asked.

34

It was Hammersmith's clue, so Fey let him take the lead and run with it. She caught Rhonda's worried look, but Fey knew she couldn't stop him.

Monk agreed to continue to follow up on Waverly's connections to April's brother, and stay on the probe into Waverly's big carjacking arrest.

Brindle and Alphabet were hot to find the identity of the other Hispanic man in the photos recovered from April's car. Under normal conditions, they would have started with the files at Organized Crime and Intelligence Division, Detective Support Division's Gang Unit, ATD, or RHD. For obvious reasons, those resources were not available, so Fey brought everyone on board concerning her liaison with Ethan Kelso and Thistle One. With the option of going to a source outside the department, Brindle and Alphabet now had a back door entrance to start their search.

Hammer and Nails took Hammer's personal van to the Computec location, on Ventura Boulevard, close to Waverly's residence, with Fey following in her department car. Hammer had already checked the detectives' office and cars for bugs, as Fey had requested, with negative results. The trio, however, still watched for vehicles tagged to their tail.

The drive took twenty minutes, and Fey felt like praying the entire way. They needed a big break, and Waverly's computer files could be the catalyst.

Computec had a small storefront in a strip mall on the wrong side of the boulevard. Not that there was anything specifically wrong with the north side of Ventura Boulevard. The difference was strictly a Valleyism, a perceived preference for the south side of the boulevard because it was closer to the exclusive homes the boulevard separated from the riffraff of the Valley's north side.

The difference made as little sense as not buying a home in Beverly Hills because it was in the 90211 zip code as opposed to the 90210 zip code glorified in the Aaron Spelling teenage soap. Still, rents were higher on the south side of the boulevard, and some storekeepers were willing to pay them. The three rules of real estate in L.A. were the same as anywhere else—location, location, location.

"Can I help you?"

Fey didn't care for stereotypes, but the geek behind the counter appeared to revel in the nerd look. He was tall and lean, elbows jutting out to give him a birdlike appearance. Adhesive tape fastened the bridge of his heavy glasses together, a plastic pocket protector stored an assortment of pens, and a bow tie was secured at the neck of the unironed, short-sleeved white shirt. Letters on a name tag identified the wearer as Norman. There was a patch of beard under his nose that Norm had missed during his morning shave.

"You've got to be kidding, right?" Fey said. She couldn't help herself.

Norm smiled. "A little bit," he said, quickly catching on to Fey's cynicism. "But you'd be surprised how this getup inspires confidence in many customers." There was a certain conceit to the twinkle in his eye. "On my off hours, I run marathons and help coach my kid's high school track team. I wear contacts, comb my hair straight back, shave properly, and act as if I don't know cyber space from outer space. If I were a superhero, I'd be called the Chameleon."

Fey chuckled. "Don't go changing to try and please me," she said, half-singing. "We need you just the way you are."

"The propeller head, not the runner?"

"Right," Fey said. She took out her identification and introduced Hammersmith and Rhonda.

Hammer stepped forward and handed over the receipt recovered from Waverly's desk. "Any chance you remember this transaction?"

Norm took the yellow slip of paper and scrutinized it. "Sure," he said after a couple of seconds. "Alex was a good customer. He lived around the corner. I was shocked when I read in the papers about what happened to him."

"How about this specific transaction?"

"Of course," Norm said. "Alex came in and picked his computer up the day before he died. It was the last time I saw him."

"What was wrong with the computer?"

Norm waved the receipt. "It says right here we replaced the hard drive. Alex always backed up his hard drive on disks, so he probably only lost a day's work, but he was still pissed when the laptop crashed on him."

"Do you know what made the hard drive crash?"

"Who knows and who cares? Alex just wanted the laptop fixed. I did it for him overnight, simply stuck in a new hard drive. Thirty minutes' work, tops."

"Do you usually turn around repairs that quick?"

Norm shook his head. "No way. But I knew Alex was a cop and used the laptop in his work. Plus, he was a very good customer—he bought the laptop and his home system from me. The quick turnaround was a special service. He said he needed it in a hurry because he might have to leave the country."

Rhonda jumped on the statement "Did Alex tell you what he was working on or where he was going?"

"He never told me what he was working on," Norm said, shaking his head. "But I got the impression he was going to Mexico."

"Why?"

"I don't know," Norm said. "I guess because he was messing around talking to me in Spanish, and then we were comparing notes about fishing down there."

Rhonda and Hammer exchanged looks, and Hammer took over questioning again. "This hard drive you replaced," he said, "do you still have the old one around?"

Norm paused. The three detectives watched him as if he were a cartoon character whose brain machinations had been revealed by the illustrator—wheels turning.

"Can I see your identification again?" he asked, suddenly wary.

"Sure," Hammer said, taking out his ID card this time instead of just his badge.

Norm scrutinized it and handed it back.

"Why the reluctance?" Hammer asked.

Norm's skinny shoulders rose and fell. "No reluctance. I guess I just wanted to make sure I was dealing with the right people. I mean, I know Alex was some kind of spook, and I didn't want to end up helping the bad guys."

"I bet you're an *X-Files* fan," Hammer said.

"I also like Oliver Stone films."

"A real conspiracy freak?"

Norm pushed his glasses up on his nose and pushed back a lank lock of dark hair that had fallen forward. "Yeah. I guess so."

Hammer leaned his hips against the service counter. "Alex is dead. We're simply trying to get to the bottom of some facts that don't jibe."

Norm's features scrunched up in thought. "Alex coded all his files," he said. "Even if you recover his hard drive, you won't be able to get into the files without knowing the code."

Hammer reached out and gently took hold of one tip of Norm's shirt collar. He pulled it toward him until Norm's ear was close to Hammer's mouth. "I'll wager you know exactly what Waverly's codes were. I figure you and he were close enough that you helped him work them out."

Norm tried to pull away, but Hammer held on to him. "I really think you need to start helping *us* out a little."

"Don't you guys need a warrant or something?" Norm was not at all sure he liked how the situation was developing.

Hammer released his hold on Norm's collar, hoisted himself onto the countertop, and swiveled his legs over to Norm's side. Standing up, he put his arm around Norm.

There was a tinkle from the bell over the store's entrance door. A man with a computer component under his arm walked in and observed the scene with a startled expression on his face.

"Can we help you, sir?" Hammer asked.

The customer looked at Fey and Rhonda and then back to Hammer, who was still standing with his arm around Norm.

"My son is having a problem with his CPU," the customer said hesitantly. "I don't understand much about computers, but my kid is a whiz." He set the offending piece of equipment down on the counter in front of Hammer. "He's a good kid. I told him I'd bring it in and get it fixed."

"Maybe it needs a new framistan," Hammer said.

"A what?"

"A framistan. It's what drives the heliotrope."

"Heliotrope?"

"Yeah. I had one once, but the wheel fell off."

The customer stared at Hammer.

"Have you tried kicking it?" Hammer asked.

"Well, no, but—"

"Works wonders. A new framistan will cost you an arm and an ovary. Silly to spend that kind of moola when all it may need is a swift kick."

"I don't know . . ." the customer said dubiously.

Hammer gave Norm a squeeze. "I tell you what—you take this little baby home, hook it up, and boot it up with your old size elevens. I think you'll find it will work fine. If it doesn't, bring it back in, and me and Norm will strip it down and hack around with it." Hammer took the glasses from Norm's nose and slid them across his own face. He frowned and tried to look intellectual. "What do you say?"

The customer picked up his computer component without another word and fled the store.

"I could get to like working here," Hammer said.

Norm reached out and took his glasses back. "I guess you don't need a warrant," he said. "Why don't you come in the back with me and we'll see what we can find."

Hammer nodded at Fey and Rhonda. "Amazing how you can get cooperation when you need it."

Fey gave him an amused smile. "How long do you think this will take?"

Hammer shrugged. "No telling. First we have to find the right hard drive. Then it will have to be taken to a clean room, opened up, and diagnosed for what caused it to crash. After that it will have to be repaired, placed back in a computer, and old Norm and I will have to play cyber detectives to see what we can find."

"You feel up to covering it?" Fey asked.

Crossing his hands over his chest and rubbing his arms, Hammer waggled his head. "Sure. I'm doing okay for now. I'm only half dead. I've got a long way to go before I'm ready for the grave."

"You sure?"

"Yeah. What do you have in mind?"

Fey sighed. "Maybe a wild goose chase. Maybe a more direct line. I don't know yet, but I want to try something and I want to take Rhonda with me."

"Oh, sure. Abandon the wounded," Hammer said, placing the back of one hand to his forehead in a mock swoon.

"Sarah Bernhardt, eat your heart out," Rhonda said, critiquing Hammer's performance. "If he can make jokes," she said to Fey, "he's doing fine. Let's blow this pop stand and leave Geekville to the geeks."

"Beware of geeks bearing gifts," Hammer said to their departing backs. Didn't know I was a geek god, did you? It's all geek to me. Next, we'll hear from the geek chorus?"

"I think they let him out of the hospital a little too soon," Fey said. "His sense of humor is still warped."

35

PULLING INTO the small Ash House parking lot, Fey and Rhonda clambered out of the police vehicle. They had made two other stops since leaving Norm to Hammer's mercies at the Computec store. The first was a large chain drugstore, the second the jail ward located in County-USC Medical Center.

Ash House had begun life as a church. The two-story rectangular building had been the starting place for what eventually became the worldwide bilking ministry of Reverend Otis Shaker. Shaker had filled his church pews with fervent, blind-faith followers who were willing to throw money at him week after week, believing Shaker could lead them to salvation.

Fey had learned the story of Reverend Shaker shortly after she met Ash, the FBI agent who had become her lover. Ash had been born out of wedlock to a folksinger whom Shaker had impregnated. Knowing who his father was, but never having met him, Ash had chosen to be known only by the name his mother had bestowed on him.

Through time and events, Ash had eventually inherited the church and converted it into a private residence. When Ash himself passed away from the terminal disease that racked his last days, he had left the converted church residence to Fey.

Not knowing what to do with the building, as she couldn't face actually living in it herself, Fey had taken an idea to the board of the institute Ash had founded with money left to him by his disreputable father. The board had provided funding and guidance to convert the building into Ash House, a hospital and orphanage for crack babies, babies born with fetal alcohol syndrome, AIDS babies, and other infants who had no family to care for them.

When April Waverly had given birth and entered a dissociative state where she could not care for her newborn child, Fey's influence had caused the infant to be placed in protective custody at Ash House.

She had given no thought to her action at the time, beyond thinking it was a good idea. Now, however, Fey wondered if she had subconsciously foreseen some type of scenario where she would be able to use the infant's placement to her possible advantage. Experience often dictated actions that could mean the difference in the type of desperate gamble that Fey had in mind.

At the jail ward of County-USC Medical Center, Fey and Rhonda had been forced to wait forty minutes before the doctor caring for April Waverly was free to see them.

"Physically, she's in no apparent danger," Dr. Wagner had told Fey in response to her queries regarding his patient. "Her mental health, however, is another story."

"What exactly is her mental health condition?" Fey asked.

Wagner shrugged. "Technically, she's in a dissociative state. In layman's terms, this type of condition is brought on when the mind goes into overload—when a shock, or a series of events, is of such great mental impact the brain shuts itself down to avoid completely shorting out. There is no way to tell when, or if, she will come out of it."

"So, she is mentally nonfunctioning?"

"Completely."

"She can't, or won't, respond to questions?"

"I would say *can't* is the correct operative word."

"Is she faking?" Fey asked.

"Definitely not. It is practically impossible to fabricate a dissociative state for a long period of time. She has not responded to any stimuli, and we are having to tube feed her and catheterize her."

"She just lies there?"

Wagner nodded. "Staring into space."

"What if I need to transport her somewhere?"

Wagner appeared to give the question some thought. "Well," he said eventually, "there are no physical complications, but I still have to consider that the patient has only recently given birth. What exactly do you have in mind?"

Fey's explanation led to a scowl, but the doctor could find no reason to deny the request. What Fey was suggesting couldn't hurt his patient, and it might help.

It was with only a small pang of guilt that Fey hid the fact that she hadn't told the doctor everything she planned. Not even Rhonda knew the reason for Fey's side trip to the drugstore, as she waited outside in the car at Fey's request. Fey wanted to try things the simple way, but if that didn't work, she needed another card up her sleeve.

In the Ash House parking lot, an ambulance pulled into the spot next to Fey's vehicle. An attendant and a sheriff's deputy emerged. Together they opened the rear doors of the ambulance to reveal another deputy and Dr. Wagner sitting on a low bench next to a stretcher bearing April Waverly.

April's eyes were open, but she appeared completely oblivious to the scene around her. The attendant lifted a wheelchair out of the ambulance and spread its seat open. The deputies struggled awkwardly with April's unresisting form, but were eventually able to lift her into the waiting conveyance.

Wagner watched as April was strapped into the wheelchair. She offered no resistance. She was not limp, not rigid, not cognizant, not anything. It was as if the lights were still on in a house, but the residents had all gone on a long vacation.

Dr. Wagner and the attendant propelling the wheelchair followed Fey and Rhonda. The two sheriff's deputies traipsed along at the rear of the party.

Fey pulled open the large, carved oak entrance doors and entered what had once been the church nave. In her left hand, she carried a plastic bag in which her drugstore purchase formed an odd bulk.

The builders involved in the conversion process had taken care to preserve as much of the original church character as possible.

Stained glass filtered and colored the light streaming through the high, vaulted windows above the main floor, of the old chapel. The scenes depicted in the windows were of innocuous landscapes, clouds and sun rays, doves with olive branches, and Celtic designs.

One window, however, dominated all the others from its position behind where the altar once stood. It was the window Ash had designed himself when he took residence. The colored glass patterns displayed a brutal scene of a winged, sword-wielding St. Michael—the patron saint of police officers—dressed in white, togalike robes. Sun rays parted the heavens to all like beacons from the Almighty across the saint's muscular shoulders. One of St. Michael's sandal-shod feet pinned a red-winged, horned-and-tailed Satan firmly to the ground. The adversary's arms were raised in false supplication. The sword in St. Michael's hand was pressed to the throat of his foe—pausing before the final thrust.

The window was as impressive as it was inspiring, and from below its grandeur a matronly woman came forward to greet Fey. She wore a severe, black business suit with a white blouse and a single string of pearls. A small coronet was pinned to the bun of hair piled on top of her head, and she walked with a slight limp.

"Hello, Sister Ruth," Fey said with real affection. "How are you?"

"Fine, my dear. Busy as always, but fine." She hugged both Fey and Rhonda.

Fey had lured Sister Ruth, who was a doctor in a nursing order, to Ash House from another infant hospital/orphanage in San Diego where the two had first met. While Sister Ruth still maintained contact with her past home, she now devoted the great majority of her energy to Ash House. Under her tutelage other nuns from the Sacred Heart nursing order had come to work at Ash House, their devotion leading to its success.

"Who do we have here?" Sister Ruth asked, turning to April.

"This is April Waverly," Fey explained. "I arranged for her baby to be sent here a couple of days ago."

"Oh, yes," Sister Ruth said, clapping her hands together as if preparing for prayer. "And what a delight she is. A lovely baby."

Fey introduced Dr. Wagner. Wagner made several apparently sincere noises about having heard of Sister Ruth and being impressed by her work. It was a nice gesture, and one the elderly nun accepted graciously.

"April is in a dissociative state," Fey explained, although Sister Ruth could clearly see April's condition for herself.

"And you're hoping that seeing her child, or having the child placed in her lap, will perhaps bring her back to us?"

"Yes," Fey confirmed.

"What do you think?" Sister Ruth directed her question to Dr. Wagner.

Wagner tugged at the lapel of his tweed jacket. "I've known this type of thing to happen on rare occasions in other situations, but usually the patient either comes out of the dissociative state on their own, or a much larger shock to the system is needed."

"I agree," said Sister Ruth, "but I don't see any harm in trying."

"Neither do I," Wagner said. "That's why I agreed to bring April here."

Fey was getting impatient. "I don't mean to break up this medical convention, but before you present each other with plaques and flowers, can we bring out the baby?"

Sister Ruth adjusted her round-rimmed glasses and gave Fey a stare full of rulers whacking knuckles. "One of these days, young lady, you'll discover a vein of patience and manners."

Rhonda giggled and received a hard look of her own.

"As for you," Sister Ruth said to Rhonda, "don't make out you're not as bad as your boss. I've heard all the stories."

"Yes, ma'am," Rhonda said, chastised. "Sorry."

Sister Ruth escorted the entourage farther into the open space at the center of Ash House, and into a small reception area defined by a couch and two armchairs set atop a large rug on the polished hardwood floor. Between the armchairs was a round rosewood end table with a spray of flowers in a vase.

"Would you like to come with me, Dr. Wagner?" Sister Ruth asked.

Wagner glanced at April and then at Fey, as if wondering if it was safe to leave his patient in Fey's care.

"Don't look at me in that tone of voice," Fey said. "I'm trying to

help the woman, not hurt her. I'm the one who stopped a couple of
dozen cops from shooting her. Remember?"

Wagner nodded his acquiescence and scurried off with Sister
Ruth.

Around the reception area, several rooms on the first floor had
been turned into miniature hospital wards filled with incubators,
cribs, and enough high-tech medical equipment to build a rocket
ship from the parts. Other nuns in nursing whites bustled about,
busy with their duties. Fey caught a faint whiff of medicines and dis-
infectants that was particular to this incarnation of the building.

On the rug in the reception area, Fey set her drugstore purchase
on one of the reception area armchairs. Standing up, she caught
Rhonda watching her. Fey smiled slightly, but did not comment on
the unasked question. The two deputies and the ambulance attendant stared at their feet. April stared at nothing.

Within a few minutes, Sister Ruth returned with Dr. Wagner. In
her arms, swathed in a pink blanket, Sister Ruth held Baby Waverly.

The baby gurgled happily as Fey and Rhonda gathered around
for a peek. The tiny bundle had a full head of black hair and huge,
round brown eyes that possessed the glint of intelligence.

"She's beautiful," Rhonda said, reaching to take the baby from
Sister Ruth's arms.

Fey swallowed hard. This was going to be difficult for her. The
sexual abuse and physical beatings of her father had left Fey incapable of bearing children. It was a loss, she told herself repeatedly,
that didn't matter. Being confronted by the miracle of a newborn
infant, however, always stuck a knife into Fey's psyche, creating a
devastating lust for what might have been.

The infants that were the usual residents of Ash house did not
affect Fey in the same way because they were not perfect miracles of
birth. They were usually caught in a maelstrom of drug and alcohol
addiction. In their own way, they were as ravaged by life as Fey had
been.

The sight of Baby Waverly, cooing away happily in Rhonda's
arms, was a completely different situation. Fey would have died to
have carried such a baby in her womb, to have given birth to such

blessed perfection. Fey both hated and craved Baby Waverly at the same time.

Gritting her teeth, Fey knew she had to focus on the job. Taking the baby from Rhonda, she turned to where April Waverly sat, spaced out and unaware, in her wheelchair.

When the attendant had secured April in the wheelchair, he had done so by the use of a seat belt at waist level, and another higher strap that ran across April's chest and under her arms. April's hands had been placed in her lap, where they were curled in lifeless repose.

Fey felt the warmth of Baby Waverly wiggling happily against her breasts. She had always hated that feeling, and made a habit of never holding the babies of friends because of it. Moving quickly toward April, as if trying to get rid of a hot potato, Fey bent forward and placed the baby in April's lap.

The blanket fell open, partially uncovering Baby Waverly's kicking and gurgling form.

She's perfect, Fey thought with despair. Every maternal instinct she'd spent years fighting to suppress rose up inside her with a devastation that carried a physical kick.

Fey knelt down to make sure the infant would not slip from its perch. She looked up into April's face. Nothing had changed.

Fey moved April's right hand so that it cupped the baby's head. She then moved April's left hand to the baby's stomach. The actions had no effect.

"What's the matter with you?" Fey hissed through clenched teeth. "She's your baby," she said. "She's perfect." The last sentence was delivered with jealous venom.

"Fey—" Rhonda started.

Fey jerked her head around. "What?" She saw the others grouped around her, staring. She had planned on starting a scene, but this was not the path she had anticipated taking.

"What are you all staring at?" Even Fey herself was startled by the depth of rancor in her voice. "She's the child's mother, for hell's sake, and she doesn't give a damn."

"Detective Croaker, you're out of line," Dr. Wagner said. "She's not capable of giving a damn."

Fey stood up. Her abrupt movement scared the baby, changing her happy cooing to a cry of fear.

"Somebody needs to give a damn about this baby," Fey said. "But all anybody seems to be worrying about is the mother's fragile feelings. Give me a break."

Fey turned back to April. "You don't deserve this child," she yelled, on the verge of screaming—her own, true emotions driving her on. She bent forward and grabbed April's shoulders, shaking them. "This is your baby! And you don't care!"

Dr. Wagner put his hand on Fey's shoulder. She whirled around to face him. "Get your hands off me!"

"I insist you stop immediately. This woman is my patient."

"She may be your patient, but she's my murder suspect!"

"Where is your compassion?"

"Where was hers when she was pumping bullets into the back of her husband's head?"

Wagner spluttered in confusion and anger, "You can't treat people like this—I'll report you."

Fey's face had turned a blazing red, capillaries filling with the hot flush of blood. "You can do what you damn well please, but I'll tell you something—this woman doesn't deserve this baby. She doesn't care whether this baby lives or dies." Fey turned back toward April and bent down to grab the woman by the arms. "You don't care, do you?" she screamed into April's face. "You don't deserve this baby, and I'm going to make sure you never see her again."

Fey grabbed the bay from April's lap, pulling the now screaming child to her chest. She turned away and took several steps to one of the reception area armchairs. With her back turned to the group she bent over as if in pain, a loud sob breaking from her throat.

Rhonda, Dr. Wagner, and Sister Ruth watched in horror as Fey straightened up and turned back to face them with the baby in her arms.

Fey's rage appeared to grow. "You don't deserve this miracle," she screamed at April. "Don't you know that there are people who can't have babies?" She looked down at the baby in her arms, loathing seeming to cross her face. She let out a scream of distaste and suddenly threw the baby the short distance separating her from April.

Rhonda and Sister Ruth gasped in shock.

The baby hit April in the chest with a sickening thud and dropped into April's lap.

The force of the blow knocked the head off the cheap, drugstore baby doll Fey had substituted for the real thing before throwing it. The head of the doll rolled away from the plastic body in April's lap and dropped to the floor. It bounced once in the dead silence, and turned over before coming to a stop with one eye open and the other closed.

As everyone stood in a frozen tableau, the headless torso remaining in April's lap gave voice to the mechanical word "Mama" in a high, squeaky tone.

April's head creaked down, as if on a hinge, and she actually looked at the broken toy in her lap. A tear formed in her left eye and trickled down her cheek. Her hands twitched. Another tear followed the first.

Suddenly, the damn burst, and a plaintive wail of emotional pain erupted from April's mouth with soul-shattering force.

36

D<small>R</small>. W<small>AGNER</small> had been furious with Fey, and he wasn't the only one. Sister Ruth was flustered with agitation, and even Rhonda was upset with Fey for not preparing her for the shock.

Fey accepted the verbal abuse from Wagner. She had done what she believed necessary to get a reaction out of April Waverly. She did not believe an end always justified the means, but in this case she felt vindicated. She had not done anything illegal or immoral. Unethical, maybe, but that didn't count.

April's wailing had continued rising to a hysterical pitch. She had hugged the broken doll to her chest and would not release her hold until Sister Ruth offered her the real Baby Waverly in exchange. April cradled her baby gently, but her own tears continued to the point where she could not catch her breath.

Wagner, stating that April couldn't take any more, gave her a sedative. Fey did not object. She had pushed things as far, if not further, than she dared. April was still strapped into the wheelchair, and the sedative took effect quickly. As she slipped into sleep, Sister Ruth retrieved Baby Waverly and strode away without another word to Fey.

Wagner, however, was not without voice. Fey let him blather on until she became weary of the tirade, and then held up a hand to stop him.

"You can do what you like, but your patient is still under arrest," Fey told him. "I suggest you get her back to the jail ward, and I expect you to notify me when she comes around enough to be interrogated."

Wagner's face purpled. "How dare—!"

Fey cut him off. "Spare me this high-horse nonsense. I did my job, which is more than I can say for you. If it wasn't for me, she'd still be a vegetable. Now she has a chance, and so does her baby."

"What kind of chance will either have if the mother is convicted of murder?"

"Have faith, Doc," Fey told him. "Life is full of odd twists." Twitching her head at Rhonda, she turned to leave the home. "I'll be back," she said to Wagner, in her best Terminator impression.

Outside in the car, Rhonda finally gave her opinion. "You're hell on wheels, aren't you?"

"Helen Wheels, that's me, all right. I spin 'em here, I spin 'em there, I spin those damn wheels everywhere."

Rhonda sighed, releasing tension. "Okay, but how about letting me in on the plan next time?"

"What's the matter? You don't like surprises?"

"No."

"I bet you even peek at the last page of a mystery novel."

"I confess," Rhonda said. She held up her hands like a fugitive at gunpoint. "I get about halfway through a book, and I can't take the tension any longer."

Fey chuckled. "Are you serious? I was just trying to be funny. Do you still read the rest of the book once you know the end?"

"Of course. Once I know the end, I can enjoy the ride."

Fey drove away from Ash House and regained the freeway.

"Well, I don't know how any of this is going to come out, but I think the next page of this investigation is interviewing Ron Harper's widow."

"I'll see if I can live with the anticipation," Rhonda said. "Do you have an address?"

Fey nodded as she changed lanes. "I called personnel earlier. Harper's wife is named Linda. Personnel shows her living out in Agoura."

Rhonda sighed again. "Why do you think that if we looked up

the word *fun* in the dictionary, this interview would not be listed as a definition?"

Forty-five minutes later, Fey pulled into the driveway of a pristine ranch-style house with a view of the rolling Agoura hills—an oasis of country life just outside the city limits.

Fey's instinct told her there was someone watching, but she could find no evidence of a tail, nor did there seem to be any other reason for the precognition.

Linda Harper answered the door to Fey's knock with a bright smile that faded when Fey showed her identification.

"Not Peter." she said. "Please, not Peter." Linda Harper put her hand up to her mouth, her eyes filling with tears.

Fey was confused. "I'm sorry," she said. "I don't understand. Who's Peter?"

Linda Harper took one step back from the verge of cracking. "Peter is my son." Her voice still held the jagged edge of hysteria. "He's an L.A. sheriff's deputy. He works out of the Lennox Station."

Fey was still confused. She frowned. "We're not here about Peter." At least she didn't think they were.

Linda Harper's chest heaved as she took in a lung-filling gulp of air. "I'm sorry—it's just . . ."

The penny dropped for Rhonda. She reached out and took Linda Harper's hand. "You thought we were here to tell you something had happened to Peter."

Linda Harper shook her head and started to cry. Rhonda put her arms around the woman.

"The last—" Linda Harper hesitated, still in Rhonda's embrace, and then started again. "The last time two detectives came to my door, it was to tell me my husband had died." She took another deep breath. "Ever since then, I've had nightmares—horrible dreams about detectives coming to tell me Peter is dead." She sniffed and took out a tissue to dab at her eyes. "I'm sorry. I feel so foolish. It's been over a year since Ron died. Everybody tells me I should be getting over it, but I can't. It's not that easy."

"I know," Fey said. Those two words were generally used as a placebo—an insincerity offered as a bridge to move on to other issues. There was something in the quality of Fey's voice, however, which made immediate emotional contact with Linda Harper. She reached out her hand and drew Fey into the embrace with Rhonda.

It was a strange experience for Fey. She had never been able to bond well with other women, but here she was, experiencing an emotional catharsis, sharing a group hug with a potential witness in an ongoing murder investigation.

Linda Harper eventually pulled herself together. "I'm being rude," she said. "Please come in." Standing aside, she ushered Fey and Rhonda into a home that appeared to be well cared for, but comfortably lived in. The floors displayed woven Indian rugs over large Spanish tiles. The formal living room, where Linda Harper escorted her guests, had white couches unspoiled by use.

Fey could see through to a family room, where the furniture appeared to be far more comfortable and, possibly, handmade. Making a conscious decision to put Linda Harper on more vulnerable ground, Fey did not stop in the living room. Instead, she kept walking to the family room and took a seat in a cozy armchair that matched the couch.

"These are beautiful," Fey said, referring to the chair and couch.

"Thank you," Linda said with obvious pride. "Ron made them."

Her statement confirmed Fey's suspicions. "The coffee table also?"

"Everything you see in here," Linda said with a sweep of her hand, which indicated end tables, a bar, and shelf units.

"I'm impressed."

Linda sat down on the edge of the couch near Fey. Rhonda moved to look out the windows into the backyard with its view of the local hills. Her choice was to become as invisible as possible and let Fey handle the interview.

"Did you know my husband?" Linda Harper asked. "Or is this something to do with pensions and benefits?" She was polite, but there was apprehension in her voice.

Fey reached out and put a hand on Linda's arm. "I didn't know your husband, Linda, and we're not here to give you any kind of bureaucratic hassle. I'm investigating the murder of Alex Waverly. He worked with your husband at ATD."

"I knew Alex," Linda said. "I couldn't believe it when I heard on the television about what happened to him."

"How well did you know him?"

Linda shrugged and sat further back in her chair. She seemed to become more relaxed. "I met him once at a Christmas party. It was after Ron had died, but I had been invited because there was going to be a posthumous presentation. I went with my son. I also met Waverly's wife while I was there. To be truthful, she didn't seem the type to do anything violent. She was a mouse who barely said a word the entire evening."

Fey hesitated for a second, struggling to decide on the correct approach. Linda sensed the hesitation and picked up on it immediately.

"What is this about? What do you want from me?"

"I'm not exactly sure," Fey told her honestly. "There is more to this investigation than is apparent—"

Linda nodded her head. "I was a cop's wife for thirty years. I understand the complications—especially in the kind of work Ron ended up doing for ATD." She placed her hands on her knees and spread her fingers. "Despite my earlier show of emotion, I'm tougher than I appear. Ask me what you want, and I'll do my best to answer your questions."

"Okay," Fey said. "I need to know about the circumstances surrounding your husband's death."

Linda turned her head to look at Rhonda. "Come and sit down," she said. "Ron told me a long time ago how interrogations work. You don't have to follow procedures with me. I've been waiting since Ron died for someone to ask me questions."

Fey leaned forward in her chair as Rhonda took a seat next to Linda on the couch.

"You've been waiting to be asked questions?" Fey said. "Why?"

"Obviously, you don't work with ATD, or you would know how Ron died," Linda said. "That means you must be investigating that bastard Vaughn Harrison, and I'll do anything to help you get him." Linda paused to steady herself again. "You see, Vaughn Harrison killed my husband, along with that little slut of his, Mary DeFalco."

37

THE SHOCK of Linda Harper's statement demanded a detailed explanation and an infusion of caffeine. Linda led Fey and Rhonda into the kitchen.

"I was married to my husband for over thirty years. I was with him through the police academy, through his rookie year, through assignments in narcotics, vice, and child abuse. I was with him as he climbed the ladder from policeman to captain. And none of it changed him. He was a hardworking, by-the-book cop. He was a good father and husband. His therapy was working with his hands. There wasn't anything he couldn't fix or build. We were growing old together, putting on weight together, but we still made love and giggled like we were kids."

"I take it something happened to change all this bliss?" Fey said. She took a sip of coffee and placed the mug back on the handmade kitchen table.

Linda nodded. "He took the job as commanding officer of ATD."

"What happened exactly?"

From a tiled counter, Linda picked up a framed portrait of a young man in a police uniform. It was the type of shot taken during graduation ceremonies at the police academy. Linda hugged the photo to her chest.

"Everything changed when Ron went to ATD. Suddenly, he stopped talking about his work. I understood that to a certain extent. What he was doing was considered top secret, and Ron wasn't somebody to take a classification such as that lightly. If something were secret, then you didn't speak about it to anyone else."

"Understandable," Fey said.

"Sure, but that was the least of it," Linda said. "Ron hadn't been there long when he began to complain vehemently about the changes the department was going through." She ducked her head toward both Ronda and Fey. "You've both lived through it. The past couple of years have been tough on all cops. Since the riots, the department has been a whipping boy for every liberal with an ax to grind."

Fey smiled. "Now you sound more like a cop than a cop's wife."

Linda smiled. "I know, but complaining about such things wasn't Ron's way. He simply got on with doing his job without letting outside influences affect him. But now it was as if he were trying to convince himself that things were getting out of hand—as if he were trying to justify something."

"And what do you think it was?"

"I think Ron stepped into more than he could handle at ATD. I think things were being played fast and loose. I told you Ron was a by-the-book cop. I asked him about it once, and he would only say that things were difficult for him because he played by the rules, but apparently there were no rules when playing against terrorists."

"Tequila rules," Fey mumbled.

Rhonda nodded her head in agreement, remembering Fey's adage that when you drink tequila, there are no rules.

"What?" Linda asked.

"Nothing," Fey told her. "Just an old saying. What did Vaughn Harrison have to do with all this?"

Linda Harper poured more coffee. "He came to see me once. Said he was worried about Ron, but that was pure crap—that man has never been worried about anyone other than himself. I think he came to see if Ron were talking to me about what was going on at ATD. When I told Ron about Vaughn Harrison's visit, he was livid.

He tore out of here like someone had set his pants on fire. He was gone all night. I was terrified, especially when I received a call from Peter."

"Your son?"

"Yes. I told you, he's a sheriff's deputy working patrol in Lennox. Apparently, he and his partner had been responding to an unknown trouble call that night when they were ambushed, supposedly by gang members. Their car was shot up, but both Peter and his partner were uninjured. None of the shooters were caught, and no leads were ever uncovered as to which gang it might have been."

"Obviously, Ron came home at some point," Fey said, prompting Linda.

"Yes. He came home late the next morning. He was pale and shaken. I asked him what had happened—where he'd been—but he wouldn't talk about it. I told him what had happened to Peter, but it was as if he already knew. When Peter came over later that day, Ron just hugged him and started to cry. It was the first time since Peter was born that I had ever seen that occur."

"Why were you suspicious of Vaughn Harrison?" Fey asked.

"Will you agree with me that you don't spend thirty years as a cop and not develop a sixth sense when something isn't right?"

Fey and Rhonda nodded.

"Well, you don't spend thirty years as a cop's wife and not know which way the wind is blowing—and this wind was blowing in straight out of the sewer. Harrison's conversation with me, Ron's overnight disappearance, the ambush of Peter by some unknown gang members on the same night—you can't take things like that into a court of law, but you can still add them up for yourself." Linda's tone was defiant. Her voice had raised in pitch with her emotional intensity.

"You're preaching to the choir," Fey told her soothingly. "I don't know how it all connects yet, but I'm sure it does. What about Mary DeFalco?"

Linda suddenly seemed to deflate. "I love my husband. He never strayed from home. He wasn't a tomcat like so many other cops we knew, but that witch of a vixen has something that men—not even good men like my Ron—seem able to resist."

Fey thought about Waverly's funeral, of Mary DeFalco hanging on John Dancer's arm, not for support, but to claim possession. She dredged up another memory of Mary DeFalco in John Dancer's ATD office with the scent of sex hanging heavy in the air.

"Are you saying your husband had an affair with Mary DeFalco?"

Linda Harper toyed with her coffee cup, scratching the handle with a long fingernail. "No woman likes to admit to her husband having an affair. Ron and I had become the best of friends during thirty years of marriage. We still made love, but it wasn't the passionate, hanging-from-the-chandeliers type of lovemaking that men of a certain age seem to lust for. That bitch threw it out there like it was bait on a hook, and she caught my Ron." Her voice changed to an all-girls-together conspiratorial tone, and she tried to make light of the situation. "My mother once told me God gave men both a brain and a penis, but he only gave them enough blood to work one at a time."

Both Fey and Rhonda snickered, but there was pathos behind the laughter. There was too much truth in the statement.

Fey felt as if she could read Rhonda's mind. "I know what you're thinking," she said. "You're thinking, not Hammer, but you're wrong. He may be strong enough not to stray from you, but he will be tested over and over again. He'll look, and he'll wonder, and there's not a damn thing you can do about it."

"Not Hammer," Ronda said.

Fey shrugged. "Suit yourself. But don't ever come to me and say you weren't warned." She brought her attention back to Linda Harper. "How did you find out about the affair?"

"You must be joking," Linda said, raising her eyes sharply to meet Fey's. "A wife knows. I didn't want to admit it, but I knew. There were a hundred things, starting with attitude, moving through weight loss, new clothes, and more attention to personal hygiene. I'm not stupid. And then there was the divisional Christmas party—the same one where I met Alex and his wife. Mary DeFalco was there, and I saw her make eye contact with Ron. She thought she was being cute, but I saw Ron squirm. I knew then without a doubt. Ron wasn't a good liar. He'd played by the rules for too long. There was nothing I could do. Nothing I could say. I had to live with it. It tore me up inside, but I knew it would end at some point."

"Why?"

Linda set her coffee mug down and pushed her fingers through her hair. "Mary DeFalco was not the type of woman to stay with a man like Ron for long. He wouldn't be exciting enough for her, he wasn't powerful enough for her. There was nothing he could give her." She paused, a sad smile sliding across her face. "There was also something else. Mary DeFalco was a tramp. Ron may have been cheating on me, but she was also cheating on him."

"What do you mean?" Fey asked.

"You know what cop Christmas parties are like?"

"I've been to enough of them," Fey said. "They're usually pretty staid affairs. Everyone is on their best behavior because they're with their spouse and it's Christmas. Nobody actually lets their hair down."

"That's right," Linda agreed. "The drunken, act like a child, throw up, do stupid things on a dare, grope anything in sight parties are reserved for cops only—no outsiders allowed."

Fey knew exactly what Linda was talking about. Cops believe they are the only ones who get it. Spouses don't get it. Noncop friends don't get it. Even prosecutors from the district attorney's or city attorney's office are not considered to get it the same way cops do. Unless you are out on the street making arrests, putting your damn life on the line day in and day out, you just don't get it. The big It. What every cop talks about to other cops. What every cop feels inside. The one thing that can't ever be shared with anyone but another cop.

The drunken, act like a child, throw up, do stupid things on a dare, grope anything in sight parties were only for those who got it. It was a bullcrap excuse at best for bad behavior, but that made it no less valid.

"At the Christmas party the year before Ron died—the staid, be-on-your-best behavior Christmas party—I saw Mary DeFalco sitting alone at a table with Vaughn Harrison. The party was almost over. Ron and I were getting ready to leave. I had gone to use the bathroom, but as I was coming out I saw Mary slip under the table. They thought nobody was looking—thought she would be hidden by the long tablecloth. I almost couldn't believe what I was seeing when she unzipped Harrison's pants, took his penis out, and started to suck him."

Fey and Rhonda would have laughed if Linda Harper hadn't been so damned serious.

"What did you do?"

Linda waved her hands around. "I was rooted to the spot. I watched her working on him, and then it was as if Harrison knew somebody was watching him. He turned toward me, and when he saw me he laughed."

"Damn," Fey said.

"You think Vaughn Harrison was threatening your husband? You believe he was behind the attack on your son?" Rhonda asked.

Linda Harper nodded her head. "I think Ron was against what was happening in the division—I think he found out more than Harrison wanted—and then Harrison set up the attack on Peter as a warning to Ron. I also believe Mary DeFalco bewitched Ron to be sure he was towing the line. I think she was screwing him to find out if he was being true to Harrison."

"That's a mighty big leap of faith," Fey said.

"Perhaps," Linda said, "but I don't think so. You didn't live with the man for thirty years. You weren't there the night Peter was attacked. You didn't see Mary DeFalco looking at your husband. And you didn't see that bitch sucking off the man who was driving your husband into the ground by making him go against every principle he had ever believed in."

Linda started to cry, trying to talk through the sniffles. "When we got home from the Christmas party that night, I took Ron into the bedroom and made love to him as if we were twenty instead of fifty. His fling with Mary DeFalco was so damn pathetic, I actually felt sorry for him. I knew guilt would be eating him up, but I never knew how much."

"What happened next?" Fey asked.

"Next?" Linda almost screamed. "He went to work the following day and blew his brains out in the bathroom."

38

"ANY IMMEDIATE thoughts?" Fey asked Rhonda as they walked away from Linda Harper's residence.

"Are you asking me if I think the suicide was legitimate?"

"That would appear to be the sixty-four-thousand-dollar question."

Rhonda walked to the passenger side of the detective sedan and talked to Fey across the roof. "On the surface it sounds legitimate. A man in Ron Harper's state of mind could be pressured to the point that he thought suicide was the only way out."

"I agree," Fey said. "But the question remains—did he jump or was he pushed?"

Rhonda nodded. "Or, in this case—did he pull the trigger or was he shot?"

Fey shrugged as she unlocked the car and slid in.

"I have this feeling we're not getting anywhere," Rhonda said. "I feel like a dog chasing my own tail. Every time we turn around, the answers to this case seem to be further and further away."

"Patience," Fey counseled. "I know that word is foreign to your vocabulary, but it's one you need to come to grips with. A case is like a Rubik's Cube—you have to keep twisting everything this way and that until, when you least expect it, it all clicks into place." She pulled the car out of the driveway and drove sedately away. Almost immediately, she sensed something. She checked the rearview mirror, but there was nothing out of the ordinary.

Rhonda shifted in her seat and adjusted her seat belt. "I never was very good with that stupid toy. It raised my frustration level to the point where all I wanted to do was smash the damn thing. I'm beginning to feel the same way about this case."

Fey laughed. "Remind me never to frustrate you."

Rhonda raised her eyebrows. "Yeah? Well, you're not exactly known as the patience poster child."

"I'm old. I'm entitled."

"Get off it, Fey. You've always got it together. You've got so much confidence, it makes me want to spit." The tone of the sentiment made it a compliment, not a condemnation.

"What?" Fey's reaction was so violent she almost turned the car into the oncoming lanes. "I'm about the least together person I know! You're the one who has it together." Fey waved one hand around in exasperation. "I mean, you and Hammer are the perfect duo. Everybody walks in fear of the pair of you."

Rhonda blew air through her lips and then said, "There are days when it's damn hard work trying to live up to the Hammer and Nails image. Sometimes, I wish I could allow myself the pleasure of screwing up. It's like women who try to turn themselves into Martha Stewart—there's this unobtainable image they are trying to emulate, and nothing they do is ever enough to get them there. Even Martha Stewart isn't Martha Stewart."

"Now, there's somebody who's probably set the women's movement back several centuries," Fey said. "That woman should be drawn and quartered, and put out of everyone else's misery." Fey added a falsetto to her voice. "Stop me before I hostess again!"

"I don't know," Rhonda said, repressing a laugh. "That image is strictly a media creation. Like I said, even Martha Stewart isn't Martha Stewart. I just think women end up being their own worst enemy at times."

"Probably," Fey agreed. "I know I certainly do. I've screwed up so many times in my life, I've lost count. All you can do is learn from your mistakes and move on, which I know is easier said than done."

Rhonda was silent, staring out the window.

"What's this all about, anyway?" Fey asked. Thoughts of Rhonda's reaction to Hammer's being put in the hospital flashed through her mind. Something was up. "I've never heard you talk this way before."

Rhonda made a gruntlike noise in the back of her throat.

Instead of taking the freeway back to the station, Fey had chosen to drive one of the canyon passes that would take them from Agoura through the foothills and drop them down onto Pacific Coast Highway. From there, it was a short run to the station.

The road in front of her twisted and turned as it wound through the mountain pass. She kept her eyes on the road, driving automatically as she sorted through the vibes she was getting from Rhonda. Suddenly, a feeling of premonition sent a chill down her spine.

"Are you pregnant?" The word blurted out of her.

There was a pause before Rhonda, still looking out the passenger-side window, answered in a small voice, "Yes."

"Holy cow."

"Yeah, and I don't know what to do about it."

Fey saw a turnout approaching and pulled into it. The small stopping area on the side of the road was used for slower vehicles to get out of the way so faster traffic could pass. Fey put the car into park but did not turn the engine off. She had pulled into the turnout and stopped in order to give her full attention to Rhonda. One part of her subconscious, however, was aware of the cars that passed them—checking for anything familiar. Her precognitive sense was working overtime.

"Does Hammer know?" she asked. "I assume Hammer . . ." She trailed off.

Rhonda sighed. "No, he doesn't. And of course he is," she said, answering Fey. "And don't ask how. I told you, it's tough being perfect all the time."

Fey released her seat belt. She thought about what Rhonda must have been going through during the interview with April Waverly. "Are you worried about what Hammer will say?"

"No," Rhonda said. "I think he'll be delighted. He's never let me down, and I doubt he'll start now. He's big on personal responsibility." She paused slightly, as if having difficulty opening herself up further. "It's not his reaction I'm worried about," she said after a second. "It's mine. I'm old enough to have kids who could be having kids of their own."

"The word is grandmother," Fey said, trying to lighten things up a bit.

"The dreaded G word," Rhonda agreed, smiling.

"Okay," Fey said. "If Hammer isn't the problem, what is?"

Rhonda released her own seat belt and turned to face Fey. "I don't know if I can go through with this. I'm scared for the baby," she said. "Healthwise, I mean. You know? Me having a baby this late in life." She bit a hangnail off her left thumb.

"There's more," Fey said, pushing.

"I'm also scared about what this will mean to my career," Rhonda said in a rush. "I'm scared of the changes a baby will bring into my relationship with Hammer. I'm scared of having a baby. I'm scared of having to be a mother." Her words were now coming out in a speeding torrent. "I'm just flat out terrified!"

Rhonda started to cry, and Fey reached out to embrace her.

39

ALPHABET AND Brindle were impressed with the setup Ethan Kelso had established for Thistle One. The headquarters of the security/intelligence corporation were housed in an unobtrusive series of rooms above a group of ground-level businesses established in one of Santa Monica's older buildings. The only indication of Thistle One's existence in the building was a small wall plaque—bearing the logo of a Scottish thistle—attached to the brick facade near a door that opened into a tiny, featureless lobby.

An intercom buzzer and electronic surveillance determined who gained entrance to the inner sanctum. Once a subject had been cleared for admittance, an interior button was pushed, causing the rear wall of the small lobby to slide aside, revealing a narrow stairwell.

For some reason, the design reminded Alphabet of Del Florio's Tailor Shop from the old *The Man From U.N.C.L.E.* television series. He still occasionally watched the show late at night on the TNT channel. Alphabet had always wanted to be a spy ever since he'd first watched the program as a kid. He had come to accept, however, that with his luck, he would have ended up as Maxwell Smart instead of James Bond. It was bad enough that he had to become a cop who was closer to Gunther Toody than Joe Friday.

While the outside of the building was purposely misleading, the interior of the Thistle One offices was resplendent with the old-world charm of a British men's club. Hunter-green carpet played host to dark leather chairs and couches. The pale, beige walls were covered with hunting and racing prints in heavy frames and other British sporting memorabilia.

But even the appearances of the offices were a sleight-of-hand misdirection to hide the state-of-the-art computer, phone, electronic, and surveillance equipment that were the company's heart.

Alphabet's first comment had been that Thistle One had enough spy apparatus to support a midsized country. Brindle had not argued.

"That's because there is more spying going on inside every big city in this country than George Smiley could have ever dreamed about," Ethan told him. "Industrial espionage and corporate spying are the fastest expanding businesses in the world."

"Is there a difference?" Brindle asked, sitting in Ethan's rosewood-paneled office.

"Industrial espionage deals with product secrets," Ethan explained. "Corporate spying has more to do with personnel and business ethics—hostile takeovers, insider trading leaks, that sort of thing."

"And your company engages in these practices?" Alphabet asked. It was difficult for him to hide the censure in his voice.

Ethan chuckled. "Relax. I'm still one of the good guys. Thistle One is strictly in the deterrent arm of the business. We get hired to prevent secrets from being leaked. We catch industrial spies and corporate snitches. The closest we come to proactive spying is the dissemination of false information. If a competitor of one of our clients gets burned by false information, they think twice before trying the same tactics again."

Earlier in the day Brindle and Alphabet had hooked up with Ethan after Fey had given them the go-ahead to use Thistle One in trying to identify the suspect holding the burning cigarette to Ignacio Ramos's cheek in the photos recovered from April's car. Ethan had put his people to work on the information and asked Brindle and Alphabet to come back in a few hours.

When they returned, Ethan had given them a quick tour of the facilities and introduced them to the team he was dispatching to shadow P.J. and T-Bone.

The surveillance team was an odd blend. Boone Coltrayne was

an LAPD legend. Ethan had picked Boone up when it was clear that retirement on his Santa Barbara horse ranch left him craving the edge that came with police work.

Boone Coltrayne had himself been a mockingbird. His infiltration of the American Revolutionary Council had led to the indictment and conviction of the top five council leaders. Every LAPD academy recruit learned the story of how Boone was later ambushed by five members of a Libyan hit squad in retaliation for his actions against ARC. Although shot seven times, Boone went on the offense, reloaded twice, and killed all of his assailants. The filmed reenactment of the event was enough to cool the blood of even the most eager rookie.

There was much more to Coltrayne's story. Ethan Kelso was one of a few select individuals who knew the complete truth of Coltrayne's undercover activities, the ambush, and Boone's later revenge on the people who sent the hit squad. He was the first man Ethan approached when he was opening Thistle One, and Boone was now a full partner in the operation.

Large and imposing, Blue MacKenzie was an ex-CIA operative who owned a well-known muscle gym called Derringers. Like Coltrayne, he missed the jazz of being in the field. It hadn't taken much for Ethan to convince him to join Thistle One.

Trinity Valance was a thrill seeker with a mind sharper and quicker than most computers. Ethan had recruited her directly out of college, and she'd proven herself over and over again to be a valuable asset.

The last member of the surveillance team was Ramon Quintana. He was small in stature, but big in presence. He had run a much smaller agency specializing in deterring industrial espionage, and had been agreeably absorbed into Thistle One when both companies were competing for the same contract.

After being briefed by Ethan, Brindle, and Alphabet, the surveillance team had left to locate and follow P.J. and T-Bone. If needed, they would be able to call in other operatives, but the core team would first evaluate the situation to determine the need for later assets.

"What about sleeping?" Alphabet asked.

"They'll spell each other for a while in the field," Ethan explained. "If the surveillance goes on too long, I'll send a replacement team. If I know this lot, however, they'll stay with this to the end. All of them function on only a couple of hours' sleep a day to begin with."

"They must collapse afterward," Brindle said. "I know I would."

"I'm sure they do," Ethan agreed. "But their powers of recuperation are amazing. They collapse, but within a few hours they're ready to go again."

Ethan led the way from the team conference room to the more intimate quarters of his office. He flipped open a buff-colored file envelope, withdrawing several sheets of paper, which he brought back to a grouping of chairs where Alphabet and Brindle were sitting. He rested the file envelope and its remaining contents against one leg of his chair.

Skimming the papers first, Ethan then handed them off to Brindle. Alphabet moved to where he could read over her shoulder.

"Those are the individuals and situations my people have identified as possible terrorist targets in the L.A. Area in the coming days. They used the same criteria the Anti-Terrorist Division uses when establishing threat assessments—everything is geared toward events or visiting dignitaries whose presence may pose a threat to the security of Los Angeles."

"How do they know?" Brindle asked.

Ethan shrugged. "Some threat assessments are no-brainers, such as the pope coming to town. Other possible targets have to be anticipated by judging the political climate at any given time—which radical groups have become strong enough to pull off a terrorist act, which groups have fallen from favor with outside terrorist supporters, such as the Libyans or the Colombians. In many ways it's a guessing game. It's what separates the type of police work the Anti-Terrorist Division does from normal, routine police work. ATD's job is to anticipate terrorist acts and take action to forestall them from happening."

"That must make their work very frustrating," Alphabet said. "The only way to tell they're doing their job is if no terrorist actions take place in Los Angeles."

Ethan nodded his head in agreement. "ATD runs surveillance on approved groups or individuals who have been identified as possible terrorists."

"Who approves the groups, and what do they base their criteria on?" Brindle asked.

"With probable cause, ATD can establish a thirty-day investigation on a target. After that period, they have to prove to a police commissioner there is something beyond speculation in order to continue the investigation. If they can't support their initial probable cause, the investigation is terminated and the files redacted."

"Thirty days isn't much time to establish whether or not an individual or a group is a terrorist organization," Alphabet said. "It must make for a mad scramble toward the end."

"No doubt," Ethan agreed. "When I worked for ATD, there was a lot of pressure on informants and other sources—sometimes very intense pressure. Threat assessments, however, are another matter entirely. They are done not on specific terrorist groups or individuals, but on possible terrorist targets—rallies, visiting dignitaries, that sort of thing." He added two lumps of sugar to his milky tea. "For instance, the president is coming to town next week, but right now nobody appears to be gunning for him—the threat assessment is very low."

Brindle shuffled to the pages of information Ethan had supplied. "Prince Charles?" she queried, seeing the name in the text.

"Yes," Ethan nodded. "He'll be in town in two weeks for a goodwill junket. The only threat may come from some IRA fanatic, but despite a strong Irish presence in the city, there's very little threat directed at the prince. He does a lot of good work and he's well liked, despite America's image of him as a goofball with big ears. Anyway, the IRA gets too much of its funding from America. They don't want to kill the golden goose by crapping on the doorstep."

"What about Di?" Alphabet asked jokingly. "She may have hired a hit squad to take Charles out."

Ethan chuckled. "I doubt it. With him gone, her scandal value would be cut in half."

Brindle shuffled the papers again. "What about this next one?"

Ethan nodded. "I don't know how it fits in as a possibility, but it's the most likely candidate to correspond with the scenario we're building. The Central American Solidarity Conclave has been holding unity meetings and speeches all week. Our information shows the Central American delegates attending the conclave have also been meeting with California representatives to discuss more volatile issues."

"Have there been any problems?" Brindle asked, looking up from the typed pages.

"Everything appears to be going well, but you never know," Ethan told her. "The culmination of the conclave will come on Sunday, when everyone involved will attend the World Cup qualifying soccer match between Mexico and the United States. The game will be held at the Coliseum."

"Today is Friday," Brindle noted. "Is there any indication the game is a terrorist target?"

Ethan sighed. "To be honest, no, there isn't. But it's the only current event with any kind of Mexican or Central American connection. Right now Thistle One's researchers are trying to find a connection between your boy Ramos's Catalan cartel, their rivals, the Oro de Dios cartel, and anyone connected to the Central American Solidarity Conclave. We're trying for drug connections, political connections, family connections—anything that would indicate we're on the right track. If we come up with anything, then we'll worry about what they're planning."

"This is a bit outside your normal frame of work, isn't it?" Brindle asked.

"The venue, perhaps, but not the actual scut work. My people are actually enjoying themselves. It's giving them a break from corporate intrigue."

"How good are your people?" The question displayed Alphabet's people skills at their clumsiest.

Ethan frowned. "My people are the best. Not just the best money can buy. They are the best under any qualification. And I can prove it."

"Really?" Alphabet was taken aback by the timbre of Ethan's voice.

"Really," Ethan said. "The photos recovered from April Waverly's car?"

"Yeah," Alphabet said, indicating he was on the same page of music after the subject change.

Ethan's expression switched to one of satisfaction. "It only took my people three hours to identify your unknown suspect."

40

"LUCIAN SANTIAGO," Brindle said casually. On the desk in front of Fey, she placed the Polaroid photo of Ignacio Ramos being burned on the cheek by a cigar. With a long fingernail, she pointed to the face of the now identified person who leered into the camera while holding the cigar to Ignacio's cheek.

Fey was quick to react. "Santiago? As in Don Diego Santiago, head of the Oro de Dios cartel?"

"His grandson," Brindle told her.

Leaving Ethan Kelso and his people from Thistle One to do their job, Brindle and Alphabet had raced back to West L.A. Station to rendezvous with Fey and Rhonda.

After their brief stop in the canyon road turnout, Fey and Rhonda had driven back to West L.A. in companionable silence. Fey knew there was little she could do, other than to be a friend and sounding board, to help Rhonda struggle with her new challenges. There also appeared to be little she could do to deal with her own concerns. The persistent feeling she had that somebody had them under surveillance would not let her relax. Fey did not want Rhonda to think she was acting paranoid, so she fought the urge to employ any dry-cleaning techniques while driving. Still, her eyes often flicked to the rearview mirror, looking for any sign of a tail, any indication there was somebody following them, but she saw nothing.

It was late afternoon by the time Fey pulled back into the police station parking lot, but to Fey the day seemed to be endless. She was emotionally drained, and needed something positive to pick up her energy level again—something like Brindle and Alphabet.

"How did Ethan's people come up with an ID so quickly?" Fey asked.

"Beats me," Brindle said. "But I have a feeling the files Ethan has established at Thistle One are even more extensive than those kept by ATD."

Fey nodded. "I'm sure they are. Thistle One doesn't have to answer to the police commission and justify the existence of its files."

"I also have a feeling," Alphabet added, plunking his bulk into a chair next to Brindle, "Ethan took a lot of ATD files with him when he left to open Thistle One."

"How can you say such a thing?" Fey asked in a mocking voice. "That would have been unethical."

"And your point is?" Alphabet asked, returning the sarcasm.

Rolling her eyes, Brindle interjected herself into the discussion. "Actually, Thistle One already had established files on the Catalan and Oro de Dios cartels. With NAFTA taking many jobs south of the border, much of Thistle One's security work revolves around Mexico and the disruptive factions there.

"Monk wasn't kidding earlier when he said Tijuana is experiencing a Latin version of the Al Capone mob wars. There have been seven Baja prosecutors and a police commander killed this year alone. The assassination of Adrian Santiago by the Catalan cartel was simply everyday business. The Catalan cartel held the upper hand politically, and there was no way they were going to let the Oro de Dios cartel muscle in on their action. When Adrian became influential enough to threaten the term of the Catalan cartel's pet politician, Ignacio and the other male members of his family were brought in to take Adrian out."

"Did you get all this from Ethan?" Fey asked, looking for a second source confirmation of the information Monk reported.

Alphabet nodded. "Yeah. His people seemed right on top of this stuff. Like Brindle said, they've been dealing with this type of thing ever since more and more American companies have started taking U.S. government–sanctioned advantage of cheap factory labor on the other side of the border."

"How did they get on to Lucian Santiago?" Fey asked, picking up the photo from the table and taking a hard look at it.

"Thistle One has an exhaustive file on who's who in the zoo down there," Brindle explained. "Everyone known to be connected to either cartel is in the Thistle One database. Their expert on the situation, a guy named Warrick, knows many of the players on sight. He recognized Lucian Santiago as soon as he saw the photo."

"Is Lucian that big of a player?"

"In some ways, yes, and in others, no."

"Thanks."

Brindle chuckled. "Sorry, but it's true. Lucian is part of a new breed of gangster emerging from the mire. He is a member of a loose-knit group referred to as Los Juniors. The group consists of young men from the upwardly mobile Mexican families who have been given every advantage their parents' money can buy. They have connections, Catholic school admittance in San Diego, university educations, and the ability to pass with ease on either side of the Mexican border. The problem is, Los Juniors are returning the favors shown them by becoming virtually high-class hit men for the cartels."

"It's a new fad," Alphabet explained. "The cartel kingpins have become famed for having members of Los Juniors by their sides, as if they provide a protective shield. Because Los Juniors are protected by their family money and position, they have become untouchables—they murder, rape, and rob at will and nobody is doing anything about it."

"And Lucian Santiago is part of Los Juniors?" Fey asked.

"A rising leader," Brindle told her. "He's been going to the university here for the past three years, but his position as a leader of Los Juniors is cemented by being Don Diego Santiago's grandson. Not only is he from one of the richest families in the state of Baja California, it is also the family that runs the second most powerful cartel in the area."

"With visions of being the most powerful," Alphabet added.

Fey was silent for a second. "Wait a minute," she said eventually, giving the pair of detectives a twisted look. "You just tried to scam something past me, didn't you?"

Alphabet and Brindle smiled. "Just seeing if you were listening, boss," Alphabet said.

"Exactly what university is dear old Lucian attending?" Fey asked.

"UCLA, of course," Brindle told her angelically. "Didn't we make that clear?"

Before Fey could respond to this minor bombshell, somebody cleared his voice in the doorway to the office.

All four detectives turned to see the tall physique of Vaughn Harrison leaning against the door frame. He waved his clawed fingers at the assembled group.

"Sorry to interrupt," he said. "But I was wondering if I could have a private word with Detective Croaker?"

41

FEY IMMEDIATELY realized there was no way to tell how long Harrison had been standing in the doorway, or how much of the conversation he had overheard. What good would it do having Hammer sweep for listening devices if they weren't more careful about the integrity of their own security?

It bothered Fey. She had dealt with media leaks and other outside intrusions into an investigation before, but she'd never had to worry about keeping an investigation from those in command of the department. Suddenly, she was faced with being betrayed by her own kind.

Harrison stepped into the room, and both Alphabet and Brindle stood up from their chairs. Fey waved them down. At the same time, she pointedly turned over the photos that were arranged on the conference table.

Standing up herself, she nodded at Harrison. "Let's talk outside," she said, walking past him and through the doorway.

He glared at Rhonda before turning to follow Fey. Outside the office, he saw Fey making for the stairwell that led to the detective squad room.

"Let's go out on the roof," Fey said over her shoulder. She moved on, not waiting for a reply or to see if Harrison was following her.

On the second floor, Fey turned down the hallway that led past the vice unit's office and the bathrooms. She pushed open a fire door at the end of the hallway and stepped out onto a roof extending over a small section of the station's first floor that wasn't covered by the second story.

In the center of the roof area, the building's generators and air-conditioning units stuck up like so many pimples on a debutante's chin. The noise they emitted blocked any chance of conversation being surreptitiously overheard or recorded.

Fey stood on a small running track that ovaled around the exterior machinery. At one time, the track had been expensively installed to encourage officers to run on it to keep fit. The constant noise of the air conditioner and generators, however, discouraged even the best of stay-in-shape intentions.

"So, what can I do for you?" Fey asked. She had turned to face Harrison with her arms folded across her chest, her hips shot to one side, body language speaking volumes.

With difficulty, Harrison struggled to keep his temper in check. "I didn't come here to cause problems."

Fey shook her head in a slow, cynical manner. "Do you know what the three most common lies are?" She proceeded to give the answer without waiting for a response. "'The check is in the mail.' 'Honest, honey, I won't come in your mouth.' And 'I didn't come here to cause problems.'"

"Fey—"

"Yes, Vaughn?" Fey's tone of voice made a mockery out of Harrison's condescending use of her first name.

Anger straightened the deputy chief's spine into a rigid spear. "Be very careful, Detective Croaker. I came here to extend an olive branch. You're bordering on insubordination."

"I don't think so," Fey said. "Insolence, maybe, but not insubordination. I've been rude to you, but I haven't disobeyed anything you've ordered me to do." She smiled and then added, "Yet."

Harrison gave her a steel-edged stare, but then cleared his facial expression with a smile of his own. This one was genuine. He even gave a small chuckle, but the sound of it was lost as a generator kicked in and raised the surrounding noise level considerably.

"Okay," he said. "You've made your point. You're a tough broad, and you aren't going to be pushed around." He gestured with his clawed hand. "You've brought me up here where there are no witnesses and you can be as insolent as you want. So, why don't we cut to the chase—put our cards on the table."

"I love a man who knows how to flog a dead metaphor." Fey said. Her stomach was churning. She knew she could be digging her own grave by verbally abusing Harrison, but she couldn't help herself.

Fey's psychiatrist, Dr. Winter, had explained how snide vocal remarks were a defensive mechanism—Fey's way of keeping control over a situation with aggressive verbal intimidation. Dr. Winter had even explained alternative responses to Fey that were designed to overcome her habitual reactions, but Fey was damned if she could remember any of them right now.

"You're coming to the party a little late," Fey told Harrison. "If you wanted to play nice, you could have done so right from the very beginning. I have a feeling the only reason you want to see my cards is so you'll be able to judge how much damage control you need to worry about."

Harrison scowled. "I thought perhaps you and I had been on the job long enough to be on the same page of music."

"And what is that supposed to mean?" The generator cut out just as Fey finished speaking, which made her last words sound as if she were shouting.

Harrison reached inside his jacket pocket and removed a thin cigar equipped with a wooden tip to draw the smoke through. He took his time peeling off the cellophane wrapper and using a wooden match to light the tightly rolled tube of tobacco. In the silence created by the generator's plug being pulled, he puffed several times before answering Fey.

"Can you honestly tell me you like the way this department is going with all of this community policing crap?"

Fey wasn't at all sure what this had to do with the investigation of Alex Waverly's murder, but she was willing to play along for a while. A good detective knows you always go where an investigation takes you, not where you take the investigation. "It's what the citizens want," Fey said. "What I like doesn't enter into it."

"That's a bunch of malarkey," Harrison said. He blew a stream of smoke out through his nostrils. "The citizens don't want community policing, they just think they do. What responsible citizens really want is for us to protect their families, recover property, put assholes in jail, keep dope from being visible on the streets, and to do it all with a minimum of fuss. If we can do those things, you won't hear anyone talking about reaching out to form a better understanding between the police and the public."

Fey shifted the weight on her feet and refolded her arms. "If you really believe that to be true, then you're so high up in your ivory promotion tower, you have no idea what's happening on the street. This isn't the seventies and the eighties anymore. Police work has changed. The public's priorities have changed. They don't want service delivered with a smile and a nightstick anymore."

"Yes, they do," Harrison said, meaning it. "The majority of them just don't want to come forward and admit it. Most of the public only want to be safe in their homes. They don't want to be policemen."

"Police officers," Fey corrected. She shook her head. "You're the worst kind of anachronism. What you're actually saying is men want to be safe in their homes so they can beat their wives, molest their kids, and shoot dope without being harassed by the police. As long as they do it in private, it's not a problem as far as you're concerned."

"Now who's throwing sexist generalities around?"

"Monkey see, monkey do," Fey said. "There are a hell of a lot of citizens who are coming forward to get involved with community policing. We have to listen to them."

"Why?" Harrison asked. "Most of them are nothing more than do-gooders with too much time on their hands, or rabble-rousing lowlifes with political agendas that support anarchy and stifle the police so they can line their own pockets." Harrison jabbed his cigar in Fey's direction. "You know that's the truth. I know you do."

"Maybe, maybe not," Fey conceded. "But what does any of this have to do with the murder of Alex Waverly?"

Harrison paused for a moment. "This is our city," he said. "We have to take it back before the animals run it over. And the first thing we have to do is get rid of the chief—make it impossible for his contract to be renewed. He is bringing this department to its knees. I know you don't agree with the direction he's taking. You know in your gut this community policing crap is a losing proposition. Do you think the community is going to be able to stop hard-core criminals? Do you think the community has any clue how to stop terrorists?" The questions were rhetorical, and Harrison quickly rambled on. "We've been given the wake-up calls—the World Trade Center in New York, the federal building in Oklahoma, the Arndale shopping center in Manchester, England, the subway system in Tokyo. Terrorism is everywhere. Los Angeles is not exempt. Terrorism is here now, just waiting for its chance to explode in our faces and tear our city apart."

"And what do you propose to do about it?"

"I propose to get us back on track. We have to bolster our intelligence-gathering apparatus instead of allowing the ACLU and others to take away every tool we have for anticipating terrorists by demanding we destroy intelligence files. We have to punish those who threaten us and reward those who bring us useful information."

Harrison was sounding more like an extremist himself with every word. Fey figured he'd read too many chapters out of the *Do-It-Yourself KGB*. She didn't interrupt, however, waiting to see where Harrison was going.

The deputy chief took her silence as acquiescence. "I want the chief gone in order to make L.A. a safer place. You want to solve Alex Waverly's murder. Okay, fine, I'll make you a deal. Give me a week and you can solve the hell out of the damn thing. I'll even give you the murderer on a plate. Until then, back off. Give me the chance to start bringing this department back to greatness. Alex was my man. Don't let his death go in vain. Let me finish what he started."

This last revelation stunk like Limburger cheese. Fey wasn't at all sure that Alex had been Harrison's man. He may have been working for him, but his loyalties were another thing altogether.

"What happens in a week?" she asked.

"We'll have what we need—the chief on his way out."

"How?"

"Don't push this."

"Don't push what? It's a reasonable question."

"Come on, Fey. Help me take our city back."

"Exactly what part of this city is ours?" Fey asked. "Hell, you don't even live within the city limits. You just get to suck at the public teat along with the rest of us day workers. What gives you the arrogance to think you can hinder a murder investigation in order to fulfill your own political agenda? You're no better than any of the other bureaucratic hyenas feeding on the public carcass."

Harrison jammed his cigar back in his mouth. "I gave you credit for being smarter than this, Croaker. I want to bring you on board. You want to play hardball, fine. I admire your balls. What do you want? Let's make it happen."

"I want to get a couple of things straight," Fey said. "First, I don't have balls. Secondly, who died and made you king? I hate the crap that's going on in this city. I wonder every day why the hell people think they can tell the police how to do their job. These same concerned citizens would never dream of telling their doctors how to do an operation, or a plumber how to clear a sink, but they all think they can tell the police how to fight crime. But do you know what the truth of the matter is? They can tell us. We work for them. Not one of us—not me, not you, not the chief—has the right to tell the people how their police department is going to be run. We may be in a mess, but turning the police department into a fascist force to impose the will of those in charge will only lead to disaster." Fey took a step forward. "There isn't anything you can do that will stop me taking you down if you're dirty."

"Don't get in my way, Croaker." Harrison's voice rose to a loud growl as the generators switched on again. "I'll squash you like a cockroach."

"Funny thing about cockroaches," Fey said, knowing there was no turning back. "They'll still be around when the rest of us are worm food."

42

MARY DEFALCO thrust her hips forward to meet John Dancer's frantic lunges. With her arms over her head and her hands bracing herself against the headboard of her bed, she locked her ankles behind Dancer's buttocks and pulled him to her as she sensed his release explode.

There was no threat that anyone would stumble upon or interrupt their rutting, but to Dancer, the danger inherent in screwing his secretary while on duty was still very real. It added spice to the erotic tryst, bringing to Dancer a sexual urgency he hadn't known since his youth.

Nobody questioned the pair when they had signed out from the division within five minutes of each other. Dancer had made a production of everyone knowing he was on his way to a meeting with the police commission. Mary simply and quietly signed herself out to a late lunch.

Taking his plain detective sedan, Dancer had arrived at Mary's apartment in Silverlake ten minutes later. He used her backup gate opener to park in the lot beneath the complex. He waited in the car until Mary pulled her new Ford Taurus into the spot next to his.

Unable to suppress his anticipation, Dancer virtually attacked Mary as she left her car. Grabbing her in his arms, he kissed her and crushed her against him. He was delighted when she responded by grinding her pelvis against his leg in a manner that told him she couldn't wait for him either.

They rolled against the side of the car for a few moments, tongues and lips forced against each other with bruising passion.

"Inside," Mary eventually gasped, pushing at Dancer's hand, which had made its way up her skirt and was rubbing against her heat. "Inside, you can have everything."

Dancer growled, but controlled himself enough to allow Mary to lead him into the complex's elevator.

Inside the boxlike conveyance, the pair again embraced. Slim and light, Mary put her arms around Dancer's neck and pulled herself up to wrap her legs around his waist. With his back against the wall of the elevator, he ran his hands over her buttocks and felt his pulse race beyond any sexual urge he'd ever experienced.

Their intimacy had started the day before in Dancer's office. It had been late in the day, with most of the ATD crew either off duty or in the field. Mary had come into the office and had begun rubbing Dancer's shoulders. He'd been surprised by the action, but had no thoughts about objecting.

Ever since the last curtailed sexual session with his wife, Dancer had been fantasizing about Mary DeFalco. She had been giving him signs of being open to any advances he might make, but he had feared exposing himself to ridicule and rejection.

He had almost gone for it earlier yesterday when Mary had been coming on strong just before Croaker and her crew had walked in. The interruption had both startled and scared Dancer, but later, when Mary first rubbed his shoulders and then moved her hands down to caress his chest, Dancer knew he was willing to risk everything to have her.

When she'd closed and locked the door to his office, he'd made no objection. And when she'd turned to him, removing her blouse and bra, he'd been incapable of speech.

They did it for the first time right there in his office. Lying back on his desk, Mary had squirmed uncontrollably, biting his shoulder to keep from crying out. She had then taken him home with her and had run him through a gauntlet of sexual gymnastics that left him exhausted and satiated in a manner he had never experienced before.

When he'd dragged himself home, he had been prepared with numerous excuses for his wife. When she didn't bother even to ask him where he'd been, Dancer was more determined than ever to take Mary again. Guilt was neutralized by lust.

On Mary's part the coupling with Dancer was far more than sex. The sensation caused by the friction from genitals rubbing together was pleasant, but the power she felt as she controlled Dancer, as she had controlled other men, swept through her like a tsunami. For her, sexual lust paled by comparison.

Over her years with the department, she had entranced and seduced officers, detectives, sergeants, lieutenants, captains, commanders, and now a deputy chief—the man who, with her help, she believed would soon be chief of police. And if that help meant stepping down in rank to screw a lieutenant who was possibly threatening to rob her of her goal, then Mary had no hesitation in using her sexual prowess.

Vaughn Harrison turned Mary on like no man had before him. She fed on the potency he exuded. In her heart, she knew Harrison's rise to power would not stop at police chief. With her beside him, he would hold the fate of the city in his hands.

The years had been kind to Mary. Despite her age, her looks had not faded. She could still turn the head of any man she chose. Before Vaughn Harrison came along, the flirtations and sex had all been a game to Mary. She reveled in being a kept woman, knowing she was the one doing the keeping, knowing she could make men grovel for her sexual favors.

Harrison had been the one man who had set her afire, and she would do anything to keep him. Screwing Dancer was only a small favor, she even kind of enjoyed it—intuitively sensing how quick and strong his need for her had become.

As she pulled him into the warmth between her legs, she reached out to bring his head down against her breasts. He moaned as he released into her, and she matched him with a verbal cry of her own orgasm.

Later, she lay snuggled against Dancer's chest. He was propped up on her pillows staring into space. She ran her long fingernails down his chest.

"What's wrong?" she asked. "Feeling guilty?"

Dancer brought his attention back from the beyond and moved his hand to caress Mary's breast. "No, nothing's wrong," he assured her. "Certainly not guilt. I'd have to be a fool to feel guilty. You're wonderful."

"I know I am," she said with a laugh, but she was thinking that he was a fool. "But something is bothering you. What is it?"

Dancer took a deep breath. He started to say something, and then changed his mind and said, "Nothing."

"Come on. Don't make me drag it out of you." Mary raised her head to look into his face. She reached up and ran a hand gently down his profile. "You can tell me. I'm safe. After all, who can I tell? I'm your secretary and your lover. I want to help—even if the only thing I can do is listen."

"Mary, you are truly a wonder," Dancer said. "I can't believe we've found each other after all this time."

This was the part Mary reveled in. She had Dancer hooked good and proper. He would never be able to wiggle away from her until she was ready.

She removed her hand from his face and reached down to grasp him. He was instantly hard.

He would tell her everything.

And he did.

Later that night, Mary again snuggled against a male chest. This time, however, it was a misshapen hand with only three fingers that played with the nipples of her breasts.

Vaughn Harrison's house, elevated above Topanga Canyon, was soaked in testosterone. Heavy furniture and dark colors with swathes of burgundy dominated the high-priced-decorator's idea of a man's castle. Harrison had paid for the dubious good taste, and paid willingly. He felt it displayed his position in the world, especially when he stared through the picture windows and out over the vast canyon below.

During their lovemaking in the bedroom, Harrison had channeled all of his anger at Fey into a driving rhythm that Mary had absorbed with an abundance of pleasure. She sensed his frustration, and did everything to pleasure him.

After sending Dancer on his way with promises for the future, she cleaned herself up and rushed to Harrison's home to be there when he returned. She had news for him—news she knew was important.

The immorality of running from one man to another didn't enter into her head. Dancer was nothing more than an assignment. Harrison was love.

"We are getting close," Harrison said. "A couple more days and the chief can kiss his big blue butt good-bye."

Mary wiggled closer to the source of her obsession. "Did you see the articles in the paper today on the press conference he held yesterday to announce he's applying for another five-year term?"

Something akin to laughter rumbled in Harrison's chest. "The fool. Doesn't he realize that his only supporters are do-gooders, liberal freaks, and minority organizations who are trying to manipulate him? He doesn't stand a chance."

Mary frowned. She rubbed her hand through Harrison's chest hairs and raised her head to look at him. "If he doesn't stand a chance, then why are you putting yourself through all of these machinations?"

Harrison rolled over and pinned Mary beneath him. He worked his way between her legs and entered her. She moaned with pleasure.

"Because, my lovely Mary," Harrison paused to answer her question, "in this politically correct climate, you can never underestimate the cowardice of a police commission and a city council who also have their own agendas. They don't give a damn about what's right for the city. The only thing they care about is keeping themselves in office, and if they will make more political points by reappointing the chief, then you can be assured that's exactly what they will do—the good of the city and the people they serve be damned."

Mary pushed herself toward Harrison's slowly motioning pelvis. She moaned and clutched her hands in his hair.

"Tell me about Dancer," Harrison said, refusing to lose himself in passion.

Mary moaned again and didn't answer. She lifted her hips and bucked against him. Harrison used his weight to pin her hips to the pale green sheets of the bed.

"Tell me," he said.

Mary gasped for breath before speaking. "He's coming apart," she said. "He is questioning everything that has happened—questioning the actions you have set in motion."

"What's he going to do?"

"He talked about going to Croaker."

"Croaker!" Harrison pulled out and moved away from Mary. She almost whimpered.

"I don't know if he will, but he talked about it," she explained rapidly, reaching for Harrison and grasping his erection. "I think he's too scared to talk to Croaker, but it's in his mind."

Harrison was distracted. "He is rapidly becoming the weak link in this chain. You must watch him. Stay close to him. If he breaks, we'll have to handle him before he goes to Croaker."

"What about Croaker?" Mary asked. She wouldn't mind seeing that bitch put in her place.

"You worry about Dancer. I'll deal with Croaker when the time comes," he said, reaching out to entwine the fingers of his maimed hand in Mary's hair and pull her toward him.

He had told Croaker he needed a week. It had been a calculated statement. He'd made it to throw her off the scent. He didn't need a week. He only needed two days.

43

TRINITY VALANCE popped a Benzedrine pill into her mouth and then offered the tube of uppers to Alphabet.

He waved her off. "No thanks. I already ate."

"You don't know what you're missing," Trinity said as she adjusted her position in the plush driver's seat of the Thistle One surveillance van.

"What I'm missing is getting arrested for possession of a controlled substance."

"So take me in, Officer," Trinity said. She extended her hands to be cuffed.

"Sorry, ma'am. I can't accommodate you. I'm out of my jurisdiction."

"You can say that again," Trinity agreed. "Way out."

The van was parked in a dirt lot across the street from a Bob's Big Boy restaurant. The restaurant itself was located at one end of the Boulevard Agua Caliente—the main drag running through the town of Tijuana, Mexico.

Located across the street from the bull ring and a short distance from the Agua Caliente racetrack, the restaurant franchise served around-the-clock coffee and classic Tex-Mex favorites such as fat burgers, enchiladas, and greasy fries.

"What the hell are they doing in there?" Alphabet asked.

Beyond the plastic statue of Big Boy—the traditional, freestanding franchise logo of a chubby kid in red-checked pants with black plastic wavy hair—Alphabet could see P. J. Hunter and T-Bone sitting in a booth next to a dirty window. A waitress in a green uniform brought them coffee.

"You ever see the movie *Casablanca?*" Trinity asked. She adjusted the earphones connected to the parabolic microphone pointed at the restaurant window.

"Sure."

"Everybody who was anybody went to Rick's Café, right?"

"Yeah, so?"

Trinity adjusted the direction of the microphone slightly, trying to zero in on P.J. and T-Bone. "So, in Tijuana—where life is filled with border intrigue—everybody who is anybody goes to El Big."

Alphabet stretched in his seat. "You're putting me on, right? A Bob's Big Boy restaurant is the local hotbed of espionage and conspiracy?"

"Spooks, spies, and private eyes," Trinity confirmed with a nod of her head. The pupils of her eyes had dilated into huge saucers from the drug she had ingested. She had stopped fiddling with the equipment and was sitting back in her seat, but she still appeared to be vibrating. "Cops, reporters, lawyers, government officials—instead of chasing all over town for information, they all go to El Big and the information comes to them."

The parking lot of the restaurant was beginning to fill with breakfast customers.

"See the men sitting at the tables next to our boys?"

"Yeah." Alphabet switched his attention to a group of stolid-looking men who shared several tables near another section of windows. When they entered the restaurant, they had set down their briefcases, pulled out cellular phones, and appeared to convert their area into an informal office.

"They are *ganaderos,*" Trinity told him, "businessmen who make their money in the livestock business." She moved her hands on the van's steering wheel and pulled gently back and forth on it, swaying to her internal rhythms. "In the afternoon, they will leave and groups of cops and reporters will take their place. Later, once darkness falls, the politicians, the snitches, the drug czars, and the gunslingers slither in."

"How do you know all this?"

Trinity rolled her head around on her neck, trying to relieve tension. She spoke slowly, as if sifting through a memory. "I was in town in 1994 when Colosio was assassinated."

"The Mexican presidential candidate?"

"Yeah," she acknowledged. "I've never seen anything like it. Thistle One was doing security work for a corporation whose profits on this side of the border were disappearing down a sinkhole. It was a routine assignment—find the leak and plug it. When the assassination occurred, however, the whole situation became a moot point. There was a group of ex-cops called Groupo Tucan who handled security for Colosio. The local cops were tipped that Groupo Tucan were behind the assassination attempt, giving the assassin access to Colosio. We had contacts within the local cops and knew they didn't have the equipment to handle all of the surveillance and interrogations, so we helped out. In return, they gave us the leak we were after."

"And what did all of that have to do with El Big?"

Trinity began drumming her fists gently on the steering wheel. "It's where everything happened—making contact with the cops, delivering the equipment, getting the info back on the leak. El Big is where it all happens."

"Sounds like a dangerous place to hang out."

Trinity shrugged. "Not really. It's considered hallowed ground— intrigue only. No bloodshed."

Alphabet grinned. "Is there a sign on the door: 'No shirt, no shoes, no guns, no service?'"

"Close," Trinity agreed. "Hey, hey," she said quietly, suddenly sitting up in her seat. "Now we're cooking with gas. That's Lucian Santiago and some of his boys." She began fiddling with the parabolic microphone again. The van's tinted windows hid her actions.

Alphabet brought up a pair of binoculars and focused on the new arrivals, who were shaking hands with P.J. and T-Bone.

"My, my," he said. "Isn't that cozy."

• • •

The day before, while Fey was having her rooftop discussion with Vaughn Harrison, Ethan Kelso had called to check in with an update. Speaking to Brindle, he advised her that the Thistle One surveillance team had located P.J. and T-Bone at Parker Center and had settled in for the duration.

With a questioning glance at her partner, Brindle asked if she and Alphabet could join the surveillance team. Internally, she could feel the momentum of the case building and was taking a chance on where the break would come from.

Ethan said since Fey was footing the bill, her people could do whatever they wanted. On a side street near Parker Center, Alphabet had parked behind the surveillance van occupied by Trinity Valance and Boone Coltrayne. Coltrayne got out of the van and explained that Blue MacKenzie and Ramon Quintana were entrenched several blocks away.

"I know this may seem like a dumb question," Alphabet had said, "but if MacKenzie and Quintana are several blocks away, and we don't have a visual on P.J. and T-Bone's car from here, how are we going to know when they take off?"

Coltrayne then opened the passenger door of the Thistle One surveillance van and pointed to a screen displaying a city grid. Trinity twisted a knob and an insistent beeping noise filled the air.

"You bugged their car?" Brindle had questioned.

"Sure," Trinity said. "In fact, we double bugged it in case the first bug fell off or malfunctioned."

"It's illegal to use surveillance equipment without going through channels," Alphabet said.

"Illegal for the police department," Trinity said. "But not for a private security firm."

"You're working for the police department," Alphabet said. "That makes you an extension of the police department. You're acting as our agent."

"So? What's your point?"

Alphabet sighed. "So, if we can't use electronic surveillance equipment, neither can you as our representatives."

Trinity looked at Coltrayne. "I don't think I want this job anymore. They're trying to take all the fun out of it."

Coltrayne put his hand on Alphabet's shoulder. "With you and Brindle, there are six of us working this caper. Even if we all drove separate cars, there is no way of guaranteeing we won't lose the subjects or get burned. If we use the bugs, it makes our job safer and easier. Do you have any doubt the chief would authorize the use of electronic surveillance? It's his butt that's on the line. Somehow I don't think he'll pick nits."

Alphabet tapped the grid screen. "Show me how to use this thing," he said in an abrupt about-face, and climbed into the van's passenger seat.

Leaving Alphabet in the van with Trinity, Coltrayne went to join Brindle in the unmarked detective sedan. Bringing a portable radio turned to a frequency above the normal police bands, Coltrayne made radio contact with Quintana and MacKenzie before sliding down in his seat to wait.

The surveillance had started off in a routine manner. The Thistle One units sat and waited to the point where they believed P.J. and T-Bone had slipped through the net. Twice, Alphabet cruised through the Parker Center lot on foot to verify the detective sedan assigned to their quarry was still parked in its original location.

A scan was done for other ATD vehicles, in case P.J. and T-Bone might have become paranoid and taken another unit, but that didn't appear to be the case as the two suddenly emerged from the glassed edifice of the LAPD headquarters. In their regular car, they pulled onto Temple Street, the tiny electronic bug attached to their bumper emitting a strong signal.

The three surveillance vehicles began their shadowing convoy, the occupants once again feeling a rush of adrenaline. When the first stop was the cleaner's, however, and the second stop was a Fat Burger, where T-Bone wrapped himself around four of the half-pounders with everything, attention began to lag.

"I do hope these boys are going to lead us somewhere exciting," Coltrayne said to Brindle. They were following the play from several hundred yards behind Trinity and Alphabet, who were on the point in the surveillance van. Quintana and MacKenzie were paralleling the action using side streets.

"Any chance they've made us?" Brindle asked.

"I don't think so," Coltrayne said eventually. "The only way they could know about the bug is if they sweep the car every time before they get in it. That's not standard procedure, and it would mean somebody from the department's electronics unit coming down to do the sweep. You and I both know the LAPD doesn't have the resources to provide individual anti-bugging devices."

"I don't know," Brindle said. "All it would take is a battery-powered tape recorder. You run that over the car and it would pick up the bug. Crude, but effective."

Coltrayne shrugged. "If you want to be a pessimist, go ahead, but I think these guys are acting too cool. If they thought they were under surveillance, there would be indications that they were hinky."

The coolness of P.J. and T-Bone's actions continued until they took a pizza and a six-pack to P.J.'s apartment. It was close to midnight.

Neither ATD detective was married. P.J. was divorced with two kids he rarely saw since his ex-wife moved back with her parents in San Francisco, and T-Bone, being what he was, had never been married to anything else but the department.

"Isn't that sweet?" Alphabet said. "Do you think they're having a sleep-over?"

"What I think," Trinity told him, "is they're waiting for instructions from Harrison, or whoever is running this caper."

Alphabet settled back into his seat and closed his eyes. "Wake me in two hours," he said. "I'll take the second watch."

Trinity had waited for three hours, and wouldn't have awakened Alphabet even then if P.J. and T-Bone hadn't put in a sudden appearance.

"Wake up, love bucket," Trinity called out to her newfound friend. "We're moving."

Alphabet had shaken his groggy head, felt his bladder tighten, and checked his watch.

"Why didn't you wake me up?"

"A guy like you, who really knows how to show a girl a good time on a first date, needs his rest," Trinity said as she pulled the van away from the curb.

"Anybody ever mention that sarcasm suits you?" Alphabet asked.

There was no deception in P.J.'s driving as he hit the San Diego Freeway and headed for the border. T-Bone sat on the rear seat with his legs stretched out into the space where the front passenger seat should have been.

The surveillance convoy had no problem staying far enough back not to be spotted, and there was no challenge to the straight-ahead driving. When it became clear, though, that a border crossing was imminent, Alphabet called Brindle on the cell phone for a quick conversation regarding the sanity of their actions.

"In for a penny, in for a pound," Brindle had said. "If Fey was down here faced with the same decision, she wouldn't back off."

Alphabet knew she was right. If they lost P.J. and T-Bone now, there was no knowing when or where they would be able to pick them up again. Also, this trip did not appear to be a tourist junket. Fey had said the caca was due to hit the fan, and whatever P.J. and T-Bone were up to was probably the precursor to that action.

When it came down to it, Alphabet knew they didn't have any real choice. There would be no problem regarding passports. Only identification—such as a California driver's license—was required to cross the Mexico–United States border in either direction.

"Let's do it," he said, pointing for Trinity to head for the border crossing. "I've always wanted to be part of an international incident."

Behind Trinity and Alphabet, the two other surveillance vehicles lined up for the border crossing.

Still watching the windows of the Bob's Big Boy, Alphabet saw Lucian Santiago release his grip on P.J.'s hand and turn to the large Tongan. T-Bone simply stared at Lucian with no other reaction. Lucian ignored him—a dangerous thing to do, Alphabet thought—and turned back to P.J. Two other men had entered the location with

Lucian, but they stood back from the table, facing the entrance to the restaurant.

"What are they saying?" Alphabet asked Trinity, who had her hands pressing the parabolic microphone's earpieces to her head.

"Small talk," she said. "Lucian's asking if they had any trouble at the border."

"That statement would make more sense if the trip had been the other way around. Nobody worries about getting across the border into Mexico."

"Unless you're smuggling," Trinity said. "Then you always worry."

"What gets smuggled into Mexico?" Alphabet asked.

"You mean, besides cars, trucks, stolen jewelry, works of art, white females for the slave trade circuit—"

"Okay, I get the point." Alphabet tried to interrupt the tirade.

"—guns, explosives," Trinity continued.

"Okay, okay," Alphabet said, finally getting Trinity to shut up as she started to listen to the earphones more carefully.

"Lucian's asking if they brought the money. Hunter's telling him yes, and something about other items." Trinity was breaking down the conversation she was overhearing into brief statements. "Hunter is asking if Lucian would be willing to handle another small problem."

"What small problem?"

"Shush!" Trinity said, waving one hand at Alphabet while still pressing the earphones to her head with the other.

"Lucian stated his men would handle any problem if the price was right. Hunter has assured him it is." Trinity continued her verbalizing of the overheard conversation.

P.J. suddenly stood up and moved away from the window with Lucian.

"Damn," Trinity said. "I've lost them." She fiddled with the microphone, but found no joy.

Quietly, Alphabet radioed Coltrayne and the others—who were parked nearby but out of sight—and rapidly brought them up to date.

The two other men with Lucian came out the front door of the restaurant together, eyes sweeping the parking lot, alert for trouble.

"Bodyguards?" Alphabet suggested when he saw them.

"Probably," Trinity agreed.

Lucian and P.J. came out next, followed by T-Bone playing rear guard. Together the group walked over to the ATD detectives' car. When P.J. unlocked and lifted the trunk lid, it effectively acted as a barrier, cutting him off from the sight of the surveillance van and also making the parabolic microphone ineffectual.

P.J.'s arm appeared, handing a briefcase to Lucian. It disappeared again and then reemerged to deliver several long, wrapped packages to the men with Lucian. They took them eagerly. Lastly, P.J.'s arm could be seen gently handing over a second briefcase to Lucian, who took it almost reverently.

"Guns in the long packages," Trinity said, making an educated guess.

"With money in the first briefcase, and explosives in the second," Alphabet added.

Their guesses were based on long experience coupled with the inferences from the scenario itself.

Alphabet rubbed the bridge of his nose. "Looks as if war is about to break out."

44

FEY HAD gotten a better night's sleep than either Alphabet or Brindle, but not by much. She at least hadn't been trying to sleep in a sitting position with one eye open, one eye closed, with ears pricked for any sound out of the ordinary.

Nevertheless, with the weight of the case hanging on her and the specter of Vaughn Harrison haunting her dreams, her sleep had been troubled and too short.

At four in the morning, she realized the sandman had fled for the duration and she dragged herself out of bed to attend to overdue personal chores.

Turning on the strategically placed lights in her rear yard, she walked out to the rear corral area and wooden stalls that housed her horses. Two years earlier, the stalls had burned down during an attempt on her life. She had rebuilt them with the insurance money and they were now better than ever, with a built-in, automatic watering system and more space for feed and tack storage.

Constable and Thieftaker both nickered as Fey approached. She turned them loose in the corral area and lunged the horses to calm them. Afterward, she rubbed both horses down, brushed their coats, mucked out their stalls, and changed their feed. She checked the water in the corral trough, and split a bale of hay open in the middle of the steel-ringed dirt area.

She rubbed the muzzles of the two horses and stroked and patted

their necks. She talked softly to them and soaked in the uncondi-
tional love they emanated.

Fey's neighbor, Peter Dent, and Lori, a local teenager who knew
the truth that horses were far more interesting and rewarding than
boys, looked after Constable and Thieftaker when the demands of
Fey's work made it impossible for her to do so. The arrangement
worked well for all concerned, and Fey returned the favors when
opportunities presented themselves.

Returning to the house, Fey was greeted by Brentwood and
Marvella, who caterwauled at her and rubbed themselves into a
frenzy around her ankles until she paid them some attention and fed
them.

Soon Fey could feel her stress level starting to build again. That
she was in a vulnerable position didn't bother her—she'd been there
so many times before that it was starting to feel natural—but it did
bother her that her people were also hanging themselves out. They
were displaying their loyalty, but they were also trusting her to see
them safely through whatever crisis presented itself.

Harrison would take her down if he ever had the chance, but
whatever he was planning had to be stopped. And somewhere along
the line Alex Waverly's murder also had to be solved. The murder
had become almost a side issue within the greater political manipu-
lations of the department.

Fey thought about this as she got ready for the day. It was time to
refocus the investigation on the murder of Alex Waverly. If she
could solve that conundrum, the bigger picture might shrink into
perspective.

She made a mental list to track down Rhonda immediately and
initiate an interview with April Waverly. She also had to find out
where Hammer was in his computer investigations.

The phone rang. "Hey, boss." Hammer's voice came down the
line. "Hope I'm not waking you."

"Don't worry about it. Me and Pinkerton's, we never sleep," Fey
said. "Actually, I was wondering about you. Thought maybe you'd
either died on us or decided to take a vacation."

"Sorry about that," Hammer said. "This project took longer than
expected."

"How are you feeling?" Fey asked, trying to keep her priorities straight.

"Let's not talk about that right now," Hammer said, not realizing Alphabet had previously said much the same.

"Why do people keep saying that to me? I'm beginning to feel like a mushroom."

"What?"

"People are keeping me in the dark and feeding me crap."

"At least you're more polite than normal."

"I'm trying to watch my weight and my mouth these days," Fey said. "Now, give. If you don't want to talk about your condition, get my day off to a good start and tell me you've cracked the case."

"Not quite," Hammer told her. "But we're getting closer."

"Tell Mother all," Fey said.

"You're not going to like some of it."

"Tell me something I don't know," Fey said, sighing. "Save the bad news for last. At least by then I'll have swallowed another half a cup of coffee."

There was a rattling of papers at Hammer's end. "We've been on this thing all night," Hammer said eventually. "Once Norm got with the program, he turned out to be very helpful. I had the idea, but I couldn't have pulled off the reality without his technical expertise. We weren't able to recover all of the data in the hard drive, but what we've got is good stuff."

"Yawn, yawn," Fey said. "I'll stipulate to your hard work and brilliance, and I don't want to spend all morning listening to you make excuses for not being perfect. Can we cut to the chase?"

Hammer chuckled. "Waverly may have been a rock-and-roll kind of guy in the field and with the ladies, but he also knew how to cover his ass. He kept everything he did in files on the computer. He kept a running journal—dates, times, activities, justifications, theories, plans, informants—everything, including files on his fellow ATD detectives, as well as Vaughn Harrison, and how Waverly was running April's brother, Ignacio, as his personal undercover informant."

"You're kidding," Fey said.

"The files on Hunter, T-Bone, and Harrison make interesting

reading. If we can find corroboration, those three are going down big time."

"The problem will be finding the corroboration," Fey said. "What about Ignacio Ramos?"

"From what I can tell from the files, Waverly first hooked up with Ramos while he was working RHD, prior to busting open the carjacking ring."

"Was Ramos part of the ring?" Fey put her coffee mug down to swat gently at Brentwood, who had jumped up on the kitchen counter and was attempting to bat the antenna on the portable phone.

"It looks that way," Hammer said. "Waverly documented his contacts with Ramos. He must have had him on some other low-level squeal and Ramos rolled over on the carjacking ring in order to get out from under."

That was an old story that Fey knew well. She also knew that cops could be brutal when it came to not letting an informant get out from under. You kept the pressure on them to give you more and more information. Put simply, it was blackmail, and cops desperate for the next big bust could be as vicious as any blackmailer when it came to putting the screws to their victims.

"How does April Waverly fit into all this?"

"I'm not sure," Hammer said. "But maybe she was part of the hold Waverly had over Ramos."

Fey thought about that for a beat. "Okay. What else do you have?"

"Once Waverly made the transition to ATD, he took Ramos with him. There are files on several cases he was working with Hunter and T-Bone, but they don't seem connected to anything we're interested in, and it's pretty clear Waverly was keeping Ramos as a private source."

Fey was also aware of how that worked. Detectives jealously guarded their best informants. Whether they were kept on a string for money, revenge, or working off lesser crimes, a good informant was like a precious gem to be guarded at all costs.

"How the hell did he end up on the roof at Bunch Hall?"

"Waverly used Ramos as his entry to Lucian Santiago. Santiago was going to school at UCLA. When Waverly set his sights on Santiago and his cronies, Ramos was the logical choice to use as a direct conduit. I don't think Waverly knew at first how dangerous things were going to be for Ramos because he doesn't start documenting the connections to what happened between the Ramos and Santiago families in Mexico until later. After that, it was too late to pull him out without losing the foothold he'd gained."

"Why did Waverly target Santiago?"

"This is the part you're not going to like."

Fey drained her coffee cup. "I'm braced. Go for it."

"Waverly was working directly for the chief," Hammer said without inflection.

"What?"

"He was the chief's agent in ATD," Hammer continued in a hurry. "There's a whole file, like a diary, documenting his meetings with the chief, information he passed on, everything. The chief must have known something was brewing in ATD under Vaughn Harrison's direction, and he sent Waverly in there to sniff it out and bring it down. Waverly quickly realized Hunter and T-Bone were running a mockingbird in connection with Lucian Santiago. Waverly also documents his belief that Harrison, along with Hunter and T-Bone, and probably Danny Ochoa—the mockingbird—were in bed with Santiago and cooking up some action of their own on the side."

"We've been conned," Fey said when Hammer paused for breath. She could feel anger building inside of her.

"Looks that way," Hammer agreed.

"The chief sent us in blind. If we'd had that information, a whole lot of people might not have ended up getting hurt."

"Boss," Hammer said, his voice full of concern. "Don't do anything stupid."

"Me?" Fey said. "You must be joking. Stupid is my specialty. It's what I do best."

"Boss, wait!" Hammer's voice was abruptly cut off as Fey disconnected.

45

Trinity Valance tooled the Thistle One surveillance van west-bound along Agua Caliente Boulevard and through the curve turning it into Tijuana's Avenida Revolución—the major north-south highway running through the center of town.

"I don't like this at all," Trinity said.

Alphabet agreed with her but kept his counsel to himself. After the transfer of packages and briefcases from the ATD detective's car to Lucian Santiago and his men, the two groups had immediately gone their separate ways.

"What did you hear?" Alphabet had asked.

Trinity had still been fiddling with the parabolic microphone. "Not enough," she said. They had been able to pick up the conversation through the restaurant window, but not when P.J. had blocked the mike with the car trunk lid in the parking lot. "We must have missed something while they were walking through the restaurant— before they came outside."

"Why is it the good guys never get a break?" Alphabet's question was rhetorical. It was well-established fact in law enforcement that a suspect could shoot a bent-barreled, corroded small-caliber gun blindly over his shoulder, in the pitch-dark while falling down, and hit a policeman hidden behind a brick wall. Cops, on the other hand, could be expert sharpshooters, using well-cared-for weapons, firing off entire magazines of bullets under perfect conditions, and never touch a suspect standing five feet away. Sod's Law to the nth degree. "They didn't say anything more about the other little job P.J. mentioned at the table?" Alphabet pushed.

"They didn't talk about anything that I could pick up." Trinity tore the earphones off her head and threw them at the tinted windshield in frustration.

Coltrayne had come on the radio at that point, demanding to know what was going on. Alphabet had quickly filled him in and a decision was made to follow Lucian and his people and let P.J. and T-Bone go.

The contact between the two groups had been established, and Alphabet had documented the meeting on film. It seemed more important at that point to stay on Lucian, as his group appeared to have been tasked with carrying out whatever plan had been agreed upon.

From the parking lot, Lucian carried both briefcases, leaving his men to carry the long parcels that had been handed to them from the trunk of the ATD detectives' vehicle.

The parcels were obviously weapons, but nobody in the area seemed to be paying the least bit of attention. Alphabet felt as if he had fallen through the rabbit hole and had emerged into another dimension where the rules of civilized behavior were completely alien to what he considered normal.

"This is Mexico," Trinity had reminded him, as if reading his mind. "Not only is it Mexico, it is also the border. This is the Wild West out here. Normal doesn't apply."

"Where are the cops?" Alphabet asked.

"Looking the other way. Lucian is one of the Los Juniors. He is one of the untouchables."

"Where's Elliot Ness when you need him?" Alphabet wondered aloud.

Lucian approached a beat-up station wagon at the other end of the parking lot. The wooden panels on the sides had been stripped of their protective lacquered coating by years of sun and neglect. The standard white paint job covering the rest of the car was chipped and rusting and had turned a dirty smudge color. A chrome roof rack was pitted and only half there.

Sliding into the driver's seat, after placing the briefcases inside through the open rear window, Lucian had keyed the ignition. The engine turned over on the first try. Clearly, it was kept in better shape than the vehicle's exterior.

Trinity had fired up the surveillance van and pulled out to follow the station wagon a few moments after it passed. Coltrayne and Brindle quickly came up and took over the point position. Without a bug on Lucian's car, the surveillance would have to be an in-sight job.

Trinity also allowed MacKenzie and Quintana to pass and drop into position behind Coltrayne and Brindle. As Aqua Caliente Boulevard turned into Avenida Revolución, MacKenzie and Quintana peeled off to parallel the surveillance on Boulevard Reforma.

From their position at the rear of the clandestine convoy, Trinity stated her distrust of the situation.

"I have a very bad feeling about all this," she said.

"Anything in particular?" Alphabet asked. "I mean besides being in a foreign country, dealing with criminals who the local law either can't or won't touch, and having those same criminals provided with weapons by L.A. cops?"

"No," Trinity said. "That about covers it in a nutshell."

Trinity kept the van several cars behind Coltrayne and Brindle. If Lucian were paranoid enough to employ dry-cleaning techniques as a matter of drill, MacKenzie and Quintana would rejoin the convoy and the three Thistle One vehicles would trade off the point position in an effort to remain undetected. Lucian, however, appeared oblivious even to the possibility of anyone daring to follow him. Tijuana was his kingdom, and the peasants wouldn't dare revolt.

"Something has got to start making sense soon," Alphabet said. "Otherwise my brain is going to go into overload. We've got one murdered detective, one mockingbird who found out he couldn't fly, one missing detective who nobody wants to talk about, a hack writer who had the crap beat out of him, and now we've got two other detectives playing footsies with murderous scum from south of the border. I'm beginning to feel as if I'm stuck in the middle of a kaleidoscope—surrounded by fractured images."

"The bottom line is we're dealing with a passel of bad cops who are rewriting the rules," Trinity told him. "Whatever they're planning, it appears to be almost ready to go down."

Alphabet nodded his head. "Keep your fingers crossed and hope we can trip them up."

It was clear the quality of the bars, clothing shops, and curio stores was higher than that of those closer to the border end of the wide boulevard.

There was moderate traffic as Lucian unknowingly led the convoy past the Palacio Fronton, where tourists flock to watch and bet on jai alai games. Across the street was a large open-air gathering of glassblowers. Shelves of hand-blown glass objects formed a maze of walkways for customers to browse through.

Lucian turned right down Eighth Street, next to the artisans, and pulled the station wagon over to the curb.

Coltrayne's radio voice reached Trinity and Alphabet, telling them Lucian had parked and Coltrayne and Brindle were driving past. The Thistle One radio system was self-contained, powered by a main unit in the surveillance van.

Trinity drove across Eighth before pulling over into a spot at the curb conveniently being vacated by a rickety produce truck.

From their position on Boulevard Reforma, MacKenzie and Quintana turned left on Eighth and trekked back until they could park on the opposite side of the street from Lucian while keeping the station wagon in sight.

Coltrayne and Brindle drove northbound around the block to come back and park on Avenida Revolución, facing in the opposite direction to Trinity and Alphabet.

MacKenzie's deep voice came in over the radio. "I think we have a major problem here. Lucian's buddies are getting out of the wagon. They've unwrapped the long packages they took from Hunter and turned them into what looks like M-sixteen assault rifles. Lucian is out of the wagon as well, and has just pulled two forty-fives from under his windbreaker."

"Oh, crap!" Alphabet said.

"Have they made you?" Coltrayne asked MacKenzie.

"I doubt it," MacKenzie replied calmly. "They're not even looking at us. They're just real casual. If it weren't for the weapons, you'd think they were out for a walk in the park."

Trinity suddenly took the radio microphone from Alphabet. "Is there a bank anywhere?" she asked with urgency.

The radio was silent as the heads of all the Thistle One team members looked around.

"A bank?" Alphabet asked. "What do you think they're going to do, calmly walk into a bank in their hometown, shoot it up, steal the money, and walk away?"

"Exactly," Trinity said. "Don't you read the newspapers? Banks all over Mexico have become sitting ducks. The cops are refusing to protect them any longer, and the banks can't afford private security because of being hit by the peso devaluation."

"What does that have to do with Lucian? Doesn't his family get enough money from illegal activities that are safer than robbing banks?"

"The Oro de Dios cartel are major promoters of a protection racket aimed at the banks. If the banks refuse to pay up, Los Juniors are sent in to do the dirty work of terrorizing the bank customers and taking any available money. There's nobody to challenge them."

"Northwest corner," MacKenzie's radio voice interrupted. "Banco de Mexico."

Alphabet rolled down the van's passenger-side window and twisted the outside mirror in order to see back down the street. With little difficulty, he picked up the images of Lucian and his men as they entered the front door of a plain-fronted building with the words BANCO DE MEXICO in peeling paint across a grimy front window. After a few moments, shots could be heard coming from inside the bank and, when the front window shattered, the screams of patrons joined the commotion.

Opening the door to the van, Alphabet stepped out.

"Where are you going?" Trinity asked. "You can't get involved!"

"I don't plan on it," Alphabet said as he began jogging back to the Eighth Street intersection.

Surprisingly quick on his feet for a heavyset man, Alphabet

turned the corner on Eighth and kept moving down the near side of the street. He was remembering Lucian lifting the briefcases he'd received from P.J. and setting them in the back of the station wagon through the open rear window—*open* being the operative word.

When he was directly opposite Lucian's beat-up vehicle, Alphabet rushed across the street. The station wagon's rear window *was* open, the briefcase set just inside. Alphabet reached in with both hands and grabbed the handles of the two briefcases. Pulling the cases out through the open window, he turned to move away. Luck, however, was not with him.

The noise of rapid-fire shots scattered the screaming people on the street and bullets blasted into one of the briefcases, tearing it from Alphabet's grip. He ducked back and grabbed the case. As he did, he caught a glimpse of Lucian and his men.

MacKenzie and Quintana had been surprised to see Alphabet heading for Lucian's station wagon. They reacted quickly, however, when they saw Lucian and his men calmly emerge from the bank with several money sacks in their hands.

Almost immediately, Lucian had spotted Alphabet removing the briefcases from the back of the station wagon. Yelling in surprise and anger, he brought up his .45s and began blasting indiscriminately. The tallest of Lucian's men dropped the sacks he was carrying and unslung the M-16 from over his shoulder and fired off a rapid burst.

MacKenzie pulled away from the curb and floored the accelerator. The engine in the solidly built Dodge Ram pickup he was driving roared with power and the truck leapt forward.

Extending his twin .45s in front of him at arm's length, Lucian began running toward Alphabet, firing as he went. The shots flew wildly, his aim thrown off by the bouncing of his running.

With the second briefcase back in his hand, Alphabet scampered to the sidewalk and turned into the maze of shelving in the open-air glassblowers' market. Several of the fragile glass items near Alphabet exploded as Lucian continued to fire.

From his position on the passenger side of the Dodge Ram, Quintana slid a shotgun out from a hidden pouch under the cab's bench seat. Sticking it through the open window, he fired several controlled rounds at Lucian's men.

The two thugs dropped to the ground and scrambled for cover, splattering bullets down the rear portion of the truck's right-side quarter panel.

MacKenzie pointed the pickup truck directly at Lucian's running figure and urged the vehicle forward, over the cracked concrete curb, and straight into the middle of the glassblowers' marketplace.

Lucian was almost too late in hearing the truck engine accelerating behind him. Finally, as the truck smashed into the shelves of glass stock, Lucian turned to see what had happened.

He twisted to one side, diving and rolling as if he were a toreador escaping the rush of a charging bull. He still held his guns, one in each hand, and fired both blindly in a last, desperate attempt to hit Alphabet. Then the monster was on him.

The left front corner of the truck's bumper dealt Lucian a hard but glancing blow, knocking him upward and outward to land with a crash on a row of shelving. The shelving toppled over backward and, like a display of well-placed dominos, knocked over the shelf behind it, which in turn knocked over the next shelf in line, and onward. Glass exploded in every direction, showering down on screaming tourists and fleeing craftsmen.

Driving on, impervious to the damage the truck was causing, MacKenzie raced toward Alphabet, who turned and took the last bullet fired by Lucian high in his right shoulder. The impact spun him around, thumping him into another row of shelving, toppling it over and starting another domino effect.

Staggering to his feet, Alphabet recognized the truck racing toward him. He grabbed the briefcases and slowly began moving forward. His arm was on fire, but shock had not yet set in. He was a tough, old workhorse getting on with what had to be done.

As the truck screeched to a brake-smoking stop beside him, Alphabet tossed the briefcases into the rear bed. With the last of his remaining strength, he threw his good arm over the side panel and half-pulled, half-propelled himself into the truck bed. MacKenzie plowed through three more rows of glass geegaws to reach the street.

Behind them, Trinity had the surveillance van already in gear and moving.

Brindle and Coltrayne were also saddled and galloping.

Every image and rumor the surveillance team had ever seen or heard about Mexican jails suddenly filled their heads and turned their hearts to stone.

46

Trying to keep her temper in check, Fey marched purposefully down the harshly lighted corridor toward the chief's office. She couldn't stop thinking about how close Hammer and Nails had come to being killed in the explosion of Waverly's house. There were also the murders of Ignacio Ramos and the ATD mockingbird, Danny Ochoa. And in the middle of it all were the RHD detectives, Keegan and Hale, who appeared to be paying some kind of personal price as the investigation of Waverly's death continued.

Perhaps not all of those things could have been changed by the chief coming clean with Fey at the start, but there was certainly the chance that much of the danger her people were in could have been reduced. She was worried about Brindle and Alphabet—having no idea where they were or what they were doing.

The long corridor leading to the chief's office was surprisingly busy with Saturday morning activity. People bustled in and out of offices on either side, only to move aside as Fey plowed down the middle of the hallway like a human SCUD missile. Heads turned to watch her with the fascination usually reserved for traffic accidents. Clearly, she was ready to explode.

There were four people in the chief's outer office who all looked up as Fey blew in. Dan Ayala almost tripped over himself getting out from behind his desk.

"Detective Croaker—"

"Where is he?"

"Who?"

"Who the hell do you think? How many *who*'s are there working in this office?"

"The chief is not—"

"Get out of my way," Fey cut Ayala off again.

"You go, girl," one of the secretaries said with a laugh of encouragement. She hated the pompous Ayala and thought it was great to see a woman putting him in his place.

Ayala shot the secretary a dirty look, and Fey took advantage of his diverted attention to slide past him.

"Where do you think you're going, little lady?" Ayala asked, reaching out to grab Fey by the arm. His tone was condescending.

"You moron," Fey said through clenched teeth. "Take your hands off me."

Ayala hesitated for a fatal second, bringing an immediate reaction from Fey. Grabbing the little finger of Ayala's right hand, she twisted it away from her, giving him the choice of releasing her arm or having his finger broken. With her freed hand, she seized Ayala's wrist and raised it while continuing to twist the little finger at an unnatural angle. The pain forced Ayala onto his toes with a yelp.

"Everything you've ever heard about me being a first-class bitch on wheels doesn't even come close to the real truth," Fey said as Ayala hopped about in her control hold. "I eat pissants like you for between-meal snacks. You ever lay your hands on me again I'll break your finger off. You got that, Sunbeam?" Fey finished by twisting the finger in question an extra degree.

"Ouch! Yeah. Yeah. I got it," Ayala said, his eyes watering with pain.

Fey bent Ayala across his desk, forcing him off balance so that he fell forward when she released her hold on him. He thumped down, scattering paperwork.

"Now, there's a complete loss of dignity," the secretary who had encouraged Fey said.

"Shut up, Myra," Ayala snapped at her.

Fey continued past Ayala's desk to the chief's door. She'd set her course now, and there was no going back. Without knocking, she opened the door.

The chief looked up from surveying paperwork on his desk. "Fey," he said in surprise.

"Wait for it," Fey said.

The odd response made the chief frown, his beetle brows coming together to form one giant caterpillar. In explanation, Fey pointed to the phone on the chief's desk and, as if on cue, one of the lines lighted up. Somebody was making a call. The chief looked back at Fey.

Holding her index finger up in a gesture asking for patience, she counted softly and slowly to twenty-five before picking up the receiver and punching into the lighted line.

She smiled when she heard the familiar voices on the line. "Harrison, this is Fey Croaker," she said, interrupting the flow of terse conversation. "I figured your pathetic little snitch would be calling you to whine about being made to look like a fool. However, it's his own fault for not knowing his limitations." There was silence on the line. "How about you, Harrison? Do you know your limitations?" Fey asked.

More silence answered her.

"Harrison? Are you there, Harrison?" Fey banged the phone receiver on the chief's desk, and then put it back to her ear.

"Quit screwing around, Croaker," Vaughn Harrison's deep rumble of a voice came through the wire.

"It's over, Harrison," Fey said. "I told you that before. People are digging deep and looking to see what's hiding under rocks. Whatever you've got going ain't going to come together. Call it off, or I'm going to take you down."

"I have no idea what you're talking about, Detective Croaker. It sounds to me as if you need to take some stress time off to unwind."

"Thanks for your concern," Fey said. "But don't say you weren't warned." She hung up, turning to face the chief.

The big man was leaning forward, his platelike hands spread flat on his desktop. "What is going on?" he asked.

"You're a lying bastard who almost got my people killed," Fey replied, fighting hard to keep her voice even. "That's what's going on. And either you tell me the truth about your association with Alex Waverly, or I'm going to get you as well as Harrison."

"You think you're up to it?" he asked, showing his anger.

"Do you really want to try me?" Fey asked, unfazed.

For a second more, the chief challenged Fey with his glare and then he blinked. It was as if a switch had been thrown. His features relaxed, and a deep chuckle rose from the depths of his chest. "I should have realized when I gave you this assignment that no skeletons would be sacred."

"You lied to me. You put my people at risk."

"I didn't lie to you," the chief said. "I purposely held back information."

"Semantics," Fey snapped. "Either way, my people were in more danger than they needed to be."

"It's a dangerous job. If you or your people can't take the heat, get out of the fire."

"You want Vaughn Harrison taken down, so you pointed me at him like a gun," Fey said. "But I don't have enough yet to do the job properly. So, unless you come clean, I'll back off and let him run, and you can kiss your reappointment good-bye."

The chief appeared to debate the situation internally for a moment before gesturing Fey to a visitor's chair. "Please sit down, Fey. There may be some things I need to tell you."

47

"YOU'RE RIGHT," the chief said. "Alex Waverly was my man."

Fey crossed her legs and stared at the chief without saying anything.

The chief found Fey's silent stare disconcerting. "Look, do you want coffee or anything?"

"I just want the truth for a change. Besides, who are you going to send for it? Ayala?" She had already explained what had transpired in the chief's front office and led to her phone conversation with Vaughn Harrison. "I wouldn't trust him not to spit in it, or worse."

The chief shook his head. He wasn't used to explaining himself to subordinates. He knew Fey's moral code would not allow her to throw her lot in with Vaughn Harrison. However, it was also clear that if Fey backed down, Harrison could very possibly get his way.

Despite the legal and moral duplicity of his actions, which were not common knowledge, Harrison had the support of the department rank and file, while the chief had the support of the vocal ethnic communities and the reformists. Between the two, the press were selling papers by playing one side against the other.

The chief fully believed Harrison's actions had gone beyond backroom, backstabbing politics and into the realm of murder and insurrection, but without Fey there was no way Harrison's transgressions were ever going to be revealed. He needed both Fey and her people on his side. He might not retain his position as the LAPD's chief of police, but if he went down, Vaughn Harrison would go with him.

"What do you know about Alex Waverly's personality?" the chief asked.

"As far as I can tell," Fey told him, "he was a callous, thrill-seeking, egotistical womanizer who thought playing cops and robbers was a great game."

"I'd say that was a fair assessment." The chief sighed. "He was also a shit stirrer. He enjoyed pitting friends and enemies against each other and watching the fireworks. If he could be in the middle of those fireworks, then so much the better." While he talked, the chief stood up and walked across the office to a small cabinet. He removed a bottle of scotch and two glasses. "It's early in the day, so let's call this medicinal," he said, pouring healthy measures into both glasses. He sat down again, handing Fey one of the glasses, and took a deep swallow from his own.

"Drinking on duty?" Fey questioned, taking a sip from her own glass.

"RHP—rank has privilege," the chief said. He took another swallow of scotch before continuing. "Waverly had another trait, albeit a strange one in this day and age. He was certainly immoral in his personal life, but in his professional life as a cop, he was unbending when it came to the law."

"Unless it applied to him," Fey said.

The chief shrugged. "There are people who believe the job can't be done playing by the rules."

"And there are those who would argue that getting the job done is no excuse for breaking the rules," Fey said.

"Are you prepared to throw stones from the porch of your glass house?" the chief asked pointedly.

"Not me."

The chief smiled. "As I'm sure you're aware, many of the detectives working specialty divisions such as ATD, RHD, or Organized Crime and Intelligence Division often hang out together."

"The perceived elite separating themselves from area detectives.

An incestuous bunch along the lines of fraternal organizations," Fey agreed. She knew all about one hand washing the other.

"Waverly was drinking buddies with P. J. Hunter and T-Bone Rawlings. From alcohol-lubricated comments by Hunter, Waverly began to suspect Vaughn Harrison was manipulating events and investigations within ATD for his own purposes. He was pressing Hunter and Rawlings in their investigation of a possible terrorist group called Los Juniors."

"To call Lucian Santiago and his compatriots terrorists is a bit off the mark. They are really no more than common crooks," Fey said.

"Maybe so, but Harrison apparently saw potential for whatever scheme he had in mind and was pressing Hunter and Rawlings for information. Unbeknownst to me, Harrison had authorized the planting of a mockingbird within the group—pulling Danny Ochoa out of a nonproductive investigation and setting him after Lucian Santiago at UCLA, where Santiago was attending school at his father's wishes."

"I would have thought going to school was not real high on Lucian Santiago's list of priorities."

"It's all about appearances," the chief told her. "He would have been the first Santiago to have gone to a university. It was a matter of honor."

It was Fey's turn to shrug. "Was all of this before or after Waverly busted the carjacking ring?"

"After." The chief shifted his bulk and swallowed the last of the scotch in his glass. "He was on a high after the carjacking arrests and he thought he was onto uncovering another big scandal—this time within the department itself."

"I take it he'd begun to take his press clippings seriously. Thought he was Super Cop or something."

"I suppose," the chief said. "He came to me and convinced me Vaughn Harrison was up to no good. I was already aware of Harrison's ambitions, and perceived him as a personal threat."

"So, Waverly offered to become your agent in ATD," Fey said, anticipating what was coming.

The chief nodded. "Yes. After I gave him the go-ahead, he convinced Hunter and Rawlings that he could help them with the Los Juniors investigation."

Fey's brain was still racing ahead of the story. "And they convinced Harrison that Waverly would help them get the job done, and the next thing you know, Waverly's off to ATD."

"More or less," the chief agreed.

"What part do Keegan and Hale play in this sordid scenario?"

"They were Waverly's partners at RHD. When Waverly transferred to ATD he became the inside man in their operation, while Keegan and Hale operated as his controls. I don't know how much either one knows, or even if one or the other was possibly in collusion with Harrison—after all, Harrison is the deputy chief in charge of both ATD and RHD. I confronted both of them after Waverly's murder, but neither one would talk about the situation. They wanted the murder investigation for themselves, but when they weren't forthcoming about what Waverly had been doing, I could no longer trust them. That's why I brought you in."

"Where is Keegan now?"

"I don't know. According to my information, Hale has gone missing as well."

"Oh, great," Fey said sarcastically. "Congratulations on your control over the situation. Why didn't you tell me all this up front? Why did you let my people stumble around in the dark without telling us what we were up against?"

The chief held out his hands in a gesture asking for understanding. "Because Waverly wouldn't give me straight answers. You were right when you called him an egomaniac. He wanted to wrap the whole thing up and put a big red ribbon on it before he let it go. He saw it as the coup de grâce of his career. He wanted all the credit."

"And you let him get away with that attitude?"

"I didn't have a choice. He was the only link I had to what was going on."

"That still doesn't explain why you kept your knowledge to yourself."

"I did it because I needed you to come at the situation from an unbiased perspective. I had no proof of what Waverly was telling me, and there were times I believed he was actually setting me up. I came to distrust what he told me. I needed you to confirm Waverly's findings as a second, independent source."

Fey put down her almost untouched glass of scotch. She stood up. "So, what you're telling me is that you put my people in danger to protect your own position. It's all politics as usual."

"Don't be naive. Of course it's politics as usual. What did you expect?"

"I don't know," Fey said. "Maybe honor and loyalty, but I guess those words aren't in your personal vocabulary."

The chief parted his lips to expose the top row of his small, pointed teeth. "But they are words in your vocabulary, so I know I can rely on you to pull the rest of this investigation together in a way that will leave the department in the best possible light."

"And you in the best possible position for reappointment?"

"You can't do one without the other. You want to run with the big dogs, you have to be prepared to be bit."

Fey looked down at the floor and took a deep breath. Looking up again, she squared her shoulders. "You're right. My people and I will do the right thing, but don't ever let your guard down, because given the chance I'll bite back—hard."

48

"**Y**OU GOT shot while you were down in Mexico?" Fey couldn't believe what she was hearing.

After leaving the chief's office, Fey had been forced to make time for a mandatory court appearance. Eventually, her turn to testify came, but was interrupted by a motion from the defense to have her testimony stricken over a Miranda issue. The motion took another hour to settle in the prosecution's favor and then it was back on the stand to give the same testimony she had been prepared to give an hour earlier. By the time she was able to return to West Los Angeles Station, it was early afternoon.

All her troops were waiting for her, filled with information and all wanting to talk at the same time.

Mexico, for hell's sake! she thought. What have we let ourselves in for?

"Actually, I'm doing okay," Alphabet said. "Thanks for asking," he attached with mild sarcasm.

"Wiseasses I don't need right now."

"Okay. I'm sorry. Let's not make more of a big deal out of this than it is," Alphabet said. He was sitting in one of the chairs in the captain's office, where the homicide unit had set up shop. "I was hit, but I was lucky—a flesh wound, really. Trinity was able to stop the bleeding easily enough, so no hospital trips, no nosy doctors, no reason for anyone else outside of this room to know about it."

"It was still incredibly foolish. There's no way we can use any of the evidence you gathered without revealing where you were and what happened. You put civilian lives in danger—in another country yet, for crying out loud!"

After Alphabet dragged himself into the back of the pickup driven by Blue MacKenzie, all of the Thistle One units had fled the scene. Using standard procedure for a blown operation, they all met later at a cantina well off the town's main drags. The spot had been chosen ahead of time as a fallback location if something went wrong.

Alphabet was bruised and battered. Fortunately, the bullet hit had been minor and the blood was coagulating even before Trinity Valance had her chance to play nurse.

Boone Coltrayne had calmly begun handling damage control. This type of pressure situation was not new to him, or as he put it, "Been there. Done that. Got the T-shirt." He used a pay phone to call friendly contacts within the local law enforcement bureaucracy. Those contacts stayed friendly due to the promise of *mordida* money, large sums of it, that smoothed the way.

The pickup truck was abandoned. The threat of *mordida* paid by the other side made it too conspicuous to take a chance. "This is going to cost your chief a bundle," Trinity had said to Alphabet as they drove away in the van.

"It's only money," Alphabet had told her, wincing as they drove over a bump.

At the border, the van went through first with Alphabet hidden in the back under a canvas drop cloth. Brindle and the three other Thistle One operatives watched from six car lengths back in another border crossing line. When the van wasn't stopped, everyone began to breathe again. Brindle was also able to drive through easily.

The trip back to L.A. was a straight, foot-to-the-floor speedway ride, the team barely even slowing for the checkpoint on the American side of the border.

A clean dressing, a clean shirt, two prescription-strength pain pills, and a temporary sling hidden under a jacket got Alphabet kick-started again. Mexico already seemed like some kind of bad hallucination.

With Fey's own return to the station, the explanations and wood-sheddings had begun.

Alphabet was still trying to press his point. "Look, we got away with it. We got the money, and we got the explosives. We may not be able to explain them, or do anything with them, but then, neither can Lucian Santiago and his boys."

"You think that's going to stop them?" Fey asked. The shock of the situation was making her angry. "There's always more money and more explosives."

Alphabet shook his head. "I was only trying to do the right thing."

"The right thing would have been to abort the surveillance on this side of the border!"

"Sure! Would you have backed off?" Brindle asked harshly. "You would have done exactly the same thing we did. I've worked for you long enough to know how you operate."

She was probably right, Fey thought. Still, she pressed her point. "You work for me," she said. "That means you do as I say, not as I do." Fey threw up her arms, gesturing both mock surrender and for the bickering to come to an end. "Okay, what's done is done, but don't think for a New York second that if Harrison pulls off whatever he has in mind, he won't take all of us down with the chief. We've lost track of all the major players. Who knows where Hunter and Rawlings are, let alone what Lucian Santiago and his crew are planning for next? We have to start looking for all the connections in this damn case, see if we can figure out what they mean, and then decide what we're going to do next. I have a bad feeling time is running out on us, and if we don't hurry we're going to get slammed."

Off to one side of where Hammer was sitting, Monk Lawson had perched a buttock on the corner of the large oval conference table. The look on his face was grim. He was the only one among them who had a family to look after. He was absolutely loyal to Fey, but going down in a blaze of glory was not an option he took lightly.

"This is ridiculous," he said. "Are you telling me Hunter and Rawlings are supplying money, guns, and explosives to known terrorists, and we can't do a thing about it?"

"Not without laying ourselves out." Fey explained the obvious, knowing Monk already knew it: "Anyway, what happened in Mexico is not going to wash in a court of law on this side of the border."

Alphabet grimaced as he moved his shoulder. He spoke through tight jaws. "There's also still nothing tying any of this to Vaughn Harrison. It doesn't make sense to pick off the little fish if it won't lead us to the shark himself."

Shuffling a stack of computer printouts, Hammersmith spoke up. "There's more to what I found out from Waverly's files than what you allowed me to get through this morning. I think it will clear up a lot about what's been going on."

Fey leaned back in her chair and stretched. "Okay, but let's get fresh coffee all around. My caffeine level is dropping below critical."

The six detectives shuffled around the coffee machine filling mugs and groping through a bag of bagels.

Fey had checked the detective squad room upstairs when she first returned to the station, and Frank Hale was indeed missing in action as the chief had said. His people upstairs were covering for him, but it was clear to Fey—who had covered for more than one missing detective in her day—that they were worried.

She didn't yet know what roles Keegan and Hale had played in everything that was going on, but she was beginning to have some theories.

With everyone sitting around the conference table again, Hammer spread his printouts in front of him.

"Okay," he said. "Waverly's files tell us a lot about what was going on. He kept a running documentation of his activities—not only those things connected to this case, but everything he was working on at ATD or had worked on while at RHD. Before transferring to ATD, he had already connected with P. J. Hunter and T-Bone Rawlings as drinking buddies, and knew they were running a hush-hush scheme for Vaughn Harrison involving Lucian Santiago."

Fey interrupted to talk around a mouthful of bagel. "That's when he went to the chief and they hatched their conspiracy to have Waverly infiltrate ATD."

Hammer nodded. "Once working for ATD, Waverly partnered up with Hunter and Rawlings. The problem was that Harrison didn't immediately buy into bringing Waverly into the fold. Any other case was okay, but Harrison made sure Hunter and Rawlings kept Waverly at a distance where the Lucian Santiago investigation was concerned."

"When exactly was this?" Brindle asked. She had one of her hands resting on Alphabet's good arm. Fey had observed the bodily contact and was wondering if she was about to have another sexually connected pair of detectives. An unlikely pairing it would seem, but nothing would surprise her.

Hammer looked down at the printouts. "This was shortly before Ron Harper committed suicide—Waverly even reported his belief that there was more to Harper's death than was apparent, but it doesn't appear that he had any evidence to back up his feeling."

"How did he handle being frozen out of the Santiago investigation?" Alphabet asked.

"From what I can tell, Waverly had been planning ahead. He knew Hunter and Rawlings were running a mockingbird in the group, so he added his own bird into the mix."

"Ignacio Ramos," Fey said.

"Yeah. Waverly had used Ramos to infiltrate the carjacking ring. He apparently had his hooks into Ramos over a major theft—he was basically blackmailing him into being a snitch—and wasn't going to let him wriggle off. Waverly documents that Ramos wasn't too keen on taking on the assignment. This didn't sit well with Waverly, since he knew Ramos was risking prison time by denying him. Evidently, Waverly's suspicions were aroused, and he did some digging and came up with the connections between the Ramos family and the Santiagos. He also came up with Ramos's sister, April."

"I can see it now," Fey said. "Waverly must have used the threat of laying April out to Santiago in order to make Ramos do his bidding."

"What a bastard," Rhonda said from her position behind Hammer. "But if Ramos was known to Lucian, how could he possibly infiltrate the group?"

"Waverly set him on Danny Ochoa," Hammersmith explained. "Waverly knew Ochoa was the mockingbird who'd infiltrated the group as Daniel Sousa. He pointed Ramos at Ochoa and told him to get whatever information he could about what was going on with Lucian Santiago."

Rhonda nodded her head. "But there's still one question," she said, voicing the thought of everyone in the room. "Why did Alex marry April Ramos?"

49

Fᴇʏ ᴀɴᴅ Rhonda waited patiently in the small interrogation room at County-USC Hospital for April Waverly to be brought down from the hospital's jail ward.

The homicide unit's meeting at the station had continued for another hour before Fey and Rhonda left. Hammer had provided further information recovered from Waverly's computer files, and a long discourse was initiated on what needed to be done next. It was clear Hammer and Alphabet both needed rest before they could reasonably pursue any further investigations. Brindle was game to continue, but she'd also been awake for over twenty-four hours and needed to get her head down.

The three of them were sent home to take a break while Fey and Rhonda went to interview April Waverly. Monk's assignment was to touch base again with Ethan Kelso. It still needed to be determined if any further connections had been established between the Santiagos' Oro de Dios cartel and any emissaries from the Central American Solidarity Conclave. The conclave had run its course peacefully enough through the week, but there was still the soccer match at the Rose Bowl on Sunday. If he had time, Monk would also attempt to get a line on Hunter and Rawlings, and dig for further details regarding Keegan and Hale.

From Waverly's files, Hammer had produced the information

that Keegan and Hale were working as Waverly's control officers. "It's possible," Hammer had said, "that if Harrison found out what Waverly was doing, he also found out that Keegan and Hale were in on the operation."

Brindle asked the obvious follow-up question. "You think Keegan disappeared after Waverly was killed because he was afraid the same thing could happen to him?"

"Or he was afraid of what would happen to his daughter," Fey said.

The theories went round and round, some far-fetched, others with a ring of truth about them. Fey knew they were getting closer. The crevices in the case were getting deeper and deeper, but they still needed to find the lever that would split the investigation wide open.

Now, waiting for April to appear, Rhonda was deep in thought. She was sitting on a wooden bench attached to a side wall. A matching bench on the opposite wall was the only other furniture in the room. Fey stood near the benchless back wall, leaning her shoulder blades against the metal paneling.

Plucking at her lower lip, Rhonda spoke at last. "If Lucian Santiago was going to school at UCLA, why would Hunter and Rawlings risk taking explosives, guns, and money to Mexico for delivery?"

"That's a point," Fey said. "I hadn't really thought about it." She frowned. "Perhaps, after the situation with Ramos and Ochoa on the roof of Bunch Hall, Santiago felt it was too hot to hang around. He may be a big-fish Los Junior in the Tijuana pond, but in L.A. he's just a little fish in a big ocean."

"Do you think it's possible Hunter and Rawlings took the contraband to Santiago in Tijuana as a show of good faith—a way of coaxing Santiago back across the border to carry out whatever Harrison had in mind?" Rhonda asked.

"Maybe," Fey said. "Possibly, it was a way to challenge Santiago's machismo. Taking the contraband into Mexico wasn't much of a gamble, especially if bribe money had been spread around. It was a calculated risk, nothing more. If it got them what they wanted, perhaps it was worth the chance."

Before they could speculate further, the door to the interrogation room swung wide and April Waverly was ushered inside.

The small woman looked even more frail than when Fey had last seen her. April's cheeks were sunken, and there were dark smudges under her eyes that looked like bruises against her sallow skin. Her hair was dirty, and strands of it fell across her face. The hospital smock she wore hung on her like a limp rag, and the paper-thin slippers provided by the hospital jail ward did little for fashion and less for warmth.

April took one look at Fey. "My baby . . . my baby?" she asked. Her voice was a plaintive cry.

"Your baby is fine," Fey said. She took the woman's hands on her own and was distressed by their icy coldness. She could feel the shivering vibrations coming from the whole of the frail body.

Fey looked up at the deputy who had brought April down from the ward. "Quickly, bring some blankets," she said. "This woman is freezing."

Fey wrapped her arms around April. When she sensed the deputy hadn't moved, she looked back at him. "I need those blankets now, not next week." Her voice and authority appeared to get through and the deputy moved away. Fey figured he was the type who didn't like to take orders from a woman.

She moved April to the bench opposite Rhonda and sat down with her, keeping her arms wrapped around the woman's slight frame. "Can you see if you can dig up some hot soup?" she asked Rhonda. "There has to be a commissary somewhere in this place."

Rhonda didn't question the instructions and slid out through the interrogation room doorway. There was no doubt April Waverly needed warmth both inside and out.

Fey gathered April against her chest and rocked her back and forth as if she were a child.

When the deputy returned with the blankets, Fey took them and wrapped them snugly around April. "Where's the doctor?" she asked.

"There's only an on-call doctor on the jail ward at the moment," the deputy told her. "The guy whose shift it is called in sick."

Probably out playing golf, Fey thought.

Rhonda returned bearing a tray with a bowl of steaming vegetable soup. Fey dismissed the deputy with a flip of her hand, and returned to her ministrations. Behind the now closed door of the interrogation room, Fey fed the soup to April, trying to get more into her than on her.

April spluttered and protested weakly at first. Gradually, though, as the warmth of the blankets and the smell of the soup did their job, she began to swallow more easily. When the soup was gone, she leaned back against the wall and again asked, "My baby?"

Fey's guts twisted. The truth was that April didn't belong in jail. Whereas it had suited the needs of the investigation to keep April in custody, it had hardly been the best thing for April. In her dissociative state, it had not mattered much whether the charge was murder, or attempted murder for shooting her husband's corpse. But Fey had been the one to cruelly force April to resume conscious thought, and then had callously abandoned her back into the barely substandard care provided by the hospital jail ward.

The woman's torment was clear on her face. She had been forced to murder her husband under the threat on her brother's life, had her baby ripped from her through stress-induced labor, and then had the shock of thinking her baby was being thrown at her by Fey.

Fey also realized that April was in a country that was possibly still very strange to her. Also, if she judged American justice on the same scale as she was familiar with in Mexico, who knew what she believed was going to happen to her?

Fey took a deep breath to steel herself against the rawness of her emotions.

"Your baby is fine," she told April. "You'll get to see her soon, I promise."

April nodded.

"Do you understand what I'm saying to you, April? Do you speak English?"

The small woman nodded. "I speak English not so good," she said, her accent pronounced. "But I understand you, and I speak more now than before I come here."

Fey reached between the edges of the blankets to hold April's hands. "I know this is very difficult, but there are some things I need to tell you, and some questions I need to ask. After that, we'll see about getting this mess cleared up." Fey took a deep breath, trying to think of the best way to proceed. "It is true you shot your husband and he is dead."

"Oh, Holy Mother, I am so sorry." April started to rock and cry. Fey put her arms around her and held her tight.

"April, it's going to be okay. Alex was already dead when you shot him. You didn't kill him."

"What do you mean?" April's statement was a wail of confused anguish.

Fey could feel tears spring to her own eyes as she tried in English, and her dimly remembered, broken high-school Spanish, to explain the situation.

50

EVENTUALLY, WITH time and patience, Fey and Rhonda helped April understand the circumstances surrounding her predicament. The trickiest bit came in getting April to comprehend that, even though she didn't actually kill Alex—only shooting into his corpse—the fact that she didn't know Alex was dead when she shot him could technically still make her guilty of attempted murder.

April's grasp of English was passable, but the nuances of the law were difficulty to convey. She finally seemed to accept what Fey and Rhonda were trying to explain, but there was still a doubt that she fully comprehended. An interpreter would have helped, but there was not one readily available.

Taking a break, Rhonda made another run to the hospital cafeteria. She brought back coffee for herself and Fey, and more soup for April. This time April was able to feed herself, and appeared to be far calmer than before.

Setting her half-empty coffee cup on the floor, Fey turned and began the next phase of the interview. Knowing there was no way the district attorney's office was ever actually going to file charges against April—even though the statute was on the books—she didn't bother with Miranda rights.

It was easy to explain their knowledge of the photos and note from April's car, because Fey had brought them with her. April broke down when she saw the photos again and asked repeatedly about her brother and if the police would do anything to help find him.

Rhonda kept her mouth shut when Fey did not tell April about Ignacio's death. Coping with the death of her husband was enough of a burden for April without the additional shock of her brother's murder. Fey also omitted the details about April's house being blow up, wary that too many jolts to her system could push April over the edge again.

There was too much at stake for Fey to worry about ethics. She had to use anything she could to get April to talk to her—and what Fey had was April's baby. It wasn't pleasant, and it wasn't nice, but pleasant and nice were not what big-city police work was about. If you expected pleasant and nice, you became a florist, not a cop.

"In Mexico, especially in towns near the border, everyone does something for the *sindicatos,*" April said. When she spoke slowly, April's accent was more easily understood. It was not that she didn't speak English, it seemed, as much as she did not use it with regularity. "You must choose one side or another. If you do not choose, you starve. My father and brothers worked for Hector Catalan, the brother of Don Emil Catalan. We were very powerful, and very rich." April's voice held more than a touch of pride.

Nice work, Fey thought, if you don't mind being murderous scum.

"Do not judge me," April said, as if Fey's thought had been written on her face. "My father did what he had to do so his family would survive. My brothers also."

"But your family didn't survive," Rhonda said, trying to get April to focus before she went too far into self-justification. It was a strong verbal blow—a risk Fey might not have taken—but it was too late to take it back.

Tears began to leak silently from the corners of April's eyes, but she appeared to maintain her composure. "They came and slaughtered us like pigs in the street," she said. "My father, my mother, my brothers. Everyone except for Ignacio and me."

"How did you escape?" Fey asked. She hoped to keep April's

story moving, not give the woman time to dwell on the horror of the situation.

"Ignacio had taken me to town to do the shopping. It was not a chore he liked, but he was the youngest of my brothers." April pulled the blankets more tightly around her shoulders and appeared to sink into their folds. "We returned after the killings. The Santiagos had left three men behind to kill Ignacio and me when we returned, but Ignacio was more than they were. He killed two of them, and I . . . I killed the other." April's hesitation was only minimal before she made her declaration of murder with a twist of arrogance.

Fey and Rhonda remained silent. There was no passing of judgment, neither one knowing what she might have done in the same circumstance.

"Ignacio was also a coyote," April said. The term coyote referred to somebody who was paid to smuggle illegal immigrants across the border into the United States. "He knew the paths through the hills and across the border. I was angry with him because he would not stay to bury our family, but I also knew he was right. If we had stayed, we would also have died."

"What happened when you came to California?" Fey asked, still trying to keep the story moving along.

"We came to Los Angeles. Ignacio knew some Catalan people here and they took us in. Once I was safe, Ignacio wanted to return to Mexico to take revenge, but I begged him not to go—not to leave me. He was the only blood I had left in the world. I could not stand the thought of losing him as well."

Strangely, April appeared to find strength in telling her story. It was as if sharing the horrors of her past was somehow relieving her of their burdens—distancing her from the overwhelming pressures that had brought her to her current state.

"How did you and Ignacio become involved with Alex?" Fey asked.

April actually wadded up spital in her throat and expectorated onto the tiled floor of the interrogation room. "I'm glad he's dead," she said. The ferocity of her words was daunting. "He was a filthy dog who would do anything if it got him what he wanted. Ignacio did not go back to Mexico, but the Catalan people would not let us stay with them unless Ignacio worked for them. He agreed, and began helping to rob jewelry salesmen downtown."

Fey had heard about the teams of thieves who preyed on the jewelry salesmen who plied their trade by carrying their wares from store to store. The salesmen's merchandise was usually carried in oversized, rectangular black suitcases, marking them as a target every time they exited their cars or came out of a business. Thieves, working in packs of three to five, would follow a target until an opportunity presented itself for them to snatch the case of jewelry. Most times, the cases were stolen without incident, but sometimes the crimes became physically violent—the gang of thieves leaving the salesman dead or injured in the street.

"Alex caught Ignacio and two other Catalan men stealing a jewelry case. Ignacio knew that without him, I would have no choice but to become a *puta* for the Catalans, so he offered Alex a deal."

"What kind of a deal?" Rhonda asked when April paused. She already suspected what was coming.

"Ignacio became a *puta* for Alex," April said simply. Both Fey and Rhonda knew she wasn't talking about a sexual whore, but an information whore—a snitch.

"He should have gone to jail," April continued. "Alex kept pushing Ignacio. If he didn't give information, Alex would tell the Catalan people about Ignacio and they would kill him. Alex also found out about me, and what had happened to our family. He used all of it to make Ignacio dance.

"It was very dangerous. I begged Ignacio to stop, but he couldn't. He tried to get away by promising Alex a big arrest. He had heard about a gang on the streets that were using guns to steal cars from people."

Fey caught Rhonda's eye. April was talking about the carjacking ring Alex had broken while working RHD with Hale and Keegan.

"Alex said he would stay away from Ignacio if he gave him the information on the car stealers. I don't know. I guess it was a big deal or something." For a woman raised in an atmosphere where beatings, maimings, and murder appeared to have been commonplace, stealing cars did not seem to be of consequence—even if it was done at gunpoint. "For a while, we didn't hear nothing from Alex, but then he grabbed Ignacio again one day and everything started over again."

"What did Alex want?" Fey probed gently.

April moved around again in her blankets. "When will I get to see my baby?" she asked. "Am I going to be kept in jail?"

"You answer our questions first," Fey said, "and then we'll see what we can do about your situation and your baby."

"You are all the same," April said. Contempt was clear in her voice. "You only take, you never give. You want me to think you care, but you don't."

Fey knew it was useless to argue. There was a thin thread of truth in April's statement, but it neglected to consider that Ignacio was not an unfortunate, innocent bystander. He had been a murderer and a thief and probably got what he deserved in the way of justice—live by the sword, die by the sword.

Fey decided to play the game the only way April would understand. "You're wrong," she told April. "I'm worse than Alex. I control whether you will ever see your baby again. I control whether you will ever get out of jail again." None of that was true, but April's life experiences would make her believe it was. "Now tell me what Alex wanted." Her tone was icy.

April looked down at the floor, staring at her slippered feet sticking out from under the blankets. "He wanted Ignacio to go after a man at the school."

"UCLA?"

"Yes." April's answer was given reluctantly.

Fey stood up. "Cut the crap, April. You know damn well the man Alex sent your brother after was Lucian Santiago."

April shrugged. "Okay. Sure. You say so."

"You can also cut the broken-English stuff. You don't have any problem speaking English. You know it, and we know it."

"You know why they say Mexicans are like cue balls?" April asked suddenly, her English almost accentless. She didn't wait before providing her own punch line. "Because the harder you hit them, the more English you get out of them." She didn't pause for laughter. "You going to hit me? You going to beat me up if I don't talk to you?" The aggressive attitude was bringing color to April's face.

Fey sat down, trying to cool the atmosphere and take control of the interview again. She rethought her earlier resolve about keeping Ignacio's death from April, and decided to go for the shock factor.

"Ignacio is dead, April."

April gasped, reacting as if Fey had hit her. "No!"

"Yes," Fey said, nodding her head. "And if Lucian Santiago didn't kill him directly, he at least had a hand in the murder."

April had begun to cry.

"There is nobody left for you now but your baby," Fey said. "And there will be nobody left for your baby if you don't help us because you'll be rotting in jail." Half-lies and half-truths, all tools available to a good interrogator with no conscience. Fey pushed her self-loathing aside and forged ahead. "Why did you marry Alex?"

The question appeared to catch April off guard. "Because of Ignacio."

"I don't understand."

"Alex wanted Ignacio to go after Lucian, but Ignacio refused to do so unless Alex would marry me."

"Why?"

"Because Ignacio knew Lucian would kill him if he found out who he was, and then there would be nobody to take care of me. I was an illegal. Without Ignacio, the Catalan people would have put me on the street—just another *puta* for them."

Fey tried to follow the train of Ignacio's thinking. "And Ignacio believed that if you were married to Alex you would be safe?"

"Yes. Married to an American, I would be an American as well. I could not be made to go back to Mexico. If something happened to Ignacio, I would not have to become a *puta*. Alex would be forced to take care of me."

Fey shook her head at April's naivete and lack of sophistication, coupled with the woman's cold disregard for human ethics. April felt it was fine for her father and brothers to murder and rob, but a husband had a duty to protect his wife—even if the marriage was nothing more than a business arrangement.

"It didn't work that way, though, did it?" Fey said.

April shook her head. "Alex married me because Ignacio refused to work for Alex any other way. At first we thought the laugh was on Alex because, I knew, Ignacio would go after Lucian Santiago for his own revenge. But Alex didn't care about marriage. It meant nothing to him—less than nothing." The tears had begun again.

"Did he hit you?"

April shook her head and sniffed. "No. He didn't care enough to hit me. Sometimes he was nice to me and took me places. He even took me once to a party at his work." April's eyes cleared slightly with the memory. "But usually he just left me to do nothing. He would use me like a *puta*."

"What did he do when you told him you were pregnant?"

"I didn't tell him at first because I knew he would make me get rid of it. When he found out, he did try, but I told him I would kill him in his sleep if he made me lose the baby. He laughed at me, but he didn't do anything about the baby. I hated him for what he did to me. I hated him for what he did to Ignacio."

"And when the pictures were sent to you?"

"I knew they must have tortured Ignacio to find out about me. I knew they would be coming for me next. And I knew it was Alex's fault."

It was April's turn to stand up. In a quiet but firm voice, she stated, "I would have killed him even if they hadn't told me I had to do it."

51

IN HIS Parker Center office, Vaughn Harrison was feeling the pressure. For the first time in his life, he thought he might not succeed. That he had underestimated Croaker from the start was something that churned in his guts. He had been blind to her stubbornness and her resourcefulness.

He pushed around the paperwork on his desk, not really seeing any of it, his mind a Machiavellian labyrinth. When the murder of Alex Waverly occurred, he'd had his hooks into the personnel at RHD. It could all have been handled smoothly if they had been allowed to investigate the situation per standard operating procedures.

Providence had even presented the stupid Mexican wife as the perfect scapegoat. With Keegan and Hale in charge, April Waverly would have gone down for the murder of her husband and nobody would have blinked an eye.

Without the wife, it would still have been easy—a simple heart attack. Nothing more. With Harrison's tame RHD detectives in charge, the body would have been shifted to a coroner who wasn't too particular about his work, and bingo—death by natural causes. No fuss. No muss. Obstacle overcome. The threat of Los Juniors neutralized.

Even if the digoxin overdose had been discovered for some reason, then suicide was an easy verdict. After all, Waverly had been under a lot of stress lately. Everyone at ATD could have testified to that fact, and the termination of the brother, Ignacio Ramos—Waverly's personal mockingbird—would have assured that nobody disagreed with the determination.

Harrison had to give the chief credit for not going down without a fight. No opponent worth crushing ever did.

At first, when the chief removed the investigation of Waverly's death from RHD, Harrison had been frustrated and wary. But when the investigation was assigned to Croaker, Harrison had relaxed. He knew her track record. She'd worked a couple of high-profile cases, but so had every homicide unit supervisor. He'd felt she could be handled, controlled, or coerced.

He'd been wrong, though, and now he was close to paying the price. He could still beat her, but it was going to be very, very close. The blinders of his greater vision had focused him on the chief as his opponent, but with hindsight he could see how Croaker presented much more of a threat.

She had undermined his people at RHD. She had John Dancer on the ropes. She had overcome every effort he'd made to block the investigation, and she had personally thrown the gauntlet at his feet.

Harrison still believed in himself. He still believed in the greater vision he saw for Los Angeles and his role in that vision. He was right, damn it! He knew he was right. The wolves could not be allowed to run free in the streets. Gangs, narcotics, home invasions, street robberies, drive-by shootings, muggings, rapes, self-serving politicians, agenda-waving anarchists—they were everywhere, and without a strong leader, the department would crumble under the pressure.

The chief was just another self-important bureaucrat, not a cop. He cared only about his personal itinerary, a presidential appointment, perhaps, or a bid for mayor, then governor. His performance had shown he didn't care about the city. As for the men and women who worked for him, he exploited them at the merest whim.

Harrison caressed his clawed hand with the fingers of his other hand. The movements were gentle as if the two appendages were lovers seeking solace from each other. Staring at his hands, Harrison searched his conscience for the answer.

He was right, he eventually decided. He had to stand firm and follow through on his plan. If it all went to hell, he'd decide what action to take at that time.

Neutralizing Fey Croaker was Harrison's current top priority, and he had a pair of blunt instruments available to do the job. He picked up the phone and punched in the number of P. J. Hunter's pager.

Picking up the phone again, he called John Dancer. It was time to see what side of the line the man was on. Dancer's predecessor, Ron Harper, had come up on the wrong side. If Dancer didn't come up right, then he would have to be dealt with in a similar fashion.

Risks had to be taken, and the city couldn't afford for him to lose.

"The man is crazy!" John Dancer said to Mary DeFalco, his mind whirling with what Harrison had told him.

"Calm down," Mary said. She came around his desk, behind his chair, and placed her hands on his shoulders. She kneaded knotted muscles with strong fingers. "What's going on?"

Dancer stood up and began pacing. "He's mad—stark, raving mad."

"Who is?"

"Harrison, who else?" His stomach juices gurgled and the urge was on him to flatuate. "He's intent on going through with this craziness involving Los Juniors. He's going to let this Lucian Santiago character commit a terrorist act in the city to prove the chief can't keep the citizens safe."

"He can't keep them safe," Mary said. "And we're all aware that he can't. Perhaps this is the best thing."

"The best thing! How can you say such a thing? People could be killed! Harrison expects me to feed the criminal conspiracy section false information, keep them away from Lucian Santiago or any connections to Los Juniors."

"You can do that easily. With the help of P.J. and T-Bone, CCS will never catch on that you're leading them astray."

Dancer threw his hands up. "That's not the point. The man is talking about allowing murder to be committed." Dancer was terrified of Harrison, but he was finding something at the root of his own being that was finally rebelling.

"John," Mary DeFalco's voice was unruffled, "sometimes blood has to be spilled in order that more blood is not."

Dancer shook his head at the remark. "You're talking about the end justifying the means. Life doesn't work that way."

"Of course it does, and it has throughout the course of history."

"So what are you saying? Hitler was right?"

"Don't be stupid. What I'm saying is that Vaughn Harrison will one day be running this department. If you help him now, he'll help you later. Think about what it could mean for us. We could get rid of your wife. Harrison could move you rapidly up through the ranks. We could be together." She moved toward Dancer and wrapped herself around him. "And I know that's what Mama's little boy wants more than anything." She placed her mouth full over his, wide open and tongue thrusting.

Dancer felt himself spinning out of control. His erection was threatening to burst through the fabric of his pants. He wanted Mary DeFalco more than he'd wanted anything in his life, but at what cost?

With an effort Dancer disengaged his lips. "Mary, we can't let him do this. It's not right. Harrison thinks it is, but I've sworn to protect the people of this city."

Mary almost laughed. "And when has that vow ever been important to you?"

Dancer gave her an odd look. "I don't know," he said. "I've never been in a position that has tested it before."

Mary was sensing that her control over Dancer was not going to be enough to keep him in line. The stupid bastard was actually getting moralistic on her. He was a man who could only do it once a night, and he thought he could stand up to the power of a man, a true man, like Vaughn Harrison. He even thought she loved him because she screwed his puny little brains out. The stupid man couldn't see beyond the end of his pecker.

"Mary, you've got to see that what he's doing is wrong. This has all gone too far. I don't know who killed Alex Waverly, or how Danny Ochoa came to fall off Bunch Hall, but it's all got to be connected to Los Juniors, and Vaughn Harrison is in league with them."

"What are you going to do?"

"I don't know."

Mary knew what she had to do, however. Vaughn was relying on her and she wouldn't let him down. "Why don't you tell Fey Croaker?"

Dancer looked at the woman who had made him feel things he'd never felt before. She didn't know it, but through her love, he'd uncovered this newfound strength. "Do you think she would listen?"

"Of course."

Dancer made to pick up the phone on his desk, but Mary stopped him from lifting the receiver. "Not the phone," she said. "Harrison could have it bugged."

Dancer's eyes went a bit wild with paranoia, sweeping the office. If Mary thought the phone could be bugged, if she thought Harrison was that powerful, then the whole office could be bugged. "We've got to get out of here." He grabbed Mary's hand and pulled her out of the office with him.

It was late on Saturday, and the outer office was empty.

Striding down the long exit corridor, Dancer could feel the warmth of Mary's hand in his. He felt excitement building in his belly. He didn't know what he was going to do about his cold bitch of a wife, but he and Mary had to be together.

Outside the division's security door, Dancer headed for the elevator, but Mary pulled him to a stop by the stairwell.

"Not the elevator," she said. "It's too slow. Let's take the stairs."

"It's seven floors."

"Better seven floors than having Harrison turn up while we're waiting for the elevator doors to open."

Mary's argument made a demented kind of sense. Dancer turned to the door leading to the stairwell and pushed his way through.

The stairs were seldom used this high up in the building, and it was not unusual, especially as late in the day as it was, to find nobody in the stairwell.

"Hurry," Mary said. The urgency in her voice was all part of her plan. I should have been on stage, she thought.

Dancer's quickly moving feet fled down the first half-flight of stairs and turned to go down the second half-flight to the next floor.

Reaching the landing of the sixth floor, Mary urged Dancer on: "Faster, John. I'm scared."

With Mary following on his heels, Dancer picked up speed. As they turned from the landing of the fifth floor to the first half-flight of stairs leading down to the fourth, Dancer was almost overbalancing in his haste.

With deliberation, Mary DeFalco kicked out with the toes of her right foot and tapped Dancer's trailing right heel. As Dancer rapidly brought his right foot forward, it caught behind his left ankle.

Dancer tipped forward, scrambling for balance.

Mary placed her hand in the center of his back and shoved for all she was worth.

With a small scream, Dancer crashed down on the concrete stairs headfirst. His body rolled, over and over, his momentum sending him around the bend in the stairwell and down the second half-flight of stairs.

Mary followed rapidly after the body. On the fourth-floor landing, she didn't hesitate. She could not tell for sure if Dancer had broken his neck and was dead or merely unconscious.

Taking the 9-millimeter Smith & Wesson from Dancer's hip holster, she held it by the barrel and delivered a crushing single blow to the soft part of the cranium just above Dancer's neck. She wiped the pistol clean on the tail of her blouse and returned it to its holster.

Then, taking a deep, calming breath, she threw herself down on the body of her dead lover and began to scream.

52

$\mathcal{S}$OMETIMES AN interview becomes an interrogation, and sometimes the opposite is true. On rare occasions, the fluctuation
between the accusatory interrogation and the information-gathering
interview ebbs and flows as if it were a constantly changing tide.

Interrogations and interviews are an art, a ballet between interrogator and suspect or interviewer and witness that combines the
skills of verbal swordplay, body language interpretation, subtle physical and environmental intimidation, and mental domination.

Through their verbal pursuit of April Waverly, Fey and Rhonda
had gained an important piece of the puzzle, but they needed more.

Fey knew Vaughn Harrison's goal was to pull off a palace coup and
become chief of police. Fey was further convinced Harrison was
manipulating Lucian Santiago and Los Juniors in an effort to
achieve his own aspirations. It was Rhonda, however, who had earlier
suggested that a terrorist action within the city of Los Angeles would
change the current chief's position from tenuous to untenable.

Even a low-scale terrorist action could be used to prove the
chief's community-friendly approach to police work was unsuited for
the demands of safety required in a major city. It was also the type of
action Vaughn Harrison could manipulate from afar through Lucian
Santiago and Los Juniors. The trick came in identifying possible terrorist targets that would both appeal to Lucian Santiago and serve
Vaughn Harrison's purposes.

Ethan Kelso had been correct in his analysis that the Central American Solidarity Conclave was the only possible target currently in the area that might have even a remote connection to Lucian Santiago and Los Juniors. The conclave, which was successfully winding down, had little of consequence left on its agenda beyond its participants attending the Mexico-U.S. soccer match at the Coliseum on the following day.

At the time Ethan had presented this information, nobody had been able to see a further connection. However, with his usual efficiency, Kelso had provided a list of all the ambassadors and staff who were attending the conclave.

Fey had brought a copy of the list with her to the interview with April Waverly. One of the names might mean something to April.

When she was asked to look at the list, April was reluctant and only gave the names on the paper a cursory glance. Her emotions were in so much of an uproar it was difficult for her to concentrate.

Fey's frustration was mounting. She could sense time was running out in the case and there was more at stake than simply solving a murder. Fey had a perception of foreboding, as if waiting for the other shoe to fall. Anticipation roiled in the pit of her stomach. Murder was usually the end of a bad sequence of events, but Fey was sure the murder of Alex Waverly was only a step on the way to a far greater tragedy. Somehow, she had to find a way to stop the omen from completing its cycle.

When April wouldn't cooperate, Fey began reading the names off the list aloud. She didn't believe it would help, but she didn't know what else to do.

The names droned around the small interview room, bouncing off April with no visible effect. The small Mexican woman sat with her head bent, hair falling forward to distort her features.

The names went on as Fey continued down the list of conclave participants.

Suddenly, April looked up, her eyes startled.

Fey was not watching the woman and continued reading names off the list until Rhonda stopped her by putting her hand on Fey's shoulder. Fey paused in her recitation, and quickly picked up on April's change of expression.

"What is it? Do you recognize a name?"

April nodded. "Yes. You said Ricardo Alamar?"

Fey checked the list. Alamar was three names back from where she had stopped reading. He was listed as the attaché to the ambassador from Mexico City. "Yes. That's a name on the list. Do you know him?"

"I have an uncle with that name. He is my mother's brother. He lives in Mexico City."

"Do you know what he does?"

April had shaken her head. "No. I haven't seen him since I was a little girl."

Fey's expression was thoughtful. "The Santiagos—the people who killed your family—"

"I know who they are!" April's outraged reaction was filled with hatred and spite. "You think I do not know who the Santiagos are? You think I do not remember the bloody corpses of my own family?"

Fey held up her hands. "I'm sorry. I was only trying to be sensitive to the situation. I'm sure you're well aware of the Santiagos. What I want to know is how far would Lucian Santiago go to kill another person related to the Ramos family? Would he kill your uncle if given the chance?"

"Of course," April said. "This is a blood feud. It will run until one family is completely wiped from the face of the earth. Why do you think Ignacio would risk his life to try and bring Lucian Santiago down?"

"If Ignacio was that determined to kill Lucian, why couldn't he have simply walked up to him on campus and gunned him down?" Fey asked.

"Because Lucian had too many bodyguards with him all the time." April hesitated for a second. "And because of me. I once heard Alex tell Ignacio if he did not do as Alex told him, Alex would turn me over to Lucian Santiago to do with as he pleased."

"So, if somebody found out that Lucian was planning to kill your uncle, and they promised to smooth the way for Lucian—help him kill your uncle here in Los Angeles and get away again—Lucian would have jumped at the opportunity?" Fey asked.

"Of course," April said, as if Fey and Rhonda were particularly slow children. "Just like I would do anything to kill Lucian Santiago."

Rhonda tried a change of tack. "I understand that Ignacio pushed Alex Waverly into marrying you, but why did you go along with the program?"

April shrugged. "What else could I do? I was in this country illegally. I had no money. There were people after me who would kill me if they found me. I did not have a lot of choices."

"You were also already pregnant with Alex's baby, weren't you?" Fey asked more gently.

April cast her eyes downward again and began fiddling with the coarse material of her hospital gown. "Yes," she said. "I was infatuated with him. I met him after Ignacio began working for him. I did not understand the pressure he was putting on Ignacio. He was a strong, powerful American. A policeman. I thought he could keep me safe. I gave myself to him willingly, and when I became pregnant I was so excited. I thought Alex would love me and take care of me—it was also his baby."

Fey exchanged glances with Rhonda. For her part, Rhonda had involuntarily slipped a hand across the secret in her own womb.

April moved the hair out of her face with long, nail-bitten fingers. "Alex helped me to get false papers to protect me from the Santiagos. When we were married in the courthouse, I was so happy. I didn't know about Ignacio making a deal with Alex to make Alex marry me. I thought Alex loved me and wanted the baby." April trailed off and went silent.

"What went wrong?" Fey asked.

"I don't know. Alex became abusive. He used me like a *puta* until the baby began to show, then he went with other women."

"You knew?"

April laughed. "How could I not know? He flaunted them in my face. Told me I would be out on the street as soon as he was done with Ignacio."

"Did he tell you about his deal with Ignacio?"

"Yes." April had started to cry silently.

"Did you talk to Ignacio about this situation?"

April sniffed. "No. Ignacio was gone. Alex told me he was under-cover doing something for him. I was so scared."

Fey put her arms around April again. "And then what happened?"

"And then the pictures came—the pictures of Ignacio being tor-tured by Lucian! I knew I had to do what the note said. I had to try to help Ignacio!"

Fey turned the interview away from Ignacio—not wanting April to dwell on her brother's fate. "These other women Alex was seeing, who were they?"

"I don't know, I don't know."

"Come on, April. Help me out here. Did you know them? Did Alex talk about them? You said he flaunted them in front of you."

"He would talk to them on the telephone—love talk, dirty talk. I heard him. I would come into the room and he wouldn't even stop. He would stand there talking to his *putas* watching me."

"Did he mention any names?"

April shook her head. "I don't remember. But there was one who seemed special."

"How about a Gina? Did you hear him talk about a Gina Kane?"

"No."

Fey cast about her memory, searching for another link, another name. The memory of Linda Harper's angst-filled voice ran through her head: *You see, Vaughn Harrison killed my husband, along with that little slut of his, Mary DeFalco.*

That statement connected with other random memory bytes— Mary DeFalco on John Dancer's arm at Waverly's funeral. Mary and Dancer almost caught in a sexual clinch when Fey entered Dancer's office unannounced.

"How about the name Mary?"

April suddenly looked as if she was going to spit. "Yes. The oth-ers he would laugh about, but that one, I think she had him by the *cojones.*"

53

I T WAS late enough in the afternoon to be considered early evening when Fey convened a council of war in the captain's office. All of the team had returned to the station feeling the same anticipation as Fey. Time was running out. The conference table was piled with coffee cups, soda cans, and ordered-in pizza and salads.

Fey and Rhonda knew they would soon be forced to release April Waverly. Legally, however, they didn't have to do anything before Monday morning, and holding her in the jail ward over the weekend was the best way to keep her safe and out of the way. April's release would bring with it a fanfare of press interest. More of the facts behind Waverly's murder would be brought out, and the resulting media circus was something to be avoided for as long as possible.

While returning from interviewing April, Fey again sensed that she was being followed.

Rhonda caught Fey watching the rearview mirror more intently than normal. "Blue Plymouth, about four cars back, number-two lane—been with us since we pulled out of the parking lot," she said.

"Yeah," said Fey. "I've sensed them around before now, but couldn't get a visual fix."

"I felt the same way. Do you think they're letting us know they're there?"

"Possibly," Fey said. "Somehow, I don't get the feeling they're a threat. More like guardian angels."

"Do you know who they are?"

Fey twisted her mouth slightly as if in thought. "Maybe."

"Yeah. Me too," Rhonda agreed, well aware she was on the same wavelength as Fey. "You thinking of losing them?"

"Not really. It doesn't make much sense. If they wanted to find us again, we'd be easy to pick up. I vote we let them sit for now."

Having made their decision, neither Fey nor Rhonda spotted the blue Plymouth again on the ride back to the station. They both felt their shadow was still with them, but it had returned to being invisible.

In the captain's office, Fey soon brought everyone up to speed on the interview with April Waverly.

Alphabet and Brindle provided input from Ethan Kelso and Thistle One. In the aftermath of what had happened to the Thistle One surveillance team in Tijuana, Ethan Kelso had tapped into the intelligence grapevine for information. Money, as always, went a long way toward loosening the mouths of the local reporters and Thistle One's Mexican police contacts.

First, Ethan had reminded Fey, through Alphabet and Brindle, that the price tag on their venture was rising rapidly, depleting the chief's slush fund. Then came the information about Blue MacKenzie's driving skills bouncing Lucian Santiago off the bumper of the Dodge Ram pickup and flinging him into the shelving of the glass-blowers' market.

The injuries should have been painful, but minimal. However, the truth was far more serious. Both Lucian's hip and left leg had been shattered and, more seriously, a rib had splintered and pierced a lung. His chances of survival were currently touch-and-go.

"That should upset any plans Harrison may have involving Lucian Santiago," Brindle said. "With Alphabet grabbing the brief-cases containing the money and explosives, I think you can rule out any immediate comeback from that end of the equation." A note of pride in her voice made it clear she was on Alphabet's side in the should-he-have-grabbed-the-briefcases or shouldn't-he-have-grabbed-the-briefcases? argument.

Fey scratched at her head. "I think you're right up to a point. It sounds as if Lucian is going to be out of commission at least long enough for us to make sure he's made persona non grata if he tries to come back across the border. Somehow, though, I don't see Vaughn Harrison being the type of personality to give up on his plans so quickly. Things may be more dangerous for him now—he may have to get his own hands dirty instead of manipulating Lucian and Los Juniors—but he's hanging out too far to pull back now."

The "explosives" in the briefcase Alphabet had taken from Lucian Santiago had turned out to be nothing more lethal than canisters of CS tear gas and smoke bombs. Still illegal, but not quite as deadly as first believed. The money, two hundred and fifty thousand dollars, was impressive but not over the top. Fey knew she had better keep it under lock and key before it became a contribution to the chief's slush fund.

The Thistle One research people had also been busy checking connections between the Central American Solidarity Conclave and the Santiago and Ramos families. Ricardo Alamar was indeed April Waverly's uncle, but none of the other participants had any ties to the two families.

Alamar was a rising star in the Mexican national government, a conservative, with apparently the best interests of the people at heart. If indeed he were the target of assassins, his murder would strike another shattering blow at the already precarious Mexican political structure.

For his part, Monk brought to the table information concerning Keegan and Hale. When he was unable to produce a lead on P. J. Hunter or T-Bone Rawlings, Monk had gone to visit Keegan's ex-wife.

"Her name is Donna, and she told me she's been divorced from Keegan for almost a year. Work stress had taken its toll on their relationship, and Keegan appeared to become more and more depressed. He was drinking heavily. Donna said she still loved him, but couldn't live with him anymore."

"I take it there's more to the traditional story," Fey said. The failed-relationship tune was familiar to most detectives.

Monk wrapped his hands around a half-full soda can on the table in front of him. "Donna eventually told me her daughter, Lyric, had recently been threatened on the way home from school. Lyric is fifteen and takes the public bus home from the local high school."

"Threatened?" Fey asked.

"More like intimidation," Monk told her. "The bus was crowded, and Lyric found herself stuck standing between two men. She describes one as short and mean looking, and the other one as being built like a boulder."

"No points for guessing who those players are," Rhonda said.

Monk nodded. "Apparently, the boulder placed something sharp between Lyric's shoulder blades while the short one rubbed himself against her and touched her breasts and buttocks."

Fey closed her eyes and shook her head. "Oh, gross. The other people on the bus didn't say anything?"

"They either didn't see or didn't want to get involved. When he was done with his little physical games, the short one reached around and removed the clip from Lyric's hair. It was then sent to Keegan with a note about how vulnerable his daughter was in today's world."

"Cute," Fey said. "A fancy way of saying if you make waves your daughter will pay the price."

"You think that's what made Keegan call you?" Rhonda asked.

"Probably," Fey said.

"What about Hale?" Rhonda pressed.

"I asked Donna about Hale," Monk said. "She told me Hale is Lyric's godfather. Puts him in almost the same boat as Keegan."

Hammer came back into the room after having gone to relieve himself. His face was grave. "I just heard a news flash on the urinal grapevine. John Dancer fell down a flight of stairs at Parker Center and crushed his skull."

"You're kidding?" Fey said, in shock. "What happened?"

"Mary DeFalco was with him," Hammer explained. "She's claiming Dancer tripped and went ass over tea kettle. It was all a big accident."

"Like hell," Fey said.

"You're saying Dancer was pushed?" Brindle asked.

"And I'm saying Mary DeFalco pushed him," Fey said. She and Rhonda brought everyone on board with what they had learned about Mary DeFalco's involvement with Ron Harper, Alex Waverly, and Vaughn Harrison.

"What is it we always say?" Rhonda asked. "'In police work, the easy answer is usually the correct answer.'"

"Rhonda's right," Fey said. "Mary DeFalco keeps turning up all over this investigation. Okay, Vaughn Harrison is the mover and shaker behind the scenes, with Hunter and Rawlings as the battering rams. Somewhere, though, there is a more subtle, much more dangerous entity. My money says it's Mary DeFalco."

Fey stood up and began to walk around the conference table. She talked as she walked.

"Linda Harper damn near accused Mary DeFalco of pulling the trigger when her husband committed suicide," Fey said. "That's tough to prove, however." Fey picked up her coffee cup and walked over to fill it from the pot on a temporary hot plate. "I also saw DeFalco hanging all over John Dancer at Waverly's funeral, and almost caught them going at it when I walked into Dancer's office unannounced. Now we find out she's the only witness to Dancer falling to his death in the Parker Center stairwell. Did he fall, or was he pushed? Again, hard if not impossible to prove."

"Harper was definitely on the edge when he committed suicide," Rhonda filled in. "He knew something bad was going on at ATD, and he was being sucked into it. He couldn't do anything about it, and the guilt led him to eat his gun."

"Maybe John Dancer couldn't handle the pressure either," Hammer said. "What if he was also having an affair with DeFalco and told her he was going to spill the beans?"

"A little extra momentum is applied as he goes down the stairs and, bingo!"

"How could she be sure the fall would kill him?" Brindle asked.

"How would you be sure?" Fey asked her.

Brindle thought for a moment and then replied, "If the stairwell was empty, I'd hit him on the head with something hard. There would be no way to tell the injury wasn't caused by the fall."

"Maybe we need to look for that something hard—see if there is any trace evidence," Rhonda agreed.

Fey had returned to her chair but did not sit down. Instead, she stood looking at her unit, the cogs of her brain almost visibly turning. "April Waverly also tells us that DeFalco was having an affair with Alex. Here's a woman screwing everything in sight that could possibly have an effect on whatever Vaughn Harrison was up to. There's more than a good chance she's giving her all for a man who is manipulating her as if she were a rag doll. It's clear she has an effect on men. Harrison could have been aiming her like a gun at any man he perceived as a threat."

"And when that threat proved to be valid," Rhonda said, "Mary DeFalco was more than happy to remove it."

"Why would she do it?" Alphabet asked.

"You don't understand the first thing about women, partner," Brindle told him. "She did it for love or for power, both of which she planned on getting from Vaughn Harrison."

"How do you figure?" Alphabet persisted.

Brindle gave him a patronizing look. "Because, honey, power turns women on, especially a woman like Mary DeFalco, whose only personal power comes from what she can offer a man between her legs. She wasn't doing all of this for herself, she was doing it for a man with power, and Vaughn Harrison is the only one in the equation who fits the bill."

"I've had a thought," Fey said. She turned to Monk. "When you checked with the pharmacy that refilled Waverly's digoxin, did you ask them how long it had been since his previous refill?"

"It didn't occur to me," Monk said.

"Nor to any of us," Fey agreed. "But if Waverly was having sex with Mary DeFalco, she could have had access to both his digoxin and his water bottle."

"I'll get on to the pharmacy right away," Monk told her. "The information will be somewhere in their records."

Fey switched her gaze to Hammer and then seemed to stop in her tracks.

Hammer caught her look and quickly interpreted it. "I swept the phone lines and the room earlier today. No signs of any bugs. I'd say we were clear."

"Good man," Fey told him. "Now I want you to prepare a search warrant for Mary DeFalco's residence, office desk, station locker, and anywhere else where she might have storage access."

"What are we looking for?"

"Leftover digoxin, the old bottle that contained the pills, maybe notes or tapes. She's a controlling bitch and she's not stupid. She knows men. Just because she may be in love with Vaughn Harrison or enamored by his power doesn't mean she hasn't taken steps to protect herself should he try to disentangle himself from her. I have a feeling she's even more Machiavellian than he is, and maybe more dangerous."

"When do you want to serve the warrants?"

Fey turned to Rhonda. "Why don't you and I pay her an early morning visit and bring her down to the station. The warrants can be served while we're interrogating her."

"On what charge?"

"We don't need to charge her to interrogate her, and she's just become the number one suspect in Alex Waverly's murder."

54

As Fey pulled into the driveway of her house, she could feel exhaustion flowing over her. She parked the car in the garage, turned the engine off, and slumped back in the seat. She felt too tired even to make the effort to get out and go into the house. She closed her eyes for a moment, and used the lever on the side of the car seat to recline the back to a more comfortable position.

Just five minutes, she thought. Just five minutes' rest, and then I'll go inside.

The driver's side window was open, and Fey could hear the ticking of the cooling engine. The light on the garage door opener clicked off automatically and the garage went dark. The door to the garage was still open, however, and the cool air stopped Fey from drifting completely off to sleep.

I'm getting old, she thought. I can still play the game, but I'm getting old and tired. Still not feeling up to leaving the car, she squirmed to get more comfortable in the bucket seat.

Before the council of war at the station had broken up, several other items of business had been settled and acted upon. Even though Lucian Santiago appeared to be out of commission, Ricardo Alamar was still a possible terrorist target. If other members of Los Juniors could be compelled to take action without Lucian—or if Harrison decided to take events into his own hands by directly using Hunter and Rawlings—an assassination attempt could still be mounted at the Mexico-U.S. soccer match.

If Alamar were to be assassinated while in Los Angeles, the chief would have no choice but to let the LAPD's Anti-Terrorist Division investigate. Fey's unit couldn't use what they had seen in Mexico against Hunter and Rawlings without admitting to their own actions in that country. Without that evidence, though, there was no viable proof that ATD and Harrison were involved behind the scenes in the event.

With Harrison manipulating the investigation, he could easily lead a hue and cry that would make sure the chief would be forced to resign, or at the very least not receive reappointment.

Events showed that murder was not beyond the scope of Harrison's actions. If he double-crossed Los Juniors, or found a suitable patsy to pin the assassination on, there was no doubt Harrison would arrange it so the suspects did not get to trial.

With the chief out, and ATD receiving kudos all around for solving the case and blasting the bad guys, Harrison could write his own ticket with the police commission and the city council. He'd be chief of police before the corpses were cold.

To stop this scenario in its tracks, Fey directed Monk to alert the State Department to the possibility of the assassination attempt on Alamar. Officials from State wouldn't waste a second inventing a debilitating sickness that would have Alamar on the next plane back to Mexico.

Whatever Harrison was planning would at least be minimized by Alamar's return to Mexico. But Fey and her people had to stay on the ball in case Harrison had a contingency plan.

There were also several murders left to solve, not to mention the need to cut out the cancer represented by Harrison and his followers and destroy it before it spread its tentacles further.

Fey and her unit had decided to start with Mary DeFalco in the morning. When they saw where that action led them, they would go after Hunter and Rawlings, and from there—maybe—to Harrison.

Fey had told the deputy chief that his plan was coming apart at the seams. It had been a bluff at the time, but now maybe it was true.

There was still a long way to go, however, before an end to the game could be called.

The unit also agreed to do a preemptive strike where the news media were concerned. The circumstances surrounding Alex Waverly's death were inevitably going to come out when April was released from jail on Monday, so Fey would make the announcement herself and put the situation in the best light possible.

Hammer had gone to check on Zelman Tucker's status. There was nobody better at exploiting the press to his own advantage than Tucker. Fey knew Tucker would still be expecting a book scoop out of this investigation, especially after the beating he'd taken. Fey would never admit it to the man's face, but while she found his manner unsettling and his glee in other people's tragedy unappealing, there was still something about the guy she liked and trusted.

Using Zelman as the conduit, many of the problems with the press could be diverted. The whole investigation to this point had been unorthodox, and Fey could see no reason to change things. She liked playing it fast and loose. The chief had given her carte blanche, and she was going to take advantage of it.

Fey and the other detectives on her unit didn't agree with the way the chief was changing the department, but in a battle to be the lesser of two evils, he won hands down over Harrison. Ends never justified the means—unless they were your means and your ends.

Stretching, Fey forced herself to wake up and get out of the car. She had to go in and see to the cats. She also needed to check on her horses. She needed to shower and wash her hair.

All she wanted to do was to collapse into bed.

The cats? What was it about the cats? Fey had been in the garage for ten minutes, and was surprised the two animals weren't sitting on the other side of the back door yowling at her. Normally, they started a commotion as soon as they heard the garage door open.

Groggy with fatigue, Fey ignored the warning and unlocked the door leading from the garage into the house. Entering, she pressed the button to close the exterior garage door.

When she didn't see the cats sitting on the rug of the short hall, she called out to them. "Brentwood? Marvella? Where are you guys?"

Slinging her purse off her shoulder, she stepped into the living room. Something else was wrong. The light she kept on an automatic timer was not off, but was no longer on its normal high setting—as if somebody had turned it off, then thought the better of it and turned it back on, but only to the first setting of the three-way bulb. Fey always kept it on high.

As she began to understand, it was already too late. Something punched her hard in the back of the head, and she pitched forward—not unconscious, but dazed.

Fey's knees hit the floor with the whole weight of her body on top of them. She felt cartilage twist and scrunch, bringing a flash of clarity back with the pain. Trying to roll, she flung out an arm for her purse and the backup gun it contained. A steel-toed boot came out of nowhere and buried its tip in her shoulder, paralyzing the action. The agony was excruciating.

Before Fey could turn to confront her assailant, she was assaulted from another direction. A heavy gauze bag—like a pillowcase with a drawstring around the opening—was pulled over her head, turning everything black. She felt the bag being tightened around her neck and, in a panic, flailed her functioning arm around to it. The steel-toed boot slammed into her other shoulder.

Fey screamed in agony when she was kicked, but the sound was slightly muffled by the bag over her head.

When nothing further happened for several seconds, she tried to keep her voice steady and ask, "What do you want?"

She was crying and her nose was stuffing up. She tried to raise her arms, but couldn't. The kicks had not been random. Both had hit nerve points and sent her shoulders into instant nonresponsive shock.

"What do you want?" she implored again. She wanted to yell, to scream, but felt she couldn't breathe. Images of being helpless at the rough hands of her father flashed through her mind in a mad kaleidoscope. She didn't know if she could live with being raped again.

There was still no verbal response from her attackers.

She tried to sit up.

A living line of agony slashed across her back, and she heard the material of the thin jacket and blouse she wore tear like tissue paper. She tried to scream, but no sound came out of her mouth.

Collapsing back to the floor, Fey tried to roll away from the pain, but another strip of torment lashed out and caught her across the breasts. Again, she heard the material of her blouse tearing. A sudden memory of the tatters of the clothing Zelman Tucker had been left with after his beating leapt into her consciousness.

Again and again, in an even, measured cadence, Fey felt the straps of wide whips bite into her flesh. Curled into a fetal position, she felt as if her skin was being flayed from her body. Her mind cried out for the bliss of unconsciousness, but the fresh agony of every lash stroke brought her screamingly back to reality.

She was whimpering, assaulted from every side, unable to run, retaliate, or recover any semblance of control. She regurgitated into the sack over her head, and thought she was going to choke on the vomit.

Dimly, she heard a crashing noise. In her compressed world of darkness and pain, she could not identify the sound. There were loud, angry voices, but she didn't understand the words.

An explosion, seeming to come from above her, immediately registered as a gunshot. She'd heard enough of them never to mistake the sound. There was a retaliating crack, and an immense weight fell across her, driving what little air was left in her body out of her lungs with a whoop.

She wanted to scream, cry, die, and could do none of them. Everything outside of her felt as if it were on fire. Everything inside felt crushed and twisted.

For the first time, it registered that the lashings had stopped, but there was still a cacophony of exterior sounds that could not penetrate their meaning to her scrambled brain.

A ripping sound was suddenly close to her ear, and something sharp touched her cheek in passing, causing her to flinch. The bag was pulled away from her head and there was glaring light and air, blessed air. She gulped the precious, cool, almost painfully soothing oxygen down her ragged windpipe, and struggled to focus her eyes.

Brain functions began kicking in, and Fey realized she was staring at her carpet. She tried to move, and when she couldn't, she screamed in terror.

"Wait, wait," a voice reached her from a distance, but she continued to scream until her throat closed involuntarily.

The great weight pinning her legs to the floor was rolled away, and hands turned her gently over.

"It's okay, Fey. It's going to be okay." The voice was clearer, male and soothing.

Her eyes began to operate, and Fey looked up to find herself cradled in the arms of Derek Keegan. He was crying as he tried to smooth hair and gore from her face.

"It's okay," he repeated. "You're going to be all right. It's over."

Fey couldn't talk. It wasn't over. Unanticipated pain suddenly engulfed her as the streaks of agony from the beating seemed to come alive in a blaze of flesh-searing fire.

Fey wanted to scream, but could only whimper pathetically. She writhed in misery, her eyes rolling up in her head as her body and mind shut down, setting her aboard the *Oblivion Express*.

55

"WHAT THE hell did I get hit with?" Fey asked. She was sitting carefully on the edge of an emergency room bed, her bare legs dangling toward the floor. The thin hospital gown she wore was untied at the back so not to irritate the long, red welts that crisscrossed her skin.

Derek Keegan handed Fey a two-inch-wide leather strap. Moving slowly, Fey took the strap in her hands, turning it back and forth to examine it. The pain in her shoulders, which had paralyzed her arms, still throbbed, but the agony was receding and she was slowly recovering the use of her limbs.

"Nasty," she said, running a finger along the thin metal stripping inlaid along the length of the strap's outer edges.

"That's what did most of the damage," Keegan said. "I know."

Fey looked up from the strap to stare directly at Keegan.

"The physical marks heal eventually," he said, but did not comment further.

Fey turned the strap over in her hands again. It was about thirty-six inches long, with holes in one end as if the leather had originally been destined to become a belt. One side was tanned a deep polished brown, the reverse was raw leather with the Spanish words ECHO EN MEXICO branded in. The thin, deadly metal edges ran along either side to a point six inches from the end, which the wielder could use as a handle.

Fey handed the belt to Monk, who was standing next to Keegan in the curtained cubicle. "Book it," she said, a physical tremor running through her. She felt weak, exhausted, but knew if she gave in to the fatigue she would be out of commission for a week—a luxury she couldn't afford. She deduced for herself that the beating was meant as much to get her off the playing field as punish her. However, she was not going to give in. She was much too stubborn. She'd played hurt before and still won, and she was determined this time would be no different.

She turned her attention back to Keegan. "As you can imagine," she said, "there are more than a couple of questions you and your partner need to answer."

There was a parting of the curtain screen and a young doctor stepped into the makeshift cubicle around Fey's hospital bed. "The answers will have to wait until I'm done," he said. "I've got an emergency room full of other sufferers who need attention, so I won't take long." He flicked a thumb at Monk and Keegan. "Out," he said, his tone commanding but not superior.

"You look younger than Doogie Howser," Fey said, as Monk's and Keegan's presence was replaced by that of a short, round nurse with dark hair. "Are you sure this guy's a doctor?" Fey asked the nurse.

"He's a doctor, all right," the nurse replied with a straight face. "His golf handicap is down to two, and his malpractice insurance premiums are higher than my mortgage payments."

"Oh, in that case, carry on," Fey said.

The doctor ignored the sarcastic humor, such as it was, and turned to salving and dressing Fey's injuries. She'd already received a shot of painkiller, but the procedure started all of the injuries throbbing again.

When Fey had regained consciousness, she'd found herself in the back of an ambulance on the way to the emergency room. Keegan was in the ambulance with her, along with a paramedic.

"You were following me, weren't you?" Fey had asked Keegan through lips that felt dry and cracked. "You knew something like this might happen."

Keegan nodded his head. He was holding Fey's hand. "Yeah, but we couldn't prove anything, and there was nothing we could do about it."

"Because of your daughter?"

"Yeah," Keegan said with a thick, angry catch in his voice. He didn't appear surprised at Fey's knowledge.

Fey closed her eyes. Keegan thought she'd fainted again, but after a moment, she spoke.

"It was Rawlings and Hunter who beat me?"

"Yeah," Keegan replied. "It took us by surprise. We didn't expect them to be already in your house, and then Frank spotted their car when we were trying to find a concealed surveillance position."

"Better late than never," Fey had said weakly, and then added, "I heard shots."

"When we kicked in the door, Hunter capped a round off at us. Frank returned fire. He hit Hunter in the chest and put him down."

Fey remembered the feel of the weight on her legs. "Is he dead?"

"No. He was wearing a vest, but the pain and trauma of the bullet impact knocked him unconscious."

"Why was he wearing a vest?"

Keegan shrugged as Fey's eyes closed. "I think he was worried about being double-crossed. The whole scenario was going to crap, and I think Hunter and Rawlings knew it."

Fey had felt herself fading in the ambulance, but tried to get a few more words out. "Where are Hunter and Rawlings now?"

"Frank is baby-sitting. We called in your people. They'll be there to take over soon."

Fey had managed to get out the word "Thanks," before she faded out again.

The ER doctor eventually finished putting Fey through what seemed like more agony than Hunter and Rawlings had inflicted. Hale's and Keegan's intervention had stopped the beating from going to extremes, but there was still damage done. Fortunately, although the welts were painful, as were the cuts caused by the metal edges of the leather straps, there were no broken bones and nothing threatening permanent damage. The doctor tried to insist Fey be admitted for overnight observation, but she flatly refused. Eventually, he gave up and bandaged the injuries with so much gauze wrapping Fey thought he was trying to turn her into a mummy.

When the doctor had moved on to saner patients, Fey carefully put on a loose, sleeveless sweatshirt and a baggy pair of sweat bottoms Monk had scavenged from her house.

Fey's one concession to her injuries was to let Monk put Nikes on her feet and secure the bows as if she'd been a kindergartner. "Don't say a word," Fey told him.

"Not me, boss."

"What's the current status?"

Monk finished tying the second shoe. He knew better than to ask if Fey wanted a wheelchair ride out to the car. "I contacted your neighbor, Peter Dent. He volunteered to take care of your cats and horses and take care of securing the front door, which Keegan and Hale kicked in."

"Great. A new door is going to cost a fortune."

"Are you complaining?"

Fey thought about being struck by the leather straps. "No," she said decidedly. "What about Hunter and T-Bone Rawlings?"

"Hale had them in cuffs when I arrived. A Devonshire patrol unit is transporting them to West Los Angeles Station. Hammer and Nails will take over from there."

Fey was aware she couldn't do everything, and there was nobody else to whom she'd rather entrust the interrogation of Hunter and Rawlings. "What about Brindle and Alphabet?"

"I've got them rolling on the search warrants and probable cause warrant we'll need for Mary DeFalco. I assumed you wouldn't want to wait until morning."

"You're damn right. We have to chase this thing right now and do everything we can to keep Vaughn Harrison in the dark."

"He's bound to know something is up when Rawlings and Hunter don't check in."

Fey produced a wicked smile. "Yeah, and then he's going to start to sweat."

56

ARCH HAMMERSMITH was tingling with anticipation. He could tell that Rhonda also had the scent of blood in her nostrils. There were two interrogation rooms off the front hallway attached to the squad room. After receiving his own emergency room checkup for the bruising to his chest, P. J. Hunter had been ensconced in the larger of the two rooms. The large Tongan, T-Bone Rawlings, had stoically taken a seat when guided into the smaller room without saying a word.

Hammer had written the names Rawlings and Hunter on small bits of paper and rolled them into tiny wads. He juggled the wads around, and placed one into the heart of each fist. He extended his fists toward Rhonda. "Pick," he said.

Without pausing, she pointed to Hammer's left fist. He uncurled it, and she removed the wad of paper it contained.

"Hunter," she said, smoothing out the strip of paper.

"Aw, I wanted Hunter," Hammer complained, using a voice like a disgruntled child. "You always get to interrogate the easy suspects."

"You want to trade?"

"Not on your life," Hammer said, giving Rhonda a wide smile.

They were both on the jazz. Sex was going to be great after the dust of the interrogations settled.

Frank Hale was also in the squad room. He sat quietly at Fey's desk, where he was smoking a cigarette in violation of station policy, but neither Hammer nor Nails told him to put it out.

Hale was in for a long evening. So was Keegan, who was on his way to the station with Fey and Monk. The officer-involved shooting team would soon be descending on them over the action at Fey's house. Hale could handle that situation with no problem. He'd been through it several times before.

He wasn't even concerned about it. The shooting had been clean. Under other circumstances, he and Keegan would have probably received medals for rescuing Fey. This time around, however, there weren't any other circumstances to hide behind. Hale was aware that he and Keegan were balanced on a very thin wire, high above the ground—and there was no net below.

The only other person currently in the squad room was a district attorney called Groom, a good-looking, rapier-thin black man in an expensive suit and with a pate as bald as Monk Lawson's. He wore fashionable glasses that gave him a distinct look of intelligence which was not misleading. Groom was high enough in the district attorney's office to give most people a nosebleed.

"How do you two want to play this?" he asked Hammer and Nails collectively. He'd worked with the pair before and knew enough to give them their head and not to discuss something without including both of them.

"We've got the dynamics of a classic prisoner's-dilemma scenario working for us," Hammer said.

"We'll lay the groundwork with both Rawlings and Hunter," Rhonda said, smoothly taking over the conversation—as in sync with Hammer as ever. "You just be ready to play Let's Make a Deal when the time comes."

"I'll be ready," Groom told them.

"Let's rock 'n' roll," Hammer said. He stuck his hand out and Rhonda gave him a low five across the palm.

"Give 'em hell," she said.

• • •

The second Rhonda Lawless stepped into the interrogation room, P. J. Hunter turned on her in a verbal assault.

"I don't have anything to say to you. I'm not waiving my rights, I want an attorney, and I want to be booked so I can make bail."

"Sit down and shut up," Rhonda told him casually. She sat in one of the chairs, keeping the table between herself and P.J.

"Don't tell me what to do. You can't tell me what to do. You shouldn't even be in here talking to me. You just wait till Chief Harrison hears about this and gets down here."

"He isn't chief yet," Rhonda said, knowing full well that deputy chiefs were always referred to as chief. "And he *has* been told about your arrest. He seemed very interested. Said he's been worried about you and T-Bone recently. Said he didn't have any proof, but he had you under observation because he thought you might be possibly going rogue—whipped the tar out of a couple of low-grade suspects to get information that would lead you up the ladder on a couple of investigations. Said he'd help us any way he could in our inquiries."

P.J. laughed. "Is that the best bluff you can run? Jeez! Do you know how many times I've run crap like that past suspects? Do us both a favor and walk away now. Don't waste your breath because I ain't buying nothing." P.J. was up out of his chair again, pacing across the back of the square room.

For her part, Rhonda sat quietly. She wasn't worried about P.J. attacking her physically. She knew the trauma to his chest had done enough damage to keep him away from physical violence for a while. She'd also known P.J. would call her bluff. After all, it was a bluff, and a transparent bluff to any cop who had spent any amount of time as an interrogator. But her statements had been more than a bluff. They were a way of winding P.J. up, getting him strung tighter than a snare drum.

"Next you're going to be telling me about the prisoner's dilemma," P.J. said.

Rhonda smiled. P.J. was going to do the interrogation for her. She settled back as comfortably as she could in the hard chair and waited for P.J. to self-destruct.

• • •

"The prisoner's dilemma," Hammer said to T-Bone Rawlings's rocklike countenance. "How many times have you explained it to a suspect?"

Rawlings continued to do his impression of a statue. He hadn't spoken or moved perceptibly since Hammer entered the room. His wide buttocks were spread across the seats of two chairs, his feet planted firmly on the ground as if they had taken root. His arms were folded across his chest, and his eyes were unfocused, as if he were meditating.

None of this bothered Hammer unduly. He knew inside the human boulder in front of him was a scared little copper who had heard every horror story about what happened to cops in prison.

"In case, by some miracle, you've forgotten," Hammer plowed on from his perch on the top of the room's small table, "the prisoner's dilemma still works just the way it was taught to all of us in the academy.

"You have two suspects in custody." Hammer paused and patted the Tongan's thick arms. "That would be you and P.J.," he said, making the obvious point. "These two suspects have committed a crime, or a series of crimes, during which somebody has died as a result."

Hammer patted T-Bone's arms again. "That's called murder, like what happened to Alex Waverly, Ignacio Ramos, and Danny Ochoa." He then returned to his lecturing voice. "The suspects are kept isolated from each other."

The arm pat again. "Does any of this sound familiar?" he asked. He waved a hand in front of Rawlings's face. "Hello, anybody home?"

When Rawlings didn't flinch, Hammer returned to his discourse. "Both suspects are given the same offer: If you confess and testify against your accomplice, your prosecution will be reduced to a minimum—unless your partner, who has been given the same offer, also confesses. Then both of you will be given the maximum sentences for all crimes except murder one."

Hammer patted Rawlings's arms again. "Be sure you're listening, because this is important. If your partner confesses, however, and you don't, you will be charged with murder one and the DA will be guaranteed to seek the death penalty."

Hammer stood up and moved to the door of the room. "Okay, contestants, you can't discuss your decision with anyone and time is ticking. We'll be right back after this commercial break to see if you have the winning answer."

Hammer opened the door to the interrogation room and stepped out. He turned and stuck his head back into the room. "Isn't this great?" he asked as a parting shot.

"The first three things I learned when I got out of the academy," P. J. Hunter said, "were deny everything, admit nothing, and demand proof." P.J. had wound down his own bastardized version of the prisoner's dilemma for Rhonda. "You don't have anything you can use on T-Bone or me. If you did, you wouldn't be trying to cut a deal."

"That's where you're wrong," Rhonda told him calmly. "The thing is, we aren't all that interested in you or T-Bone. Yeah, you're going to take a fall, but you don't need to fall all the way if you give us Vaughn Harrison."

P.J. laughed. "You sound like a broken record. The prisoner's dilemma only works if the players involved can't trust each other. T-Bone won't say a word—you can write that in stone—and there is no way I'm going to give you anything either. Would you say anything if you and that butt hair you call a partner were faced with the prisoner's dilemma?"

"Butt hair? I'll have to quote you."

"You're ignoring the question."

Rhonda was silent for a second before saying, "No, I wouldn't say anything and neither would Hammer. And do you know why?"

"Why?"

"Because we have the intestinal fortitude to take responsibility for our actions. You don't, and neither does your partner."

"How do you know?"

"Because if you did, you wouldn't be in this mess in the first place. Mark my words, one of you will confess all. It's the only logical way to minimize your losses."

P.J. shook his head. "No way."

"What about Vaughn Harrison? Do you really think he'll do anything to save you? He's going to go down with your help or without it. Without your help may take longer, but he'll still go down eventually. And when he does, he's going to give you and your partner up with all the enthusiasm of a big dog rolling in manure."

For the first time, Rhonda saw a look of worry flash through P.J.'s eyes.

"Think about it," she said, and left him to stew.

"Well?" Groom inquired when Hammer and Nails rejoined him in the squad room. "Who's going to roll over?"

Hammer looked at Nails. She shrugged.

"Give it time," Hammer said to Groom before heading for the coffee room.

Hammer came back with two mugs of coffee. Groom already had a mug sitting on the desk near his right hand.

"What do you think?" he asked Rhonda.

She waggled her hand. "It's a tough call. P.J. asked me if I would talk if you and I were faced with the same decision."

"What did you tell him?"

"I told him the truth."

"Okay, but did you tell him that you'd talk or keep closed?"

"I told him the truth," Rhonda said, refusing to give anything else away.

Hammer handed her a coffee mug. He waited for her to take the first sip before saying, "You'll have to cut down on this stuff or the baby will come out as wired as a ferret on uppers."

Groom looked up sharply at Rhonda. "You're pregnant?" he asked. "Congratulations!"

Rhonda had choked on her coffee. She began coughing and slopping the rest of the coffee around in her mug. "You bastard," she said to Hammer when she regained her breath. "How did you know?"

Hammer shrugged. "I know you better than I know myself."

Groom was smart enough to remain quiet.

Hammer reached out and took Nail's hand. "It's okay," he said. "Whatever happens in life, we face it together."

Rhonda swallowed hard.

The two detectives stared at each other, one smiling, the other fighting tears.

"We better check on our contestants," Rhonda said eventually. "It's time to see who gets to play the bonus round."

"I told you the first time you stepped through the door," P.J. was adamant, "I'm not saying another word about anything. I deny everything, I admit nothing, and I'm demanding proof."

"In that case," Rhonda said, still in shock from Hammer's intuition, and actually glad she didn't have to get into the middle of a messy confession, "the best thing you can do is stick your head between your legs and kiss your butt good-bye."

Hammer had entered the other interrogation room without much hope. He'd handled his original interview with T-Bone in a lighthearted manner, feeling there was little chance of getting through to the man. If anybody were going to crack it was Hunter. The big Tongan didn't appear to have any feelings. He wouldn't fear prison as much as his smaller partner.

"How we doing?" Hammer asked. He didn't expect a response.

T-Bone's eyes focused in from a long way off and settled on Hammer's face.

His voice when it came was a slow, gravel monotone. "I'll give you Harrison."

Hammer was as shocked as Rhonda had been when he'd guessed she was pregnant.

"Get the DA in here and let's make a deal," T-Bone said. He sighed and uncrossed his arms. "Make sure the tape is running. I ain't going down alone for nobody."

57

ITTING IN the captain's office, Hammer and Nails presented the highlights of T-Bone Rawlings's interrogation to Fey.

"When Rawlings and Hunter first began investigating Los Juniors, it started out like any other ATD investigation—a little rumor, a little innuendo, just enough smoke to indicate there might be a fire. Gradually, as they uncovered more about the group, they uncovered Santiago's plan to detonate the tear gas canisters and smoke bombs in the Coliseum stands during the U.S.-Mexico soccer match on Sunday," Hammer explained. "The Coliseum is expected to be packed—possibly a sellout by game time. In the confusion, Lucian Santiago intended to assassinate Ricardo Alamar and any of the other conclave participants nearby. Missives would then be sent to the media claiming credit in the name of a nonexistent Central American terrorist group." Unable to sit still, Hammer stood up and paced around the conference table as he spoke. "Lucian didn't care about the other conclave participants, but their deaths would be used to cover up the fact Alamar was the actual target of the assassination."

"Why do it so publicly?" Fey asked. "Wouldn't it have been easier for Santiago to take Alamar out in Mexico?"

"I asked the same questions," Hammer said. "Apparently, Santiago wanted to get out from under his grandfather's thumb and become a player on the international terrorist scene. Alamar was the target because of the blood feud started in Mexico, but Santiago saw the Coliseum setting as the perfect way to make a statement."

"Harrison already had Rawlings and T-Bone slavering for a chance to help him take over the reins of the department," Rhonda explained. "They were his torpedoes—his blunt instruments. Harrison had seduced them with his dream of a hard-line return to law and order, and had shared with them what he believed was necessary for the fulfillment of that vision. When they uncovered the bare bones of Santiago's plan, it appeared to be tailor-made for what Harrison needed.

"Santiago and Los Juniors were not an ultrasophisticated terrorist cell. They were more a collection of wanna-be gangsters with delusions of grandeur. Harrison agreed Los Juniors could be manipulated and controlled, and arranged to plant Danny Ochoa as a mockingbird."

Hammer stretched his arms behind him and worked the tight muscles across his shoulders. "When Ochoa contacted Santiago, he represented himself as having contacts with the terrorist underground." Hammer had picked up the thread from Rhonda. "Ochoa promised Lucian these contacts were aware of Lucian's plans and wanted to help by providing both material and monetary support. Ochoa further intimated his contacts could smooth the way for Lucian and Los Juniors to escape back to Mexico without problems from the police."

"All of this also appealed to Santiago's ego," Rhonda told Fey. "He was tired of going to school and doing his grandfather's bidding. He wanted to begin throwing his macho around, and needed to take a big step up in the criminal world. The penny-ante protection racket Don Diego Santiago allowed Lucian to control in Tijuana was not where Lucian wanted to be. He wanted everything, and he wanted it now. He was so impressed with himself, he never questioned Ochoa's credentials. He told everything to Ochoa, truly believing he was important enough for major terrorist backers to take him seriously."

"There's no fool like a willing fool," Fey said.

Rhonda swiveled back and forth in her chair. "The beauty of the plan—and something we hadn't picked up on—was that T-Bone and Hunter planned on being in the Coliseum as point men on the surveillance team ATD was using to keep tabs on Los Juniors. When the crap hit the fan, they planned on eliminating Lucian and Los Juniors and taking credit for killing the terrorists in the act—an act they allowed to take place."

Hammer added, "I don't think they were overly worried about whether or not Lucian actually completed the assassinations. The mere attempt would be enough for their purposes."

Rhonda nodded. "T-Bone told us the other members of the ATD surveillance team were not in on the plot. They didn't have to be. Hunter, T-Bone, and Waverly were the lead detectives on the case. In their positions as division commanding officers of ATD, both Ron Harper and John Dancer knew something was up, but they didn't know all the ins and outs. Harrison was controlling them, making sure they stayed in line."

"And we all know what happened when they didn't," Fey said.

"Yeah," Hammer agreed. "But T-Bone flat denies he and Hunter knew anything about what happened to Harper and now to Dancer."

"Sure," Fey said. "Put the blinders on and do what you're told— the old Nazi philosophy."

"There's something else as well," Rhonda said. "T-Bone told Hammer that both the mayor and our chief were scheduled to be at the game along with a number of other city dignitaries."

"Not out of a love for soccer, I'm sure," Fey said. "I doubt any of them know which side of the field the baskets are for the puck to go in."

Hammer laughed. "Another fan, I can tell."

Fey shrugged. "Give me a break. At least I can spell *soccer*, which is more than most people legally in this country can do."

"Soccer puck, soccer ball, what's the difference?" Rhonda said. "The point is, the mayor, the chief, and the other dignitaries are going to the game as a public show of support for the Central American Solidarity Conclave. T-Bone didn't flatly admit it, but he gave the strong impression that if the chief and the mayor just happen to get trampled in the panic, or die in some other manner in the attack, then so much the better."

"Either way," Hammer said, "Harrison figured he could pull off his palace coup and seize control of the department. If the chief survived, Harrison would manipulate circumstances to make him resign. If the chief and mayor were actually eliminated, then Harrison would have an even easier time dragging the department back to the paramilitary, jackbooted middle ages."

Fey felt a wave of weariness sweep over her. "All the changes, pro and con, that the department has gone through since the ninety-two riots would all be for *nada.*"

"The man is a megalomaniac," Rhonda said. "He doesn't give a damn about the department, just about his vision of a world where he's been made king."

Fey's head was spinning. She was feeling rough. Actually, she was feeling very rough. She hadn't had the strength to get into the middle of Rawlings's interrogation herself, and had been happy to leave it in the capable hands of Hammer and Nails. Once back at the station with Monk and Keegan, she'd crashed in the officers' cot room for a few hours' sleep, letting events proceed without her. It hadn't been near enough rest, but it was all she was going to get for a while.

"Did T-Bone tell you anything about what happened on the roof at Bunch Hall?" she asked.

"Yeah," Hammer replied. "Ramos screwed up trying to get close to Los Juniors. Lucian rumbled Ramos's true identity and grabbed him. That's when the torturing took place and the photos that were sent to April were taken. Ochoa was party to Santiago's interrogation of Ramos, but he couldn't do anything about it without giving his own identity away. According to what Ochoa told T-Bone and Hunter, Ramos held out for a while, but eventually spilled his guts. He told Santiago about Waverly and April and that ATD was investigating Los Juniors."

Rhonda had switched from coffee to Coke, and she used a swallow to lubricate her throat. "T-Bone said they freaked when Ochoa told them about Waverly. Harrison calmed them down, and told them he would handle the situation. Ochoa had also told them about the photos of Ramos being sent to April with the orders to kill. Santiago believed it would work, but it was too tenuous for Harrison to rely on. He couldn't know how April felt about her brother or about Waverly."

"I can see how he would think that way," Fey said. "So, he came up with the digoxin in the water bottle as a way of making sure. Once he used T-Bone and Hunter to put the squeeze on Keegan and Hale through Keegan's daughter, Harrison could then control the investigation of Waverly's death and make sure it came back as a heart attack."

"Between April Waverly's actions and the chief assigning us to investigate, that plan got screwed up big time," Hammer said.

Fey thought about the incidents. "Things must have gotten pretty ugly for Ramos to give up his sister," she said.

"You saw the body," Hammer said. "All of us think we'd be brave if we were being tortured, but not many people can stand up to that kind of abuse. How much more could you have taken?"

"Don't even ask that question," Fey said. "Okay, so how did Ramos end up on the roof of Bunch Hall, and what happened with Ochoa?"

"From the best I can piece together, when the media picked up the story of Waverly being shot by his wife, Ramos was no longer needed alive. Ochoa was in over his head. He wanted out, but T-Bone and Hunter kept pushing him, forcing him to stay in tight with Lucian and Los Juniors. However, he couldn't stand by and let Ramos be murdered. He convinced Santiago that if he wanted the backing of the terrorist groups Ochoa maintained he represented, then Santiago had to keep clean. Ochoa told Santiago he would turn Ramos over to his contacts and they would make Ramos disappear. Santiago saw the sense in this and agreed."

"Santiago really wanted to be a big wheel," Rhonda put in. "He was willing to give up the pleasure of killing Ramos for a chance at Alamar in the Coliseum and the backing of Ochoa's supposed terrorist group contacts."

"We still haven't put Ochoa and Ramos on the Bunch Hall roof," Fey said.

"That's the easy part," Hammer told her. "Once clear of Santiago, Ochoa contacted T-Bone and Hunter and arranged to meet them at their usual rendezvous spot—the roof of Bunch Hall."

"How bad off was Ramos by this point?"

"He was moving under his own power, but his mind wasn't all there." Hammer stopped pacing and came to lean on the edge of the conference table near Fey. "T-Bone told me when they met Ochoa and Ramos, they weren't sure how they were going to handle things. Up to this point, they had gone along with everything Harrison wanted. They'd bought into his scheme—to set up and then thwart a terrorist action in Los Angeles. They were going to be heroes, but now everything was suddenly crumbling around the edges."

"So, what happened?"

"Ramos happened. At some point on the roof, he came to life and tried to escape what he must have thought was a plan to kill him. He'd already been stabbed when Santiago had been torturing him. He was disoriented and ran for the edge. Ochoa tried to stop him. There was a struggle, and before T-Bone or Hunter could do anything, Ramos pushed Ochoa over the edge. Hunter and Rawlings grabbed Ramos, but he was further gone than they thought and went into a seizure."

"Cardiac arrest, probably," Rhonda added.

Hammer nodded. "The exertion was all too much on top of the torture he'd suffered, and he died on them right then and there. With Ochoa over the edge and another dead man on the roof, T-Bone and Hunter cut their losses and split the scene."

"What a pile of self-serving bull!" Fey said. The anger in her voice was colored with frustration. "Does Rawlings actually think we're going to accept that everything that happened on the roof was an accident?"

"It's going to be difficult to prove otherwise," Hammer said. "I know what you're saying, but Rawlings and Hunter were the only ones on the roof. Hunter isn't talking, and Rawlings has cut a deal. He's going to put everything in the best light possible for himself."

"Okay," Fey said. "I don't like it, but I guess nobody is asking for my opinion."

"It was the turning point for Hunter and Rawlings. Like Ochoa, they were in over their heads. The only choice they had was to keep running. Harrison was promising to protect them, but he demanded they do as he told them. It was the only way they thought they could come out clean."

"I take it they recontacted Santiago?"

Hammer nodded. "Harrison still wanted Santiago to carry out the assassinations in the Coliseum, so Hunter and T-Bone made contact and told Santiago they were Ochoa's replacements as Santiago's connections to the terrorist underground. They salved Santiago's ego, and told him they would still supply the guns, explosives, and money for the job."

"Aside from everything else," Rhonda said, "I think Rawlings and Hunter were caught up in taking Lucian Santiago out. They crossed a line somewhere and couldn't get back. Taking down Lucian Santiago was their only justification for what they had become involved in."

"Like blowing up Waverly's house and almost taking us out," Hammer said.

"That was T-Bone and Hunter?"

"Yeah. Once they found out Waverly was working against them, nobody was sure how much he had learned or where he was keeping the information. They put the squeeze on Hale and Keegan with the threats to Keegan's daughter, but things got sticky once we took over the murder investigation instead of RHD. Harrison told Rawlings and Hunter to destroy Waverly's house. They knew we would get there sooner or later and it was decided to send us a message at the same time, maybe slow us down long enough for Harrison to get his master plan back on track again."

"T-Bone maintains nobody was supposed to get seriously hurt," Rhonda said.

"Yeah. Right," Fey said. "I can't see any of us buying that lie. They didn't care who got hurt."

"T-Bone admitted to using the inlaid metal belts to beat Tucker in order to find out what he knew about Keegan's disappearance. They also used the belts on you, planning to hamper the investigation until after the soccer match on Sunday. They used the belts because it was the same MO that had been used by Santiago on

Ramos. They still thought they could wrap this thing up in one big package, blame everything on Santiago and Los Juniors, and make it all go away."

"Obviously, they didn't know they'd been followed to Mexico."

"No clue," Hammer agreed. "When I told T-Bone that Lucian Santiago was lying in pieces in a Mexican hospital just waiting to spill his guts, he damn near turned white."

"Since when has Lucian been ready to spill his guts?" Fey asked.

"So, I told a little lie," Hammer said, and then grinned. "It was worth it to see the expression on the big man's face."

Fey was almost too tired to laugh. She still had recurring chills, and the thumping behind her right eye was affecting her vision. Her mouth was dry, and her stomach kept rolling over involuntarily. Medication was easing the pain of the cuts and welts, but it wasn't helping much.

"What you're telling me jibes with most of what Keegan and Hale told me," she said. Fey had spent time talking to both men about their roles in the plot. "When Waverly convinced the chief to send him into ATD to get the goods on Vaughn Harrison, Keegan and Hale acted as his control officers. Waverly had essentially turned himself into a mockingbird inside the department, and standard procedure was being followed as in similar operations." Fey shifted gingerly in her chair, trying to organize her thoughts. "Waverly, however, played everything close to his vest. Keegan and Hale didn't know what was going on with him half the time. When Vaughn Harrison found out about Waverly being a plant, he approached Keegan and Hale and tried to recruit them. When they didn't respond as Harrison wanted them to, he had T-Bone and Hunter threaten Keegan's daughter."

"Frigging pukes," Rhonda said with feeling.

Fey tried shifting her weight in the chair again and winced slightly. "Yeah, well it was enough to put the fear of the devil into Keegan, especially after the chief took the investigation into Waverly's murder away from RHD." She picked up her coffee mug and took a swallow of the tepid contents. "Keegan couldn't take the pressure. He was already drinking too much and feeling the loss of separation from his family. He was also a good cop and couldn't live with what was going on. He tried feeding us information through Tucker, hoping that somehow we could sort everything out.

"Keegan was in touch with Hale, and when it looked as if things were getting completely out of control, they began following me to try and be there if needed without jeopardizing Keegan's family."

"How did Keegan think his disappearance would keep his family safe?" Rhonda asked.

Fey shrugged. "He felt if he wasn't around to be a threat to Harrison, his family would be left alone. He wasn't cooperating with Harrison, but he didn't appear to be hindering him either."

"It's time we take that bastard down," Rhonda said.

"I agree," Fey said. "And I think I know just the little lady who is going to lead us to him."

58

Fey felt like hell and looked worse, but there was no way she was going to back off before the investigation was completed. Pushing hard on both her own team and the lab rats from SID had produced several pertinent facts.

The first good lead came from SID. Alana Giles, the department's brightest trace evidence analyst, called with the news.

"You were right," Alana told Fey without preamble. "We found traces of hair, skin, and blood on the butt of John Dancer's duty weapon. I've also talked to the coroner. He said the injury that actually killed Dancer could be consistent with a blow from the gun butt. He was glad we gave him the heads up—said the injury could have easily been put down to a blow received while falling down the stairs, but coupled with the trace evidence from the gun, it's clear what happened."

"Can he make it good enough for court?" Fey asked.

"As good as it can be," Alana said. "The proper testimony will put the findings beyond reasonable doubt. The coroner's inquest will definitely return a verdict of death at the hands of another."

The second lead came when Monk finally was able to track down the pharmacist who provided the refill prescription of digoxin found in Waverly's pocket.

"He wasn't much pleased about being hauled from a warm bed,"

Monk told Fey in reference to the pharmacist. "Didn't want to take my word for it that the information couldn't wait."

"My heart bleeds," Fey said. "Let him tell it to the complaint board at Internal Affairs. What else did he have to say?"

"When Waverly ordered the refill, it was the second time in a week the script had been filled," Monk reported. "Waverly claimed he'd lost the first one. The pharmacist did check with Waverly's doctor before providing the refill, but he didn't really think there was anything odd about the request. Waverly was a regular customer and had never tried to get extra drugs before. There was no reason to believe he hadn't lost the first prescription."

"So, if we can find the first prescription bottle, it could give us the leverage we need," Fey said.

"It would be solid evidence," Monk agreed.

"Then make it so," Fey told him.

Armed as they were with search and arrest warrants, the statement was Monk's cue to take to the streets dragging Brindle and Alphabet along.

"Remember," Fey told the trio as they made for the door. "You're going after a killer. Don't make mistakes."

Still at the station with Fey, Rhonda asked, "When are you going to bring the chief up to speed?"

The same question had been nagging at Fey, but she had tried to ignore it. Now, however, with both Hammer and Nails watching her, she knew she had to confront it.

"My orders from the chief were to go wherever the investigation led."

"That's not an answer," Hammer told her.

Fey shot him a dirty look. "The chief is first and foremost a political animal. If he gets involved at this stage of the investigation, do you think we'll ever be allowed to wrap this up properly?"

Hammer exchanged glances with Nails. "Not a chance," they said in unison.

"Is that what you want?"

"What we want is Vaughn Harrison," Rhonda said without hesitation. Hammer nodded his agreement.

"Then we'd better get him fast," Fey told them. "Because in another few hours the chief and his toadies will inevitably find out what is going on, and they'll be all over us whether we want them to be or not."

It was a few minutes short of 5 A.M. when Brindle knocked on Mary DeFalco's front door.

"She's not going to like having her beauty sleep disturbed," Alphabet said from where he was standing on the left side of the front door.

"Tough beans," said Brindle. "I can't remember the last time I got any beauty sleep—disturbed or otherwise."

Monk had gone around to the back of the residence with a uniformed officer. Another half-dozen uniforms had taken up positions around the small house, located in a middle-class area of Pacific Division.

Brindle pounded on the front door again and rang the doorbell several times. After a few moments of continued silence, a light was turned on in the hallway behind the frosted-glass windows flanking the front door.

"Who is it?" Mary DeFalco's angry voice shouted the question.

"Mary? It's Detective Jones," Brindle said. "Open the door. We have a warrant."

There was no response from inside. Time ticked by.

"Don't be stupid, Mary," Brindle called out.

Still no response.

"Open it," Brindle said to Alphabet.

Stepping back to give himself room, Alphabet brought up what the department lovingly termed an Arkansas toothpick—a thick, round, four-foot-long metal bar with a point on one end and a claw hammer on the opposite. Thrusting the bar forward, Alphabet jammed the claw-hammer end into the door frame near the dead bolt lock.

Brindle had her gun out in her right hand. With her left hand she plucked the radio off her belt and spoke into it, telling Monk and the other officers at the scene what was happening.

As Alphabet heaved his weight against the metal pry bar, the door popped open quicker than if he'd been using a key.

Brindle flashed through the opening. The radio was back on the belt of her jeans, but her gun was still out, pointing ahead of her in the low ready position. She moved quickly down a short hallway and into a living room, trusting Alphabet to be behind her.

The house was neat and tidy, the furnishings comfortable and of good quality, but without being noticeably expensive. A beige pile carpet, showing signs of wear down the center walkways, ran wall to wall through the rooms.

"Mary?" Brindle called out. "Don't be stupid. This is how people get hurt."

"Come out, come out, wherever you are," Alphabet said in a loud voice. "Olly, olly, oxenfree."

"Shut up," Brindle told him. "This isn't a game."

"Sorry," Alphabet said, clearly not taking Brindle's chiding seriously. He had left the metal pry bar at the front door and had his own 9-millimeter gripped in a meaty palm.

Off to the right, there was the noise of wood splintering. Alphabet stuck his head through an open doorway and observed Monk tumbling in through a rear door.

"Got her?" Monk asked, seeing Alphabet's head.

"Not yet," Alphabet said. He withdrew his head to follow Brindle. He had disposed of his sling for the time being.

At the base of a stairway, Brindle called up to the floor above, "Come on out, Mary, and keep your hands where I can see them. You're making me very nervous. This isn't necessary."

"Yes, it is," Alphabet said in a low voice. "She's been watching all the cop shows on television. Of course this is necessary."

"Quit screwing around," Brindle said. "Is the lower floor secured?"

"Secured," Monk told her, coming to join the two detectives at the bottom of the stairs.

"Do we go up?" Brindle asked.

"Don't have much choice," Monk told her. "Unless you want to back off and wait for SWAT."

"The hell with that idea," Alphabet said, and started up the stairway.

Brindle stepped in behind her partner, dogging his footsteps. Monk was right behind them.

At the top of the landing, there was a room to either side. Both had closed doors.

Without hesitating, Alphabet went to the room on the right and kicked at the door. His foot slammed into the hollow core construction directly beside the door handle. The door blasted open, and Alphabet went in low and fast with Brindle right behind him.

Following up on Alphabet's assault, Monk moved quickly to the door on the left. Using more caution than Alphabet, he grabbed the handle of the door, twisted it, and flung the door open. He pulled his body back away from the door, and then moved forward to take a cautious look inside.

The room was the residence's master bedroom. A lamp on a nightstand was turned on. Rumpled sheets and blankets were piled on the bed. They were yellow and gold, matching the paint on the walls and other items used to decorate the feminine, almost childlike room.

Moving inside, Monk could see the door to the master bathroom was closed. Since Mary DeFalco was obviously not visible in the bedroom area, Monk had to make a decision.

"Anything?" he called out loudly to Brindle and Alphabet.

"Nothing," Alphabet said as he stepped into the room behind Monk.

Monk swore softly and then moved forward. Mimicking Alphabet's earlier actions, he kicked at the door leading to the master bathroom. The door sprang open, slammed against a wall, and almost closed again.

A scream came from inside the bathroom, and then Monk was through the door with Alphabet climbing up his heels.

Mary DeFalco was crouched in the bathtub, a portable phone clasped in her hand, and wearing nothing but a diaphanous, nylon shorty nightgown.

She screamed again and threw the phone at Monk. He ducked

and the phone sailed past him to clout Alphabet in the head. Alphabet grunted and swore.

Monk charged forward, arms out to ward off Mary's flailing fists. She was screaming and crying, twisting away from Monk as he wrapped his arms around her and drove her back against a wall.

"Calm down, calm down," he told her, but it did no good. Mary had worked herself into a state of hysteria.

Leaning forward, she sunk her teeth into Monk's ear.

For Monk, enough was enough. He jabbed a balled fist into Mary DeFalco's stomach, driving the wind and the fight out of her.

Unfortunately for Monk, it also drove the contents of her stomach out of her and across his shoulders.

"Crap!" he said in disgust.

"No, it's puke," Alphabet advised him, laughing as he gingerly stepped forward to assist by restraining Mary's arms and clicking a pair of handcuffs over her slim wrists. "Crap comes out the other end."

59

WHEN FEY entered the interrogation room at West Los Angeles Station, she couldn't help but compare the tiny office to a room at a no-tell motel—turnover was brisk, and people rarely stayed over an hour.

Mary DeFalco sat on a hard chair and was buttoned into an old overcoat Brindle had retrieved from a closet in Mary's house. On her feet, she wore a pair of fluffy slippers Brindle had similarly rescued. If things had gone easier at the house, the detectives might have let Mary get dressed properly. As things were, she was lucky she wasn't sitting in the interrogation room wearing nothing but the shorty nightgown and a frown.

"Hello, Mary," Fey said as she sat down in another hard chair on the same side of the table as Mary.

Mary didn't respond.

Fey sighed. "Look, you're in some trouble here, Mary, but there are a number of things that can still happen, and maybe something can be worked out." Even as she said it, Fey knew the platitude sounded weak. Mary DeFalco was going down big time for murder, and there wasn't much anyone could do about it.

After taking Mary into custody, Monk and the others had searched Mary's residence from top to bottom. It was Monk who eventually struck lucky. Refuse collection in Mary's neighborhood was on Mondays, which meant there was almost a week's worth of garbage piled in the can on the side of Mary's residence.

Since the outside of the can was stenciled with the address of Mary's house, and since it was kept in Mary's backyard behind a closed gate, there would be little trouble in court proving the ownership of the garbage it contained. Working in the early morning light, Monk had poured the contents onto a large canvas sheet taken from the back of his detective sedan.

Pawing through eggshells, coffee grounds, empty frozen juice cans, and the other detritus of Mary's throwaways was not exactly stimulating work, but it was necessary. Monk uncovered two items: an empty, amber-colored prescription bottle clearly marked with Alex Waverly's name, and a lump of gelatin capsules squeezed empty of their contents. There was little doubt SID would discover digoxin residue inside the pierced gelatin caps.

Fey now took the prescription bottle and the lump of gelatin caps out of a bag she had brought into the interrogation room with her. She set them in the middle of the table, and silently watched Mary struggle to keep her eyes from straying to the items.

Fey was worried. At the same time that Monk and the others had been at Mary's house, Hammer and Nails had driven to Vaughn Harrison's residence. They had neither search nor arrest warrants. However, they hoped to find Harrison and have him accompany them to the station voluntarily.

They had arrived at Harrison's house at five-thirty to find nobody home. The deputy chief was not in his office either. Nor was he logged out to any police crime scene.

Harrison was off duty. He had no obligation to tell anyone where he was or what he was doing. Under normal circumstances, there would be nothing suspicious in the fact he wasn't at home, even at five-thirty in the morning. But circumstances weren't normal, and Fey knew something had gone wrong. Her feelings were intensified when Hammer and Nails further reported Harrison was not responding to his pager.

It was Brindle, however, who added the capper to the situation. While still at Mary DeFalco's house, she retrieved the phone Mary had thrown at Monk.

Using a gadget she'd picked up from Arch Hammersmith, Brindle covered the receiving end of the phone. By pushing the redial button, the phone produced a series of electronic noises as the last number called was redialed. The gadget over the phone translated the electronic noises into numbers on an LED readout.

It didn't take Brindle long to verify that the last number called from Mary's phone belonged to Vaughn Harrison. The call had gone out at five-fifteen. At five-thirty, when Hammer and Nails had arrived at Harrison's residence, Harrison had been gone.

"He's panicked," Brindle had told Fey.

"Vaughn Harrison doesn't panic," Fey said. Her stomach felt queasy with anticipation, but she was still determined to see things through on her terms. The politicians could fight over the remains later.

In the interrogation room, Mary DeFalco's eyes eventually drifted to the items on the table. "What are those?" she asked.

"Don't play stupid, Mary," Fey said. "The game is over. I told Vaughn Harrison that a long time ago, but he refused to believe me. All of this could have been avoided if he had been able to control his own ego and let events run their course."

"I don't know what you're talking about."

"Of course you don't, Mary. I always get my people to yank police secretaries out of bed, drag them down to the police station half-naked, and search their houses because it's how I get my kicks."

"Whatever gets you off."

Kid gloves were not going to do any good in handling Mary DeFalco.

"How long were you screwing Ron Harper?" Fey asked bluntly.

Mary laughed. "Why? Are you jealous?"

"How about Alex Waverly? Did Vaughn Harrison ask you to let Waverly get into your pants? Couldn't you see he was using you like a pimp uses a whore?"

Mary's eyes flickered with anger at Fey's statement, but she kept her mouth shut.

"Why are women so stupid?" Fey asked. "Why is it we're the ones who always end up dropped in the crap because of the games men insist on playing?"

Fey had taken another dose of pain medication, and was feeling half-human again. She knew, however, that her reserves were getting low and she needed to pace herself so she didn't collapse.

The clothing she'd worn from the hospital had been replaced by a black, oversized sweatshirt, black leggings, and black jodhpur boots. She kept the items in her locker at work for serving search warrants when her regular dress clothes might get dirty, or for emergencies. When the earthquake had struck Los Angeles in 1994, she'd been stuck at work for three days and had been glad to have the change of clothing on hand.

Fey was playing a strong hunch. She had no solid proof that Mary was involved with Vaughn Harrison, but it was the only scenario that made sense. It was also the simplest reason for Mary to get close to any male who could have been a threat to Vaughn Harrison.

There was also the panicked phone call to Harrison when Brindle, Alphabet, and Monk had shown up on her doorstep. Monk was currently busy getting PIN records from the phone company to establish how often Mary called Vaughn Harrison's home or office from her residence.

"Do you love Vaughn Harrison, Mary?" Fey asked. "Is that why you did it?"

"Did what?" Mary answered Fey's question with a question.

Outwardly, Fey didn't change the expression of concern on her face. Inwardly, she registered that Mary hadn't denied being in love with Vaughn Harrison.

The theme Fey was laying out for Mary was one where the blame for Mary's actions could be laid on the doorstep of another. Fey was trying to get Mary to shift the responsibility for her actions to Vaughn Harrison. Easier said than done, but still achievable.

Fey pointed at the prescription bottle and the remains of the gelatin caps on the table. "Was putting the digoxin in Alex's water bottle your idea or Harrison's?"

"Don't you have to read me my rights or something?" Mary asked. She was still belligerent, but Fey could work through that emotion.

"Sure, I could read you your rights," she said. "But then everything gets complicated. I'm just trying to help you out here—woman to woman—trying to help you see the light and give you a path to follow. I don't need statements from you. I don't need a confession. You're bought and paid for already." Fey pointed again at the items on the table. "It was your tough luck the garbage pickup at your house had already come and gone for the week when you threw those items away."

"I've never seen those things before," Mary said. "They were planted."

"And everyone in prison is innocent," Fey said. "I've heard it all before. I suppose we also planted the blood and hairs on the butt of John Dancer's gun."

The statement took Mary by surprise. "But—" She caught herself and stopped.

"But what?" Fey asked. "*But* you thought you'd wiped the butt of the gun clean? *But* you didn't hit Dancer with the gun butt? But what?"

Mary didn't reply. She stuck a thumbnail in her mouth and began chewing on the skin around it.

"How did you get yourself in so deep, Mary? How long did you think you could keep getting away with murder? Do you think Vaughn Harrison is going to come riding through the door with a lance in his hand to rescue you? Grow up, Mary! You're facing murder one charges for killing at least two police officers! You're facing the death penalty unless you can give up something that's going to dig you out from behind the eight ball."

Mary had started to cry.

"There's no future in going through this alone," Fey said in a softer tone. "Do you think if Vaughn Harrison was in here right now, he wouldn't be rolling all over himself to dump you into six shades of shit?"

"Shut up," Mary wailed. "Shut up! Shut up! Shut up!" She covered her ears and curled into a modified fetal position.

"I don't care who you screwed or why you screwed them," Fey said. "It's always the women who have to do the dirty work. Don't go down for a man, Mary. Don't go down for somebody who doesn't give a crap about what happens to you."

"He does care. He does."

"Then where is he?" Fey asked. "You called him." She ran with her best guess. "You told him we were at your door. You told him we were breaking into your house. You told him we were coming to get you. You were scared, terrified! You told him we must know everything. Didn't you?"

"No! No!"

"Yes! Yes, Mary. You told him all of those things. You were there every time he needed you. You were there to let him know Ron Harper was going over the edge. You were already sacrificing yourself, your body, and your self-esteem to Alex Waverly when Harrison found out Waverly was the chief's man." Fey picked up the prescription bottle and waved it in Mary's face. "You were there for Harrison when Waverly had to be silenced. And you were there when John Dancer somehow became a threat. You've been there every time, but where is Harrison when you need him? Where is he, Mary? Where the hell is he?"

Mary DeFalco was into full-fledged crying. Tears streamed down her face and she was gulping for breath.

"Give him to me, Mary." Fey's voice had dropped to a gentle, lulling tone. "Don't let him dump you in it any deeper than he has already. Give yourself a chance to come at least a small way back." Fey reached out a hand and placed it on Mary's shoulder. "Where is he, Mary?"

Mary gulped and sputtered. She wiped her eyes and nose on the cuffs of her coat.

Eventually, she was able to force out the words. "You can't stop him. He's going after the chief."

60

"CRAP! CRAP! Crap!" Fey said. She was getting more pissed off at herself by the second.

"Has Harrison gone completely out of his head?" Rhonda asked. "Why would he risk going after the chief? Even if we did get charges brought against him, Harrison has every chance of beating them in court. Right now all we have to tie him to the conspiracy and murders are the statements of two coconspirators and a bushelful of gut instincts."

Hammer spoke up in agreement. "Any defense attorney worth spit could make those things go away without breaking a sweat. The statements will be looked at as questionable because of their self-serving nature, and a copper's gut instincts aren't worth squat in a court of law."

"I don't know," Alphabet argued. "We've also got Waverly's computer files, plus whatever Keegan and Hale can tell us."

Hammer shook his head. "I don't think Harrison is even aware we've been able to recover Waverly's computer files. But that's all for the lawyers to figure out. Harrison could still think he's far enough removed to bluff it out. I don't think he's panicking yet."

"He isn't panicking," Fey said. "But he is doing what he believes is right. In his mind, taking the chief out is the only option he has left. No matter what happens in or out of a courtroom, his career with the department is over. He'll never become chief—and that's what all of this has been about: one man's attempt to grasp what he considers the brass ring."

The homicide team was gathered in the detective squad room. As it was Sunday, there were no other detectives on duty.

Fey was flopped in the swivel chair behind her own desk. "I know Harrison. I've seen how he thinks and operates. He truly believes he has to save the city from itself. Rhonda called him a megalomaniac earlier, but I think it would be closer to say he's suffering from a messiah complex."

"Maybe he's got a stalker mentality going," Brindle said. "You know, the if-I-can't-have-you-nobody-can rationalization," she explained when the other detectives looked at her. "If I can't run the police department, you can't either."

Fey nodded. "Could be, but it doesn't do us any good sitting around here debating psychology. We know the last thing Mary DeFalco did before we arrested her was call Harrison. Now he's in the wind. Does anybody here want to take the chance he's not going after the chief?"

There were no takers for her offer.

Monk hung up the phone on another desk, where he'd moved to get away from the noise of the team's conversation. "The chief isn't at home," he said. "I just woke up his wife. She said he has a standing Sunday tee time with the mayor at the Conquistador Country Club. She gave me his beeper number."

Fey sat up sharply in her chair. "Activate his beeper, then," she said. "Punch in the number of my cell phone."

Monk picked up the phone again and began dialing the beeper number from his scribbled notes. He knew Fey's cell phone number by heart.

"What about getting patrol rolling?" Alphabet asked. The Conquistador Country Club was at the northeast corner of West Los Angeles, set among the exclusive homes of Pacific Palisades.

"We'll go ourselves," Fey said, getting to her feet.

"But—" Alphabet tried.

"No buts." Fey cut him off. "Do you want to try and explain all of this to communications? By the time we get people to believe us, we could be there."

Alphabet could see the sense in Fey's statement and moved rapidly toward the squad room door with the others.

Monk hung back to wait for Fey, watching as she fiddled with something in her purse.

"What are you doing?" he asked quietly, so the other detectives couldn't hear.

Fey looked up. From Monk's expression, she could see he already had a good idea what she was doing.

"Funny," Fey said. "I have no idea how my cell phone got turned off in my purse."

"You're as bad as the rest of them," Monk said as he followed Fey to the squad room exit. "You've planned to force this confrontation from the start."

"Not exactly from the start," Fey said. "And I would have preferred things to be somewhat more under control, but you go with what you've got."

"We're talking about people's lives here," Monk argued.

"We're not talking about people, we're talking about the chief. He's supposed to be the top cop. He's a big boy. It's time some of the upper echelon faced the same types of dangers faced by the lower ranks of the thin blue line."

"You're playing God."

"Somebody has to take the role."

"Fey." Monk grabbed Fey's arm and pulled her to a stop at the top of the stairwell.

Fey rounded on him angrily. "Do you want Harrison to walk away from this?" she demanded. "Hammer and Nails are right. Harrison is directly or indirectly responsible for the deaths of four police detectives, the corruption of several others, and attempts on the lives of yet others. He's put the city at risk, and is willing to do whatever it takes to enforce his vision on the rest of us." Fey knew she was on borrowed time. She only had so much go left in her. If she backed off or slowed down, shock and the physical cost of her injuries would catch up with her. She didn't have the strength to argue. "Do you want this department dragged through the mud backward in court as lawyers for Harrison weave and bob their way through the circumstantial evidence? Do you want all of us to face cross-examination about every minute action we've taken in this case and every other case we've ever worked? Hasn't the LAPD been through enough in the last few years?"

"You can't assassinate the man."

"I don't intend to assassinate him. I just want to catch him with enough evidence so he can't walk away. If that means using the chief as a staked goat, so be it."

61

THE CONQUISTADOR Country Club was a fashionable golf club located south of Sunset Boulevard and a dozen blocks from the beach in the middle of the Santa Monica Canyon. The vast rolling fairways and greens were immaculately groomed, seeming to exude pride from playing host once a year to one of the major golf tournaments on the pro tour.

To belong to Conquistador, it wasn't enough for your yearly income to be in the high six figures. In addition to having money, you needed just the right connections to secure your recommendation to the membership committee—no white-trash, lottery-winning millionaires need apply. Exceptions were made, however, for celebrities or power brokers. The mayor and the chief of police could get a standing Sunday morning tee time without breaking a sweat or paying a cent out of their pockets. Quid pro quo went a long way in Los Angeles, as it did in any big city.

As Monk turned the wheel of the detective sedan, sliding around the corner from Sunset Boulevard to the residential street leading to the country club entrance, he posed a question. "How can we be sure Harrison will choose this location to go after the chief? For that matter, how would he even know the chief is out here playing golf?"

Fey was turned in her seat, watching through the rear window as Hammer and Nails followed them around the corner in another detective sedan. Alphabet and Brindle completed the convoy in a black-and-white slick top, a model that was now part of the detective vehicle fleet.

"If Harrison is going after the chief, he's got to do it fast. If he hesitates, the whole game board will change against him, and he will have lost any chance of carrying out his plan. Harrison is a deputy chief. He would be familiar with the chief's routine. Knowing the chief has a standing Sunday morning tee time with the mayor would be common knowledge among the department's command staff."

Monk nodded as he braked hard next to the Conquistador clubhouse. He was out of the car before the cars following him had imitated his screeching halt.

Fey was slower. The wounds to her back and chest had started burning again.

"Are you okay?" Rhonda asked, seeing Fey's distress.

"Fine," Fey said. "Just get out there and find him."

Rhonda still hesitated, Hammer beside her.

"Go!" Fey said. "Go!"

The duo sprinted away, dragging Brindle with them.

The parking lot was already a quarter full with the cars of early morning golfers. Several duffers had stopped to stare as the detectives had spilled out of their cars and headed rapidly toward the course.

Alphabet stopped beside Fey.

"How about we take the easy route?" he asked as he and Fey passed a line of golf carts.

"I'm with you," Fey said. She clambered gingerly into the passenger seat, leaving Alphabet to drive one-handed.

A course employee came out of the cart room. "Hey! What are you doing?" He started running as Alphabet pulled away.

"Call a cop, why don't you?" Fey yelled back at the man, who had stopped to talk rapidly into a two-way radio he'd taken from a clip on his belt.

"Don't you just hate little people who think they have power?" Alphabet asked. The golf cart was rapidly moving along, but Alphabet's tone of voice betrayed no hint of tension, as if he were simply taking a casual spin around the golf course.

"I hate important people who misuse their power more," Fey replied.

On the course ahead of them, they could see their detective compatriots fanning out to cover as much ground as possible. Monk was well ahead of everyone, his sprinter's build a testimony to the shape he was in.

Groups of golfers sputtered and yelled as the detectives raced across fairways. One particular foursome was enraged when Hammer bent down and scooped two balls off the fairway.

In the golf cart, Fey and Alphabet bumped along, swerving around obstacles and making their own path through the course.

"There!" Fey called out, half-standing in the golf cart and pointing toward a group of golfers on the green of the eighth hole. The chief's bulky silhouette, a huge bowling ball, was clearly defined against the morning sun.

Another figure approaching the group turned and spotted the detectives. He immediately began running. Against the bright sun, it was almost impossible to see who the figure was, but there was no doubt in any of the detectives' minds.

Monk was closest to the figure and kicked in an extra burst of speed. He launched a tackle at the legs of his quarry, managing to trip him, but not wrap him up.

Vaughn Harrison rolled away from Monk's grasp. He clambered back to his feet and continued to run toward the chief. He was not displaying a weapon, but that didn't mean he didn't have one. It did mean nobody could justify shooting at him yet.

Fey knew the mayor would be with the chief, but had no idea who else was with them.

Monk was back in pursuit, but Fey and Alphabet were rapidly catching up. The bouncing of the golf cart was killing Fey, but she refused to give in to the pain. Even though Monk had been right when he accused her of trying to manipulate the situation, she did not want anyone killed. She had hoped to force a confrontation with Harrison, in front of witnesses that would have worked to secure his guilt in court. A showdown on a crowded golf course was not the controlled environment she had envisioned.

"Don't do it, Vaughn!" Fey yelled. "Don't be a fool!" She was wasting her breath and knew it.

As Harrison approached the chief's group of golfers, three of the figures began running away. Harrison clearly had a gun in his hand now, but the chief stood firm behind his golf bag.

Harrison's running feet propelled him onto the green as he brought the gun in his hand up into a two-handed shooting position. The fingers of his clawed hand were wrapped around the gun butt in a death grip. The surgeons who had molded it back together could be proud of their handiwork.

Monk was too far back to stop Harrison, who moved forward relentlessly toward the chief.

Harrison didn't waste time on words. As his gun came up on target, his finger started to squeeze the trigger.

"No!" Fey yelled, both in pain and fear as the golf cart chewed its way onto the green.

There was the sound of gunfire, but flame spat out of the chief's golf bag, not out of the muzzle of Harrison's gun.

Fey immediately realized the chief had been concealing a gun behind his golf bag and had fired before Harrison could get off a shot. She'd been suckered—the chief had been prepared for a deadly confrontation with Harrison, and had only been waiting for Fey to drive Harrison toward him.

Hit in the shoulder by the chief's bullet, Harrison stumbled—his gun coming off target—and then Monk crashed into him from behind. Fey stepped from the golf cart as Alphabet pulled it to a halt. She wanted to jump in and help Monk, but she had pushed herself too far already. She could barely stand up.

On the ground, Harrison roared and bucked away from Monk. The gun, still grasped in his disfigured hand, whipped around and clouted Monk on the side of the head. The blow stunned Monk, who loosened his grip and gave Harrison the opportunity to wiggle away.

Fey had her own gun out, but held her fire when she saw the spreading blood high on Harrison's shoulder.

"It's over, Vaughn," she said. "I told you before, but you had to push it."

Harrison was on his knees, his gun pointing at the ground. "You're fools, all of you. We could have made a difference in this city. We could have taken it back from the perverts, the politicians, and the violent animals who prey on the weak. You can't do that by being weak yourself. You have to tame them—beat them into submission—fight fire with fire." He was gasping for breath.

"Put the gun down," Fey commanded.

Hammer and Nails were arriving on the run behind her.

Harrison started to raise his gun, turning it inward toward himself.

"Fore!" Hammer yelled as a distraction, and threw one of the golf balls he'd picked up. The orb struck Harrison on the forehead, but as it bounced off there was the sound of a shot and a black hole appeared in the same spot where the golf ball had struck an instant before.

Harrison's body flopped backward onto the ground, his legs, bent at the knees, trapped beneath him.

Fey's head whipped around. She saw the chief holding a 9-millimeter in his hand.

She felt a flush of anger and despair flood through her, and spat out one accusatory word.

"Why!"

Epilogue

ℐ᎗T WAS two nights later when the crew reconvened in The Blue Cat. The wind down to the case had included a harrowing gauntlet of explanations, press conferences, damage control, arranging for the release of April Waverly and her reunion with her baby.

T-Bone Rawlings was still spilling his guts, looking for a deal, but P. J. Hunter and Mary DeFalco were bought and paid for. All the ducks were in a ragged row, but there was still paperwork that needed tying up, and administrative spaghetti that needed untying.

The chief was being played as a hero. The *Los Angeles Tribune* headline read, MAYOR PRAISES TOP COP FOR SAVING LIVES IN GOLF COURSE SHOOTOUT. The internal investigation leading to the crushing of corruption and murder within the police department was applauded as a sign of the old department ways being rooted out.

Everyone in Fey's unit wanted to vomit. They had discussed speaking out, but there was nothing to be gained. There was no way to prove the chief acted any way but honorably.

Cynicism reigned.

Fortunately, there had also been time to catch up on sleep and lick wounds. Sitting around The Blue Cat's largest booth, everyone felt only half-dead, which was as good as things got when you worked homicide.

Tuesdays were a slow night by The Blue Cat standards — just a clutch of regular faces keeping beat with the soft groove of the Tab Nelson Trio. Booker wasn't rushed behind the bar, and there was nobody crowding the table where the homicide unit detectives had established themselves.

There were, however, several guests who had insinuated themselves into Fey's unit for the evening. Keegan and Hale sat together at one end of the large circular booth. They had returned to their Mutt and Jeff routine, both wearing dark suits, white shirts, and skinny black ties. Booker had accused them of impersonating the Blues Brothers. Noticing their glasses were empty, they had accused him of impersonating a bartender.

Wearing lime green golf pants and an organdy polo shirt, Zelman Tucker was practically preening over his acceptance into the inner circle. He offset the seriousness of Keegan and Hale with a flow of patter that would have done well onstage at any of the local comedy clubs.

"Do you ever wonder," Zelman said in his best Andy Rooney impersonation, "if someone has a multiple personality and they threaten to kill themselves, is it considered a hostage situation?"

Everyone laughed, glad for the release of tension, and Tucker took that as his cue to continue. "How about if you shoot a mime, do you have to use a silencer? And if it's called tourist season, why can't we kill them?"

"Enough, Tucker," Fey said. "This isn't *Star Search.*"

"No, wait, I've got questions that need answers. Why do they sterilize the needles for lethal injection? If a mute kid swears, does his mother wash his hands with soap?"

"Tucker, you are a sick puppy," Fey said, not able to stop herself from chuckling with everybody else.

Sometimes the only thing you could do was laugh.

"I knew you loved me," Tucker said. "So, what's it gonna be? You gonna give me the inside scoop and let me write the book? I paid my dues. I've still got the black-and-blue marks to prove it."

"We'll see," Fey said. She had her own black-and-blue marks from the beating, along with a few psychological hiccups she wasn't ready to confront yet. "The chips are still falling."

"Yeah, but when they settle, I'm gonna write the book with you or without you, so you might as well help me out. It's one way to make sure your name gets spelled right."

"Let's get real," Fey told him. "The politicians are busy covering their asses on this one. There's never going to be a way to get the truth into print."

"Okay, so we'll do it as a novel—change the names to protect the guilty."

Fey gave the reporter a hard glare. "Don't push me, Tucker, or The Blue Cat will become off-limits to you."

Tucker looked over to see Booker scowling at him.

Fey caught the exchange of expressions. "Hey, a girl's gotta have someplace she can go to unwind without being hassled."

"I've been eighty-sixed out of worse places than this," Tucker said, retreating to his beer. He took a large swallow to hide his grin.

Monk was making wet circles on the table with the bottom of his frosted beer glass. "I think the capper to the whole story is what happened to Lucian Santiago."

"I think you could see that one coming," Fey said.

"Yeah, but right there in his grandfather's hacienda—some hit man waltzes in and puts two bullets in Lucian's head while he's in traction, and then waltzes out again. That's cold, man."

"That's life in Mexico right now. Gangland warfare. An-eye-for-an-eye stuff. If it can happen here, it can happen there. You saw what happened on the golf course."

"Not if you read the papers," Monk said pessimistically.

"So, you think Lucian's assassination was ordered by Ricardo Alamar?" Brindle Jones asked. She was dressed in a tight, low-cut sweater and jeans.

"Maybe not directly by Alamar, but certainly by somebody connected to the Ramos family," Fey said. "Once Alamar found out why he was being whisked out of the country by the State Department, you can bet he tracked down the source and had something done to eliminate the threat aimed at him."

"What happens now?" Brindle asked.

"Hard to call," Fey said. "How about you guys?" she asked Keegan and Hale. "Internal Affairs making any noises in your direction?"

"Maybe," Hale said. "But we've run that course before. The

chief ain't exactly sending us roses, but he doesn't seem to be after our asses either. It's like you said, the politicians just want this to go away."

"The bigger question," Keegan said, "is how the chief reacted to being used as a staked goat?"

Fey shrugged. "He called the tune. I just danced to it. I may have stepped on his toes a few times, but I still got to the end of the cotillion. Somehow, after what happened on the golf course, I think he set us up, not the other way around."

"What does that mean?"

"It means don't be looking for her name on any promotion lists in the near future," Tucker translated.

Monk spoke up again. "A lot of what happens next depends on if the chief gets reappointed. After this mess, it's unfortunately a good probability. The chief has come out looking like a hero. Harrison may have gone about things all wrong, but I'm not sure how far off the mark his philosophy was."

"Yeah, but what good is it going to do him?" Rhonda asked. "He's leading a rebellion in hell right now." She was sitting next to Hammer nursing a trendy cranberry juice. Her forearm was resting on the table with Hammer's hand clasping hers from above. For them, it was an unusual public show of affection.

Fey smiled at the duo. Rhonda had told her Hammer knew about the pregnancy. It wasn't common knowledge yet, but that would only be a matter of time. She was glad they looked happy, but wondered how they were going to face the challenges ahead.

"It was a wild ride," Hammer said.

"That it was," Fey agreed. "I know we all have a rotten taste in our mouth, but you all did a good job under tough circumstances. I'm proud of you."

"You're the leader of the band, boss," Alphabet said, raising his bourbon tumbler in her direction. "We just do what we're told."

"If that were true nothing would ever get solved in this Division," Fey said. "I just hope the next murder we handle is straightforward for a change."

As if responding to fate, Fey's beeper sounded.

"Oh, no," everyone groaned. They wrapped their hands around their glasses and hung their heads.

Fey removed the small, black electronic box from her belt and pressed the message-retrieval button. She smiled. "Low battery alarm," she said, showing everyone the LED readout.

A cheer went up from the table.

Hammer signaled Booker and called for another round. When the drinks arrived, he held up his glass and offered a toast. *"Vita continuat."*

"What the hell did he say?" Tucker asked.

"He's showing off," Rhonda told him. "It's the Latin translation of the homicide motto."

"What's the translation?"

The detectives all looked at each other in tired resignation before responding in unison.

"Life goes on."

About the Author

A twenty-year veteran of the Los Angeles Police Department, Paul Bishop is a Detective III in charge of the Sex Crimes and Major Assault Crimes units for the West Los Angeles Detective Division. He has worked many varied assignments throughout his career, including a three-year stint with the department's Anti-Terrorist Division.

As a detective, Bishop was named Officer of the Year in 1992 and again in 1993. In 1994, he was accorded the Quality and Productivity Commission Award for the City of Los Angeles.

The author of seven novels, including the previous Fey Croaker mysteries, *Kill Me Again* and *Twice Dead*, Bishop was born in England in 1954. He emigrated to America in 1962. Between police work and writing, he enjoys his family, playing soccer, reading, teaching, and a variety of other interests.

He is currently working on the next Fey Croaker novel.